Redtail

An Erotic Paranormal Romance Western Adventure

Devon Layne

Redtail

An Erotic Paranormal Romance Western Adventure

ELDER ROAD BOOKS
BELLEVUE, WA

Contents

Devon Layne

Cast List

Twentieth Century

Cole Alexander Bell: Narrator. Teen on a cattle ranch in Wyoming.

Earl Bell: Cole's father.

Sarah Alexander Bell: Cole's Mother

Mary Beth Alexander: Cole's cousin, next door neighbor (only half a mile away), and first lover. Three years older than Cole.

Angus Arthur Alexander: Mary Beth's father, Sarah Bell's older (9 years) brother.

Lily Alexander: Mary Beth's mother.

Laune Wickersham: High school classmate and Cole's first kiss.

Sid Davis: High school classmate and Cole's friend.

Geneive Murrieta: High school classmate and Cole's first girlfriend.

George: Ranch foreman.

Joe Teini: Sheriff of Albany County.

Isabelle 'Izzy' Gonzales: Librarian at Laramie Public Library.

Ashley Kay Brewer: College classmate and Cole's girlfriend.

Chet and Celia Brewer: Ashley's parents.

Philemon Morgan III: Lawyer in Salem, OR.

Phil Morgan: Lawyer in Salem, son of Philemon.

Obert Calhoun: Neighbor rancher.

Nineteenth Century

Kyle 'Redtail' Wardlaw: Young enforcer for the sheriff in Laramie City, Wyoming. Cole's host.

Laramie Wyoming: Half Cheyenne girl living on Centennial Ridge with her mother.

Theresa Ranae: Laramie's mother.

White Horse: Laramie's father. Cheyenne brave.

Kaylene: Laramie and Kyle's daughter.

Robert Hood: Kaylene's common law husband.

Mildred: Kaylene's daughter.

Caitlin Forster: Young whore at Bertha's Wild Ride. Geneive's host.

Ellen Jane: Older heavyset whore at Bertha's.

Cal Despain: Sheriff of Laramie City. Joe's host.

Maria: Young Hispanic whore at Bertha's.

Bill Campbell: Old prospector. Philemon's host.

Kat Tangeman: School teacher. Kyle's fiancée.

Arthur Alexander: Banker. Eventual husband of Kat.

Artie Alexander: Kyle and Kat's son, raised by Arthur.

Bonnie Alexander: Kat and Arthur's daughter.

Redtail

1
The First Time

WHY IS it that everybody wants to know about your first time? What kind of voyeurs are we? Do we just want to compare to see that we weren't the only ones who were somehow disappointed? Or to prove that our experiences were so far better than everyone else? Or to participate vicariously in something we lost long ago? The first time. The first time.

Well, I was in Seattle for a conference on cattle-breeding. Why the hell they held a conference on cattle-breeding in Seattle is beyond me, except it was hot as blazes in Omaha and Seattle was a nice temperate eighty-two.

So, of course, I'd heard about it. Guys had told me I had to try it. I'd read about it. I decided, 'What the hey! I can do this.'

Well, it wasn't at all what I expected. The first time I looked at it, I thought it was pretty disgusting. And slimy. And the smell—it was definitely something you had to get used to. I'd made it this far, though, and I wasn't going to back down now. I kind of held my breath and stuck my tongue in and slurped. It took a couple minutes and when I could breathe again, I grabbed a shot of tequila. A minute later I dove in again. It's definitely an acquired taste, but after eight times, I was feeling pretty satisfied. Hell, I was a connoisseur. I hadn't even had tequila after the last four.

So yeah. Not exactly what I expected, but I'd eat oysters again.

Okay. I know that wasn't the first time you wanted to hear about. And no, I'm not here to waste your time. I know I'm a smartass, but I really do want to talk about this. I'll pay extra if you'll put up with me a little longer. I think I'm going crazy.

Yeah. Back to the first time.

Freshman Year

IT WAS BACK about the time the economy was going to hell and it was affecting us ranchers just like everyone else. Prospects were bleak and Dad had taken a mortgage on the ranch for the first time in—well, as far as I knew, ever. I was thinking I might join up after high school and go to college on the GI Bill if they still had one by then. Circumstances changed and I still figured I'd serve after college, but then when Dad died, there was no one to run the ranch and I couldn't turn my back on Mom and… well, everybody. But I'm getting ahead of myself. That was later.

School was tough on me that year. Not the studies, but all the girls in Laramie had blossomed over the past summer and there they all were in school with new tits on display and makeup on. I'd put on a couple inches and a few pounds and was getting as many looks as I was giving. I think girls get just as horny as guys do, you know? Well, now I do know, but then it was a new revelation to me.

Laune Wickersham. She wasn't the prettiest girl in my freshman class and she didn't have the biggest tits. But not having much in the way of tits, she most of the time didn't bother with a brassiere either. Those are the times I remember most about freshman year. Laune would look across the room at me in Algebra with those big brown eyes and I'd sprout a boner. Then I'd glance down at her chest—well, hell. Of course, I looked at her chest. I looked at every girl's chest—and she'd have these two little points pushing her t-shirt out. A lot of times, she'd just wear a t-shirt with some kind of vest or jacket over it, but it always seemed like when she looked at me in Algebra, she'd kind of have her vest pulled back so I could see her little blossoming buds.

We only had ten minutes between the last bell and when the bus carted us country kids off home. Laune lived in town, but it was more than an hour on the bus for me to get back to the ranch. As soon as I got home, I had chores to do and then supper. Dad would ask me at the dinner table every night how much homework I had and if I'd done it on the bus. Usually I got most of it done on the bus, but I knew that after dinner I had to finish it because before bed Dad would ask if I was done. He'd take a look at my work and nod his head. I don't think he ever understood anything that I was studying. Not that he was dumb, but he worked on the ranch next door more than he studied until he was eighteen and entered the service. He was smart, but he wanted a son that was smarter and that went to college.

I did, but I didn't finish—not right away. Dad was in an accident the summer between my freshman and sophomore years as a Cowboy at the University of Wyoming. In the fall, there was just too much to be done on the ranch, and all this other stuff that's going on. I took a year's leave of absence and said I'd go back when Dad got better, but he died before we got that far. Ahead of myself again. Sorry.

Anyway, back to Laune; it had started snowing that day early in December and they decided to get the busses moving early. It was pretty chaotic because the busses were already having a hard time getting through. They let us out of class as soon as the first bus got there, but it was almost an hour before mine showed up. I was standing outside freezing my buns off when Laune walked up to me. She lived in town and said she was walking home.

"When are you gonna ask me out on a date, Cole?" she said. Just like that. Like she was waiting for me to ask her out.

"I reckon when I get a driver's license next summer," I said.

"Don't know I can wait that long," she said. Then you know what she did? She stood up on her tiptoes and kissed me, right there in the school bus parking lot. And it wasn't no peck on the cheek or lips. She put her tongue right in my mouth. It fuckin' took my breath away, I'll tell you. I had a boner and she was rubbing right up against it. "You always make my titties ache when you look at me in Algebra," she said. "I sure wish you could drive."

I tell you, when I got to bed that night, the old cowboy got a workout.

Course, by spring, she and Sid got together and she stopped showing me her hard nips in Algebra. Wouldn't you know she got pregnant and they got married when we were juniors? I guess in a way that worked out pretty well for me. I sure wasn't ready for kids.

School would be out in May and I was really looking forward to getting a driver's license so maybe I could at least date some *other* girl in town. But that was still six months away. You see, out on the ranch it was almost half a mile to the nearest neighbor. And that happened to be Uncle Angus and Aunt Lily's place. Uncle Angus was Mom's brother. Their kids were all a little older than me. The youngest, Mary Beth, was a real sweetheart, but she was eighteen and a senior when I started high school. I hardly ever saw her except at holidays or when the families got together.

GUESS THAT'S HOW that started. We all had Christmas dinner together over at their house that year. The two older Alexander girls were home with their husbands and babies, so I guess me and Mary Beth hung out a little.

"You gonna get it on with that Laune Wickersham?" she asked.

"What are you talking about?"

"Everybody saw you kiss her in that snowstorm three weeks ago. My little cousin got something going?"

"I didn't really kiss her," I said, blushing. "She sorta did all the work."

"You be careful with her. She's lookin' for a meal ticket." I started to object, but Mary Beth cut me off. "I know she's a nice girl and all. I'm sure she don't mean no harm, but her family—well, they ain't very nice to her. She'd do about anything to get away from them and you're a real good catch."

"You gotta be kidding. A stringy fifteen-year-old like me? What have I got to offer?"

"A nice ranch. Good people. And you ain't bad lookin', you know? Just be careful."

"Ain't nothing gonna happen anyway," I groused. "I can't drive into town till I get a license. What about you? Who's trying to get into your knickers?" I thought I'd turn the tables on her, but I couldn't think of a single guy I'd ever seen her with at school.

"Who'd want to go out with me?" she snapped. "Hell, I'm bigger than you are."

"Not for long. I grew another two inches this fall. Just 'cause you're tall don't mean you ain't beautiful."

"Cole! Hush! Don't go telling your cousin she's beautiful. It'll give her a swelled head. And perky titties like Laune's. Hell, you've already gotten more than I'm likely to ever get."

"You don't mean you've never been kissed, do you?"

It was Mary Beth's turn to blush.

4

Sally Ann's kids were playing with Christmas presents on the floor and while they hadn't been paying any attention to us, we'd been talking softly on the sofa. Our Dads were all in Uncle Angus's office drinking whisky and watching some game on TV. The Moms were in the kitchen and dining room.

I stood up and took hold of Mary Beth's hand.

"Come here with me."

"Where?"

"Just around the corner over here," I said, leading her into the hall down by the bathroom. I took a careful look around and then I kissed her. I wasn't very skilled, but I'd had one more than Mary Beth had and she kind of melted into my arms. When I touched her lips with my tongue, hell! I thought she was going to scream. But she mashed her lips against mine and let her tongue follow mine wherever it went.

"You gotta be careful with that!" she whispered, looking down the hall. She'd stepped back a bit and looked a little panicked. She looked at me with fire in her eyes.

"I'm sorry, Mary Beth, but..."

"Shut up." She closed the distance between us and laid another one on me, practicing everything I'd just taught her and making up stuff on the fly. Then she pushed me away and rushed back to the living room just as Aunt Lily called everyone to Christmas Dinner. I slipped into the bathroom and managed to get the cowboy pretty much under control in my jeans before I showed up at the table.

YOU MIGHT THINK that started Mary Beth and me kissing at every chance we got, but it was pretty much a one-time thing. I mean, we were friendly and all and she went out of her way to say hi at school. We even sat next to each other a couple of times on the bus when her best friend Beckie was sick. We talked a bit and she said how she was sorry when she heard Laune and Sid had got together. But there wasn't much else between us, though when she said she was sorry about Laune and Sid, she took hold of my hand and squeezed it and didn't really let it go until we got back to Centennial. I didn't think anything about it other than all the thoughts I'd had about her since that kiss on Christmas and the cowboy got another ride in my hand saddle that night. *But shit!* She'd warned me off and I was just thankful that she still treated me like she liked me as her cousin and was genuinely sorry I'd had my heart broken. Sorta.

It was Mary Beth's graduation that really changed things.

Uncle Angus gave her a car. A ten-year-old Chevy Cavalier convertible. Mary Beth loved it.

The car was a pig.

It was black with a gray fabric interior and red racing stripes. But the passenger door was just battleship gray primer paint because it had been wrecked at one time. It had a couple of nicks in the soft top and duct tape stretched across them to mend it. The floorboard was just about worn through. It had 215,000 miles on it and I think Angus must have paid $800 for it. Probably cost that much to insure.

Well, Mary Beth had this dream about taking the car on a road trip all the way to Oregon. She wanted to see the ocean. But the damn thing had an oil leak and she put a quart of oil in it every time she filled the tank with gas. That's what got me involved.

"Cole, would you help me fix my car?" she asked after she'd pulled into the drive. It was Sunday afternoon, which is the only reason I wasn't out in the fields. I'd probably ride herd later in the summer to give the ranch hands a break. I'd go out for three weeks and each of them would come in for one week in rotation. It was pretty good. I liked being out with the cattle when we moved them to high ground. I wouldn't go up till after my birthday, though. I'd been busy in the fields since school got out and had the first cutting of hay that I'd bale on Monday.

"What's wrong with it?"

"Pop said the oil pan gasket leaked. I drove all the way to Cheyenne and got a new gasket, but Pop says I have to fix it myself. I don't mind doing it, but I don't know how and I know you do."

"Well, yeah. Ain't nothing to replacing a gasket. Let me go ask Dad if he's got some goop for it. We'll pull it into the barn where the blocks are." Dad fixed everything and he started me running for tools when I could hardly walk. It's not like I love cars or anything, but I can fix it if I have to. For my cousin, I'd do it. Anything.

We pulled the car into the barn and onto the blocks—a pair of short ramps that raised the front end up about a foot.

"We gotta drain the oil first. Did you get oil for it?"

"Are you kidding? The way it's been dripping oil, I bought a case and put it in the trunk," she laughed.

I handed her a pair of coveralls and she looked at me strange.

"Your Pop said you had to fix it. I'll show you how." She pulled them on over her shorts and one of those tops that ties in front. That was reason enough to get her into coveralls. I wouldn't be paying any attention to the car at all if I was looking at that the whole time. I pulled on a pair, too.

We slid under the car and I positioned an old enamel wash tub under the oil pan and fit the socket on the plug. Mary Beth put her hands on the handle and I helped pull enough to loosen the nut. Oil started spraying out right away and I laughed at Mary Beth with oil on her face. She glared at me, but she was pretty proud she'd just drained the oil out of her car anyway. We pulled the tub out from under the car and poured the old oil into the drum dad kept there. The co-op came by to pick up drums from the ranchers once every six months or year, however much it was needed. They filled our gas tank and the LP tank for the stove and water heater, too. After the pan was drained, we loosened the bolts holding it and then pulled it out to take a look. I showed Mary Beth how to clean it and we examined it for cracks. It seemed to be okay, but I swear that gasket had never been replaced. It was a mess and we had to scrape the bits and pieces off before we gooped it up and sealed the new gasket in place. Then we slid under the car again and I had Mary Beth bolt it up. I gave each of the bolts an extra turn after she finished and we put in the plug.

We put four quarts of oil in the little four-cylinder engine and then started it up and rolled it back down where it was level. We watched pretty carefully to see if it started leaking or over-heated or anything, but after about fifteen minutes it looked good. We went into the shop and used degreaser to clean ourselves up and Mary Beth took off her coveralls.

"Thank you, Cole. That was the second nicest thing you've ever done for me," she said.

"Huh?" Yeah, I'm quick on the uptake. She didn't need to explain, though. She just pulled my head to her and put a kiss on me that made me forget about what I was doing. I guess I got a little carried away, 'cause there was a grease-mark on that tie-together blouse she was wearing, right over her left boob. Mary Beth just glanced down at it and grinned.

"I better go home and get this scrubbed out before Mama sees it," she said. "But since it's already got a mark on it..." she pulled me in for another kiss and put my hand right back on her boob. Oh man! I was in heaven. I squeezed it gentle like and she moaned into my mouth and we made out like bandits for about ten minutes. Well, then she really did get in her car.

"Cole, how would you like to go for a ride on your birthday?" It was Sunday and my birthday was coming on Saturday. I couldn't think of anything I wanted more for my birthday than going for a ride with Mary Beth.

"Yeah. You think we could get away?"

"We'll let 'em all have cake and ice cream and then I'll take you to see the fireworks. Okay?"

"Thanks Mary Beth. You're the best." I leaned in and kissed her again a little and she drove away.

IT ALL WORKED just the way she said it would. I baled and loaded the first cutting that week, but other than feeding the horses and pigs and tending to normal chores, there was no work on my birthday. It's good when your birthday is a National Holiday.

I'm a firecracker. You know, born on the Fourth of July. In fact, on the Bicentennial, 1976. That was Dad's joke. He lit a fuse in October and on the Fourth he got fireworks. It was cool, really. Dad and I were close in a kind of rough way. He wasn't above beating my ass with a belt if I smarted off to Mom or if he caught me smoking behind the barn. Of course, he explained after that last one that if I was going to smoke I had to do it where I wouldn't burn the barn down. Then he showed me his favorite place to light up out in the woodlot where there was even the remains of an old stone chimney to toss our butts into. Then we lit up together.

Shit. That was a long time ago.

Back to my birthday. We had a big family barbecue Sunday afternoon. Then when everybody was sitting around just being lazy, Mary Beth turned to me like it was a sudden inspiration.

"I never properly said thank you for helping me fix my car Sunday, Cole," she said loud enough for everybody to hear. "How about if I take you to see the fireworks in Laramie? I'll even spring for sodas. Would that be okay, Aunt Sarah?" My mom looked at us like we'd just grown two heads. Mary Beth and I had always been polite to each other, but we'd never gone out of our way to do things with each other.

"That's awfully nice of you, Mary Beth, but if you are driving and spending all that money on gas and oil, I think Cole should spring for the sodas. Don't you think so, Lily?"

"It sounds fair." *Shit. Where could I get money for sodas?* I had maybe five bucks scattered around my room. Mom called me over and whispered in my ear.

"Take twenty dollars from the cookie jar on the kitchen counter and be sure you treat your cousin nicely. If she'd rather have a malt, you get her one."

"Yes ma'am," I said and ran into the house. Ten minutes later, Mary Beth and I pulled out of the driveway.

Once we were well out of sight, about a mile down the road, Mary Beth slowed down. As soon as she caught my eye she grinned and floored it. The little Cavalier fishtailed down the road spewing gravel and a cloud of dust out behind it. I didn't think that 95 horsepower engine with a three-speed automatic would do that. I think the garden tractor had more kick in it. But Mary Beth had her fun and we laughed all the way into Centennial. That's when she really surprised me. Instead of turning right to go into Laramie, she turned left and headed toward the mountains. I didn't think the little car could make it over the pass, but she only went a few miles. She turned off onto the USFS road we use to get a truck up to the high pastures. She scraped bottom a few times, but we finally came out at the loading ramp where we'd drop supplies a couple times during the summer and where I'd be unloading my horse next Monday.

"What are we doing here, Mary Beth?" She reached across the console and pulled me to her for a big kiss.

"We're making out," she declared. "I've waited long enough, Cole. I'm eighteen and will be nineteen in two months. I'm outta high school and headed to Boulder this fall. I want to know what it's all about. Cole, I want you to make love to me."

"Wow! I mean. Why me, beautiful? I'm honored and all, but I don't know nothing. And I'm your cousin."

"Because you're my cousin. Do you think I'd risk my reputation and getting a disease and all with somebody like Billy Summers? That makes my skin crawl. But you wouldn't do that to me. And I'd never do it to you."

"But…"

"Let's just take my 'emergency supplies' out of the trunk and go find a nice quiet place to make out and see what happens," she said, giving me another kiss. She sure took to kissing quick-like. I was punching a hole in my jeans, I was so hard. We grabbed her emergency kit and set off down the trail the other way from where we knew the cattle would be grazing. The trail opened up into a smaller meadow and we looked around to be sure none of the hands had come out this way looking for strays, but there was a gully between us and where the herd was and there wasn't much chance of them being on the north side. Her emergency supplies kit was put together with a nice blanket, plenty of water, a few energy bars, a flashlight, knife, and compass. And a big box of condoms.

"You're really prepared for emergencies," I laughed.

"Well, I've only been on the pill for a few weeks and I don't trust it yet. Beckie was on the pill and look at her."

"Beckie's pregnant?"

"Don't you go telling anybody. Tuesday, I'm driving her over to a clinic in Cheyenne. They'll take care of it and nobody here will ever know. We'll just be safe, you know?"

"Well, if we get that far, sure. Mary Beth, I just think the world of you and I don't want anything bad to happen to you. Outside of school, you're really the only person I call a friend. I don't want to do anything that would make you stop being my friend."

"Honey, here." She reached for my hands and squirted some of that hand sanitizer in them. Then she did the same thing herself. "I know we haven't been mucking out stalls or anything, but this way at least we're not spreading any diseases with our fingers. Now come here and kiss me. Make me believe I'm as beautiful as you say I am. Just kiss me, honey."

Well, I don't know if it was me doing the kissing or her. I guess we both contributed. I just know that she was running her hands all over my body, including places that nobody else's hands had ever been. And she wasn't objecting to me exploring either. I don't know how long we kissed, but when I felt the soft round flesh and hard little point of her tit in my left hand, I had to pull away and look.

She'd managed to get my t-shirt off and I got her shirt opened up. My hand was up under her brassiere cupping a handful of heaven. I looked up at her face and she had her eyes closed and the prettiest smile on her lips I've ever seen. I leaned down and kissed her just a brush on her cheek and squeezed a little again. But it was a tight space.

"Let me show you how to take it off, honey." I reluctantly pulled my hand out from under her bra and she lifted up enough to slide her arms out of her shirt. Then she rolled toward me. "Look. See where it fastens in the middle of my back. There's three little hooks and eyes. You've got to unfasten it." It took me a little struggle as I had to sit up so I could use both hands.

"Who helps you get this contraption on?" I asked.

"I fasten it in front and then slide it around and put my titties in the cups and my arms through the straps. It's a lot easier that way and nobody has to help. Course, if you were there, I'd let you help me." The straps came loose and she shrugged out of it. There were her titties sitting on her chest right in front of me and God and everybody. "You're staring, Cole. Don't you like them?" There was a real note of fear in her voice and she reached for her bra.

"Oh, Mary Beth! That's the most beautiful thing I've ever seen. Don't cover 'em up, beautiful. Please let me just look at you for a minute. I've seen pictures and all, but Lord Almighty! There just ain't anything like this. You're so beautiful, I just want to hold you and look at you and touch you and kiss you and…"

"Well, what are you waiting for?"

I pulled that sweet girl into my arms and let my hands walk all over her bare back as I kissed her and pressed her boobies against my chest. In all my life, I never felt anything like this. I kissed on her neck and shoulders and cupped her breast in my hand. I didn't know too much about it, but I sure wanted to kiss those little brown points and give them a little suck. She seemed to be of a like mind and cradled my head in her hands as I put my lips on her nip. She moaned and I figured I must be doing something right.

Now I was no ignoramus. Sid's brother kept us supplied with copies of *Playboy*. Sometimes those *Forum* stories that had me spurting without even touching the cowboy. But the reality of holding an almost naked girl in my arms and sucking on her tit was nothing like I was prepared for. I stroked up and down her belly with my hand and when I switched my lips to the other breast, my hand came up to comfort the first for its loss.

Mary Beth pushed me back and I flopped onto the blanket. She was on top of me kissing her way around my chest while I kept her boobies warm with my hands. Hell! I did not know that my nips were sensitive like that. I could feel my cock start throbbing in my pants and sat bolt upright. I practically threw her off if I hadn't wrapped my arms around her and held her tight.

"Oh shit!"

"What is it, honey?" she said with some alarm.

"Oh God! I'm sorry, Mary Beth. I'm sorry. I didn't know I'd… Oh shit." I was so embarrassed I was ready to crawl home. I have to say I wasn't being very manly now that I'd come. I had tears in my eyes when she looked up at me.

"Oh, honey. Don't go crying. What's wrong?"

"I… I come in my pants. I'm sorry."

"Oh," she sighed like it was a relief. "You come just because I was kissing you and you were holding my boobies? Really? Oh, honey. I really turn you on that much?"

"Mary Beth, you're the most wonderful woman I ever met. And that ain't just because were sitting here half naked. What you do to me, I didn't even know was possible."

"Well that's good. Beckie told me that I'd enjoy it more if I got my man off before we made love. She said the first time she did it, he was in her and it was over before she got her engine started. I figured it would be harder to do than just me kissing on you."

"I'm just so embarrassed to fill my pants like that."

"Hey. We're young. I've never done the things we're doing and I guess you haven't either. I come a little one while you were sucking on my nips. It was just so dreamy. So don't be embarrassed. Let's just get you out of those wet, icky jockeys. And you can do the same for me."

"Really? You still want to… you know?"

"Honey, my panties are probably just as wet as your jockeys."

She set about pulling my boots off and then my jeans and under-shorts. They were plenty wet and sticky all right. She used the dry panel to wipe things up and then damned if she didn't get some of that sanitizer soap and rub me down. The cowboy was ready to ride again in no time. She just looked at it and kept stroking on it.

"What do you like, honey?"

"I like what you're doing. A lot. Maybe too much unless you think it's best if I come twice. Oh Jesus, Mary Beth." She stopped stroking me and laid back.

"Now you do me," she said. I moved my bare ass around so I could reach her boots and pulled them off. Then I unfastened her jeans button and unzipped them. She shivered as the zipper came down.

"You okay, beautiful?"

"Oh yeah," she sighed. "I'm just excited. Cole, nobody's seen my pussy before 'cept the OB/gyn when she examined me and put me on the pill. Certainly, no boy. I want you to see me like I just saw you. I want you to touch me in all my special places." Well, that was pretty much invitation enough and I pulled her jeans and panties down off her hips. She lifted up a bit so I could get them off and I saw the most beautiful light brown tuft of fur come into view between her legs. Everybody in my family is kind of dark blonde or light brown. Mary Beth was light brown, up and down. When the jeans were off, I ran my hands up both legs and she parted them a little so I could see. "Do you like it, Cole?"

"I like everything about you, Mary Beth. You're beautiful. But, I don't know what to do. What do you want me to do next, honey?"

"Just kind of lie here beside me and kiss me some more? Is that okay? And you can let your fingers do the walking and finding more places to touch. Just be real gentle and when you get close, I'll show you where my little button is."

Well, that's what we did. We kissed and touched. I found her damp curls with my fingers and the slippery channel between her lower lips. She didn't want me to push a finger inside her, but she guided it up to her clitoris and taught me how to rub her just a little right alongside it. And she *did* come. Then we just held each other for a few minutes.

"That was so much better than doing it to myself," she whispered. "I'm so ready to make love to you, honey."

"Do you want me to… like… lick it first? That's what I read was supposed to happen."

"Those are just stories. I mean, sometime, I'd like you to lick it. And sometime, I want to suck on your cowboy till you come in my mouth. But just now, I just want you to push yourself inside me and tell me that I'll always be your favorite cousin and you really do think I'm beautiful."

"There's no question about that. You never think you're beautiful because you're tall. But I'm taller than you now. I don't know what other reason you have to think you aren't beautiful. You've got the sweetest face in the world. You've got the deepest green eyes I've ever seen with those little flecks of gold in them. I could look into your eyes all day." While I was talking, Mary Beth was busy, too. She tore open a condom and pushed me back then figured which side was right side out and started to roll it onto my dick. I wasn't quite hard, but it didn't take a second of her playing there for me to come up full. It was a strange feeling rolling on one of those things. It cut in and put pressure all around my hard-on. When it was finally in place and I'd managed to pull the couple of caught hairs out of it, she lay back and opened her arms and legs to me.

"Come to me, Cole. Be my very first lover and let me be yours."

I got between her legs and positioned myself where I'd felt her tiny opening. I looked into her eyes and she nodded. I pushed forward. I didn't get very far.

"I know you want to be gentle, honey, and thank you. But you gotta push through that barrier. I know it'll hurt a little, but I want it. Just, when it breaks stop and let me get used to you. Do it, honey. Do it."

I did it. She gasped a little and squinted her eyes. I tried to stop, but just kept slowly sliding in, encouraged by her pulling at my hips.

There was a flash of a shadow on my left shoulder and I jerked my head around and saw a redtail hawk diving toward the meadow. My mouth was open, but it was that hawk that let out a long shrill cry.

Traveling: Loving Laramie

IF YOU WATCH an old western on television and see a big bird screeching down out of the sky, chances are it isn't an eagle's cry you are hearing. The masters of the air have wimpy little voices. It's almost a whistle. But that's not very dramatic so the Hollywood types went hunting for a bigger sound that would match the majesty of the National Symbol. They came upon the Red-tailed Hawk. That predator isn't as big as an eagle, nor does it fly quite as high. But its scream will fill a valley and freeze its prey to the spot.

My eyes snapped back to my lover, my sweet, sweet cousin, who had me wrapped tight in her velvet sheath and was moaning under me with her eyes tightly closed as I sank my full length into her.

"Oh my God, Mary Beth!" I said, closing my own eyes in ecstasy.

She slugged me.

I don't mean slapped. I don't mean love-tapped. She caught me with a round-house right to the jaw that knocked me clean out of the saddle. Or in this case, onto a saddle with the horn poking me in the ribs. Two beautiful horses, a buckskin and a pinto grazed near us.

What the fuck?

I retreated a little. She was staring at me while she reached to pull up her buckskin trousers.

"Don't call me by your white whore names, Kyle Wardlaw! Go back and practice some more."

"Wait, Laramie! I don't know what happened. You musta misunderstood me. I said, 'Oh my God, oh yes!' That was it. Sweet Laramie, don't get dressed. It'll be good. I promise."

"It hurt."

"But the hurt part is over. Don't give up before we get to the good parts."

Something was really wrong here. I was hearing the words coming out of my mouth, but I wasn't saying them. Laramie? Who the hell was this girl in buckskins who looked so much like Mary Beth that I still couldn't tell the difference? And, where was I? The woods around me looked different and even the little meadow—it smelled different, sweeter. And now I was picking up more than the voice coming out of this body. I was hearing what he was thinking, too. It wasn't all that pretty.

Kyle genuinely believed that if he got between the girl's legs and started pumping, she'd be fine. It was his first time and all he knew about sex came from watching horses and cows and listening to the whores where he lived. It wasn't my fight. I was getting out of here.

Well, that was a problem. I tried to jerk myself back into my real body, but all that happened was that this Kyle jerked back so hard he practically cracked a rib on that saddle horn. How the hell was I supposed to get back to me? And what was happening to poor Mary Beth?

The girl moved toward Kyle to see if he was okay. He was groaning, but I suddenly felt him tense and knew he was going to grab her and force her. Shit!

No! I screamed in his head. I stopped the hand as it was rising. I put him in his place and told him to sit still and be quiet. I could feel his consciousness receding and suddenly I had full control of the body. Maybe I could get out of this without having the half-breed girl kill us. *Half-breed?* So that was it. The things that Kyle knew were slowly seeping into my consciousness. Laramie's mother had run off Cheyenne father and went to a reservation in Montana in 1872. Laramie and her mother had come back to live where her ancestors had.

And damn, she was beautiful. I could tell now some of the subtle differences between her and Mary Beth. Her hair was a little darker. Her eyes were like coal. And just as likely to catch fire.

"Laramie," I said, finally making Kyle's mouth work as I raised my hand slowly to her cheek. "Beautiful girl, I'm sorry I hurt you. You made me so excited I got carried away. I never want to hurt you. You are the most beautiful girl in the whole of southern Wyoming. Even your name is like you are the spirit of the territory. Let me show you how much I like you." I was stroking her cheek and little by little she was leaning into my hand. I shifted down off the horn of the saddle and just leaned back, pulling her with me. She came a little hesitantly, but leaned in until I could reach her lips and kiss her.

She jerked back away from me and looked at me curiously. She touched her lips.

Kyle, you idiot! You didn't even kiss her?

"It's okay," I whispered. "You'll like it. Taste my lips with your tongue. Just like I tasted you."

What followed was about the sweetest most exciting thing I've ever experienced in either body. You've got to remember that when Laune walked up and kissed me in the bus parking lot, she pretty much smashed her lips against mine and rammed her tongue in my mouth. I was a little gentler than that when I kissed Mary Beth that first time, but I didn't have much experience to go by and after the first one, we were zero to sixty as soon as our lips touched. Not so with Laramie. She bravely and tentatively touched my lips with hers and pulled back as if I'd bite her.

"That's it," I whispered. "Come here and kiss me, Laramie."

She leaned in again and I made my lips as soft as I could and opened them slightly. She kissed me softly. Her tongue licked lightly at my lips and she was surprised when mine touched it. She pulled back a little and smiled then she came back for more. I just got lost in her. While we were kissing, my hand slid up under her buckskin shirt and I started playing with her tits. She didn't wear anything under her buckskins and they were almost as soft as she was. I was beginning to see and feel more differences between Laramie and Mary Beth. Laramie was just a little smaller in the chest and was skinnier overall. I guessed she was pretty athletic and ate a lean diet. But her nipples were every bit as sensitive as Mary Beth's and looked like they could be twins. I pulled the shirt up and over her head. She was beautiful, shy, and even a little aggressive as she started pulling at Kyle's shirt. I helped as best I could getting it off over my head and suggesting in my mind that he could do with washing his clothes and his pits.

Laramie didn't seem to mind too much and we went back to kissing with our bare chests pressed against each other. In any timeline and with any partner, I don't think there will ever be a feeling that I like better than having my bare chest pressed against a girl's bare breasts. We rolled over onto the coarse horse blanket. I pushed my pants off my legs, having to kick my boots off first. Laramie saw what I was doing and pulled her own trousers off. She lay back as if she expected me to just get on like Kyle had, but I lay down beside her instead. I kept kissing her and leaned down to kiss her little nips while I let my hand wander down her flat tummy to her sparsely-haired pussy. I wondered if maybe she was a little younger than Mary Beth so didn't have as much hair. Well, I didn't care. Whatever this timeframe was, she was an adult and an equal participant in what we were doing.

I found her slit was wet and slippery. She shuddered and moaned when I found her clit and started playing with it. Her eyes snapped wide open as she looked at me with a mix of fright and elation and came with a howl. She pushed me away. I thought maybe I'd gone a little overboard with the girl and we were back to square one, but her eyes trailed down my body (or Kyle's) to a pretty impressive erection. Without another word, she threw a leg over me and got her pussy opening lined up with my cock and started sinking down on it. She was moaning and practically jumping up and down on my cock like a wild thing. I could feel the come boiling up in my balls and opened my mouth howl my own orgasm. Just as my mouth opened I saw the shadow and heard that unmistakable screech of Redtail.

Loving Mary Beth

"OH, LARAMIE, I love you!" There was a moment's disorientation as I felt the world roll me over and turn me inside out.

She slapped me.

I looked down and shook my head. Staring up at me were those green eyes with gold flecks that I'd come to love over the past few weeks.

"What did you call me? What? Am I so big you think of me as a whole city?"

"Ma… Mary Beth," I panted. "Beautiful. You are just so beautiful. Don't you think Laramie is just one of the prettiest words you ever heard? I had to scream and I didn't want it to be vulgar. I didn't want to yell 'Oh fuck!' because you're too beautiful for that. But I just had to yell something and Laramie was the prettiest word I could think of." Jesus, I was working harder to put this right than Kyle had with Laramie. I had no idea what had happened to me. I just knew that Mary Beth was the reality that I knew and I wanted her to be the center of my being.

"Oh Cole. I don't know if I should believe you or think you're full of shit. Do you love me, Cole? Like you said?"

"I do, cousin. I hardly know what love is all about, but I love you more than just as my next-door neighbor cousin."

"Well, I love you, too, but you know we can never be like a couple, right?"

"What?"

"I want to make love to you whenever we can get away. I want to feel you kissing me all over. I want to suck you sometime and feel you spurt your cream in my mouth. But we can't be a couple. We can't be boyfriend and girlfriend or anything else, honey. You know that, right?"

"Yeah. I guess I know that, but I don't want this to just be a fuck we had to lose our virginities. You know?"

"I know, honey. And it isn't. It isn't even over yet today, so let's not borrow trouble from tomorrow."

"Can we just love each other?" I asked. "Can we just—when we're together—forget about what can and can't be? Beautiful, you just gave me the most wonderful gift of my life and I haven't even begun to show you how wonderful I think you are."

"That's my Cole. Let's get that used condom off and get you ready for another round. I'm sure ready. That was terrific!"

So that was my first time. It's funny how your mind works, isn't it? I mean if anyone really knows how the mind works. In those first few strokes when I was inside Mary Beth, every one of which I remember clearly, I also spent a whole afternoon making love with a beautiful half-breed girl sometime back in the 1880s or 90s. And I remember every single thing that happened there, too. It's like I have two different people's memories in my head. I remember other stuff that was floating around in Kyle's head. I know his horse was the buckskin and its name is Bolt. We were the same age, but I don't know when his birthday is. And it was his first time, too, though he'd got a different idea of what was supposed to happen. Apparently, I only got the surface thoughts. I kind of took control when I discovered he was going to be an ass.

I don't think he *really* is an ass. I think he meant right, but just didn't know what he was doing. I hoped he and Laramie would work things out—partly because I was hoping that someday I'd get to ride in his head and body again and… and make love to Laramie again. I meant it when I told Mary Beth I loved her. But damn. When I screamed 'Laramie, I love you,' it wasn't just my orgasm talking.

I wish I knew if she was real.

2
WWJD?

REMEMBER THAT phrase all the religious nuts were using? Carol Ann Meyers came up to me one day in the hall at school senior year when I was having a particularly bad meltdown. I hardly remember what it was all about at the time, but it seems to me that it might have been the day I found out Sid got Laune pregnant. I couldn't believe how stupid either of them had been. It wasn't like I still wanted to date Laune, but she had been kind of special during my freshman year and every once in a while, when no one was looking, she'd still open up her vest and show me the hard points of her nipples sticking into her t-shirt. Then of course, she'd follow it up with some catty little remark like "Too bad you didn't have a driver's license," and sigh. She'd run off and join Sid someplace and I'd be standing in the hallway with a boner.

It's just that Mary Beth had taught me really well. First, to keep my pants zipped and if I couldn't do that to keep my cowboy covered. Her friend Beckie had real problems that summer she got pregnant. Mary Beth took her to Cheyenne and got an abortion, but then Beckie got so depressed that she almost killed herself. She didn't go to college that fall like she planned to with Mary Beth. Instead, she went back to fooling around with the same guy that knocked her up the first time and this time when she got pregnant she told him and he married her. I saw her the next summer and she was carting around a little baby and had a big bruise on her cheek. I could just see Laune and Sid being in the same situation only worse. They weren't even out of high school yet. What the fuck was she thinking?

Anyway, I guess I was taking it out on my locker when Carol Ann came up beside me and laid a hand on my shoulder.

"There, there, Cole," she said. "WWJD?"

"Huh?"

"What would Jesus do?"

"Oh." Only what I heard got jumbled up a little and I started thinking immediately, "What would Jason do?" I kinda liked Jason Bourne. I'd read all of Ludlum's books. You gotta have something to do when you're riding herd up on the ridge. Hell, he'd just pick up a ballpoint pen from a desk and jab it into Laune's gut, right into the fetus so she'd abort. Then he'd use the same pen and jam it into Sid's eye so far it came out the back of his head, the stupid fuck!

Except Jason was way too cool for that. He'd just walk away. Laune was nothing to him and she looked happy. Sid was going to suffer enough on his own. What was it to Jason Bourne? It's not like one of them is going to hunt him down.

And that's where I differed with Carol Ann. Apparently to her, what Jesus would do was to loudly lecture Laune and Sid in the hall about the evils of premarital sex and how they were cursed to a life of misery because they didn't follow the Lord.

I guess Jesus and I were both wrong and Jason was right. Last time I heard, Laune and Sid had three kids in three years before they figured out what caused it. Sid went straight out and got clipped. They moved up to Casper and Sid fixes computers for a living. He was always good at that. I guess they're happy. What Jason would do is just walk away.

It's what I should have done with Kyle.

First Girlfriend

FOR A WHILE there, I thought that I was going to get transported to the 1800s every time I had sex, but Mary Beth and I disproved that the first weekend of August when I got down from my time with the herds. There isn't really a whole lot to do up there unless something spooks the cattle or a few wander off. Mostly the dogs take care of things, but there's always a rider nearby. The worst things we watch for are thunderstorms and cougars. Thunder and lightning are the things most likely to spook the cattle into a stampede. Cougars? Well that's where some of the wandering cows end up. You gotta be careful to keep the dogs away from the cougars, too.

But when I got back, I had two days off before I had to start baling the second cutting of hay. I called Mary Beth the day I got home and told Mom and Dad that now I had my license, I'd like to go camping for the weekend. Dad tossed me the keys to the truck and told me I had work to start on Monday and not to be late. How cool is that? I loaded my camp gear in the back of the truck, and hung my rifle from the rack in the rear window and by dinner time I was on the road. I knew where to drive to, though, and it was straight through Centennial. Beckie lived just beyond Miller Corner and that's where Mary Beth had her Cavalier parked with all her gear. We tossed it in the back of the truck and headed for the mountains.

We made a stop at the first truck stop on I-25 to get another box of condoms and then high-tailed it to Boulder. Mary Beth wanted to show me where she'd be living this fall and we both just wanted to be a long way from where anybody knew us or knew that we were related.

We set up camp in the state park on the Front Range in a place that might not have been completely legal, but once the tent was up and the air mattress was inflated, we hardly came out of the tent again all weekend. At first, I was a little nervous, but it hadn't been all that bad the first time I traveled back, so maybe it wouldn't be this time either. I didn't need to worry because we made love all weekend long and I never left the tent with Mary Beth. Apparently, it wasn't sex that sent me time-traveling. I was tempted to tell Mary Beth all about what happened, but decided that this was one of those things that you just don't tell anyone. Besides, who wanted to put a damper on that weekend?

We did get up and broke camp on Sunday afternoon. We drove into Boulder to walk around the campus. I was a little sad and maybe jealous that she'd be gone in just a few weeks. We wandered around and ended up in this big circle area in front of the library. Mary Beth looked around like she was getting her bearings and then stood right in the middle of the courtyard. She called me to her.

"Kiss me," she said.

"Here?"

"No. On my lips. Come on. I want a really good one."

There was still a summer session going on and people were walking around, but I walked over to her and started a slow easy kiss. I remembered what I'd done with Laramie and just caressed her lips with mine, tickling them with my tongue. It didn't stay slow and easy all that long.

We got pretty hot, even though I tried not to let my hands get carried away. I could hear some laughs and a rude comment or two, but I just ignored it. This was what Mary Beth wanted.

When she pulled away she looked into my eyes. I called them witch's eyes. Green with those gold flecks. You'd think she could see right through you.

"Every day I'm here on campus, I'm going to come to this spot. I'm going to close my eyes and think of you kissing me right here—on the lips. And you'll know how much I love you, Cole." She just took my hand and led me back to the truck. You gotta love a pickup truck with a big bench seat and a middle seatbelt. She was tucked under my arm all the way back to Beckie's.

Well, the end of August came and Mary Beth moved. I volunteered to drive her down, but her parents were pretty set on doing the job themselves. The night before she left, we both left our houses and met in the big pasture halfway between us. We made love out under the stars until it was almost dawn.

"Cole, you got to promise me that you'll not sit there moping around all winter. You got a driver's license now. You can go into town and pick up a girl for a date and have some fun. I want you to do that, Cole. I might meet someone I want to have some fun with, too. Remember, we aren't a couple no matter how much we love each other. We're never going to get married and have babies. But honey, I'll always be your lover."

MY SOPHOMORE YEAR in high school started kind of sad, but I saw the sense in what Mary Beth said. I'd pretty much finished my growth and was 6'3" and a slim 195. But I was strong and wiry from working on the ranch all summer. I guess some girls like that look.

One of them was Geneive Murrieta. Her dad ran a Basque restaurant in town and it had a really good reputation. It was the kind of place where they just seated you at a long table with everyone else who came in and served most of the food except your entree family style. She was pretty damned cute, too. I suppose she wouldn't have seemed so short to most guys, but her 5'1" put the top of her head just below my collar bone. I could put an arm around her waist and carry her on my hip like a baby. Everything about her was tiny. Tiny feet. Tiny hands. Tiny titties. Yeah, you guessed it. A tiny pussy, too.

I found that out on our third date. We went to a movie and when we got back in the truck, she was all over me. She had the cowboy out of my pants and her tiny mouth around its head before I got out of the parking lot.

"Easy there, sweetheart," I said. "I don't want any accidents if I hit a pothole. I'd like to keep that cowboy intact."

"You better find a good place to park then, boyfriend. Otherwise I'm going to straddle your lap right here and plant my pussy all over your friend."

I didn't think it was that great a movie, but who understands chick flicks? Once I got us out of town and onto a nice quiet farm road, Geneive was naked in a flash and pulling at my clothes. I got stripped down which involved moving out from under the steering wheel and being practically thrown on my back. I had a condom out and barely got it rolled on before Geneive was sinking down on my pole.

"What's got into you, sweetheart?"

"You."

"Yeah. I sure am and you are tight around. I'm not going to last long at the rate you're going."

"Go ahead. Fill me up. I wanted this from our first date. Third date is the charm."

She was a vigorous lover and even though her titties were small, compared to, say Mary Beth or some of the girls who sported double-Ds already at 16, they were really sensitive and she came three times before I finally unleashed a load. Geneive collapsed on top of me, protected by my arm from hitting her head on the steering wheel. She just lay there panting until I started to shrink out of her and reached down to grab the condom.

She looked at it like she hadn't known it was there.

"Why'd you put that on?" she asked. "You think I've got a disease?"

"Condoms prevent lots of things besides disease," I said.

"I don't care if I get pregnant. I love you."

"That's not a one-sided decision to make, sweetheart."

"You mean you don't love me so you wouldn't get me pregnant?"

"I care about you just enough to make sure neither of us gets saddled with a kid when we're not even seventeen."

"I still wouldn't have cared. I hate school. I'd rather sit at home with a baby."

"And eat what?" I asked. "Is your daddy going to just feed you from the restaurant every day without you lifting a hand? Or did you think I'd marry you if you had my baby and go to work at Walmart so you could stay home with that precious little one?"

"You wouldn't do that, would you?"

"No, I wouldn't. So, the best thing is not to have a baby. Now, I'll practice with you all you want. You're pretty amazing and I could really fall for you. But this cowboy don't go in that corral without rubber boots."

I pretty much figured that ended our fucking and probably our dating, but I was in for a surprise. Geneive pushed me back and slurped my soft cock into her mouth. I started to respond almost instantly.

"We don't need rubber boots for this, do we?" she asked, grinning.

"No sweetheart. You can have as much of that as you want. I'll even return the favor."

"Really?" There was a mad scramble in the truck and somehow, we managed to fit a sixty-nine around the steering wheel. There was a little leftover taste of the rubber on her pussy, but that disappeared pretty quickly and was replaced by a flood of sweet juices that were all hers.

I wasn't very proficient at pussy-licking. Mary Beth and I had done it a couple times and it wasn't like I didn't like it, it's just I wasn't always sure I was any good at it. Based on Geneive's response, though, I seemed to be doing pretty well. And all the noise she was making as she sucked on my cock was sending a bunch of new thrills up and down my spine and straight through my balls.

"Sweetheart, I'm about to come. I can't hold back." She didn't change her rhythm or her position so I just relaxed and buried my nose in her puss while I let 'er rip. I swear, Geneive came with me, even while she was swallowing my load and bathing my face.

I'm NOT MUCH on sports. I'll watch a football game and cheer for the Cowboys just like anyone else, but when it comes to playing sports I figure if it isn't done on horseback why bother? In case you're a Dallas fan, you should know I'm talking about the University of Wyoming Cowboys, not the North Dallas 40. Mostly, though, that just means that I'm a tall skinny guy who doesn't play basketball. Kind of narrows down the dating pool. With Geneive that was a moot point. Once in a while I'd attend a high school ball game if there seemed like a reason to—like I was meeting Geneive at the game and then leaving. She became really special to me really fast. It seemed she'd set her sights on me the first day of school and I wasn't complaining.

We used ballgames as an excuse to date and Dad raised his brows a little at my sudden interest. I noticed he never got more specific than "Who won?" the next morning. I always remembered to check in with Sid to find out before I went home. We'd managed to stay pretty good friends in spite of the fact that Laune still teased me once in a while.

"I guess you really like us girls with tiny titties," Laune whispered to me in the hall one day. "Do Geneive's stand up in little points and push her t-shirt out when you look at them like mine do?" Then she giggled and ran down the hall to grab Sid's hand before I could respond. *Sid, what did you save me from?*

Of course, she was right. There was something about those little bumps on Geneive's chest that just cried out for me to catch them in my lips and tongue them until she came. And for Geneive's part, I think she caught Laune one day because the next day I couldn't help but notice there were no bra straps showing through her t-shirt. She was wearing a pair of bib overalls over the t-shirt—it was all the fashion among the town-girls—and it seemed like every time I looked at her, one tit or the other was poking her t-shirt out just to the side of the bib. I walked around bow-legged all day.

I never will understand girls and fashion. There were at least a dozen city-girls wearing some form of bibs that day—full overalls, shorts or cut-offs, and even one who'd cut the crotch out and sewed it into a mini-skirt. The ranch girls all hated the idea of wearing 'work clothes' to school and even though we had a pretty fair selection of skin-tight blue jeans, they were usually some Guess or Gloria somebody brand and not the usual work Levi's or Wranglers. And those tight jeans were always topped by a cute shirt, sweater, or blouse. A lot of country girls came to school in dresses, but some of those were forced to by their parents. We still had some pretty strict notions of propriety on the ranches.

Well, as it happened, this was a Friday and I had standing permission to stay in town on Friday night to go out with friends after school and then to whatever ballgame there was that night. The fact that Geneive and I seldom actually made it to the game didn't matter.

"Well, hers or mine?" Geneive asked as we drove away from the school. I glanced over at her trying for just a second to figure out what she was talking about. She'd pulled off her jacket when she got in the truck and unbuckled the straps on her bibs so the front fell forward and just the dangling buckles were over her shoulders. She'd worn a white t-shirt and her dark tits were clearly visible under it. I swerved and got my eyes back on the road. "Well?" she asked again.

"Darlin', I don't know what 'her' you're talking about. I can't see nobody else but you."

"Sweet-tongued devil. You know what I'm talking about. Laune's been showing you her tits for over a year now. Even her boyfriend knows about it. She spent half the day today pointing him at mine. So, you like mine better or Laune's?" she repeated.

"I'm stickin' with what I said first. I mighta looked at Laune a little. It's hard not to. But I got eyes for nobody but you."

"Good. Let's go out on Comanche Road to that abandoned barn you showed me. I want you to get a better look at these."

I swung north out of town like she told me to and when she slid over to sit in the middle seat I put my arm around her. I had to look again, 'cause all I felt was skin. That t-shirt had come off as fast as her bibs went down. She pulled my arm around her as she leaned against me and put my hand on her right tit.

"I love that you love them, Cole. I love that you want to look at me and touch me. I love that you always want to make me feel good. You're different than anybody else, lover. You're gentle and still get a little rough when we both get going. Just enough most of the time." Her hand was in my lap and had unzipped my pants to ease the pressure down below. "Don't you know I want to do everything with you?"

"God, Ginny, we do just about everything and I can't get enough of you. Just let me get us to that barn before I drive off the road."

I did get to the barn and Geneive showed me a bunch of stuff that we hadn't done yet for the next six hours. I know you're thinking I should know all this stuff by now, but besides Geneive, I'd only been with Mary Beth and that one amazing time with Laramie. Mary Beth and I were learning the basics from each other, but neither of us had much experience to teach the other. Laramie had scarcely known what sex was and had never been kissed when we met.

I didn't want to ask about where Geneive got all her knowledge. She'd say something about "online" or "I saw this on a site." But I didn't think that could all come from just browsing the web.

Like kissing.

I know I talk a lot about screwing Geneive, but that wasn't all we'd do. There were times when we'd just lie there together for a while and kiss and kiss and kiss. She had the softest lips ever just caressing and loving at me. And then she'd turn into the most insistent open mouthed and all-tongue kisser on the planet. I never knew what to expect when her lips touched mine.

Tonight, she wanted me to do a kissing tour of her body. Of course, I spent a long time on her lips. But I guess I spent just as long kissing up her face, her eyes, her ears—that little spot just behind her ears that always seemed to drive her crazy. Then down her neck and throat that was vibrating the whole time with her moans. Oh yeah, that hollow in her shoulders at the base of her neck—some reason that's like a huge target for me and I just loved that she was letting me or actually asking me to kiss her all over. I was afraid she might be ticklish there when she scrunched her head to that side a little but she pulled it back upright to give me better access and just whined as I let my soft lips move under her shoulder bone to the top of her chest.

I love to kiss and suck her tender nipples, but I had the feeling she wanted me to try everyplace else instead of focusing on them. I couldn't resist just a little tongue lap across those hard points she'd been showing off all day. Then I continued down her sides and across her belly.

"There! Cole. Oh God! Right there. What are you doing?" I was just kissing her sort of above her pelvis to one side. She tensed up and moaned long and loud. "I loved that, Cole! I loved that! I didn't know I was so sensitive right there. Oh Lord! that was intense. No, not again.

Don't touch it again right now. It's too sensitive there." I glanced up at her face and from where I was, I could see the hard points of her nipples sticking out even further than usual.

Do you know how many little hollows there are on a woman? I mean places where there's a little dip in the skin like the top of the shoulder and under the shoulder bone on her chest and at the base of her neck and the little indent I'd found that was so sensitive above her pelvis and that spot where her thigh muscles have a tendon that connects and there's a hollow spot on either side of it and behind the knee and at her ankle. Every single one of them seem to have nerves that are right at the surface and each time I found one, Geneive would moan and lift up off the seat of the truck arching her back. And when I finally reached the center—when her legs fully parted and she let me find the source of the heat I felt on my face—I touched the sweetest nectar I'd ever known. I kept up with just kissing for a minute but I couldn't resist dipping my tongue in and bringing it slowly up across her clit. When she screamed this time, she was shaking all over and I quickly moved up to hold her in my arms while she sobbed against me.

"Oh Cole. I love you, baby. I don't know how you did that to me. I just loved it."

"You told me what to do, Ginny. I never would have known. I loved that I could do something to make you so happy."

"Do something else to make me happy," she said. "Get that cowboy dressed and put him in me. Make love to me some more, honey. Tell me how I can make you happy."

By nine o'clock, we were both pretty damned happy—and hungry. We drove in to the Sonic on Grand in town. We ate, but we did as much feeding each other and cuddling in the truck as we did eating. I don't know what that carhop thought when I rolled down the window for her to take our order and the smell in the cab rolled out. Her eyes kind of shot open in surprise, though, and I think she blushed. Could have been just the color of the lights in the drive-in, though.

I HAD A long talk with Mary Beth over Thanksgiving. Geneive and her folks went to visit relatives over the holiday. Mary Beth said she was happy for me and that I should have all the fun I could with Geneive. She wanted to know if I wanted to stop seeing her.

"I don't know what to say to you, Mary Beth. I love you. Sure, Geneive and me have a lot of great sex, but we've never really talked about being anything more serious than we are. I don't want to cheat on her, but I don't feel the same about her as I do about you."

"How about if we just cool it until Christmas and see if you develop deeper feelings for her, then," Mary Beth suggested. That might sound real generous and all, but the fact was we were lying naked in each other's arms in the hay loft of the horse barn at the time. It was Saturday night and Mary Beth was headed back to Boulder Sunday. I grinned at her.

"Yeah. Maybe we should not do this again until you get back at Christmas. After tonight, I mean."

"After tonight. Show me that thing you did on our sides, again, honey. I think I'll need to remember that when I get back to school. Like every night." We rolled together again and I made love to Mary Beth softly and gently until we fell asleep under a big quilt we'd brought along.

THE CHAT NEVER came. I got out of school December 18, but Mary Beth didn't get home until Christmas Eve. Any thoughts I had about getting together with either of my girls were shattered when Dad came in and said we had a sick herd. We had about 900 steers in the feedlot with over three hundred nearly ready for January market. A virus could kill our chances at January income if not kill our cows altogether. We had over five hundred yearlings in the back pasture getting ready for the spring drive to the upper range. Dad opined that some of the cows he bought at auction were sick and had spread the disease through the whole herd.

When your herd is sick there ain't no holidays.

We had to administer antibiotics and vaccine to every single one of them. Mom was out in the pen with Dad and me and the two winter hands. Mom kept track of the tag numbers as we shot the cows up. I was sent out with the front-end loader to dig a hole and scoop up the dead cows and dump them in the pit. We couldn't put them in the pasture, so I had to dig the pit in frozen rocky ground nearly half a mile south of the feedlot. It was pretty brutal. We lost fifty head, mostly from the young stock we'd just bought.

But it got worse. Uncle Angus called on Christmas morning and said his stock was coming down with the same virus. We hustled over and shot up another eight hundred head.

I was beat. So was everyone. We'd heard from half a dozen other ranchers that the virus had hit all over the county. Vaccines and antibiotics were getting to be in short supply and it was going to wreak havoc on all of us this winter.

I drove the front-end loader back to the equipment barn after I finished covering in the pit where I'd dumped eighty head. It was dark and before I reached the barn I slowed the tractor to a stop and looked up the snowy mountain where we'd have cattle this summer. I felt his presence before I heard his call.

Traveling: Caitlin

KYLE WAS RIDING into town on Bolt and I was riding in the back of his mind. He jerked his head around as if he heard someone talking, but just shook it off and sped his buckskin up as they headed toward town.

I guess I was so exhausted when I stopped the tractor that it didn't throw me as much to be inside Kyle's mind and body. He was just riding—a comfortable position for me. I just settled back to watch what was going to happen. It seemed Kyle was exhausted from a long trip, too. I'd almost come to believe it was a one-time thing and would never happen again, but here I was in a Wyoming that had no cars or trucks.

That didn't mean there was no traffic. Kyle guided his buckskin around a mule train and handed the reins and a couple coppers to a stable boy to go take care of. He just grabbed his saddlebags and went into the saloon. He was hungry and had an itch that he wanted scratched. I wondered where Laramie was. The only reason I wanted to come back was to see her. But I didn't know where she was so I'd have to ride along with whatever Kyle had in mind for a while.

What he had in mind was a steak and a couple beers. It was way too burned for my taste, but Kyle thought it was as good as it gets. As soon as he finished eating and paid with a silver dollar, he headed around the bar and showed a token to the doorkeeper. He was let through and I found myself in a roomful of half-naked women and a few cowboys.

There was a squeal from across the room and a little redhead came launching herself into my arms and planted a mouthwatering kiss on my lips and deep into my mouth.

"Mmm. Caitlin, you little wildcat. Get me a bath and scrub my prick. I want it buried deep in your cunt in half an hour."

"You sweet talker, Kyle. I saw you come in to eat and got a bath ready. It's in our room. Come on, stud. Make me scream."

I followed Caitlin up the stairs, staying just outside Kyle's consciousness. That little ass sure looked good as she tugged us along. I decided to just let this play out. Caitlin was out of what remained of her clothes and stripping Kyle out of his as quickly as she could. Something had changed here. My first trip into Kyle, he didn't care how dirty he was or what he smelled like. Now, before he even thought about bedding this very willing and perky girl, he wanted a bath and he wanted his clothes washed.

Caitlin got right into the tub with me and started scrubbing the dirt from my face and hands. Then she moved down and kept washing, grasping my cock, and stroking it to full erection. She ground herself against me and captured my mouth with her lips and tongue again.

Kyle stood up in the tub, holding Caitlin up by her ass cheeks, and stepped out. Caitlin dropped to the floor and grabbed a towel to start drying him. She dried herself when he was finished.

"Come on, wild one. Let's get that sweet cunt of yours in bed where it belongs." He picked her up and deposited her in the middle of the bed climbing in after.

"Oh Kyle. Kiss me. Do all those things you do to me. I missed you so much." *Damn. Is this a whore or is she his girlfriend?*

"Now you just settle down and let old Kyle take care of you." With that, Kyle started kissing on Caitlin. When he got down to sucking on her nipples, Caitlin was writhing in the bed, moaning and pleading for more. His fingers dipped into her folds and began smearing the fluids around, paying special attention to her little bud. Caitlin was rapidly rising to an orgasm.

"No one makes me feel like you do, Kyle. Yes. Just a little more." Caitlin tipped over the top and Kyle prepared to mount her. The damn prick was using all the things I taught him with Laramie to make the whores go apeshit over him. I read in his thoughts that Caitlin was only one of several who competed for his time, though she was his special girl. I figured it was time to up the ante a little and make him work more for his praise. I slipped past his consciousness and took control of his body before he could thrust into her.

"What are you doing, Kyle? You can fuck me now. I'd do anything for you."

"And I love that about you, Caitlin," I said. "I love it so much I've got something special for you tonight. You just lie back and enjoy."

With that, I pushed back and kissed each of her nipples before trailing kisses all down her stomach. I found each of those little concave spots I'd discovered and kissed and licked them until she was writhing on the bed. I kissed that little spot just above her hipbone and before my tongue had slid down to her fuzzies, Caitlin lit up again. I didn't stop there, though. I kept moving down and when Caitlin felt my breath parting her short hairs she jerked upright.

"What are you doing?"

"You got in the bath and scrubbed this sweet little cunt up for me. Now I'm gonna eat it all up." I dove in. There was still a trace of soap on her hair and skin, but it wasn't enough to deter me. I grabbed Caitlin behind the knees and rolled her up so her pussy was easier to get to. Geneive always loved it when I rolled her up in a little ball and started tongue lashing her pussy. Caitlin seemed to agree. Her scream was so loud that a minute later someone pounded on the door and pushed it open.

"You hurting her?" demanded the bulky presence.

"No Saul. Go away!" Caitlin screamed. "He's wonderful. Do it again, Kyle. Do it again."

The door closed behind the bouncer, and I dove back into Caitlin's snatch. This time, just before she peaked, I rose up and shoved my cock straight into her pussy. I clamped my mouth over Caitlin's as she screamed again and receded into the back of Kyle's consciousness to leave him to the thrusting and moaning. Even back here, it was a great ride. We all came together and collapsed into a sleeping mass on the bed.

I made an important discovery that night that I didn't have time for when I last visited. Kyle needed sleep, just like anyone else, but I didn't. While he slept with his redheaded beauty tucked into his arm, I was free to roam around his mind and pick up a lot of information that wasn't normally in his conscious mind. It was about all I could do. I could feel Caitlin pressed up against me and occasionally Kyle would breathe deeply and I'd smell the fresh soapy scent of her, but I couldn't see anything with Kyle's eyes closed and I hadn't managed to connect to his hearing while he was sleeping. So, I spent that night picking up bits and pieces of a man I didn't really care to know. Why the hell would I get plunked down into such a sewer?

Well, it wasn't all his fault, I suppose. He'd grown up an orphan, living on the streets and running errands for food or scrubbing out pots behind one of the brothels. He'd pretty much grown up on Front Street, right where he was now sleeping. As soon as he was old enough to hold a gun, he started practicing with it and he'd killed a man in a fight when he was 13. He was considered a slow starter in the brothel where he lived for not having taken any of the girls until he was sixteen. That hadn't been the end of it.

The bloody battles of early territorial Laramie were gone and the little town was preparing a big celebration next month for Wyoming's statehood. But there were still men who thought nothing of getting what they wanted by intimidating or killing others. Kyle was sort of an enforcer. The name and image that came up most frequently in his thoughts was Cal Despain. Sheriff Cal Despain. Sheriff Despain used seventeen-year-old Kyle for 'secret' jobs. That word had been so pounded into his mind that during the night I was unable to pry out what the secrets were.

While I was surfing around Kyle's memories, I finally located Laramie—or at least a general direction where she'd been when we had our last encounter. The bastard hadn't even been back to visit her since he took her virginity almost a year ago. I was going to remedy that situation before I went back—at least if I could.

WE WOKE UP in the morning to the exquisite feeling of morning wood being sucked into a very wet and willing mouth. It was really distracting to me that I was completely locked inside Kyle's body, so even though I was conscious and feeling the blowjob long before he woke up, I couldn't tell who was going down on me until Kyle woke up and opened his eyes. That is, unless I wanted to take over the body and wake it up. It was tempting, but I was determined to just ride along and learn at this stage—except for that little demonstration last night. So, I could feel all the sensations, but I couldn't really participate much. Okay, I finally took control long enough to thrust my hips forward and bury my cock a little deeper in the willing orifice, but that woke Kyle up and I retreated to watch as he opened his eyes.

Redheaded Caitlin was gone. Instead, a big, buxom brunette was bobbing on our morning wood. As slight as Caitlin was, this girl was big.

"Ellen Jane, what do you think you're doing?" Kyle yawned.

"I'm gettin' you ready for a ride, dahlin'. Making sure you got the nuts to give me what I want."

"And what do you want, you big ol' pig?"

"I wanna scream like you made Caitlin scream last night. She came out after you went to sleep and was so shaky on her legs she couldn't service another cowboy for two hours. I want to know what that's like and she told me some fine tales."

Kyle shuddered a little at the thought of planting his face between those thunder-thighs. I guess I joined him a little, but I was pretty proud of myself, too. If my little escapade with Caitlin last night made it harder for Kyle to cheat his women of pleasure, I was happy. I didn't really care if every whore in the brothel rode his mustache.

"You won't smother me with that big butt of yours will you, El?" Kyle groaned.

Ellen rolled off Kyle onto her back and spread her legs.

"These legs might be big but they spread wide, kid. And Caitlin made me scrub the bush before I came to see you."

"Thank Jesus for that," Kyle muttered as he rolled over on top of Ellen and headed for breakfast at the Y. I gave him a nudge, though, and reminded him that he couldn't take short-cuts. If he didn't want me to take over he had to start at the lips with one of those kisses that started a girl's engine. Surprisingly, Ellen received his offered kiss with tenderness that seemed out of character with the brassiness of the big woman. And she surprised Kyle with how good a kisser she was. Kyle was a little out of breath when he pulled his face away and our hard-on was almost painful.

"Ellen, you sure can kiss."

"My old man was a good kisser before he got hisself killed. That's the one thing I miss most working here. Most of those cowboys, I wouldn't kiss if they tripled my wages. Is that how you got Caitlin so riled up last night?"

"Well, it was a start, but not the finish," Kyle said. He kissed Ellen again and then started working his way slowly down the big woman's body. To his credit, he spent the time to make sure he found every spot on her big breasts and bulging tummy that might pleasure her. I think they were both surprised when he found that spot just above her pelvis and below the fold of her belly that made her gasp and moan. I'm pretty sure no man had ever managed to touch her there. When Kyle reached her hairy pussy, Ellen was moaning and grabbing at the sheets. Her legs were spread out like a teenaged cheerleader. It took a few seconds for Kyle to lick his way through the hair and fat labia, but when he took his first long lick of the plentiful juices from her vagina to her clit, Ellen nearly came off the bed. Kyle began a steady assault on her clit, keeping his elbows up and wedged against the clamping effects of her legs on his head. Ellen's pleasure escalated vocally and a gush of juice poured out of her pussy and into Kyle's mouth.

"Oh Kyle! Get up here and plant that big cock of yours in my cunt! Ride me like a wild horse. Let me have that pole all the way up inside. Fuck me, little man! Ellen's got everything you need right here!"

We got the wildest ride of my life. I'd never been with a woman the size of Ellen and I didn't think Kyle had either. She wasn't just big; she was strong. Kyle was hanging on for dear life as if he was breaking a wild horse. Ellen screamed and rocked her hips and beat Kyle with her heels until he hooked his arms under her knees and pressed forward with all his strength to pound into her. The explosion dizzied Kyle as he spurted into the big whore. He collapsed forward onto her tits and Ellen wrapped her arms around him and crushed him to her.

"Thank you, Jesus," Ellen kept whispering. "Thank you for bringing the spirit of my man Harry into this boy. Thank you, Jesus."

"I gotta tell you, Ellen. That was a hell of a ride. But it would sure be a hell of a lot easier to get my tongue in that sweet snatch of yours if it wasn't so hairy." He spit a little and pulled a couple of coarse hairs from his mouth. I don't think he realized what he was starting with those words, but I bet the cowboys at the Bertha's Wild Ride Saloon were going to have something new on the menu.

Kyle managed to get dressed in clean clothes and strap on an impressive pair of revolvers that stayed firmly holstered, but looked to be Smith & Wesson Model 3s. I was curious that he wore guns in town. Laramie was becoming more civilized as Wyoming headed for statehood. I was sure open guns would be frowned upon by the town marshal. Kyle looked at himself in the mirror as he placed his black hat on his head. I'd never thought to make him look at himself. It was the first time I actually saw what I looked like in this era. We were pretty close to the same build. He was a little shorter than me, but still tall for a man of that time. Most striking, however, were the intense blue eyes and hair so pale it was almost white and hung to his shoulders. I had blue eyes in my own body, but though light, my hair was much darker than Kyle's. He cut an impressive figure and I could see why he was a bit vain.

HE HEADED OUT of the hotel after a quick breakfast and walked out of the brothel area and across to Main Street. Laramie had four principal arteries and a number of cross-streets by this time. It had cleaned up Main Street where the respectable businesses were. There was a mercantile, chemist, and even a barber shop. All the less reputable businesses, brothels, saloons, and card rooms were on Front Street. Kyle stopped in front of the sheriff's office.

"Cal? You there?" he called at the door.

"Get your butt in here and quit yowling on the street," a gravelly voice commanded. Kyle obeyed.

Sheriff Cal Despain appeared to be a hard man. He'd risen to the position of sheriff on the coattails of the famous N.K. Boswell. Boswell was still around and had a big ranch southwest of town. It was a historic place in my time. I couldn't remember from my history class if he was still warden of the prison in 1890 or not. Despain worked on Boswell's ranch and when the opportunity came, Boswell stood him for election as sheriff. Folks still had a healthy fear of Boswell and Despain was elected without competition. Even the women of the town had voted for him.

"Did you get the goods?" Despain demanded.

"Yessir. Just like you said. The stage was hit by a gang of three. They killed the driver and guard, but told the three passengers to just stay in the coach and they wouldn't be hurt. One of the robbers climbed up top and tossed down the strongbox. Another was down under the carriage. When he crawled out from behind, the guy who seemed to be giving the orders gave him a nod and I saw him light a fuse hanging out of the back. The one from up top gave the horses a smack with the whip and they took off like crazy. About a hundred yards down the road, the whole coach blew up."

"Clever. They dynamited it. Well, how'd you get the money."

"I just followed them nice and quiet to their camp and as soon as they settled down for the night I shot all three of them. I stripped them of everything like you said and burned everything that would burn. I loaded my mule with the strongbox and led their saddle horses with all their tack up into the mountains. After I cleaned out their saddlebags, I dumped a saddle in a dry gulch up high where the snow will come early, then set the horse free. A few miles later I did the same with the second horse and then the third. I took the strongbox to our cache and came into town. I didn't even need to take anything for expenses since the robbers had plenty in their saddlebags for me to get my pole greased and have some fun."

"Good. It won't be long now before we can split things up and have all the money we need for life. You'll either die a rich old man or some jealous husband will shoot you climbing out of his wife's bedroom window." They both laughed at the joke.

"Thank you kindly, sir, but I'd much rather *live* a rich man than die one."

"Smart. But it's time to ride again. Sit down." Kyle sat across from the sheriff and looked at him expectantly. It was the first time I looked into Cal Despain's eyes. There was something wrong there.

So far, I'd figured I was the only time-traveler there was. In fact, I hadn't convinced myself yet that what I was experiencing was anything more than a mental aberration or some kind of wild dreams. I had an extremely lucid dream of being in a different time that only lasted a few seconds in real time. I had no evidence that it was anything else. But looking into Cal Despain's eyes, I saw something wrong—as though someone else was looking out of them. I was making no effort to control Kyle at the moment, but I simply observed what he saw. The sheriff's movements were jerky and a little off, like someone else was moving his hands as he unfolded a map on the desk.

"You need to pick up your mule and head north. You've got ten days to get to the Big Horn. Pick up supplies in Casper and stay off the main roads from then on. Follow the Big Horn River until you reach Gypsum creek and set up a dry camp on the cliff overlooking the confluence. Just wait. It might take a few days, but don't give away your location. You'll see two men head into the canyon below you. As soon as you do, take a strongbox down and wait in the trees where you can't be seen. Within hours, a posse will come through and there will be a shootout. While they're busy with the posse, crack their strongbox and empty out as much as you can. Then haul your ass out of there. Leave their strongbox and go. Get back here as quick as you can but stay off the main roads until you are south of Casper."

The instructions were so specific that Cal Despain had to have a vision of the future. I rummaged around Kyle's brain for a while and discovered that Kyle simply accepted Despain's knowledge of the future as equivalent of his glimpses of things that I brought to him. Kyle thought it was all normal. *Shit!*

I walked out of Cal Despain's office wondering who the time-traveler was that inhabited him. Then I heard Redtail's screech.

Dumped

I WAS SHIVERING when I came back to my body on that tractor. It was still running, but it was an open cab and no protection from the wind. It had started snowing and I'd just been sitting out there looking up at it for like twenty minutes. I went on to the equipment shed thinking about what I'd just experienced. Hell, having a wet dream like that stopped out in the cold December air? I had to be crazy. I headed back to the house and went to bed.

I slept well past noon.

I decided that I'd better call Geneive once I got up and had some food. There just hadn't been time in the past week. I sure wasn't expecting what I got.

"Cole? Cole, before you say anything, please listen to me. I'm sorry. I mean I'm really sorry about this, but I have to break up with you. I can't take it."

"Geneive, honey, I'm sorry I haven't been able to talk to you since school got out. It was the cattle. We had to do what ranchers do. It's all over the county. We don't need to break up over it."

"It's not that, C-Cole. Honest. It's me, not you. I know that sounds like it came out of some lousy movie that I dragged you off to. But it really is. I can't do it now. I can't tell you why, so please don't ask me for reasons. I had more fun with you than I'll probably ever have in my life, but I just can't do it now. I'm sorry, Cole. I'll see you in school."

She hung up the phone and I stood there staring at it. What the fuck? Everything was fine when school let out. We'd gone to one of those dumb chick flicks, and then we'd gone to our favorite place and screwed our brains out. I didn't get her home till three o'clock in the morning and I dragged in about four. The next day all hell broke loose. Now all of a sudden, she just says she can't take it and breaks up with me. I was too confused to be mad, too sad to be angry.

I was still staring at the phone when it rang again.

"Hello."

"Cole, it's Mary Beth. You get some rest after all the work?"

"Yeah. I just sort of woke up about an hour ago."

"I was just thinking that maybe we should have that talk we were going to have."

"Oh."

"You okay, honey?"

"You going to break up with me, too, Mary Beth?"

"Too? Oh God! She didn't! Don't you ever think I'm going to do that, Cole Alexander Bell. I might not be the one and only in your life forever, but I am forever in your life."

"Mary Beth, she just said she couldn't take it all of a sudden. I don't know what happened." Tears were starting to fill my eyes at the shit all started to stink at once.

"Cole, pack your backpack and tell Uncle Earl you'll be back on New Year's. I'm on my way to pick you up."

"Huh?"

"Cole, do it now."

"Yeah. Okay."

I hung up the phone and went to see Dad. It was two days till New Year's Eve. What the hell was I going to tell him?

"Um… Dad? Mary Beth says she's got a New Year's surprise for me and to tell you I'll be back on New Year's Day. Um… okay?"

"Angus said she had a surprise for you," Dad laughed. "Something about a college party she was taking you to. She really sprang it on you just now? You better pack your bag."

I ran upstairs and started cramming stuff into my bag. I had no idea what I'd need, so I put one of everything in it. Or two. I ran back downstairs to find Dad looking out the front window as Mary Beth came tearing down the drive.

"Um… see you in a couple days, Dad?"

"Yeah. Here." He handed me five twenties. "Your cousin thinks the world of you, Cole. Make sure you're nice and don't embarrass her in front of her friends. And… be safe. I ain't gonna tell you not to have a drink or not to screw a pretty coed, but make sure you aren't drinking and driving and that you use protection. And keep an eye out for your cousin, Cole. She's like a daughter to me as much as to Angus."

"Thanks, Dad. Uh… where's Mom?"

"She went over to Alexanders' around noon. I'm going over after chores for dinner and to play cards. I expect she knows you're going. Don't worry about it."

"Okay. 'Bye, Dad."

I ran out and jumped in Mary Beth's car. She honked the horn and waved at Dad on the front porch and then we were tearing out of the drive and down our dirt road toward town.

WHATEVER MARY BETH had told our parents, or her dad to tell my dad, we weren't headed to Boulder for any college party. She put us on the highway to Cheyenne and two hours after we left, we were checking into the Holiday Inn on I-80.

"Mary Beth, this is expensive! You can't pay for three nights here."

"Not just three nights here, but three meals each day. You get to buy condoms."

"Darling…"

"Save that for when we get into the room. And this place has a nice pool and hot tub, too. That's part of why I chose it." We rode the elevator up to the third floor and Mary Beth led the way to the room. She unlocked the door and handed me a key. We walked in and looked around. I don't think I'd ever stayed in a hotel before, at least not that I could remember—in this timeline. It was certainly nicer and cleaner than what I remembered of Kyle's room in 1890. And the bed was big enough so I could stretch out on it, I was sure. The view from the window was just the Interstate, but I didn't plan to stand staring out the window. Not with Mary Beth on this side of the glass.

I took her in my arms and kissed her. She kissed back.

"How did you ever manage to pull this off, darling?" I asked. It was too much. "The hotel. Getting our parents to agree. The money."

"Well, I told them that I thought it would be fun to surprise you with a trip to meet some cool college girls and have a party after all the crap we just had to go through with the cattle. They kind of agreed and Dad even gave me a hundred to help with expenses. The rest I saved from my job waiting tables at Castro's Diner. Tips are pretty good even though I only work about 15 hours a week."

"Dad gave me a hundred to help with expenses, too. I don't think he intended me to buy a hundred dollars' worth of condoms. But Why, Mary Beth?"

"Why? Cole, we started making love last summer on your birthday and I've craved it ever since. You've been screwing Geneive for two months now. So, tell me. Have you ever yet made love in a bed?"

"Um… no."

"Me either. And the front seat of your truck is starting to look pretty grody. I just want a weekend with the nicest boy I ever met in a room with clean sheets and all the hot water we want for showers. I want to live with you for one weekend, honey."

And we did. When that three-day stay was up, Mary Beth and I were more in love than ever. I still hurt a little over Geneive, but knowing that no matter what, Mary Beth would be there for me was pretty wonderful.

ONCE WE'D SETTLED back into the routine of school after the holiday, I found I was at a bit of a loss come Friday nights. I'd been seeing Geneive for three months and with Mary Beth back in Boulder, it was pretty lonely. It was about four weeks later, near the beginning of February that I ran into Geneive. Well, it wasn't like I didn't see her every day. We still had classes together and our circle of friends overlapped pretty completely. But on this particular Friday, I sat down with my food tray in the cafeteria and Geneive came up and sat right across from me.

"Hi. Can we talk?" she said quickly.

"Um… sure. What's to talk about? You dumped me." Okay, I was a little pissed yet, but I tried to rein in my temper.

"I know. I'm sorry." She was quiet for a while. I thought she wanted to talk.

"That's it?"

"Yeah. Really it is. I sort of got panicked. I really, really like you, Cole. I think I might have even fallen in love with you. I got to thinking of that over Christmas and looking at the present I got you and I knew you were busy on the ranch and we wouldn't see each other for a while and the more I thought about it, the more panicked I got. We're only sixteen and we're acting like we're about to get married and neither of us have ever even said we love each other. Except that one time I tried to get you to make me pregnant. I'm sorry about that, too. That made me sound like a desperate bitch who would do anything to have you, but that wasn't it really. Well, maybe that was part of it. I was just feeling so dirty about the way I treated you, I thought that wasn't fair and… And I panicked. I told you I didn't want to see you anymore. And I'm sorry. I wish I'd never said those awful words."

Well, my heart was pretty well melted, but all I could really do was reach out and pat her hand. She turned it over so I could hold it.

"Can we get back together, Cole?" Shit. Now what was I going to do. One of the things Mary Beth and I talked about on our weekend was how it was necessary to tell anyone else we got involved with that there was someone else. We didn't have to go into details, but in all fairness, neither of us wanted to go sneaking around on a girlfriend or boyfriend. Time for the proof in the pudding.

"I'd like to, Geneive. But there's… well, I've got a sort of problem… I mean not actually a problem, but…"

"Oh God! You found somebody else!" She pulled her hand away from mine.

"Wait, Geneive. It's sort of like that but not exactly. I've never had to say this before and if I could just tell you, I know you might not want to get together again, but maybe at least we won't hate each other, okay?" She sat there looking at me with her lower lip between her teeth looking like she was trying not to cry but she nodded her head. I took a deep breath and began.

"I'm in love with a woman, but we can never really be together. You can draw your own conclusions about that. We're lovers when we can be but that's not often. We got together over New Year's and talked about this. We were going to talk about whether we needed to break things off between us so you and I would stand a chance, but then you broke up with me. I realized over New Year's that I really care for her too much to ever break it off, even if we can't really be together. So, I have to tell you about it before you ask if we can get back together again." I pretty much got it all out in one breath. Geneive sat there looking at me with a puzzled look on her face—not angry or hurt, just puzzled.

"She wouldn't mind if you dated someone else?" she asked finally.

"She actually encouraged it. Said I couldn't be stuck with someone who could never be more than my sometimes lover. She offered to just step aside and not see me anymore, but I refused. I'd always have to refuse that. I'm sorry if that means we stay broken up, Ginny, but I can't lie to you about it."

"Would you mind if we talk about this again later?"

"I don't mind. Just let me know when you'd like to talk."

"Tonight. After school. This evening. Just say you'll pick me up." My mouth dropped open. I nodded and she took her lunch tray to the bussing station. I don't think either one of us touched a bite.

44

3
Picking Up Pieces

WE USE a donkey to train a bull. Sounds silly, but a bull needs to figure out that he's not the alpha male. While the bull is young, under about eight hundred pounds, we just use a big old halter on him and attach it to Benji's halter with a lead rope. The bull learns to go wherever Benji goes. Of course, if he figures out he's bigger and stronger than Benji, then there's a problem. That's where the ring comes in. We watch that stuff pretty close. You don't want a bull thinking all he has to do is throw his weight around and he can do whatever he wants to. The danged thing is going to weigh more than a ton and the most common accidental death among cattlemen is being crushed by a bull. Not gored—crushed.

So, once he gets above about 750 pounds—like at three months— we put a ring in his nose. From then on, Benji's halter is attached to the ring. No bull fights against the ring more than once. When Benji digs his heels in, the bull can't move away. If Benji wants to graze someplace different, the bull has to follow. Not to mention the fact that if a bull gets feisty, Benji has no qualms about lining up on him and belting him with both back hooves. Our bulls get pretty gentle.

We had a little problem once when a young bull lunged away from Benji and his halter snapped. I don't know how long we'd had that halter, but the leather got weak along one side and when 600 pounds lunged against it, it snapped. Dad gave me the job of mending the halter.

"Sometimes you have to mend things, Cole," Dad said. "You need to know how, even if we go out and buy a new halter." So, he taught me. We had to splice new leather onto the old and glue it, then use an awl to punch holes so I could force a needle and thick thread through the holes. It looked pretty damned good when I was finished, though it was bulky as hell with all the new leather.

Dad didn't put the halter back on the bull, though. He had a ring in his nose by that time. Instead he said he wanted us to test the mend. We've got all kinds of scales and weights around the barn, so Dad looped the halter around a beam in the barn then attached a lead rope to it. He tied the other end of the rope to a 500-pound weight balanced on a board. I'd learned about fulcrums in school, so he had me holding the other end of the board about six feet the other side of a stall half-wall. When everything was set he warned me to keep my chin back and let go of my end of the fulcrum.

I did. The board flipped up in the air and the weight tipped off the end. It fell about three feet and came to the end of the lead rope. It was almost like watching a bungee jumper get to the end of the rope and then bounce up. The weight stopped, sprang back a bit, and then fell to the floor. I looked up and my newly repaired halter was snapped again.

"Son," Dad said, "sometimes when something breaks there's just no way to patch it so that it's as strong as it used to be. You either have to treat it more gently or replace it."

Patches

GENEIVE AND I got back together. In fact, we got back together with some pretty loud yowling that very night. Now that she knew my dick was regularly if not frequently in someone else's pussy, she didn't balk so much at me wearing a condom. I still sensed a kind of yearning in her, though, as if she wanted to share something more with me than our admittedly hot sexual relationship. I assumed it was because she was still fixated on having a baby, but I just wasn't ready for that kind of commitment.

Spring break didn't match up for me and Mary Beth. I told her I'd come down to be with her, but she said not to bother because she had exams and a huge paper due. She was up to Laramie over her spring break the week before mine and we managed to squeeze in some good loving. But that meant that I had a whole week that I could devote to Geneive. I wondered if she could get away or if her parents would frown on the two of us going off together for a few days. Well, it turned out they did.

But Geneive and I did get one break that was what I wanted most. Her parents ran the restaurant, so they left the house at eight to prepare for the lunch crowd. Geneive didn't have to be there until she helped serve dinner at four. I visited Ginny from nine till three and we made love in her bed. I'd learned a few tricks on the advice of Mary Beth about covering my truck seats with a one of those fleece blankets you can get at Walmart for like five bucks. During the winter, we'd needed one over the top of us, too, but we kept the truck pretty warm and fogged over with our body heat.

Being in bed with Geneive changed things. In the truck, there was always a kind of desperation to get to the end because we were going to freeze if we didn't heat things up. She had a small bed, but it was bigger than the seat of the Ford. The house was warm and we didn't need to rush things. For the first time, I stood up in front of Geneive and undressed her, slowly, paying attention to every detail I uncovered. The little mole on her left shoulder blade. Hell! I'd hardly ever seen her bare back unless we were trying to hump doggy-style in the confines of the truck. There really just wasn't room for that! I loved the way her shoulders sloped, the curve of her spine, the flare of her butt. I paid the same kind of attention to her back that I had paid to her front a few months ago, just before we broke up. I hoped that wasn't a sign.

She shivered as I kissed the back of her arms as she stood facing a mirror with me behind her. I could glance over her shoulders and see her standing there facing me while I kissed all along her shoulders and the back of her neck. I found the same kind of sensitive indents on her back as I'd found on her front. Just below her shoulder blades. The small of her back. The crease of her butt and the ledge at the bottom. The back of her knees. I moved to take her to the longed-for bed, but Geneive was fascinated with our image in the full-length mirror on her closet door.

"Wait," she whispered. She pulled her vanity chair in front of the mirror and pushed me down in it. "Watch us," she said turning back to face the mirror. I had a pretty good view just by tilting my head to the side a little as Ginny reached between her legs and found my cowboy. She backed her little bubble butt up against my stomach and started to sink down, guiding me into her from behind. I leaned back a little to give her more room to maneuver.

That sight—watching my condom-covered cock disappearing into my little lover's body—was almost more than I could take. I reached around and fondled her, not dwelling on any one spot squeezing her tits, but letting my hands stroke the whole length of her torso from her neck down onto her thighs. Her fair skin gained a pink tint as she rose toward her climax, rising and falling on my cock as we watched in the mirror. She put her hands in the air, stretching as far as she could so I could slide my hands down her arms and her smooth pits, following the curve of her body to her hips where I helped lift and drop her. When she came, she pushed herself down as far on me as she could, gasping when I touched bottom in her vagina. That was all it took for me to start filling that condom.

We made love again, this time stretching out on the bed and just luxuriating in the feel of softness under us as we shifted positions, trying things we'd never managed in the truck. After lunch, she led me back to her bedroom and we collided in another love-making session, this time finally managing the doggy-style that had been thwarted in the truck.

We went five days like that. She even suggested trying anal as she always loved it when I tickled her rosebud with my finger. That proved to be the only unsuccessful thing we tried. Things just wouldn't fit together without both of us having pain. Well, that was okay with me. Between Ginny's pussy and her mouth, my cowboy was getting everything he could ever desire, and between him and my tongue, Ginny seemed pretty pleased as well.

The weekends were always different for Geneive's work schedule. She spent all day Saturday and Sunday at the restaurant, and I'd been rushing through my chores during the week so I had quite a bit of catch-up to do over the weekend at the ranch. Dad told me to expect to spend Saturday on the roof of the equipment shed as we'd taken some damage during the heavy snows this year and didn't want water damage to the equipment. So, Friday night Ginny and I had a tearful but loving good-bye.

"I'll see you Monday in school and maybe we can slip away for an hour after before I go to work," she said. "I've had so much fun loving you this week, Cole. I could really be gone on you."

"Don't think I don't love you, Ginny. I do. I can't turn my back on Mar… her. She means the world to me."

"Someday I hope to know what it is you feel for her and have you feel it for me, too," she said.

"I hope that day will come."

"I can't wait for us to go back. I mean, to the way it was before," she whispered as I was leaving.

WELL, WE WEREN'T going to be making love every day in her bed come summer. Before school was out, Dad told me that we'd lost a cowboy for the drive this spring and since I was nearly 17 he figured it was time I took a turn riding the range this summer. Truth was, I kind of liked that idea. Last summer I'd spent three weeks on the range while each of the other hands got their week off. I liked it. Unfortunately, it meant that I wouldn't be seeing Ginny until my week break over my birthday in July. I was trying to figure out how that would work out with Mary Beth being home and me wanting to spend time with her, too. Well, I'd just have to figure out how to handle that in July. As soon as school was out at the first week of June, I was in the saddle and headed for the upper range.

From there on, it was just more watching and seeing that our herd didn't get mixed up with anyone's besides the Alexanders' when we were on the open range. Mostly, we had enough private range, but cattle have a mind of their own. Ginny once asked me why people thought cows were so dumb. I laughed and told her it's because most folks never get to know them before they cook 'em.

It was while I was in my tent at night that I started having dreams. These were different than when I'd traveled back in time. Then I'd known I was actually in the body of Kyle Wardlaw and I could see and hear and feel with his body. I recognized what happened when I slept as dreams. Sure, I had my share of dreams about Mary Beth and about Geneive. But I started dreaming about Laramie and Caitlin, too. In my dreams, they were just as real as Mary Beth and Ginny. I guess that I should have expected the wet spot in my sleeping bag the first time I dreamt about Laramie. I'd dream her right there in my sleeping bag with me—not in her time, but in mine. She never changed, always such a lean hard body beneath or on top of mine.

Dreams of Caitlin were exhausting. She was aggressive and demanding of my loving. Caitlin was willing to try everything and pushed past the pain of anal sex to give me the ride of my life. And it was me screwing her, not Kyle. I woke up as tired as when I'd gone to sleep.

Of course, dreams of Mary Beth and Geneive were as much fun and there were nights when my dreams had leapt from one to the other taking me from bed to bed to bed. Those were the really exhausting nights. Who knew dreaming could be so tiring.

I got to thinking, though. I loved Mary Beth; there was no question about that. What we shared was something special. She could just imagine my kiss once every day when she stood in that spot at college where I kissed her. I wondered if Laramie ever went to that place where we made love and imagined me kissing her. We were somewhere in these mountains, but the terrain and landscape had changed in the past hundred plus years. There'd been some logging and a lot of cattle roaming these hills since Laramie and me. Still, if I could find a place where I could remember just one of her kisses, maybe that would mean something.

I WAS OFF chasing down a steer we'd seen go over the ridge about dawn. Something had spooked the herd during the night and all three of us were riding to get them back in one valley. Buttercup and I took off up the ridge and then set about tracking down where the stupid steer had gone. I hoped I got to it before a cougar did. The dogs were guarding the herd while the three riders hunted strays. I rode a crisscross pattern down the western slope. This section had been logged once, but it was an environmentally conscious group that got the contract from the BLM and they'd taken only every third tree that was over ten inches in diameter. There were a lot of stumps and a couple of logging roads that had been cut through. I heard the stupid bovine before I saw it. His rump was in the air and he had one foreleg curled under him and the other stuck out like he was kneeling before this giant Douglas. I looped a rope around his neck and tied it off to my saddle horn. Dismounting I approached the beast whispering soft comforting words. Steers aren't violent, but if they get spooked and throw twelve hundred pounds against you, you're in bad shape.

This dumbass had come through next to the tree and let his foot slide down a marmot hole. He was trying to lift it the way his leg would normally bend, but that just brought pressure up against the root it was under. I didn't really have anything I could cut the root with and wouldn't want to swing an axe that close to the animal anyway. I debated myself and decided to get the camp shovel out of my saddle roll. Carefully and slowly, I dug out under his leg until he could sweep the leg out from under the root. He jumped up and bolted, but that was why I had the rope tied to my saddle horn. Buttercup dug in and the steer came to a screeching halt. I laughed at him as the two of them planted their feet and stared at each other. I grabbed my canteen and took a long swig of water, then went back and filled in the hole. Let the damned marmot dig a new one.

When the hole was full, I leaned back against the tree and took another long drink of water. The canteen was still at my lips when I heard the hawk's lonesome scream.

Traveling: My Baby

I STILL HAD the canteen to my lips when I felt the rolling gait of my horse beneath me. I was following the directions that Cal gave me, stocking up in Casper and then moving cross-country into the mountains. I was back in Kyle's body and let him do the driving as I settled into the back of his mind to watch and learn. It was late June, but still pretty cold out here.

I couldn't figure out why I didn't totally freak out when I got ripped out of my body and planted into Kyle. In spite of the fact that I was in a different place and time, being in Kyle was sort of comfortable—like I belonged there. My thought processes changed, too. When I was in Kyle, that was my reality. My 'real' life was more like a dream. I knew I was there, but it was remote. What I felt in this time was what was real. Not that I felt the same things that Kyle did, though. As far as I could tell, he had no emotional attachment to Laramie, but was really fond of Caitlin. I liked Caitlin and could see why Kyle was falling for her, but the moment I looked into Laramie's eyes, I felt an attachment that I knew I'd never break. I fell in love twice that birthday afternoon. Once in each timeline. Somehow, that seemed okay.

I learned something else, though. Kyle could sleep and even if his body was a little uncomfortable, he rested and his mind blanked out the discomfort. I was conscious all the time and his body's discomfort was as exhausting as my dreaming was, but not as pleasant. I wondered about the whole sleep deprivation thing and started doing different meditation exercises I'd heard of while Kyle slept. It was all pretty much self-taught, so I don't have any idea if I was doing them right. Most of what I knew had to do with relaxing the body, but, hell, Kyle's body was asleep and as relaxed as it was going to get. I had to focus on relaxing my mind and that was all I had. Still, after two weeks, I got pretty good at just drifting off when Kyle slept.

Two weeks was when the action started. I had to admit that Kyle was good at what he did. In spite of the fact that he liked to dress nice when he was in town, once he hit the mountains, he dressed more like what I'd last seen Laramie in. He wore buckskins and moccasins rather than jeans and boots. When he crept up to the fugitives' camp, he was silent, even carrying the packs. And like me, Kyle was strong. While I had a few inches in height on him, he had a few pounds on me, and they were all muscle.

As soon as the gunfire started, Kyle slipped into the camp, used a small mallet to smash the lock, and quickly emptied most of the contents of the fugitives' strongbox into his bags. Kyle was a little disappointed that most of what was in the box was paper money—fifty dollar United States Notes with a picture of Franklin on the left and Lady Liberty on the right—but it made it lighter to carry. There was a good sack of gold and silver coins though and Kyle tossed a couple of them back in the box, leaving about six bundles of the paper money there as well.

When he had transferred the money and was slipping back into the woods, the gunfire suddenly ceased. He hurried back through the woods a good mile before picking his way up a steep trail to the cliff-top again. He loaded the packs of money onto his already packed mule and headed east into the Big Horn Mountains looking every bit like a grizzled prospector before winding his way back south. We actually missed Casper and came back toward Laramie from the east through the mountains.

Instead of returning directly to Laramie, Kyle followed a track west that led him to a bluff north of Laramie. I wished I had a topo map and compass so I could mark the location. Kyle didn't bother to open any of the other boxes in the cavern he entered. He pulled out a bundle of fifty dollar notes and a big handful of Morgan Silvers and loaded the rest into a box already almost full in the cave. Then he wearily headed the last fifty miles into Laramie.

I HAD TO agree with Kyle's assessment of what was needed. He climbed off the horse in front of Bertha's Wild Ride and a boy ran out to take the horse and mule to the stable and Kyle's limited luggage to his room. Kyle kept his saddlebags. In the restaurant, he had a big steak and an even bigger potato with three tankards of sour beer. He and I were both thinking more of the bath that would be waiting in his room than we were about the possibility of a hot redhead or big woman joining us in bed. After dinner, Kyle saw the bartender and settled his bill and rent with two Franklins. He got a handful of tokens in return and headed through the back door.

No bouncing redhead threw herself into Kyle's arms when we walked through the door. Otherwise the atmosphere seemed unchanged from the last time we'd been here. A young Hispanic woman approached Kyle shyly. She was a little round, but it was pleasant curves and not a lot of bulging fat. I estimated that like most of the whores she might be fifteen or sixteen.

"Senor Kyle, I have your bath ready. Will I be good for you?"

"Who are you?"

"Sorry, Senor. I am Maria."

"Where's Caitlin?"

Something was wrong. Maria hung her head and refused to look at me.

"I am so sorry, Senor Kyle. Caitlin is no longer… sir, Caitlin is dead."

That about did it for both Kyle and me. He sank down on a chair and took a deep breath. Maria knelt on the floor at his feet and kept whispering, "I sorry," over and over again. I looked up and another woman stood in front of me that Kyle recognized as the Madam—Liza.

"Kyle, Caitlin died after an abortion last week. When you came last time, she was going to tell you about it, but she got distracted. She didn't know if the baby was yours or someone else's so it is no cause for you to fret. She had Ellen and two others help, but she started bleeding and the next day she died."

"Where's Ellen?"

"She started refusing to eat after Caitlin died. She'd turn her head suddenly and mutter, 'Stop watching me. I didn't do it.' It was like she was being haunted. Two days later she left. I don't know where she went. But Maria will service all your needs, or if you want someone else, just say so."

"No," I whispered. "Come on, Maria. I need that bath before it gets cold."

It was the first time I really couldn't separate my thoughts from Kyle's. We were both so stunned and tears were leaking out of our eyes. We rose and followed Maria up the stairs to Kyle's room. Maria undressed quickly and then helped remove my clothes. I sank into the tub seeking the relief of hot water. As soon as I was settled, Maria climbed in on top of me and began washing me. Somehow, even with this lovely girl doing her best to make sure I was washed absolutely everyplace, my cowboy never woke up. When I was out of the tub and dry, I climbed numbly into the bed naked and Maria cuddled up next to me. I gently took her hand off my cock and just wrapped my arms around her.

Kyle and I both cried ourselves to sleep.

Well, Kyle slept. I just kept crying, though the tears no longer seeped from Kyle's eyes. This was ridiculous. I'd been in this time, in Kyle's head, for nearly a month. By the time I got back in my own body, if I ever did, I'd be too exhausted to ride herd. The first time I was here, it was for a few hours and only seconds had passed when I got back. The next time was longer—a couple days. All I knew was that I was freezing to death on a tractor when I woke up. How long would I have been leaning against a tree with Buttercup holding the rope on the steer if I ever got back again? What if I never got back? Did my body continue to function in my own timeline? I hadn't had a lot of lovers in my life. Well, just two back in my own time. I'd been with Kyle with three, but I'd picked up bits and pieces of memories with several others. I wasn't sure even Kyle would recognize all the whores he'd fucked. But this was the first time somebody I actually felt I knew and had a connection to and had made love to had died.

I MADE UP my mind and before daylight broke, I had Kyle up and dressed. Maria still slept in the bed as I strapped on my guns. I went straight to the stable and kicked the stable-boy awake. I got my buckskin saddled and grabbed some hardtack and jerky from the kitchen. I was off with the rising sun to my back.

I'd picked up enough from Kyle's memories to simply shove him to the back and tell him to shut up as I headed up into the hills near Centennial Ridge. I knew this territory pretty well in the 21st century. The fact that it was still completely wild in this time period caused constant distractions. I didn't know exactly where she lived, but I knew it was up this way.

It was late in the day when I finally saw a wisp of smoke across a low ridge. I rode up to the top and looked down on what could only be referred to as a hut. It looked almost like it had been a tepee, but had been walled into a permanent dwelling with the addition of a lot of branches and mud instead of a skin covering. The smoke came from a hole in the roof. I rode down the hillside, weaving in and out of the trees. There was no identifiable trail here.

"Hallo!" I called as I emerged from the woods into the small clearing.

A silver-haired woman emerged from the tent with an old rifle resting comfortably in her hands. I lifted my arms to the side to show I meant no harm and nudged the horse forward with my knees. This certainly wasn't the woman I was looking for, but maybe she knew where I'd find her.

"State your business, stranger," the woman commanded. Her voice was aged but held a cultured accent. She hadn't always lived in the wilderness.

"I'm looking for Laramie."

"That town is a day's ride behind you. You'll find it if you get moving now."

"Not the town. A girl. A young woman named Laramie. I'm looking for her."

"Kyle?" a voice said from behind the woman. The skins over the door moved and the girl of my dreams pushed past. She started running toward me and I swung down off my horse heedless of where the other woman's gun was pointed. In a dozen steps, Laramie was in my arms. I buried my face in her hair and crushed her to me. If I was going to stay in this time, I was going to stay with the woman I loved, Kyle be damned.

I leaned down and kissed Laramie softly. She took my hand and led me back toward the hut.

"This is him?" the woman at the door asked.

"Mama, this is Kyle. I told you he would come back to me."

"Ma'am," I said tipping my hat to her.

"Have you?"

"What, ma'am?"

"Have you come back to her or are you riding your fancy buckskin off again."

"I'm…" What could I say? I had no idea when I'd be jerked out of this body again and Kyle the asshole would be back. I certainly didn't want him here with Laramie and her mother. "I don't know, ma'am. I wish I could just stay here, but I don't know." She nodded her head.

"Come into the cabin, Kyle," Laramie said. She was dressed just the same as when I'd first seen her a year ago in buckskin shirt and breeches. Her mother also wore buckskin, but had fashioned it into a dress. Both outfits were decorated with bead-work.

Once inside, Laramie continued to pull me to the side where a bed of furs was piled. Nestled asleep on the furs was a little baby.

"This is Kaylene," Laramie whispered.

"Kaylene?" I asked, stupidly. "Laramie, is this… our daughter?" She nodded with her head against my chest. "I will never forgive him."

"Don't be angry, Kyle," Laramie said. "We will never ask you for anything. We didn't even put your name in the Bible. But you've come back. I knew you would come back."

"What are your intentions, young man," said the older woman.

"Mrs.… uh… ma'am, I don't know what to tell you. I won't make promises I can't keep. I love Laramie. I'll tell you that."

The woman gave me a hard look, her eyes slightly squinted. I wasn't sure if it was the squint of a gunslinger like I'd seen in movies or if she was having trouble seeing. Maybe she was squinting so she could see inside my soul. And what would she find? The asshole cowering in the back of my mind or the future time traveler? She just nodded and looked away.

I sat with Laramie and her mother who had yet to give me a name. There wasn't really much in the way of furniture. There were a couple of log stools and a split log that acted as a table. Their beds, both in the same large room, were simply furs piled on pine needles. Still, it had a homey feeling. There was even a piece of sandstone at one edge that had been polished flat and painted with fiery colors. The artwork was not primitive. I sat on one of the log stools and Laramie's mother sat on the other. Laramie settled on the floor leaning against me and nursed the baby—my daughter—as we ate a simple stew of venison and root vegetables. I fed Laramie from my bowl as she cared for our daughter.

"Ma'am," I said to the older woman, "what would be the respectful name that I should call you by?"

"Theresa Ranae."

"Miss Theresa, the repast you have set is very tasty. Thank you."

"Theresa Ranae," she repeated. "I am not Miss or Mrs. anything. I am Laramie Wyoming's mother."

"Yes ma'am. Theresa. You do not sound or look Native American. I mean like an Indian."

"I married a Cheyenne brave. My family before is all gone." I nodded. I'd heard stories like that. Family attacked and killed and white girl taken by the Indians. Well, I wouldn't make any judgments.

"Laramie Wyoming is a lovely name but how did you come by it?"

"I met someone named Laramie when I was a girl. I thought it was a beautiful name. Then we came to live in Laramie. White Horse and I were forced to move to a reservation in Montana. I named our daughter after the place my heart yearned for. Two summers ago, we returned. The soldiers did not object to a white woman and her half-breed daughter 'returning to civilization' as they said."

"White Horse was your... mate?"

"Yes."

"I've heard many stories about white girls stolen by an Indian chief. Their daughter is always considered a princess." There were tons of stories of that sort that I'd heard of. I always thought there must be a lot of Indian chiefs for so many families to have half-breed princesses in their family tree. There was even one in my family legends. I'd have to look it up sometime. Theresa looked at me sharply and laughed.

"White Horse stole my heart. I gave him my body willingly. Much as my daughter went with you. *He* was a good man and provided for us, but he was not the chief," she said letting the implication that I was not a good man rest on me.

There was no refrigeration, of course. The meat had a smoky taste so I assumed they had arranged at least a temporary smokehouse. Theresa added water to the kettle of left-over stew and put it back on the coals to heat. A never-ending pot of stew if they added fresh vegetables or meat to it tomorrow.

"Mama, Kaylene is asleep. I am going to walk with Kyle."

Theresa sighed and nodded her head. I certainly wasn't what she hoped for in a son-in-law.

Laramie and I walked out under the moonlit sky. It was early August, but this high in the mountains the night was clear and pleasant. I boldly reached out and took her hand. She leaned against me as we walked away from the hut. When it was out of sight, Laramie pulled me down to sit beneath a Mountain Douglas. As soon as we sat, Laramie pressed herself against me and offered her lips to my questing mouth. We kissed for a long time. I can't tell time when I'm kissing, but the moon had risen and it was near full dark when I first became aware of my surroundings. Both of our shirts were off and Laramie was lying atop me as I caressed her back and her milky breasts.

This woman was the mother of my daughter! I hadn't even been here for her during her pregnancy. All I had was the memory a single afternoon where we taught each other how to enjoy our bodies beneath a hot Fourth of July sun and dreams that had haunted me ever since. But I had her now. I didn't really care if I had to keep Kyle subdued in the back of my mind forever. I was going to stay with Laramie.

"I love you, Laramie," I whispered. "I've never loved any woman like I love you." Well, Mary Beth was close, but she'd made it clear we'd never be a couple. Laramie and I were a couple. We were as good as husband and wife—and daughter.

"Love me," she said as she began to grind down on my cock. We slipped our trousers off—my boots were long gone—and lay side by side as we pleasured each other. We made love long into the night.

This wasn't the howling passionate lovemaking that I'd experienced with Caitlin and Ellen or even, for that matter, with Geneive. Every physical act was an extension of how we loved each other. When I entered her wet folds, we were truly one person. When I emptied myself into her womb, I emptied my soul into her heart.

"I love you, Laramie. Remember that no matter how far I have to travel or how long before I see you again, I love you and I would give my soul to be with you."

"Who are you, really?" she asked.

"You know that. These are Kyle's hands. Kyle's heart. Kyle's lips."

"No. It is Kyle's hands and Kyle's lips, but here…" she laid her hand on my heart, "this is not Kyle's heart."

"I don't know how to answer you, my love. You may be right. It is not Kyle's heart that loves you. But I do. Across time and ages, I love you."

"What will we do then, my love?"

"I will be back as often as I can and stay as long as I can, but if Kyle returns to take his own heart back, you dare not let him be here with you." Laramie cuddled against me but in a bit insisted we return to the hut. Kaylene would need to be fed.

For the rest of the night, I held Laramie and our daughter in my arms as we slept on the furs together. I was at peace, and something told me that Kyle was peaceful, too.

OVER THE NEXT couple of days, I helped with the house and preparations for the winter. I wanted them to file land claims and to do that, they would need to winterize. Laramie carried Kaylene in a kind of sling as we worked to make the hut secure. I swung an axe until there were blisters on my hands, right through Kyle's gloves. I wanted to be sure they would have adequate wood for winter.

I shot another deer and butchered the meat while Theresa treated the hide. I was shown how they smoked the meat and kept it drying so it would not rot. There were a number of edible roots in the area and I helped dig and gather. I dug a root cellar and built an earthen wall around it and a thatched roof over it. The opening between the hut and the root cellar was small and Laramie could barely fit through the door, but they stored food like squirrels.

And each night Laramie took my hand and led me into the forest away from the house to make love. I loved her and felt contentment as we held each other in our arms. But one morning I could feel a foreboding in my heart. I needed to get Kyle away from here. I took Laramie to my saddle bags and sat with her.

"Here." I pulled the bundle of Franklins from the bag and put them into her hands. I thought better and removed ten of the bills to put in Kyle's pants. No sense leaving him without money so he'd feel compelled to come back here to reclaim it. Five hundred dollars would keep him in beer and whores for months. "It's all I have right now. Take this and go to Laramie to file a land claim. Buy as much adjacent land as you can." A sudden flash came into my mind of money hidden in Kyle's saddlebags. I don't know if he actually thought it to me or if it was an involuntary thought as I handed Laramie the Franklins. I grabbed the saddlebags and emptied them. I could feel the coins. I didn't waste time. I grabbed my knife and slit open the bottom of each bag. Sewn into the bag was a second skin that contained twenty-five double-eagles in each bag. Fifty twenty-dollar gold pieces. This wasn't California. In Laramie, Wyoming this was serious cash. I was giving her close to five thousand dollars and that could buy Laramie over a thousand acres. I gave it all to my beloved.

"Buy as much land as you can darling. Raise our daughter to love the land and love her papa, even though I won't be here. Wyoming became a State in the Union this summer. It's a state where there's women's equality. They can't stop you from filing a claim or buying land."

"I would rather have you than all this gold or what it could buy," she said.

"As would I, my love. But here is my pledge to you." I took my knife and carved in the bark of the tree the initials LK overlapping. "Laramie and Kyle. As long as a tree stands in the forest, I will be yours."

About halfway back to town the next day, I started relinquishing my hold on Kyle's body and letting his consciousness seep through. He was mad, but I held a firm grip before giving him full control.

If you ever harm a hair of her or her mother or her child, I will take you to the grave and bury you in your misery. Never tell anyone. Do you understand? Kyle mutely nodded his head as I gave him back his body.

I heard it before I saw the shadow this time. It was far away but close enough to draw me out of Kyle's body and plant me back on Centennial Ridge with a bleating steer and a pissed horse.

Verified

I LEANED AGAINST the tree as I got my bearings back. Buttercup kept dancing back and forth keeping the steer on a taut rope. I felt the bark under my hands. There was a groove where I was touching. Somebody, maybe a pioneer had blazed the tree. It's illegal these days. I looked and rubbed at the bark until I could clearly see the mark. I sat square down on my rump just staring. It was an old scar and the tree had grown out stretching the mark, but it was clear to me. LK.

That was the first I knew it wasn't all just a dream.

The rest of the summer, whenever I wasn't on an active shift, I'd ride over to that ridge and sit under the Mountain Douglas Fir. It hadn't all been a dream. I'd been here and carved our initials in that tree over a hundred years ago. I'd made love with Laramie here throughout the night. And I'd sworn that I'd love her as long as there was a tree in the forest.

It wasn't a dream.

I'd been on the range for over a month now. I knew my turn for a week's break was coming up soon. It seemed like no time at all had passed when I found myself back on my horse again, but I had close to five weeks of extra memories. It was too bad I missed all the festivities when Wyoming's statehood was announced but that really wasn't important. I was heartsick for my one true love, Laramie Wyoming Ranae. I assumed that was her last name. Her mother's name was Theresa Ranae. I wondered if my daughter Kaylene would take Kyle's surname.

I was lonelier up on the ridge that summer than if I'd been shipped off to war. The last week of July I came down from the mountain for a week's break. Dad handed me the keys to the truck and told me to remember I was due back on the mountain Monday a week.

I CALLED GENEIVE first thing and got another shock. Her mom answered the phone and told me that Geneive wasn't available to talk right now and I shouldn't really call back this summer.

What the fuck? The last time she'd broken up with me by phone, but at least she'd talked to me. Now she's having her mother break up with me? Shit! I called Mary Beth. I mean, I intended to call Mary Beth anyway, but I owed it to my girlfriend—ex-girlfriend—to call her first. Mary Beth said she'd be ready in half an hour. I used the time to get a hot shower.

You'd think that after a month and a half in the mountains, all I'd want is a soft bed, but after a very long, very hot shower and a shave, I tossed my gear in the back of the pickup truck and headed for the mountains. Half a mile from my house I stopped the truck and Mary Beth tossed her pack in the back and climbed into the cab. We were off down the road again before the dust settled.

She slid to the center seat and fastened her seatbelt before leaning into me. I wrapped an arm around her and she looked up at me.

"Where to, honey?"

"I know this place up in the Big Horn," I said.

We had a great week in that tent next to the Big Horn River and I spun her a tale about how bank robbers from Salt Lake City had come northeast and died here in a shoot-out with the posse. All the posse ever found of the loot, though, was five stacks of fifties and a few gold coins.

"What happened to all the rest?" she asked.

"Nobody ever found it. It's one of the mysteries of the mountains. Maybe we should look for it."

"You are such a bullshitter, Cole," she said, climbing on top of me again.

I guess I wasn't responsive enough, though I'm sure this was the fourth or fifth time we'd had sex that afternoon.

"You're still upset about Geneive, aren't you," she asked.

"Hmm? Geneive? Yeah. Maybe a little. It's nothing."

"Did you meet someone new? When? How could you have time? You've been up in the mountains for six weeks. Is there a mountain girl up there?"

"God, Mary Beth. You're sick. It's just a daydream. There's no one in our reality that I've fallen for."

"Then fall for me again, lover. You know that I never missed a day—even when there was two feet of snow—going to that courtyard and thinking about your kiss. I love you, Cole."

"Mary Beth, you are the best thing in my life. I love you."

YES. I'D PRETTY much resolved the major things about time travel. I didn't know *how* I was doing it, but I could recognize when it was going to happen. It was still making me crazy. I couldn't do it at will. If I could have, I'd have gone to be with Laramie and never come back.

Except there was Mary Beth. I realized I was just as anchored in this time as I was in the past. When I looked into Mary Beth's eyes, I knew I loved her just as much as I did Laramie.

It's hard to believe I'd had enough time with Laramie to really know that I loved her. I'd seen her a grand total of twice for maybe five days all told. But from that first time when she came to me in spite of what a jerk Kyle was, it was like she recognized me and I recognized her. And it wasn't just the physical similarities between Laramie and Mary Beth. I could tell the difference. Different eye color. Different hair style even though very similar color. Laramie's complexion was a little ruddier. She was half Indian after all. And she was inordinately lean. Even with milk in her tits for our baby, she was smaller in the chest than Mary Beth, but she wasn't anemic. She was just all muscle and very little fat. She lived outdoors before the invention of fast food.

And that other little bit. Our baby. *Shit!* In 1890, I was a daddy. And I wasn't there to be with my little girl and help her grow up and protect her and provide for her. If anyone had offered me the choice, I'd have bundled Mary Beth up in my arms and left everything else I knew in the present to go be with Laramie.

No one gave me that choice.

4
Time Travel Anomalies

YOU KNOW everything science fiction says about the rules of time travel? You can't be two places at the same time. You have to avoid contact with yourself in the past. Anything you do in the past could change the future. You can go 'back to the future'. From my experience, I'd say they're all bunk. I don't believe you can go back and change history. What's done is done. You're a kind of observer. It's the things that *aren't* history that you can affect.

Think about what Kyle was doing. Or rather what Despain was doing. I mean whoever the time traveler was who was giving Despain information about where to get the loot. I was pretty convinced that there was some 20th century traveler who was looking out of Despain's eyes when Kyle sat across from him. Next time I got there, I was going to look in a mirror when I took possession of Kyle and watch for subtle changes. Maybe Kyle couldn't notice it, but I could.

Anyway, I did some research about lost treasures in the library when I was in my junior year in high school. There were a ton of bank robberies in the late 1800s and early 1900s where the robbers were caught, but the money was never recovered. I suppose some of them were simply because there was a tendency to shoot first and ask questions later. You can't get good answers about where they hid the money if they're dead.

Despain was passing on all the accumulated knowledge of where the heist was going to take place and which direction the robbers were headed, where the shootout would be, and what was recovered. Kyle was there waiting for them like he was at Big Horn. When the shooting started, he slipped in, picked up the loot and left. Absolutely no history change. Clean as a whistle. So, while I was studying in school to pass stupid Algebra Two, I spent all my available spare time researching lost treasures in the Old West.

I figured newspapers were the key and most of the newspapers of that era were put on microfiche. I found out that various genealogical libraries had huge collections of old newspapers.

I knew the timeframe I was looking for, so I just started digging through every edition of every paper from the early 1890s. I found a lot.

A Broken Heart

THE FIRST TIME I saw Geneive in school—yeah, the very first day of school, just as the first bell rang—she looked daggers at me and I don't think I'd ever seen her so angry. Hell! She dumped *me*. What did I do? She marched right up to me in the hall before class even started and got right in my face. That's a good trick for a girl who's fourteen inches shorter than me.

"You bastard! Not one call! All summer and you never called me once. Who is she? Who did you dump me for? I'm going to tear her eyes out, you fucking bastard!" *Holy shit!*

"Whoa, girl! What are you on about? I come down off the mountain and call as soon as I get in the house and you won't even talk to me. You send your mother to tell me not to call you anymore. What right do you have calling me names, bitch?" I said that last a little too loudly and a bunch of people stopped in the hall and looked at us. I guess they figured there was going to be a good fight and they wanted to watch.

"You never called," Geneive insisted.

"I did. The minute I got down from the range on July 24. Your mom said you couldn't talk and I shouldn't call again this summer. What was I supposed to think? You dumped me over the phone at Christmas. This time you used your mom."

"Oh shit!" Tears sprang to Geneive's eyes. "Don't kill me, Cole. I didn't do that. Honest. I fucked up royal when I broke up with you at Christmas. I would never break up with you again without facing you. Never. Oh fuck, Mom. Why would she do that?"

"You didn't tell her to break up with me?" Geneive shook her head vigorously and tears were flying every which way. Fuck! Why do parents interfere so much? I reached out and pulled Geneive into my arms. She fell against my chest and sobbed. Mr. Carson, my Algebra teacher came out of the room and looked at us sternly.

"This is a school and we have classes. The hall is not the place to deal with your personal differences or your love life. The bell rings in... forty-four seconds. Get to class."

I bit back a retort and quickly whispered to Geneive, "Meet me after school." She nodded and rushed away. I sat down at my desk in Algebra just as the bell rang.

WHAT A WASTE. The first day of classes is a walk-through. The periods are twenty-five minutes long—just enough to get our textbooks and seating assignments if the teacher is a tight-ass like Mr. Carson. By noon, classes are out for the day. That meant that Geneive and I were free to have lunch together and not go back to class. She piled into the truck and slid over next to me like it was old times. We still had to talk, so we went to Sonic and got burgers and shakes and sat there to eat them.

"First of all, Cole, I never told Mom to break up with you. I really learned my lesson last year and if I *ever* break up with you again, it will be face-to-face just like we are sitting right now. Please don't hate me."

"I don't hate you, Geneive. I was hurt that you wouldn't even talk to me. Didn't you know I'd call as soon as I came down?"

"I... I wasn't myself this summer. After the third time I didn't go in to work, Mom got really mad at me and grounded me. I didn't mean to keep forgetting things. I forgot to let the dog out. I forgot to go to work. I forgot what shoes to wear when I was working. It's like I wasn't all there. Mom got really pissed at me. Dad, too. The more they yelled at me, the worse it got. Then when I thought you didn't call me, it got worse yet. I was like a zombie. I don't think I really snapped out of it until I saw you this morning just as the first bell rang. I was so heart-broken to think you just abandoned me."

"I won't abandon you, Ginny. No matter how rough things get, I won't abandon you."

"You would for her, though," Geneive said softly. She didn't know about Mary Beth specifically, just that there was someone else I loved. *Damn it. Two someone elses.* I admit that if I could just go back and be with my Laramie and my little baby, I'd probably abandon everything. But I also knew that wasn't going to happen and there was no sense even thinking about it.

"She'd never ask me to leave you, darlin'. I'm sorry I can't give you better. If you figure you need someone that's better than me, I understand. As much as I'd never abandon you, I'd never hold you back, either."

"That sounds a lot like love, Cole."

"Yeah. It's a lot like love."

WE STAYED AN ITEM for most of the fall and winter and it was a *lot* like love. But all the way back then, the first ripples of trouble for the family were showing up. That fall Joe Teini moved to town.

I had no idea who the hell Joe Teini was. He'd gone to high school in Laramie and then went to college a few years before I was aware of other people. He was in his mid-twenties. He was apparently rich. And he stole my girlfriend.

What would Jason do?

Well, she chose what she wanted. We'd been dating and fucking like rabbits for almost a year and a half and I'd pretty much decided she was the one. She came out to the truck on Friday night for our usual date and sat by the door. She asked me not to move the truck. She hardly looked at me as she broke up with me. But she did it face-to-face like she said she would.

"There's a group that meets on Wednesday night at the restaurant," she said. "They have the private dining room and Daddy has me on that night to help wait the tables. And there's this guy who has been really nice. And he asked me out. And I want to go. Cole, I would never cheat on you, so I'm breaking up. I really had fun this year." Tears were pouring down her cheeks and I guess there were some on mine as well. "I loved you, Cole." I reached across the seat to touch her, but her hand was already on the door handle. Lights hit the rearview mirror and a little sports car came screeching into Geneive's drive behind me. "Goodbye," she said and piled out of the truck to run to the car.

April Fool! I kept waiting for her to say it, but she didn't come back to the truck. The car pulled out around me and spun gravel into the side of my truck.

A goddamned Corvette. I couldn't believe it. She dumped me for an older guy in a black Corvette! The whole thought of it left a bad taste in my mouth. Geneive would probably be pregnant before the summer was over and he'd either dump her or they'd be getting married. I was wrong on both counts, but I didn't find that out for a few months.

I guess Geneive was my first broken heart.

MARY BETH AND I got away for spring break under the ruse that she was going to move to an apartment in Boulder and needed my help moving. She got our families to agree that I could go to Boulder to help.

I moved her.

The move from one apartment to another took about two hours. The emotional and sexual outpourings took six days.

I was in a bit of a funk. Let's face it, I'd just been dumped for a guy in a 'Vette. During the previous summer, I'd found out that Laramie and Kyle were real and not just something I dreamed or hallucinated. At least I had a bit of evidence that said they were, but there was no way I could get back. All I had were initials carved in an old tree that looked like what I remembered carving when I'd made love to Laramie and told her that I would love her as long as a tree stood in the forest.

So, having a week with Mary Beth was great therapy. As soon as we got her moved into her new apartment, we went out grocery shopping and condom shopping. The only other time we left the apartment that week was to go buy more condoms.

"Cole. Cole! Oh, my God, Cole! What are you doing?"

"I am burying my face in the sweetest muff on the Front Range," I answered from between Mary Beth's legs. And I wasn't lying either. Once I'd finally convinced her that I *really* wanted to eat her, Mary Beth was a convert. She even trimmed up her pussy hair so I wouldn't get so much in my mouth. When she arched her back and squealed for the third time she grabbed my ears and pulled me up next to her.

"No more. Please, not right now. I can't take any more. I don't care if Geneive dumped you, I've got to call her and thank her. She taught you well. Oh god, Cole. I'm exhausted. How am I ever going to recover? I love you!"

"I love you, Mary Beth. Damn, I wish life was always as simple as when I'm with you. When I'm here in bed with you, everything makes sense. You are my rock."

"You mean you just want every day of your life to be a non-stop fuckfest," she laughed.

"Hell, Mary Beth, you know I love us fucking. But I loved fucking Geneive, too. It gives me the creeps to think of that other guy fucking my Ginny's pussy. But it's more than that with you, Mary Beth. It's not about fucking—or at least not all about fucking. I can't see myself ever without you. I can't imagine life without you. Sometimes I think we'll just have to find a place where first cousins can marry and the hell with everything else. I know I'm only seventeen, but honey, you are enough for me. In fact, you're all I ever want."

"Shh. Shh. I love you, Cole. And I don't care what the laws are either. But we can be all that for each other without getting married. Honey, I want you to have a real relationship with a girl you *can* marry and have babies with. I want to live next door to my little cousins and when your wife lets you out at night, I want to be there to love you, too. She's out there someplace, Cole. That woman that can love you and still let you love me. Hell, maybe she'll even love *me*. That would be a kick, wouldn't it? Come here." I leaned over to kiss Mary Beth and instead she licked my face.

"What?"

"I'm just checking to see what a little pussy tastes like. I don't mind eating it off your face."

"Geez, you can talk dirty!"

"And look what it did to your cowboy. I think he wants to go for another ride."

"Aren't you too sore?"

"I think I just flooded the corral. Get that rubber on and do me again, lover."

AFTER OUR WEEK together, Mary Beth and I were more in love than ever. She told me in no uncertain terms, though, that I had to find myself another girlfriend and not think about her all the time.

"So, are you going to find a boyfriend and forget about me?"

"Yes," she said firmly. "I'm not going to think about you at all this year."

69

"Not going to go stand in that courtyard and think about kissing me?" I teased.

"No. Oh, Cole. Every night I'm going to lie down here in this bed and think about making love with you right here. I can't kid you. I'm going to miss you every day of the year and I'm going to hunt you down in the mountains in the summer if I have to in order to be back in your arms. But we have to date other people and we have to be prepared for not being together. There just isn't any way that we could get away with it."

"No matter who I'm with, Mary Beth, I'll always love you and I'll always be your lover. If a girl wants to be with me, she's just going to have to accept the fact that I love you, too."

We hugged each other and cried a little and then made love one more time before I got in my truck and drove north.

And then spring break was over and I had to go back to school.

I DATED A couple girls that spring before school was out. Nothing serious. Movie. Burger. Home. Little peck on the cheek and "Let's do this again. Sometime."

I think maybe girls were a little tentative about going out with a guy whose last relationship was known to be hot and heavy. I guess I was a little tentative about it, too. I just wasn't ready or willing to let anybody else get that close.

I was pretty much relieved when school got out and I mounted up the next day to ride up to the herd for the summer. At least up here, with a little luck, I'd hear a hawk and go find Laramie. I was taking the high range again during the summer. Mom convinced me to take a week's break and come home for my 18th birthday on the Fourth of July. I got delayed a couple weeks, though, because of storms up on the range. I held myself together by thinking about being back with Mary Beth. The day finally got there.

We were snuggled together in a hodgepodge of open sleeping bags and blankets on the air mattress basking in the glow of some pretty exhausting licking and kissing. I'm sure there wasn't a living thing within a mile of us. They'd all be scared off by the noise we were making. We spent five days together up in the Tetons. I thought it was a little strange how my folks never blinked an eye about me going off camping when I'd been camping on the range for two months. And I was almost sure they knew Mary Beth was going with me.

THE BREAK WAS over all too quickly and I headed back to the range. The days are quiet with the herd, but they are long. I really didn't mind. We rode twelve hour shifts, give or take, and with three of us, one slept, one cooked, and one was on the range. Of course, occasionally something happened to upset the schedule, like the thunderstorm last year that spooked the cattle and led me to that steer caught under a tree. It was different this time.

"Cole, Jack's got a belly ache. I think it might be bad," George said when I'd just got in from riding herd all night. I was ready to slide into my bedroll and be gone for the day. "I radioed your dad and he's sending a truck up to get him to the hospital. But I don't think Jack can make it to the trailhead by hisself. I think it's his 'pendix. You're going to have to grab some grub and ride back out to the herd while I get Jack loaded out. I'll try to get back as soon as possible."

"Sure," I yawned. "No big deal. Take care, Jack. You'll be fine," I said. I grabbed what was left in the coffeepot and piled some ham on a hard roll then mounted up again. Buttercup wasn't happy about turning back to the pasture, but she's a good horse and complied. We just sat out on the hill overlooking the herd while the dogs circulated.

I looked up in the sky and saw a hawk doing lazy circles high overhead. I wasn't sure if it was there or if I was dreaming. I just knew that if that hawk screamed, I was going to go see Laramie. I just thought up at it.

Screech, damn it. Take me away.

Traveling: A Winter's Love

I DAMNED NEAR got us killed. Redtail cried and I was slammed into Kyle's body hard. I jerked his head around to look for his horse before it registered that it was snowing all around. I caught sight of his buckskin a dozen paces away and turned to go get him.

"No!" Kyle screamed inside my head. I felt the bullet whistle past my head before I heard the shot. I guess body reflexes respond without conscious effort. I never left the helm, but Kyle's body spun and his hand drew the Smith & Wesson Model 3 as I dove to the ground and fired back. I watched in horror as a towering man raised his gun and then fell forward as his chest blossomed in blood.

I'd just killed a man.

I knew Kyle had killed before. I'd seen it in his memories. But that didn't seem to affect me the way this did. I'd been in control of the body when the hand drew the gun and fired. I retreated as Kyle took over, approached the man, and put another round in his head just to make sure. He ejected the spent cartridges and reloaded as he kept looking around as if expecting another enemy to emerge from the trees. The snow was coming down so heavy I could barely see as far as the trees, but I heard the horses stamping. He grabbed the dead man by the collar and dragged him to the campsite a dozen yards away. Two men slumped over a chest and a third man lay in the snow a few feet away. There were three horses and a mule hitched to a buckboard. Kyle retrieved the gun that had been fired at us and locked the bandit's hand around the grip. I rummaged around in his mind for what had happened just before I arrived.

Kyle had been waiting—right where I would have told him to. I'd read about the Wells Fargo robbery last Christmas. According to the articles, the robbers had had a falling out and killed each other fighting over the loot. I was puzzled, though. The reports said that a posse tracking in the early spring had found the campsite, the bodies, and all the gold in the Wells Fargo strongbox, unopened and untouched. If Kyle took the strongbox, that would change what was recorded in history.

We walked right past the men slumped over the Wells Fargo box and headed to the buckboard. There were three more boxes on the bed of the wagon. These, Kyle hoisted one at a time and loaded on his mule. They were lighter than I expected gold to be, but Kyle didn't open them. When he was loaded, he went to the robbers' picket line and loosened all the horses. He didn't saddle them, but left the saddles where they'd been stacked for the camp. The mule, he ponied along with his own and we headed out of the snowy pass where they'd camped. The horses stamped and headed back down the trail the way they'd come.

Kyle had scouted the area well and I wondered how long he'd been camped there waiting. The trail we took would have been treacherous in summer, but with over a foot of snow, it was nearly impassable. Our camps were meager and rations were tight for both Kyle and the animals. At the first camp, he redistributed the packs and opened the wooden boxes. Instead of gold, there were stacks of Franklins in the three boxes. Kyle distributed the bundles of money in oilcloths and put it all in the mules' side-bags. Then he broke up the boxes and used them for fuel for our campfire.

It seemed to me that Despain's time traveler had access to a lot more information than I'd been able to gather so far. How the hell did he know to tell Kyle to leave the gold and take three other boxes? Currency wasn't going to be a problem. Wyoming was a State of the Union now. This was all legal tender and easier to carry than gold. On the other hand, I had to figure out how easy it would be to cash that legal tender in my time and how durable it would be. He had to have some other plans. Whatever they were, I was making some plans as well.

It was the middle of winter and the chance that Redtail was going to swoop down out of the winter sky and snatch me back to my own time seemed remote. In my own time, I wasn't seeing more than one a year. It was winter and it seemed to me like the best place to spend it would be with Laramie.

WHEN WE REACHED Boulder, I let Kyle enjoy himself for a couple of days while he got clean and got laid. He didn't resist, though when I prodded him to keep moving north and even seemed content, somehow. I relaxed and let him be the guide as he followed the trail and then cut west after we crossed into Wyoming to pick up the Centennial Ridge, avoiding N.K. Boswell's ranch. I filtered through his memories as they came up and he seemed to actually be pushing some of them at me. He settled back in his own mind and I swear he willingly gave over control to me as we trudged through snow up to the horse's belly toward Laramie's hut.

"Hallo the cabin!" I called as I was approaching. The hides covering the opening twitched and then Laramie came out holding a rifle.

"Kyle?"

"Laramie, honey, can I stable my stock and come in?"

"Kyle!" she yelled as she set aside her rifle and did her best effort at running through the drifts to me. I slid off the horse and held her in my arms. Well, I kind of held the layers of skins that were wrapped and tied around her with the layers of cloth and coats that were wrapped around me. It was damned cold out here.

It took close to an hour to get the horse and mules stabled in the little lean-to behind her hut with her pinto and two cows. A thermal spring kept water running into their trough. Kyle had a canvas that we'd used for shelter about the size of a wagon cover and we extended the lean-to with it so that all six animals were comfortable and warm. I saw there was plenty of firewood stacked next to the hogan and there seemed to be a good haystack beside the lean-to. Laramie led me inside and unwrapped the layers from each of us. The hogan was warm—a small space with lots of furs, a fire, and four people. I greeted Theresa Ranae and she nodded in my direction then held out the baby.

My daughter. My little Kaylene. Hell, she was eight… almost nine months old now and burbling happily as she grabbed toward my wispy beard. As blond as Kyle was, the hair on his face wasn't all that thick. The hair on his head, though, was long and Kaylene loved getting her fingers tangled in it.

"You've come back," Theresa said. "How long this time?"

"I never know, Theresa," I said. "But it's winter. Have you seen any hawks circling this month?" She shook her head.

"Is that what it is?"

"The redtail hawk. Whenever he screeches, my… personality changes. The other doesn't bear you ill will, but I don't completely trust him. If we are together when the hawk cries, you must get away."

"Skin walker," Theresa said. "My husband knew of such."

"Redtail," Laramie whispered. "It is like you were among my father's people. When you are in the town of the white people you are Kyle Wardlaw. When you are with me, you are Kyle Redtail." I smiled and pulled Laramie close to me as I held our daughter in my arms and settled into the furs with the two of them.

"Have you filed a claim and purchased land?" I asked.

"There was too much to do in late summer. We needed wood, hay, furs, meat, vegetables. We needed a place for the animals. And we needed to trade for tools and bullets. I could not leave."

"We should have gone south with the People in September," Theresa said. "But you changed things. This is now her home and we'll stay here. It is not easy. But the other Kyle helped."

"He what?"

"I saw him. He didn't come near, but we could hear him cutting and splitting wood. At night, he came and built the fence for the animals and made the water trough. We 'found' a haystack less than a mile from here with wagon tracks leading away. All the wood was cut to make the shelter. Even when you are not here, he seems to want to help."

"I'll be damned," I said. I knew Kyle wouldn't hurt them, but I never thought he would help. I searched through his memories and saw that he didn't want me to be angry with him when I returned.

"I'm glad he helped," I said. "And now that I am here, I will continue to help. I will hunt and bring more wood and do what is necessary for a man to do to care for his family."

"Does that include lying with your wife?" Laramie asked. I blushed. *Damn!* Her mother was right here beside us. In fact, I noticed that the bed furs were all in one place now. I supposed the three of them slept together for warmth.

"Do not worry, Kyle Redtail," Theresa laughed. "When my husband first took me, his mother lay in the same furs. Having our family together does not need to dampen your ardor. I am an old lady, but I will relive my youth."

"I hope you live long, Mother," I said. I meant it with every fiber of my being.

It was still a little awkward. Theresa slept nearest the fire and cradled Kaylene in her arms as the two drifted off to sleep. Laramie and I kissed and I marveled again at how sweet her mouth was. I was still a little embarrassed and uncomfortable. Imagine making love to your woman with her mother and daughter in the same bed. I guess the saving grace was that there were no springs in this bed of pine needles and furs, so at least we weren't bouncing Theresa around.

Laramie seemed not to have any such compunction. I thought we'd be keeping all our clothes on and sneaking our love quietly. It was not long, though, before we lay naked with our skin pressed against each other.

"Laramie, I love you," I whispered as I stroked her milky breasts and moved my hand toward her hot center. "Throughout this life and all others. I've always loved you."

"You speak strangely, Kyle Redtail. But I love you. You bring heat to my loins when I am with you and a strange emptiness when you are gone. Fill me, Kyle Redtail. Fill me with your love."

I moved my hips and Laramie guided me into her warmth. For a moment as we joined fully together, we just lay still and enjoyed the feeling of being connected. I think Kyle was surprised that we didn't immediately start humping and I felt an involuntary twitch as my hips pushed forward. But this was another new experience—the pure joy of being connected to the woman I loved. Slowly we began moving together, each intent on the other's pleasure. I was in no rush to come to completion. I wanted to feel each ripple of her cunt as she pulsed around me and headed toward her own orgasm.

It was quiet—comparably. We'd both howled our joy to the moon on other occasions, but this time we kept our lips together and our tongues engaged as she shuddered her release, moaning into my mouth, and I filled her with an abundance of my semen.

Perhaps tonight we were making another child. I would have no trouble with that at all.

THE WINTER PASSED and the four of us grew closer as a family, even with Kyle occasionally asserting himself to go hunting or tend his animals. He was pretty docile and retreated immediately whenever Laramie came into view. I think he was content to experience love and family that he'd never known. I let him have these outings. I remembered all too well how it had been the last time as I simply rested in the back of his mind while he hunted in the Big Horn. We celebrated Kaylene's first birthday as a family.

When I was in control of his body, I slept. When Kyle had been in control last time, I was cursed to be awake all the time, even though he slept. I wondered if he had the same experience. I got my answer when I awoke one morning and discovered that I was slipping quietly in and out of Laramie, my hand softly caressing her breast. An embarrassed Kyle retreated as I came back to consciousness, but I was at peace. It was his body and I knew he enjoyed my couplings with Laramie as much as I did. I'd certainly experienced a number of his whores.

"We really need to get you to town as soon as it starts to thaw to file your claims and to buy property," I said. "The world is changing rapidly and soon all the land will be claimed."

"Who could want all of the land?" Laramie asked. "Is there not enough for everyone?"

"White men are greedy," I said. "Wyoming is big and will never have as many people as the rest of the Union. Part of that is because of the big claims of men like N.K. Boswell. His ranch keeps getting bigger and bigger."

"But, Kyle. I cannot simply go to Laramie and present a sack full of gold coins and buy land. I'm half Cheyenne. They would want to know where this money came from."

"That's true," I said. "We'll have to think this through."

"I can buy land," Theresa said. "I am white. No one would ask."

I looked at Theresa. She was getting old. I guessed she must be at least forty. Her hair gleamed silver when she went out in the sun. Still, even though she was worn and worked hard, she was definitely a white woman. That might just work.

A flash came into my mind of the railroad. I wondered where that came from and then realized Kyle was paying attention. I relaxed and let his thoughts come to mind. The rail line from Denver to Cheyenne had recently been finished. The branch line continued north to Fort Laramie, but we could transfer to the mainline Union Pacific from Cheyenne to Laramie. Kyle's thought was outstanding. Travel southeast until we reached the railroad spur at Fort Collins. Travel the spur line southeast to Greeley and board to Cheyenne. In Cheyenne, board the Union Pacific to Laramie and Theresa could present herself as moving West after her husband's death. No one in Laramie would know she boarded the westbound train in Cheyenne instead of Omaha. She would immediately deposit a few thousand dollars with Wells Fargo in Laramie and set about establishing herself and buying land.

I liked the idea and presented it to Theresa who nodded in agreement.

"If you can travel with us, we can buy proper clothes in Fort Collins that make us look like eastern farm women. I will keep Laramie hidden until we are established.

THE WHOLE SCHEME sounded too smart for Kyle to think up. Not that I think my host was dumb, but he wasn't subtle. My thoughts were apparently blocked from him as he had no idea where I came from or why. He knew whatever went on while I was in his body—all our conversations and especially our love-making. I had a feeling he was even growing fond of Kaylene. But talking to him was like talking to myself. If I really wanted information I learned that I should not try to mentally ask him questions. That confused him. But if I casually mentioned a subject aloud, his mind automatically jumped to information about it. I still didn't figure out how he thought up this scheme, though, until we happened to start talking about money. *His* money as it turned out.

"It's nearly time," Theresa said one morning looking out between the hides that covered the doorway. "There will be an early thaw. We should be ready to leave by the full moon." I nodded. The lady might be white, but she had lived among the Indians over half her life and had picked up much of their weather sense.

"How much money do you still have?" I asked Laramie. She pulled her leather pouch from under the bed furs and poured the contents out on the table. She had mostly gold coins, being harder for her to spend unobtrusively, but still a good stack of Franklins. "You need more. You have to buy land if it's already been claimed and if you are lucky, you'll get about ten acres per gold coin. You need at least a couple thousand acres in order to raise enough cattle or even sheep to make it pay. Then once you have the land, you need a real house on it. You'll have to hire some labor. And you need to buy stock. You are going to come out West as a widowed farm wife who was very successful in, say Iowa. You need more money."

I pulled my duster on and went to the lean-to where I'd carefully stowed the mule packs and started pulling out stacks of $50 bills. Kyle's alarm bells were going off, but I kept counting. I pulled ten straps out of the bag. That was $50,000. There were still at least a dozen bricks in the bags—over half a million dollars. When Kyle saw I was only taking one brick, he settled back, but I paused and watched his mind flicker with images.

So that was how he thought of going to Fort Collins and Greeley. Despain expected him to winter in Denver or Boulder then make his way to Greeley in the spring. He was to acquire a trunk, fill it with clothes and bury $100,000 dollars in it. This he was to ship to Despain. Kyle was to take the remaining money with him and return to Laramie. When the sheriff called him to his office, he'd give Despain the remaining cash. This was to accomplish two things. First, it established that a business associate had shipped his belongings to Despain with instructions to bank his money for him and use it to acquire land. Second, if the trunk and money was stolen, only a small portion was at risk. The remainder was safely with Kyle. It was clever. Even better than the system he'd thought up for Laramie and Theresa. This was 1891. There were no interstate commerce laws that governed the shipment of cash and no such thing as wire transfers.

I gave the money to Laramie and Theresa and we packed their share into saddlebags. We packed up and inside of three days we'd turned the cows loose on the lower slope where the water was running and grass was already peeking through. Then we headed southeast to Fort Collins.

THE GOING WAS only a little easier than it had been getting through in December. The Laramie River was overflowing its banks already. We weren't going to go into Laramie to cross it and I wanted to avoid Boswell's land down by Woods Landing. If Boswell recognized Kyle, he'd surely tell his protégé the next time they met. That led me to another decision that Kyle objected to. I cut his golden hair short and blackened it with a combination of grease and charcoal. I'd let his beard grow most of the winter and that I also blackened. At first glance, no one would recognize him. He headed south, avoiding Boswell by crossing at Wood's Landing at night. Theresa rode Laramie's paint and carried the baby much of the time. Laramie rode in my arms on the big buckskin. The two mules followed along docilely.

It took three weeks to make Fort Collins. We checked into a respectable but modest hotel for three dollars a night. No whorehouse on this trip.

I went out to buy the trunk and clothes to put in it. I took an assortment of women's and men's clothing, explaining to the merchant that my family's belongings had been washed away as we attempted to cross the South Platte. We had saved only the two mules, the two horses and the money in our saddlebags. I pled near destitution and got a good deal for a double-eagle. I presented the women's clothing to Laramie and Theresa and left the men's clothing in the trunk to pack the money into and ship to Despain.

We all cleaned up and I washed the coal out of my hair. From this point, Kyle was where Despain expected him to be. When everyone was safely headed north from Greeley, I'd head to Laramie with the remains of the money. I'd also sell one mule and the paint. Laramie was distraught over losing her precious horse, but I assured her that it was for the best and she would be able to buy another horse in Laramie. Probably a team for a wagon. She was going to become a respectable landowner.

The ladies that emerged from the bath were amazing. Well, I was in the room and Theresa was given the first bath while the water was hottest and cleanest. Kyle couldn't figure out why I hadn't claimed the first bath as should be my right. He wasn't disappointed to see my mother-in-law emerge naked from the tub, though. I decided I needed to do something about this response quickly and joined Laramie in the tub. She made sure my erection was fully buried and used to the fullest before we stepped out.

Her mother had already selected a dress and had brushed her long silver hair into a tight knot on her head. I wasn't sure what the fashions were in this age, but she looked fantastic, especially when she pulled a shawl up over her head. The dress I'd bought especially for Laramie was a blue gingham that slid smoothly over her graceful curves. Her mother instructed her on how to wear the various undergarments that a lady needed. When we were finally dressed, we looked the part of a western family with a husband and wife traveling with their baby and mother-in-law. They were stunning and more than one man turned his head to look at my women when they accompanied me into the dining room.

We ate a good meal and I had a beer. I think it was the first time in her life that someone other than her mother cooked a meal and served it to Laramie. It had probably been 20 years since Theresa had experienced it, if ever. They were both like kids with their eyes wide. I had to teach some basic manners to both of them, though Theresa was quicker to catch on, simply being reminded of the proper way to eat with an array of utensils beside her plate. Unfortunately, when Kaylene started to fuss, Laramie got frustrated with her fancy new dress and undergarments and just pulled the whole front of her dress down so she could nurse the baby. I quickly borrowed Theresa's shawl and draped it artfully over my wife's exposed parts. Even if breast-feeding in public was more accepted in 1891 than in 1995, I wasn't happy about every man in the place drooling over Laramie's tits.

I was getting antsy to move. We boarded the train to Greeley where I shipped the trunk and bought a suitcase and two tickets for Cheyenne. I spent a couple more days teaching Laramie and Theresa the rudiments of polite behavior, but I could feel Kyle becoming impatient to get to Laramie as well. I suggested that Theresa and Laramie stay in Cheyenne for a few days before going on to Laramie and that they should deposit half of their money with Wells Fargo in Cheyenne and then have it transferred to Laramie after they arrived. Perhaps they would even find land nearer the new state capitol, though I knew both were committed to staying on Centennial Ridge.

I WAS ANXIOUS to get going for a different reason. It was late April and I knew the hawks were returning to the upper plains.

That last night together in Greeley was precious to me. Even though we were no longer sharing the close confines of a tent or our hut on the mountain, it never occurred to us to have Theresa and the baby in a different room or bed. If anything, the confines of a double mattress were tighter than those of our sleeping furs. There was a drop-off on either side. But it made no difference to Laramie and me. We knew that tomorrow we'd be parting whether I was still riding inside Kyle or not. It was time for them to go north.

Laramie and I stripped out of our clothes and I held her in the bed while she nursed our little girl. Theresa slipped into the bed beside us and watched our loving family scene. When Kaylene had her fill, Laramie handed her over to her mother who cuddled the baby to sleep and wrapped her in the new soft blanket I'd bought. We doused the light and settled beneath the covers.

There was no pretense or slowness about Laramie and me making love. We kissed and fondled and she had me hard in an instant. I slipped my fingers into her and brought her to a good come before she crawled on top of me and put my cock in her cunt. She slid down slow and I closed my eyes trying to memorize every twist and turn and bump as my cowboy found his way home. I poured out everything I could when we were joined. I told her how much I loved her and that I was going to find a way to be sure she was taken care of. I told her I dreamed of coming back and being beside her forever. I wanted to have more children with her and raise our family on a ranch in the mountains with enough bottom land to grow feed and a garden.

All that time, I was touching her. Her hair had been washed and brushed and was like silk beneath my fingers. We had our lips locked together as we whispered and moaned into each other's mouths. I ran my hands down her sides and her back, feeling the muscles as she worked herself along my cock. I touched every one of her vertebrae and grabbed both her butt cheeks in my hands as I reached as far down as I could on her legs. I felt her heavy tits that were providing the food for our baby, even though Kaylene was beginning to eat some mashed up roots on her own. I wanted to be inside Laramie, more than just my fifth limb in her twat. I wanted my spirit to dwell in her—to be linked together forever.

Somewhere along the line as we lay there with our mixed juices flowing out of her and across my balls, I felt another hand on my shoulder and a hug as Theresa put her arm around Laramie. It wasn't anything sexual, but Theresa just lay there and held Laramie and me with Kaylene tucked in beside. She cooed and kissed at us like we were her little children and I guess we were just then. We finally drifted off to sleep and stayed in that little bundle all night long.

It was near eight in the morning when I got them on the train. I stopped for my first night's camp about twenty miles north of Greeley. I boiled water and whipped lather to a froth before scraping the whiskers from my face. As I saddled up the next morning and got ready to mount, I told Kyle I was proud of him.

I saw the shadow and heard Redtail's cry.

The Librarian

"COLE! COLE! YOU okay?"

Someone was slapping my face and I opened my eyes to the glare of the late July sun on my face. I was sweating something fierce.

"George?" The head ranch hand stopped before he slapped my face again. "Shit! What happened?"

"That's what I'd like to know. I come out here to relieve you and find you lying here asleep with Buttercup standing a few feet away. This don't look like a comfy place to nap."

"Nap? Ow. Oh, my achin' back. I musta gone to sleep in the saddle and fallen off my horse. What a dude. Every damned bone in my body hurts. What time is it?"

"Three in the afternoon. Shorty come up when your dad came and got Jack. He's in bad shape. I came ridin' out here and find you half an hour away from the herd."

"Three? Damn. Last thing I remember was about half an hour after I rode out, maybe seven hours ago."

"Well, our schedules are all messed up one way and another. Shorty and I will split the night and you go back out after breakfast. You okay to ride back to camp?"

"Yeah. I don't really feel like I hit my head or anything. I just... damn I feel like an idiot."

"Well you deserve that. Get back to camp and get some food and a real sleep before morning."

AND SO MY summer went. I came down from the upper range in time to spend two nights with Mary Beth before she left for Boulder. It was her junior year at the University of Colorado. One thing was different, though. I'd had a scare. I could remember sitting on my horse and just drifting off to sleep as my spirit headed back in time. So now if I was driving, I kept all the windows rolled up and the radio blasting. I'd slept for seven hours the last time that hawk called. I wasn't going to risk it while I was driving.

IT WAS MY senior year in high school and the year that I'd learn about heartbreak all over again.

I was surprised to see Geneive back in school and not showing any signs of being in a motherly way. I figured that as soon as she had her hands on that guy with the Corvette, she'd get herself pregnant and married. I knew that's what she wanted. She even said hi to me in the hall one day and then ran off to study with her friends. Well, I was a little relieved that there wasn't going to be any big hoo-hah when we saw each other. Like Jason would do; just walk away.

I settled into the swing of things and got my school books and Dad still checked with me after chores every night to make sure I was doing my homework. I didn't have much else to do, so there was no danger of me missing an assignment. I paid attention. Maybe I wasn't the top student in my class, but I knew how important it was going to be to have decent grades in order to get into college.

The one thing different about this year was that I started going to the library once or twice a week after school. I could spend an hour there and still get home in time to do my chores, have dinner, and do my homework. I had two missions: Find Laramie Wyoming Ranae and Kyle Wardlaw, and figure out what the next target would be for Kyle to get some loot. In fact, I'd decided that whoever he was collecting the lost treasure for didn't need to have it all. Kyle and Laramie's descendants deserved to be taken care of. It was a long slow process.

I couldn't find any record of either Laramie or Kyle in local histories. I went back through a bunch of old newspapers to see if I could find out what happened to them, but there just wasn't any information out there.

I told Mary Beth in general terms what I was trying to do—mostly about finding lost treasures—and she told me I had to go to ask a librarian. I usually just walked down shelves and pulled every book off to see what was in it.

I started with the high school library and Miss Johnson helped me a bit, showing me where I could get the local paper all the way back to when the *Boomerang* started in 1881. There were some missing issues in the microfiche, but I just had to find 1890 and read forward. There were also bound copies of the *Laramie Republican,* which was founded in 1890. I read through or skimmed through all the issues from 1890 to 1900, but never found a mention of either Laramie or Kyle.

So, I started focusing on notices of bank robberies and legends of lost treasures. For the most part, Laramie was a pretty quiet town and was likelier to have a murder than a bank robbing. There were thefts and break-ins, but nothing that amounted to a big enough treasure for Kyle to go after. Miss Johnson suggested that I try the Laramie Public Library after school and see if they had papers from Cheyenne, Casper, and Gillette. I did the same search patterns through everything the library had, but still came up blank.

I did meet a librarian, though.

It was mid-October when I asked the woman at the public library desk if there were any copies or microfilms of the *Gillette News-Record* from the 1890s. She laughed at me. Quietly. She went to a reference book at a different desk and turned the pages. Then she turned the book to face me and pointed to an entry labeled *"Gillette News-Record."* According to the entry, the newspaper began as the *Gillette News*—in 1904. Well, that was no good.

"What is it you really want to find out?" she asked.

"Well, I was looking to see if there was any news about either of two people who I think lived here in Laramie in the 1890s first. But I've been through all the local papers and there's no record of them. So, I was indulging a secret fantasy to find a buried treasure. Only problem is you can't find a lost treasure unless you know when and where one was lost. So, I was looking to see if I could spot bank or stage robberies where the money was never recovered, reports of lost mines and that sort of thing. I guess I've got too much time on my hands." I looked at her with my most winning smile. She was only a little older than me. I thought this might be her first job out of college.

"You need a life," she said. "Don't you have a girlfriend?" I shook my head. "Sports? Friends? A job?" On the last one I nodded a little.

"I'm a rancher's son. I've got plenty of jobs."

"Hmm. Well, if you really want to do this, we should go over to the University Library. They've got a much bigger historical selection and can get things through the educational lending system that I can't get here."

"We?" I asked. She blushed.

"Well, it looks like you need someone who knows her way around a library. I don't have..." she sighed, "...*a life,* either. This sounds like fun."

I arranged with Miss Isabelle Gonzales to go over to the University on Monday after I got out of school.

IT WAS ALL pretty innocent in the beginning. Isabelle was fun, smart, and dedicated to the search. I'm not sure how she arranged it, but she made herself available to accompany me to the University at least once a week and often called me with things she had discovered. I had a lot of fun with her and she seemed to enjoy my company as well. Going over to the University library so often was part of what got me interested in going to UW instead of following Mary Beth to Boulder.

Well, just before Christmas break, Isabelle and I were walking over to the U Library and she just kind of slipped her hand in mine and we kept walking. I was conscious of that hand perched in mine, I tell you. Isabelle was a pretty girl in spite of the fact that she was maybe six years older than me. I couldn't believe she would even consider an eighteen-year-old as anything more than a friend. I started for the door of the library and she just kind of pulled me the other direction and we walked out into the cemetery. UW is sort of built around the Greenhill Cemetery where the city's founders are buried. We walked through the gates and down the Avenue of the Flags.

"What's up?" I asked.

"Well, I thought of another line of research on the names you asked about." We turned left at the circle and then left again at the next avenue. "There are some amazing records for old cemeteries. This one has been around since the early days of Laramie. Even if a death notice isn't filed or published in the newspapers, it's possible for it to be listed in the cemetery records. No, I didn't find either of the names you asked about. Don't get your hopes up on that front. But I thought I'd show you what it was like here. Most of the cemetery has pretty good records, but there's this one section that is spotty. A lot of frontier cemeteries have them. It's called The Potters Field." We walked into a grassy area that didn't have much in the way of headstones. There weren't even markers at all the graves, and most of them weren't big enough to have a name.

"What is this?"

"It's the area of the cemetery where the indigent and unknown are buried. This might be the oldest part of the cemetery. Unfortunately, a lot of the people are still unknown. There are graves, but we don't know exactly what date or who is in them. It's pretty old. I thought that if you are still interested in finding information we might check more cemetery records."

"Yeah. That would be cool. Do we have to visit all of them?"

"No. Most cemeteries have now filed copies of their maps and list of names with the Family History Library in Salt Lake City. I was thinking…" She stopped and pulled me around to look at her. "Shit, Cole. This is awful of me. I'm six years older than you. But I was thinking that if you had a couple days free, we could drive over to Salt Lake City and do some research in the FHL. And maybe, when the library was closed, we could do some research on each other."

Before I could answer her or even comprehend what she was saying properly, she reached up and grabbed my head so she could pull it down far enough to kiss. The kiss was sweet and passionate and… I guess I'd say it was pleading in a way. I was surprised. I mean, I was eighteen and I'd had plenty of boners thinking about my pretty librarian, but I just figured it was pure fantasy.

"Isabelle? You really want to do something with a kid like me?"

"Cole, you might be in high school, but something about you makes you seem older—like you've got more experience than your age would suggest. I know I must seem like an old lady to you and I'm not suggesting you need to date me or anything like that, but it's been a long time since I was in any kind of a relationship and you're so nice and we get along so well that I thought if you were interested I'd like to at least have a couple days where we, you know…"

I cut off the sentence with another kiss and pulled her too me. She wrapped her arms around me out there in the cemetery and squeezed so hard I thought she'd break a rib.

"I'd love to sneak off with you for a couple of days," I said. "Let's go someplace warm and talk about it, okay?" She nodded and we turned to go.

I slipped and fell.

We'd had a couple inches of snow already, so we couldn't see all the stones. My boot heel had hit one and slid. Isabelle came down on top of me. We had snow all over us and were laughing and kissing while we struggled to get up. "Okay, who do I owe that little trip to?" I asked, wiping off the stone. It was an old one and when I finally got it clear enough to read, tears sprang to my eyes.

Caitlin Forster d. 1890.

I sat there staring and trying not to cry. The little redheaded dynamo who got off on Kyle's special treatment. Who bathed him and screamed so loud when she was being eaten that a bouncer came to check on her. Who bled to death after an abortion while I was up in the fucking Big Horn. The reality of it all hit me hard. Caitlin was buried and I'd forced Kyle to head up into the mountains to find Laramie and make love to her. That was in 1890, 105 fucking years ago. They were all dead. My lovers, my daughter, and me—or at least the me I inhabited when I was Kyle Wardlaw.

Isabelle was still laughing and pulled me to my feet, not noticing my tears as anything more that the result of the cold wind. We stumbled out of the cemetery with my arm around her shoulders and headed for the Wyoming Union. Isabelle got us coffee and we sat in a corner so we could plan our little get-away. That's when I thought of something else that was going to hurt.

"Uh, Isabelle. There might be one problem to getting away together over the holiday. I decided that before I got into anything with another girl, I had to be completely honest with her."

"You really don't like me that much, do you?"

"Yes, I really do like you that much. That's not the problem. Are we okay to just talk and be open without getting all emotional? I mean, yes, it *is* emotion, but this is difficult for me."

"You're gay?"

"Oh, God! I am *so* not gay and so damned horny… um… sorry. That sort of slipped out. But the very thought of having… special time with you is practically driving me crazy already. I just really need to tell you about this, so please don't interrupt."

"I'm sorry."

"I told you I don't have a girlfriend and that's absolutely true. But there's this girl that I'm in love with. I mean, really, really in love with. We can't ever be together as a boyfriend and girlfriend or husband and wife, but we promised each other that if we ever got involved with someone else we'd tell that person about us. I can't be with you unless you know about her."

"That's decent of you, I guess. You can't be boyfriend and girlfriend but you're in love. Are you lovers?"

"Whenever we can be."

"So why not… oh God! Your sister?"

"I don't have a sister. It's my cousin."

"Oh, thank God. I'd have been pretty squicked out if it was your sister. A cousin, I can deal with. God! My heart is racing. I can deal with this. I didn't ask you to marry me. I just want to sit on your face. Oh God! What did I say? I am such a slut. Will she be okay with… if you and I…?"

"Yeah. She'll be okay with that. Maybe a little jealous, but we agreed that we weren't going to hold out on that part of our lives. We can't be with each other, but we're with each other, if you know what I mean."

"So, okay. Now that it's out in the open, what's the problem?" Isabelle laughed.

"Well, the only problem is that she's going to be back over Christmas while school is on break and we try to get together as much as possible. I'd be taking off while she's here and…"

"And available. I got it. So, would there be a problem with right now?"

AFTER I GOT over being stunned to silence, Isabelle dragged me out of the Union and back to the truck. She gave me directions to her apartment. We practically tumbled through her door once she got it unlocked; our lips were glued together as we stripped off our coats and gloves.

"Cole, we're a little bit the same as you and your cousin, you know? I mean it might not be illegal, but both my employer and your school would probably frown on you dating the librarian. I'm not a teacher, but I'm still viewed as being a person in authority. I think we'll have to keep our relationship—whatever it is—kind of quiet. Okay?"

"Right. I think keeping quiet is a good idea."

Isabelle wasn't quiet. I guess when I filled her mouth and then filled a condom in her pussy, I wasn't very quiet either. I lay beside Isabelle fondling and sucking on her big tits. She's the most generously endowed woman I've ever been with in either life. Well, maybe Ellen, but she was big every place. Isabelle was pretty small most places but totally stacked.

"Cole?"

"Yes, Izzy?"

"That's sweet. But I have a question."

"Go ahead."

"Would your... uh... cousin want to join us on a trip to Salt Lake?"

I looked at Isabelle with my mouth open so wide her tit fell out. Was she? Did she?

"Are you making an invitation?"

"I think it could be fun."

"But you don't even know her."

"I know she loves you. That's a pretty good recommendation in my book."

"I guess we'll find out next week. Let's meet before we actually leave."

WE DID MEET. Mary Beth loved Izzy. Izzy loved Mary Beth. I was getting love from both sides. But the trip to Salt Lake did have a purpose and I was determined to get something accomplished besides wild sex. We didn't find anything on Laramie or Kyle in cemetery records or in the fifty some family Bibles we examined. But I found a whole bunch of clues to lost treasures. I made a list and photocopied all the relevant information on them that I could find. One of them would be happening in December 1891. It would be so cool to be there when Kyle picked the box of the Wells Fargo payroll that two low-life brothers stole from a stage. The brothers bought it in a gunfight with the sheriff down near Denver. The strongbox was never recovered.

Sadly, Redtail didn't screech before spring.

I took Isabelle with me when I went to Boulder over spring break. I thought it was a little strange that my parents never asked anymore if I was spending time with Mary Beth. I don't think they even knew about Isabelle. The three of us were lying in a tangle in Mary Beth's bed when she asked the big question.

"Izzy, I have to ask you something because I know Cole won't."

"What is it MB? You know I'll tell you anything."

"Sweetheart, is this going to last? I'm starting to develop feelings for you that I never thought I'd have for a woman. I just figured I'd come along for the ride, you know?"

"Don't you mean ride along for the come?" I asked. I got hit from both sides.

"Anyway. Do you have feelings for Cole and me?" Mary Beth asked.

"Oh honey, I do!" Izzy answered. "But do I think this is the be-all and end-all? Do I think we'll be together in ten years, living together and playing three-way house? God, I kinda wish. It's wonderful right now, but you're still in college and Cole's still in high school. How do any of us know what's going to happen next? With this lousy economy, the library budgets are being cut and I could end up having to move in order to get a job. I know you two have a future on the ranch with whoever you choose, but I don't know if I've got a ranching gene. I wouldn't mind reading about it, but doing it? Cole, you've always been honest with me and I'm going to be the same with you. I've been circulating my resume. Laramie Public Library isn't exactly the top of the line for librarians. I even put an application in at the FHL when we were in Salt Lake City."

I squeezed both ladies tightly.

"You don't have to make any commitments, Izzy," I said. "I am amazed every time I'm with you that you even consider being with a kid like me. Of course, I'm amazed that Mary Beth is as in love with me as I am with her. Let's just enjoy what we've got while we've got it. I'm headed back up on the high range in a couple months and I still have a dozen condoms left. What am I gonna do with them up there?"

Fortunately, I never had to find out.

Izzy and I kept seeing each other and even made another weekend trip over to Salt Lake City to do more research on lost treasure. I found a dozen stories that I felt were within the range of where Kyle would be sent. So far, he'd been only in Montana, Utah, Wyoming, and Colorado. I wasn't sure how far Despain would send Kyle. I'd found likely prospects as far as northern Nevada, Utah, Oregon, and even one in California. I recorded them all in a notebook with the necessary information, including hand-drawing maps and plotting things out on old maps that showed different landmarks than where the Interstate goes through.

Twice a week I'd go to Izzy's apartment after school and after I showed her my newest maps, we'd make love. Izzy was fun and an enthusiastic lover. But I think we both started feeling that we weren't really there for each other without Mary Beth. As the spring wore on, our romance ran down. It was just a couple weeks before graduation when Izzy called it quits.

"Hey! MB will be home in a few days. Do you want us to come over here?"

"That's nice, Cole."

"That's nice? Did you hear what I said?"

"Uh… yeah. Cole, do you love me?"

"Sure, I do, Izzy."

"No, Cole. Do you love me like you love Mary Beth?"

Shit. Now I had to figure out what the degrees of love were. No, I didn't love Izzy like I loved Mary Beth, but I didn't love Mary Beth like I loved Laramie, either. The only difference was Mary Beth didn't know about Laramie, didn't share a bed with the two of us, and Laramie probably didn't like girls all that much. At least not as much as Izzy did.

"Isn't it enough to know I love you without comparing?" I asked.

"It should be. But I guess that's what's wrong, Cole. It should be but it isn't. I know you're still in high school, but you are so sure about your life that I expect you to be sure about me, too. But you aren't. And I guess I'm not sure about us either."

"What are you saying, Isabelle? Are you breaking up with us?"

"See? You didn't even ask if I was breaking up with you. You asked about us—you and Mary Beth. This sharing has been fun, but I want somebody who is just mine. So, yes, Cole. We're breaking up. However, many you want to include in that. I took a job in Denver this week and I'm moving the first of June. I'm sorry, but… I guess you better go now."

I went. What else was I supposed to do? I wondered what Mary Beth would say when she got home and found out we'd been dumped.

I didn't wait for her to come home. I called her that night. It was fairer that way. And besides, when I cried she cried with me.

IT'S COMFORTING, YOU know, to have someone to cry with. I didn't understand that at first.

I had one more stop I was going to make that afternoon before I headed home. I bought some flowers at Safeway and drove over to the cemetery. The snow was gone and I brought a little stand to put the flowers in. It was six months ago that I discovered the little marker in the Potters Field. I'd been back once a month all winter and spring. I'd put a little cross up that I could stand in the ground so I could find the place again. I thought that if I could get a little money ahead, I'd try to buy a bigger stone for her grave.

I found the cross I'd erected and swept away the dirt and the grass from the flat marker. I made sure I cleared the whole thing. It was the only marker in the whole Potters Field that looked cared for. I jammed the planter spike into the ground at her head and put the flowers in it. Yeah, they'd be dead in a few days. Just like Caitlin. I sat there in the dark and shone my flashlight on her marker and felt tears on my cheeks. I guess tears for losing Izzy and tears for Caitlin, both.

I heard Redtail shriek and there I was in the middle of July, a year after she died, looking out of Kyle's eyes at the marker he placed and the flower he laid on her grave. It was just a couple of wild flowers, but she was a wild girl. There were tears in both our eyes when I heard the call again.

I THOUGHT A lot about grief and dying those days. Caitlin was the first lover—the first person who was really close to me—that died. And I couldn't even talk to anyone about her. I'd got from Kyle's memories that he'd ordered the stone for Caitlin's grave in the Potters Field. I'd let him know I was proud of him and I shared having found her stone. I think he was pleased we could weep together.

It had been nearly a year since my last trip into the past. It had all become truly real to me when I found the initials on that old Douglas Fir that I kept going to visit whenever I could get away from camp. And then the discovery of Caitlin's stone just made me want to go back again as soon as possible. I was despairing of ever getting back to my Laramie.

When I'd last been transported into Kyle, the first thing I did was kill a man. Yeah, it was self-defense, but that didn't matter to Kyle. He'd have killed him before the guy had a chance if I hadn't interrupted him. Then there was the death of my relationship with Izzy. Mary Beth was pretty sad about it, but didn't let it dampen her fires for me. I don't know what my folks thought about me disappearing all the time. They knew I'd had a girlfriend break-up, but I'd never introduced them to Izzy.

And that whole grief thing. Just sharing those few moments over Caitlin's grave with Kyle made me see that maybe he wasn't such a bad guy after all. He was staying clear of Laramie and Theresa in town. I figured he was in over his head with Cal Despain, though, and I aimed to get him out of that relationship if I could. I think maybe Kyle romanticized Caitlin more than he would have if I hadn't been popping in. He saw what I had with Laramie and wanted to believe he'd had that with Caitlin, too. I suppose he felt some of my residual emotions.

Well, hell. What happens when *I* die? Laramie, Theresa, Kyle—even Kaylene—they all lived a long time ago. They ain't gonna mourn for me when I go. Do you think I'll see 'em when I die? Is that what heaven is supposed to be? I reckon like the preacher says, if they do see me it will be across a deep abyss that no one can cross. That'll be my hell.

I just gotta decide when I'm gonna meet it.

5

Close Encounter

I MANAGED TO get through the last two weeks of senior year, even with a broken heart. Mary Beth getting home helped. A lot. I'd get a week off after graduation before I headed to the upper range. I'd be a free man and I intended to use my freedom for the very best thing I could imagine. First, I'd make love to Mary Beth. Then I'd ride the high range. My grades were plenty good enough for me to get into the college of my choice, and that proved to be UW. I was only going to be an hour and change away from home, but I planned to move on campus in September. It was going to be a good year. I was determined.

My whole family was there for graduation, which amounted to Mom and Dad, Uncle Angus and Aunt Lily, and Mary Beth. George, Shorty, Ham, and Jack were already up on the range, so I didn't need to rush. When I got up there, Jack was coming back down. He'd had enough of a scare with a ruptured appendix last year that he was skittish about being so far out of touch again. Well, we all face our own mortality.

No, I'm not going there. I spent a good part of my life trying to not be depressed. I'm not going back into the dumps again.

I'd made my choice of where to go to school based on three factors. If I went to U of C, Mary Beth would only be there for a year then we'd be right back where we were now only I'd be in Boulder and she'd be in Laramie. Secondly, I needed a school with a strong Agriculture program. Mary Beth majored in Business at U of C, but I was determined to get the most preparation I could to be a modern rancher.

The third reason was that I was strangely comforted by the trips I made each month to put flowers on Caitlin's grave. That stone was a constant reminder to me, not of what I'd lost, but of the reality that I lived in another life.

Do you believe in reincarnation? I was digging into that pretty hard. I mean studying Hindu and Buddhist philosophy and meditation. I couldn't abide the idea of coming back as a spider if you kill a spider and I sure wasn't going to stop eating beef or raising it to slaughter. Cows are food. Don't give me crap about levels of spiritual development. Why would reaching a higher plane in human development mean that you should give up something that was a basic part of your position on the food chain. It didn't make sense.

But I couldn't help but think if maybe going back in time and being inside Kyle wasn't just part of me reliving a previous life, you know? I had a complete set of memories of both my lives. If Kyle had remembered it any time I was in him, then I remembered it. I finally figured out that the reason he couldn't remember any of my memories was that in 1891, I hadn't been born yet. I had nothing to remember.

You know, that'll give you a headache if you think about it too long.

Bolt

"Son, take a walk with me," Dad said.

I could have said, "No, Dad, I'm going to party with my friends," but the whole family had come to my graduation and then come over to the house. Mom and Aunt Lily were fixing a big dinner and Mary Beth's sisters were coming with their families. It was almost like Christmas and it would be a long time before I could sneak off with Mary Beth.

"Sure, Dad. What's up? Is this where you impart your wisdom to me as I'm ready to go out into the world?" We both laughed. Dad had a great sense of humor and sometimes I wished I had more of it. I'd let myself get too morose this spring.

"No son. It's just that..." He turned and looked back toward the house as if to be sure no one was watching. "...Mom doesn't like us to smoke around the house." With that he pulled a cigar out of his pocket and handed it to me. He stuffed another in his mouth. Mine was already cut and waiting for a light and Dad handed me a box of matches as we got to the clearing with the chimney. We settled onto a couple of the log benches and I lit up as Dad bit the end of his cigar off and commenced to chewing. He'd quit smoking a year ago because the doctor told him his lungs couldn't take anymore. There were dark spots on them. But Dad couldn't give up tobacco, so he just chewed his cigars now instead of lighting them. He knew I just pulled on the smoke and didn't inhale it, so he'd gone easy about me pulling out a cigar at the campfire.

"Thanks, Dad." I handed him back the matches and took a big puff. I was surprised when he handed me his pocket flask and I took a pull of his whiskey.

"I've got to know, something son. I'll probably have to decide while you are up on the range this summer. Do you really want to inherit this place? It doesn't make a difference to me one way or the other. There's no pressure. We scarcely turn enough money on what we raise out here to pay the bills and there's no reason you need to feel obligated to keep it up. I've had a couple pretty good offers for the place and if you don't want it, maybe that would be the best thing for us all. It would pay for your college and Mom and I could retire to Florida and get a suntan. I mean an all-over suntan. Maybe join one of those nudist colonies they've got down there. You might not want to think about it, but your mom is a fine-looking woman. A fine woman."

"Dad. Are you saying you want out now? I don't think I'm ready to take over the ranch. If I get my degree in agricultural business like we talked, I think we can turn it around and be profitable. But it'll take me four years to get it. I want this place, Dad. It's important to me. But if it's getting you down and you can't wait for me, then I won't hold you back."

"I'm glad you want it, son. I'm worried about it, but I'm glad." He handed me the pocket flask again and I took a bigger pull this time. We just sat there in companionable silence for a while. I puffed and he spat a wad toward the hearthstone.

"Dad, there's something special about this land. It calls to me. It's like it owns me, not the other way around." How could I tell him about my experiences? They were just too unbelievable. I just knew it was important to be here.

"I've always felt the same way, son. We never talked about it much, but on the way up the hill over there when you reach the lower ridge, there's a little plot of gravestones. There are no names on them or dates, but it's where the Alexanders buried my mama and she buried her man. My grandma and great grandma are buried there. I don't know how many generations. You know grandma never got married 'cause her man got killed in Korea after he left her home pregnant. She buried him up there anyway even though they weren't married. Anyway, when it's my time, that's where I want to be buried. Just like that, too. Just a stone to mark the place, but no name or dates. You'll do that for me, won't you, son?"

"Dad, it's going to be years before we have to worry about that. But yeah. That has a kind of appeal to me, too. Nobody needs to know who I am, just that under that rock I lie peacefully on the land I love. I'll do that, Dad."

"I suppose we better head back before they send a search party out after us. I don't know what Angus will do, though. His place ain't doing any better than ours. Can't imagine why we're getting offers to buy. He might take it up."

"Dad, that would kill Mary Beth. I know her sisters have moved off and got married and don't plan to come back. But Mary Beth plans to die in that ranch house and I'd rather it wasn't soon."

"You care for her a lot, don't you, son?" What the hell was I supposed to say to that? *Yeah Dad, I fuck her every chance I get.* That would go over big. I took a deep breath.

"She's the closest and dearest relative I've got besides you and Mom. If it means I need to help her and maybe even manage her ranch and ours too, then I'll do whatever is necessary. But don't let Angus sell, Dad. Please."

"Angus is like my brother. I lived there for eighteen years after Mama died. Hell, I married his little sister. I don't know what we can do. Times are tight with that war in the Middle East and all. I thought we were done with Iraq, but then there's Bosnia and Somalia. Seems they never run out of people to fight. I'll talk to him. Maybe if we pool everything together we can make it work. You and Mary Beth could be joint owners of a combined spread. Wouldn't that be something?"

"Yeah. That would really be something, Dad."

AFTER THE BIG dinner and everybody's congratulations, I got a few gifts and then folks started to pack up. After Mary Beth's sisters left, it was just the six of us sitting around the living room. Seemed that Uncle Angus kept looking over at Mary Beth until finally she said, "All right you guys. I've got a present for Cole, too and I suppose you all want to come and watch."

Now that about knocked me over. Mary Beth hinted earlier that she had a present for me, but it wasn't something I was going to want our parents to be watching. Hell! What was this all about?

She pulled me up by the hand and we all trooped outside with our folks following. Mary Beth led us to the horse barn.

"I know you love Buttercup, but that girl's getting old. You've been riding her since you were what—eight? And she wasn't a young horse then. So, I figured it was about time you started training up somebody who could give her a rest now and then." She led me to a box stall in our barn and there was the most beautiful buckskin quarter horse I'd ever seen. He had a hide the color of a white-tail deer with a black mane, dorsal stripe, tail, and four black socks. There was a single streak of white on his face beneath the black forelock. He was young, but already stood close to sixteen hands. He was a beauty and I knew him already from hours and days in the saddle.

"Bolt," I whispered. He swung his head around to look at me. I was a step closer to believing in reincarnation.

"He's been gentled, but not ridden. You need to put a saddle on him and pony him up to the ridge with you. Just get him used to saddle and weight this summer. Let him learn from Buttercup. He'll figure it out," Mary Beth said.

"I'm going to need another saddle," I laughed.

"Well, that's what I figured," Dad said. He led me to the tack room. Things had been cleared in the crowded room. Sitting on a saddle-bench in the middle of the room was a new saddle, tan—almost the color of the horse it would sit on. It wasn't a show saddle with a bunch of silver and black trim on it. Now that I looked at it, I could tell it wasn't even new, but it had been well-cared for and recently cleaned and oiled. This was a working High Roper saddle with a solid pommel and horn and a cantle high enough to sit back in. It had a minimum of tooling and wasn't made to show off. My horse was showy enough. There was a matching headstall and snaffle bit, reins, and halter with a good lead rope. "The head gear is from your aunt and uncle," Dad said. "The saddle is from Mom and me."

I turned and hugged Dad. It had been a while since I'd done that and I regretted not doing it more often. Sometimes I wished Kyle could inhabit *my* body so he'd know what it was like to have a Mom and Dad who cared for him. I hugged Mom and then Uncle Angus and Aunt Lily together. Finally, I turned to Mary Beth. "That means you got me Bolt." She nodded and I took her in my arms and gave her a very un-cousinly kiss. "How did you ever manage to find and afford a colt like this?" I asked in awe as we looked into the stall.

"You remember Joss? My roommate freshman year?" I remembered the woman Mary Beth roomed with in the dormitory before she got her apartment. She was a big-boned gal and almost dwarfed Mary Beth—and Mary Beth is no little slip of a girl. "Her family raises quarter horses up in Montana. I went up there with her on the first winter break we had because she said her favorite mare had just foaled. This big hunk is what popped out. I bought him on the spot. Well, sorta. I made payments for him for two years and they took care of stabling and gentling him. They know their horses up there and they did a good job with him."

I turned to Mary Beth and took her in my arms again. This time the kiss I gave her started real tender-like, but it got serious real quick. I glanced up expecting our folks to be making some comment, but they'd left the barn. I looked at Mary Beth and damn, I loved that girl.

"Right here, Cole. Right now. I can't wait any longer."

"But Mary Beth," I gasped as the girl threw herself onto me and I fell back on the bales. "Our folks. They're going to be expecting us to come in. We gotta be careful."

"Cole, do you really think they don't know about us? If there was ever any doubt, the kiss you gave me after you got this horse would have taken care of that. Mom and Dad have known practically since the beginning. Honey, take me. Love me like I love you. We'll figure out the rest."

It wasn't really me doing the taking this time. I was flat on my back on the hay bales and MB got out of her britches and had herself planted on my cock before I could get my jeans down past my knees. She was all over me and I was happy to be ridden. We never did make it into the house that night. I grabbed a sleeping bag from the camp room and we went up into the loft and made love all night long.

I HEADED UP toward the mountains, ponying my new stud behind Buttercup along with my mule loaded with gear. I was taking a bunch of stuff up to the camp that the first riders couldn't carry while they were herding. After I got up to the ridge on Wednesday, Dad would bring the truck up the back way (where Mary Beth and I had our first experience together) and bring the major food supplies in exchange for Jack who would ride back down to the ranch.

The whole way, for two days, I kept watching and waiting for Redtail, but to no avail. You'd think he stayed south all spring. The guys at camp were pleased to see me and were very complimentary about my new stud. I guess they all knew about it long before I did. George had gone up to Montana to haul Bolt back before the guys headed up into the mountains. This year we had another new guy with us—Ham. He was actually hired by Uncle Angus. We'd decided that it was dumb for us to keep our herds separate on the open range and we'd divide them when we got down the mountain. Dad and Angus had been talking about this for years, but early this spring they'd sent the guys out to ride the center fence line and take down the barbed wire. As I rode up to the camp I passed fencepost after fencepost with nothing between them.

I was thankful I hadn't been snatched out of my body yet. I needed to do some scouting around. I studied the maps that I'd brought with me in a waterproof satchel. I had USGS topo maps of the entire State of Wyoming and Northern Colorado. I'd gotten a new hiking compass and studied how to use it so I could mark positions on the map. I had historical map reproductions from the 1890s for the entire Western U.S. On these maps, I'd carefully plotted out the last location known and the date of every lost treasure I'd researched. I was thinking that the next time I visited Kyle, we'd do some freelancing. Dad said the ranch was on hard times and I wasn't above producing a little miracle of my own to save the farm.

Every time I scouted out on my own, I kept coming back to the old Mountain Douglas I'd carved our initials in. From there, I scouted back as best as I could remember to the place where the tepee hut had been. I'd walked to the tree and back with my arms around Laramie and my eyes not paying attention to anything else. It had been in a clearing, but I couldn't find any clearing up in this area. I finally found a little thermal spring in an area with younger-looking trees. That had to be it.

The forest, untended for a hundred years, had grown over where our little cabin of bliss had been located. It took three weeks for me to find this area and then I was due to ride back down for my birthday celebration. I'd only be gone for five days, but I was anxious to find the landmarks I wanted before I got snatched back to wherever and whenever I was going next. After scuffing around near the spring for a while, my boot scuffed against some stone. I got down on my knees and cleared away the grass that had grown up around it. It was a pretty smooth rock. I brushed away the dirt and could see a few traces of color in the sandstone. I remembered the little scene Theresa Ranae had painted. I'd asked about the colors and paints the winter we were snowed in here. She'd told me it was all natural pigments, mostly mixed with fat. A lot like the dye job on my hair had been. She said most of it wouldn't withstand a good rainstorm if the hut was gone. I couldn't be sure the color I was seeing was something she'd put there or if it was just the natural color of the rock. Lichen grew on the rock—a remnant, I supposed, of before the forest had grown around it.

I was tempted to move the rock right now and look underneath it, but I hadn't been back in time yet, so I didn't even know if I'd been successful. I'd wait until I knew.

I waited until almost the end of summer and time for me to head down and start my first year of college. That lazy Redtail was flying circles in the sky all day long while I was out riding the herd. Just after I'd got back to camp and had had a plate of rice and beans, I heard the long shrill cry and relaxed.

Traveling: Freelancer

KYLE WAS AGITATED. He'd been on his way to meet Kat, whoever the hell that was, when the boy had run up to him and told him Sheriff Despain wanted to see him right now. Kyle told the boy to fuck off but turned his steps and headed for the sheriff's office. On the way, I saw a familiar figure cross the street ahead of us. I started to pick up speed, but Laramie looked my way, turned her head, and hurried back the way she'd come. And in that turn, I'd seen a bump. A baby bump. I turned to follow her but Kyle yowled in my brain. Despain! Now! I relented and let Kyle do the driving. I'd go find Laramie as soon as the dreadful sheriff had his fill of us.

Kyle knocked on the sheriff's door, but went on in without pausing.

"Sit down here, Kyle. I've got an errand for you. You'll need to leave tonight. As soon as we're done."

I groaned. I'd just got here and hadn't seen Laramie yet. Fortunately, Kyle was in control and the groan was inaudible.

"You got to go to Oregon and you need to hightail it." He unfolded a map and showed the exact route Kyle was to take. "There's a prospector up there. He's been there for a few months, but he's coming back to civilization. He's not carrying much, but he's not going to make it back to civilization."

"You want me to kill him?" Kyle asked in disbelief. He'd killed, sure, but he'd never been sent out to gun down a man.

"Don't be ridiculous, Kyle. You ain't a hired gun. You're a collector. Whatever reason this old guy doesn't make it, you have to be there. As soon as he's dead, you search him. I don't know rightly what he has, but I'm guessing it's a map or a deed. Whatever, he won't need it once he's gone. You get it and get back here. I'm figuring there might be early snow when you hit the mountains coming back. You just get over there, get the map and get back as soon as possible. I had the kid pack your mule. Get your horse and get out of here. Now."

I swear Kyle damned near genuflected in front of Despain. We high-tailed it out of there and straight to the stable. Kyle's Bolt was saddled and ready to ride. I didn't want to take over completely, but I damned well wanted to see Laramie again. Kyle protested, but I turned the horse to the boarding house that Kyle identified and rode around to the back. Why the hell had Laramie turned and run away from me?

Well, that thought triggered Kyle's memory of just a bit ago when he'd first seen Laramie in town. He was on his way to court his girlfriend when Laramie ran toward him. Kyle had just put his head down and held up his hands. They'd avoided each other since. That was great. Now she just assumed it was Kyle Wardlaw instead of Kyle Redtail. Kyle stopped under a window and tossed a copper at it, then sat back and let me take over. The window opened and Laramie stuck her head out.

"Laramie," I husked. "It's me. I'm back."

"Kyle! It *is* you. I love you. I'll be right down."

"No sweetheart. I've got to ride out right now. I've been sent on an errand. But you're pregnant!"

"I'm carrying our baby again, Kyle. Hurry back to me."

"Oh, I will, darling. I'm very happy! I gotta go now."

I nudged the horse forward just as another window opened. Kyle frantically tried for control and I gave it over. *What the hell?*

"Kyle, what are you doing on a horse?" asked the almost-blonde doll who poked her head out the window. This little girl was seriously cute. She wasn't tall like Mary Beth, but you couldn't really call her petite, either. She looked like she had about the right amount of meat on her bones and a generous layer of fat up on her chest.

"Damned sheriff sent me on a mission. I gotta get out of town tonight, sugar," Kyle said.

"Kyle! We were going do some sparkin' tonight. I want to come ride with you."

"You can't do that, Kat. I gotta go clear to Oregon. I might not get back before spring."

"I'll wait for you, Kyle. I ain't one of your dancehall girls. I'm sitting here at home or teaching school. That nice pregnant girl and her mama are pleasant company. Just know I'm waiting for you."

"And you best know I'm coming back," he said. "I'll see you by spring, sugar!"

Kyle nudged Bolt into a quick trot with his mule following obediently behind. I just let him go. It was coming on winter. It looked like I'd be in Kyle's head for a few months. And when we got back? Hell, I'd be a daddy again!

As Kyle pushed the animals over the Continental Divide, it was already nearly impassable. He kept muttering about why he couldn't have been told earlier. I knew why, of course. Despain's time traveler hadn't arrived much before I did. There was something about this find that had rung his chimes. I went over all the lost treasure reports I'd been memorizing. There were all kinds of lost gold mine legends that didn't have the credibility of newspaper reports of stage or bank robberies. The most famous, of course, was the Lost Dutchman, but even though one report was that it was in Colorado and another in California, the most common were that it was somewhere in Arizona. And a lost mine would be a problem if the time traveler intended to go open the mine in the 20th century. There were things like mineral rights and Federal Lands and all that needed to be dealt with.

It all bugged me. Kyle had never been sent quite this far away and it seemed senseless to go so far for a map or a deed that couldn't be transferred to the 20th century. Something stunk about all this. I couldn't remember a single lost treasure story that would send us into this part of Oregon.

Kyle didn't care. He was just doing as he was told and seeing that he was going to get his reward. Kyle was really a pretty simple fellow. I suppose that's why Despain trusted him. I mean, the kid had probably handled more gold and U.S. Government notes than anyone even in my day could ever hope to see. But he was content with the fact that he was getting "a cut," of the profit and would never begin to think of needing more than that. He always had plenty of money, but not so much as to be flashy. He bought nice things and the best whores. But he didn't own any property and he didn't flash around more money than it seemed he should have from his "guard missions" that Despain sent him out on.

It puzzled me, but I had a lot of time to think about it and go over in my mind thinking about the various stories I'd collected and the maps I'd made. I was so quiet that sometimes I caught Kyle wondering if I was still around or if I'd been called back to wherever I came from. When I followed his thoughts, they were mostly about the woman Kat, and a few about Laramie. I guess I wasn't surprised at that. He was present when I was using his body to make love to the most wonderful woman in the world. And she was pregnant with our baby. I guess what surprised me is that he thought of her fondly, but thought of Kat as a possible mate.

Hmm. Kat Tangeman, new school teacher who had met Kyle at the one year anniversary celebration of Wyoming's statehood this summer. It had taken most of the summer for Kyle to get up the nerve to court her, after Despain had sent him out again. Then Laramie had arrived and it confused Kyle because he didn't know what he should do with the two of them rooming in the boarding house next door to each other. Since that first encounter, though, Laramie had been discreet and seemed to understand. Kyle was in a panic over what he'd do when I took control and went to see Laramie instead of Kat.

I had to laugh when I finally got the whole story. We were two very different guys who occasionally shared the same body and we were in love with two women who lived next to each other. This had sitcom written all over it.

IT LOOKED LIKE we had a few months to get ourselves back in balance and for now I was just letting Kyle go about the business he knew best. It was late-October when we finally hunkered down at the foot of White's Peak to wait for the guy who was about to die. I wondered what was going to happen. Was there someone waiting in ambush? Would he have an accident? Was there a trap here somewhere?

The more I thought about the latter, the warier I became. I wasn't sure what would happen if Kyle got himself killed while I was in his mind and I wasn't anxious to find out. My distrust of Despain was rubbing off on my host as well. We set up a dry camp in the shelter of an overhang that Kyle draped with his wagon canvas. I was going to suggest that it should be painted in camouflage, but it was so filthy from use that it was the same color as the rocks anyway. Kyle changed out of his jeans and shirt and put on his buckskins. They were warmer than the city clothes, especially since he kept his union suit on. Instead of his normal riding boots, he pulled on soft fur-lined boots. He was preparing to move quickly and quietly. By day we kept watch on the trail. By night we huddled in a sleeping fur without lighting a fire.

On the third day we were there, we heard the jingle of harness. It was the first sign of life we'd had since we got here. The old man who came into view looked like a prospector and wasn't even carrying a firearm. He walked in front of a mule, using a long stick as a third leg. He was just a few feet from where we hid near the trail when he stopped short and looked around.

"I know you're there, you goddamned bastard!" the old man shouted. "You vulture. I'll make sure you never see cent one. Gnaw on these tough old bones and see what I care!" He started to laugh, but that degenerated into a coughing fit that brought the old man to his knees. The coughing didn't stop and I saw him spitting up blood.

I grabbed the canteen and pushed out of the bushes over Kyle's protests. He was instructed to wait till the old man was dead and then take what was on him. I wasn't going to let a poor guy suffer in front of me if I could help him.

"Easy, old timer. Have a sip of water." I loosened his shirt at the neck and listened to his breathing. It stopped and I started compressions on his chest. He choked and more spittle ran from his mouth, then he opened his eyes.

"Who the hell are you?" the man gasped. "You're not him. He can't even do his own dirty work, can he?"

"I've got a camp just up the slope. Let's get you warm and get some food in you. You'll make it. You just had a bad spell here, is all." After I'd given him another drink, I picked the old guy up and carried him to our camp. His mule just followed along and when he saw Bolt and my mule he just nudged them over and put his head down. I started a fire and the little shelter warmed up fast.

"Why are you doing this?" he asked when I'd given him some coffee? I don't suppose that's the right thing to do for a guy whose heart had just stopped a few minutes before, but it was all I had.

"I won't just stand around and watch a man die if I can do something about it," I mumbled. Kyle was going crazy. That was just what he was supposed to do. "Besides, I'd like to know what was so important about letting you die and searching you for a piece of paper." The old man started to laugh again, but I put a hand on his chest to calm him and he settled before it turned into a coughing fit.

"This is what he wants, then," the old guy finally whispered. He struggled to reach down into his pants like he needed to take a leak and pulled out a filthy scrap of hide. It was pretty cryptic. Kyle couldn't read, but I could make out the words and landmarks it referred to. It would take a fair amount of deciphering to make sense of it.

"Is it real?" I asked.

"Real enough. There's a chest there with over a thousand double-eagles and God-knows how many jewels." He chuckled, careful not to go too far into laughter. "He'll be so disappointed."

"Who is he?"

"You're one of us, ain't you?" The old man looked into my eyes and I saw the same kind of disconnectedness that I'd seen in Despain. I was looking at another time-traveler. He could see the same thing. "Does he know?"

"I don't think anyone knows," I said. "I didn't know there were others until I met Despain. Who is he?"

"We stay pretty well hidden. Not just from normal people, but from each other. I've been in and out of this body for forty years. But a few years ago, I met another one. Greedy little bastard. All he wanted to know was how much treasure I'd collected. I kept asking how much does a man need? He wants everything."

"I just won't give him this, then. He doesn't need any more."

"You have to. You're risking upsetting the timeline as it is. If I don't die up here and you take the map, who knows what might happen. In fact, I don't think you could avoid doing it. I'm going to die here on this trail. History records it. But it's a little vague on the exact date. Just that it will be as I'm coming down from my prospecting toward Prineville."

"Doesn't everything we do upset the timeline? I mean those treasures he's collecting are lost."

"They still are. You can only affect things in the present. Until then, you only get to pick what happens inside Schrödinger's box." Schrödinger. The name rang a bell. Something about a cat that was both dead and alive until you opened the box. Then it was one or the other. "But here's the thing. You need the tools to fight whatever his scheme is in your timeline. In this case, tools mean money. Then you just do what's right in your time."

"Sounds good. I could sure use some cash in uptime. Things are going to hell. But good old Kyle works for Despain who is the body for this other guy you don't know. I don't trust him all that much when I'm not in him."

"It's part of the risk. Let me talk to him." I was surprised, but I backed off and let Kyle take control. He was still agitated.

"Damn it! You're supposed to be dead. Why are you still alive?"

"I'm dying, Kyle. Everything is just like he said. But you've got an important thing to do. You have to bring him that map, just like he said. And I want to thank you for that and for your kindness in easing my dying. Kyle, this is just for you. Nobody needs to know about it but you. Keep it safe, and pass it down to your children. Don't let Despain know you have it. Now I'm going to die and make it okay for you." He handed Kyle a gold pocket watch. And I took control again so I could say good-bye to the old timer. I shoved the watch deep in my pouch with the map.

"You think that will do it?" I asked.

"Find the watch when you get home. You'll figure it out. And go to my mule. There are ten bars of gold. Your man didn't say to get gold, but the history says there was nothing of value on my person or in my packs. Hide them someplace where you can use them for your needs when you get back. But it's only a stopgap. The watch is your key. Fight the greedy bastard on his own turf."

The old man drew a ragged breath. I assured him that I'd do what was necessary. He looked into my eyes.

"Sure wish I knew what happened when the body you're traveling in dies. He looked up and I could see he was gone.

I retrieved the gold bars from his mule's pack and didn't check anything else. I changed into Kyle's riding clothes, doused the fire, and broke camp. I moved my horse and mule down the trail about half a mile and then went back to erase the signs of my camp and passing. I took the old man's body down to the trail where I'd first picked him up and laid him back in the position I'd found him. His mule followed me as far as the old man, but went no further. I backtracked through the woods and took my horse and mule cross-country, avoiding Prineville, and heading south.

My goal was to get out of the mountains. It was late October and damn cold. It was going to be a hard winter. I was tempted to head back home, but the Yellowstone had been a hard crossing on the way here and I wasn't about to try it till spring. But I figured there was one place we could take shelter for the winter just a ways south—Reno.

Kyle didn't seem to be displeased and I saw a flicker of lust cross his mind as he thought about the whorehouses there. He'd never been there, but had heard stories. This flash of lust was unaccountably followed by a flash of guilt. I had long ago surrendered to Kyle's tastes when I was away from Laramie, so I knew the guilt wasn't associated with that. Unless Kyle had developed feelings for her as well, but that didn't make sense. He'd been happy enough when I fucked her, but since the very first time he'd considered her hands-off unless he was in one of those strange moods where there was someone else taking control. He never quite figured that out.

WE PASSED FIVE uneventful and boring months in Reno. For the most part, I was content to let Kyle control what we did and discovered that he wasn't that adventurous. I'd always considered him an asshole for the way he was treating Laramie when we first met and then for the way he'd used my loving techniques to make the whores fall all over him. But he was turning out to be a pretty decent guy. He took a room in a boarding house rather than in a whorehouse. That was a lot cheaper. He had a few beers on Friday nights, but I made sure to steer him clear of potential fights if necessary. And he enjoyed a lady's company at least one night a week, showing them all the pleasure that he could while paying them for the privilege.

The first time Kyle found a whore in Reno, I was surprised at the resurgence of his guilt. *I been whoring all my life. It ain't like I never done it before. It never bothered me to go whoring when I'd been with Laramie. But now it's different. Maybe Kat wouldn't want me to go whoring while she's waiting for me to come back. Why do I feel bad about this? Hell, I ain't even been with her!* Kyle managed to do it anyway and each time it became a little easier.

What surprised me most was that Kyle was antsy to do something. It was with a bit of reluctance that I followed his lead into a gambling hall where instead of placing a wager, he went to see the management about a job. Inside an hour he was dealing Faro. And he was pretty good at it. I found out he'd done it before when there was time between Despain's jobs. There wasn't much action in Laramie, but Kyle had made trips to Deadwood half a dozen times in the past five years. It was good to know.

Having Kyle safely taken care of left me with nothing to do but think as I rested in the back of his mind. *How soon will it thaw so I can go back to Laramie? What else can I do to occupy my time?* During that respite, I started going through the catalog of lost treasures that I'd compiled. Kyle had never been as far west as Reno. I was tempted to go on to San Francisco since I knew there was a bank looting that would occur after the Great Quake, but we had Donner Pass between us and San Francisco. I wasn't going to attempt that at this time of year. On the other hand, if we headed northeast, we'd get to Salt Lake City. There were a good number of lost treasures in Utah, most of them in the North. I started calculating a route where we could pick up a few extra dollars before we made it back to Wyoming. It would be nice to leave Laramie with a little nest egg beyond what she had already. When I started letting those thoughts leak into Kyle's consciousness, he seemed pleased that he'd thought of such a thing. Before it had stopped snowing in the mountains in March, I packed the horse and mule and headed northeast.

THE FIRST LOST treasure opportunity overtook us when we'd been a week on the road and were near Winnemucca. I'd taken shelter in a canyon protected from the harsh wind by a small copse of trees. There was a rise near the back of the canyon where I could see down toward the entrance. I found a place where I was unlikely to be stumbled upon by any other traveler and went back to erase my trail for a mile. I'd allowed myself a small fire to heat my jerky stew, but in the waning daylight, the tiny smoke tendril would gain no attention.

Along about nightfall I heard the jangle of horses riding hard, right into my canyon. I scuffed dirt over my little fire and hunkered down to wait them out. I listened close. There had to be a dozen horses to make that much noise and then I heard the squeal of a wagon brake. There were shouts and eventually everything got quiet.

"There's no way out of this canyon, Sal. You might as well all give it up now." I heard a voice yell. Well, they weren't after me, but I still wasn't going to answer.

"Ain't no way I'll leave here alive, BJ. I got the advantage. How many men do I get to kill before you get me? You might as well just leave."

"We'll wait for you, Sal. You can't stay there forever. That gold is mine."

"You said we'd split fair and square, then you tried to cheat my boys out of theirs. Well, now you got the right of it. The gold is ours now."

There was a lot of hustle below us and we could hear two groups of men getting ready to fight. It wasn't likely anything would get started, so I kicked back with a gun in my hand and went to sleep.

The first shot was fired before daybreak. By dawn, a barrage of gunfire was being laid down on the part of both groups. I figured at the rate they were shooting, they'd run out of bullets before too long. It started to die down before noon. Finally, there were no more shots. After a few minutes pause I heard a voice.

"Sal? I still got a bullet for you, little brother."

"Yer gonna hafta come and deliver it, BJ. Ain't nobody left to back you up."

"You got any bullets, Sal?"

"Jest one."

"Come on out, Sal. It's just us."

I could see from my hiding place now. Just below me in the canyon were a half-dozen bodies and a Conestoga wagon with no cover. Behind the wagon was one man who looked like he'd already taken a couple rounds. At the opening of the canyon, there was a lone man leaning against his horse. Another half-dozen bodies lay near him and two horses were down. The nearer horses were corralled back in the trees.

"You ain't gonna win this, BJ."

"Come on, Sal. The last man alive is the richest man on earth. Holster yer gun and let's do it between the two of us. Who's really the best."

"You been taunting me with that since I was in diapers, BJ," Sal yelled. "You always said I was just the little brother and too small to ride with you big boys. Well, brother, I rode and what's mine is up to you to take. I won't kill you in cold blood, BJ. Come out and show me your gun is holstered."

"I always trusted you, Sal. Here I come." The farther man stepped out around his horse. His hands were poised above his holsters. I saw the nearer man—Sal—reach down and pick up a gun from a fallen comrade and shove it in his holster. His own gun he held in his left hand, just behind his hip. I hate cheaters. I settled back and watched, giving Kyle full control. I wasn't surprised to feel him reach for his Winchester.

The two brothers faced each other across about 20 yards of open ground. The condition they were both in, I doubted either of them could hit the other. It wasn't so, though. As soon as Sal was in the open, BJ reached for his gun. Sal's was already out and swinging to bear on his brother. Only one shot rang out and BJ fell before his gun had cleared leather. Sal walked to his brother and kicked the gun out of his hand. He picked it up and put the last bullet in BJ's head. Just when he turned around, the gun in my hands rang out and Sal fell on top of his brother.

So far as I knew, there had never been a report of a dozen bodies found in a box canyon with a wagonload of gold. That meant we had a clean-up job to do. It was going to take a while. I walked down into the canyon from our hiding place and checked all the bodies to be sure no one was alive. I heard one moan, but it was his death rattle. I was going to have to dig a big hole.

I chose the spot closest to the dead horses. They'd be the hardest to drag into a pit. I dug all the rest of the day before I finally went back to my camp and bedded down. The next morning, I dug again. Coyotes had been after the dead bodies and I figured I'd better get them buried today. When I deemed the hole big enough, I tied a rope around the horse carcasses and had the mule drag them forward until they fell into the pit. I stripped off the saddle bags, but left the saddles on those horses. Then I went through the bodies and stripped them of anything I found valuable and tossed the dead men into the pit. It took me the better part of the night to cover them up.

In the morning's light, I looked to the other horses. I tossed ten saddles into the back of the Conestoga along with the boxes that I didn't bother opening. There was feed for the animals and grazing among the junipers so I fixed a corral by stretching ropes from the wagon to trees along the edge of the canyon. Any horse that had a mind to could get out, but I was counting on herd mentality to keep them in. I was exhausted and slept like one of the dead men until morning.

After I'd fixed some coffee and stew over my campfire in the morning, I sorted things out to get moving again. I used my canvas to cover the wagon and was pleased that it fit well. I found a nice matched pair of Percherons and hitched them to the wagon and created a stringer of horses and one mule behind. The twelve animals behind me erased all sign of people having been in the canyon, even flattening out the grave as we rode over it.

As I headed east, I stopped at any town big enough to have a stable and sold a saddle. Occasionally I traded for another horse, or if I saw a fine mare, I'd buy it outright. I hired a blacksmith in the little town of Elko to make a branding iron for me and marked each of the horses with the LK brand.

There was about to be a war in Wyoming between the sheep herders and the cattlemen. Most of it would be up north where the Mormons were moving in, but it would extend south as well. It was the worst time of history for the State of Wyoming. But I could insulate my lover if she was raising horses on her new ranch. I'd bring her a herd to start with.

I stopped south of Salt Lake and boarded my sixteen horses and hired a guard for my possessions at the stable. I told them I was picking up some more horses down south a little and would be back in two weeks. It was still too early to make the crossing over the Continental Divide, but my memory told me there was another treasure about to be lost.

This was a tricky one and I was sure that Despain had decided it was okay to pass this up in favor of the old prospector's treasure map. A transport wagon headed north to Salt Lake City was about to be attacked by Uinta warriors. All that would ever be found of it would be the burned-out wagon and six dead men. The Indians took their dead from the field with them. They had no interest in the gold the wagon was supposed to be transporting. The transport had violated the sanctity of their tribal burial grounds and the Indians were pissed. I took a string of four mules with me, not knowing if this would be enough to take everything. It turned out to be plenty.

I changed into my buckskins and watched from a rise a mile away as the short battle took place. There were as many Indian casualties as white but there were many more of them in the fight. With the wagon blazing and the horses taken, the Indians took their dead and their coup and rode back to camp.

I approached cautiously, careful of any lingering hostiles. When I reached the wagon, I discovered four chests with gold ingots in them. Each chest weighed around two hundred pounds. I could lift one, but it was difficult. I loaded a hundred pounds of gold bars on each side of each of the mules. Two of the chests were already charred. I broke all four up and relit the fire to be sure they were completely consumed.

I detoured through Provo on my way back to Salt Lake City and bought a string of six matched Morgans. There was a lot of weight to haul over the mountains.

We approached Laramie from the Rock Springs Pass and made our way south above Centennial and up on the ridge. The first thing I did was locate the old hut. A year abandoned and the mud had washed through in a number of places. The sandstone slab was already showing signs of wear with the paint running together. I wedged up the rock and deposited ten gold bars under it. I proceeded to the Douglas fir where I'd made love to Laramie. I dug in the ground where I recalled a cow being stuck in the future and deposited a hundred bars deep beneath the roots.

I didn't know what to do with the rest. I hadn't explored the area enough to find a good hiding place, but I was getting a nudge from Kyle and followed it south to the point where the Centennial Ridge ended abruptly. I followed my instincts down a narrow path and found a cave. Inside I lit a branch and saw six more chests. Kyle had been putting aside his savings—his portion of what he found for Despain. If this was only a tithe of what Despain was accumulating, I was facing a really powerful enemy when I got home. I took the remaining gold bars, only a couple dozen at a time, down the path and into the cave. I did my best to hide them behind the boxes so they wouldn't shine if someone flashed a light around, but I'd just have to have faith. In my day, a thousand pounds of gold was worth more than $20,000,000. I was going to save the ranch. In addition, there were six chests under the tarp on the Conestoga. They weighed a little less than a gold chest, but I carted them down and stacked them in Kyle's hoard. He was feeling pretty pleased.

I branded the rest of my horses and mules and let them free on the upper range. Grass was peeking through the snow now and I knew they'd be okay until Laramie could round them up. I left the wagon backed up against the remains of the hut and headed back to Laramie. I'd shared fully with Kyle that the gold bars I'd hidden in the hut and under the tree were not to be disturbed. He'd restocked himself with Franklins when I was in the cave. I'd put one gold bar in his saddlebag to give to Laramie so she'd be able to hire help on the ranch.

And with the thought of Laramie we turned toward town. It had been nine months since I'd seen her. We'd have a baby. I wonder what she named this one. Did I have a son?

I was so absorbed in my thoughts as I rode toward town that I didn't see the hawk before he cried.

Buying the Farm

"COLE! IT'S YOUR shift. Grab some coffee and saddle up. Shorty's got breakfast ready." George was kicking my boots. I couldn't believe I'd fallen asleep against a tree all night. Asleep. No. I hadn't been asleep. I'd been gone. And I came back without seeing Laramie and my new son. God damn it! I could have stayed a little longer. Why did the damned hawk pull me back before I got there?

I was despondent to say the least. No one at the campfire could figure out why I woke up so morose, though. I just blamed it on falling asleep outside and saddled my horses. Bolt ponied along behind and I thought that I could probably ride him with no difficulty. I'd just spent nine months on his counterpart in 1892. I let good sense get the better of me, though, and determined not to ride him until spring. We'd be working together, though, all winter long.

I waited until the last day I was on the upper range before I returned to the slab of sandstone where the hut had once been. I guess I still had the fear that it was all in my imagination. Even if I found nothing there, what would that mean? That Kyle had betrayed me and taken all the gold? That I'd never really been there in the first place? I found the thermal spring first and then the stone. Grass had grown up all around it during the summer. I scuffed it aside and started prying at the rock. I didn't remember it being so hard to move, but then I realized that the edges were still grown over with sod. I scraped and cleaned and eventually managed to move the stone.

I didn't see anything at first. I pushed the stone back so I could reach in without crushing my hands. I felt it before I could see it. Cold and pure. I pulled out the first bar of gold. Then the second. In a matter of ten more minutes, I had ten two pound bars of gold in front of me. I dropped the rock back into its hole and scuffed grass and brush over it.

No one needed to know where I'd "found" half a million dollars. I stuffed it in my saddlebags and headed down the mountain toward home.

"DAD, CAN WE talk?" I asked. It was the second evening since I'd been back from the high range. The first was spoken for by Mary Beth. She only had another two days before she had to return to Boulder for her senior year. And I was headed into Laramie for my freshman year at UW. We'd come to an agreement, though. We were going into partnership to take over the two ranches if our Dads would let us. We just needed to keep things together until we were out of school, but we filed papers to create the Alexander Bell Cattle Company. Now I needed to speak to Dad.

"Sure, son. You know we can always talk. What's on your mind."

"I had a lot of time to do some thinking up on the range," I said. "I need to know exactly what the condition of the ranch is and our family finances. I know you always take care of these things, but I've got at least a partial solution to our problems, I think, if I know what the problems are."

"Son, it's your perfect right to know what is happening out here. I asked if you wanted the ranch so it's only right that you should know what condition it's in. In a word, it's pretty bleak. These last three years have been hard on us. There's been a recession in the beef industry and with the plague that ran through our herd last winter, we lost a ton of money. I had to buy hay for the first time in years because of the draught. Like a lot of ranchers, I took out a second mortgage to cover our operating expenses."

"Wait, Dad. Why a *second* mortgage. I thought the farm was grandma's and it didn't have a *first* mortgage."

"Well, that's true until we decided to expand the herd a few years ago. You shift capital from one asset to another. To buy more cows, we took out mortgages on the ranches."

"Dad, how much do we owe?"

"Between Angus and me, we owe close to a million dollars, Cole. We're mortgaged to the hilt and then there's your tuition coming due."

"How much are we past due?" Dad took a deep breath.

"We're not yet. January. We have a short term note for $300,000 due in January. That's why that damned Teini's offer is so tempting."

"Wait. Who?"

"Joe Teini. Teini's offered to buy us both out for double what we owe."

"Don't do it, Dad. I can help."

"I appreciate the spirit, Cole, but I'm getting too tired to fight."

"Dad. Here." I pushed a shoe box at him that weighed twenty pounds."

"Is this your life savings, son? It's pretty heavy."

"Just look, Dad."

He opened the box and picked up a bar. He turned it over. There were no marks on it. It was just a cast bar of gold.

"Cole? Is this gold?"

"I don't know how pure it is, but I'd guess it's at least 22 carat. There should be about $400,000 worth in that box. You'll have to pay an agent's fee or commission when you sell it, but that should still cover the note that's due in January."

"But how do I explain bars of gold? Cole, where did you get this?"

"You can tell the exact truth, Dad. It was found on your property. I did a lot of research on buried treasure last year, especially what to do with it if you find it. There's no tax on gold. It's yours. It's part of your land. You take it to one of those big houses that deal in gold. They deposit a check in your bank. You pay the loan. Now, Dad, there is no more where this batch came from, but I'm confident I can find more. Don't tell anyone you have this. Just go and sell it and pay the loan. Next summer we'll take the next step. We just have to be careful and not make a big deal about it. And we have to not let Joe Teini know where the money came from."

"I'm more worried about the IRS," Dad laughed. "You're sure about the tax thing?"

"As far as I can find, money you have, including gold, is not subject to any taxes. It has no history and is not income. It's not stock. I don't know about capital gains, but they'd have to prove that the gold added some specific amount to your property's value and they can't prove that unless you sell the ranch. And Mary Beth and I are asking that you and

Uncle Angus sell your property to us on contract for deed. It doesn't even need to be registered."

"Cole? What's going on? Where did you get this?" Dad was every inch the concerned parent, now. I suppose he thought I was transporting drugs or something. If he only knew how much lost treasure there was in this country—or how many people were competing for it.

"Dad, I sometimes have… dreams. One night while I was up on the ridge, I dreamed that I hid gold under a rock up there. I was just curious, so I decided on the last day I was up there to go look. I found the place exactly like I dreamed it. I didn't have to dig very far to find it."

"And you've had more dreams like this?"

"Yeah. But it wouldn't do to come up with too much all at once. This is from Mary Beth and me as an investment from our new cattle company. We formed a partnership."

Dad couldn't really speak. I could tell by the look in his eyes that he thought he'd lost the ranch. He just reached over and hugged me.

"Your grandma would be so proud of you," he whispered.

IT WAS THE second time I'd ever heard Dad mention my grandma. She died soon after he was born in 1955. He'd been taken in by his godparents, Arthur and Myrtle Alexander, who were trustees for his inheritance—the ranch next door to theirs. They were scrupulous about keeping the operations separate and accounted for. That's one of the reasons Dad and Angus had waited so long to go into partnership and mix their herds. It was also why Dad was living in the same house as Mom when he grew up and they were married when he got out of the service in '74. I was born in '76.

Family is so weird, don't you think. They say you can pick your seat and you can pick your nose, but you can't pick your relatives. I guess I wouldn't want to, really. I got pretty lucky.

Still… I miss my Dad.

6
Schrödinger's Cat

I HAVE A girlfriend. I mean, besides Mary Beth. Sweet girl who found me my freshman year of college and stuck to me like a cocklebur. There was not much I could do to shake her. Well, I didn't try very hard. Like I said, Ashley is a sweet girl and she appeals to me in a strange way. I lived on campus, even though it was only thirty-five miles home. I went home most weekends and trained Bolt into a fine working horse. I was looking forward to riding him on the range in the summer. But during the week, I stayed in a dormitory in Laramie at the University of Wyoming. I studied agri-business. The world was changing and our ranch was going to have to change, too. The damned recession that caught Dad by surprise had damaged a lot of ranchers in our area and their land was being grabbed as fast as they went under.

Okay, Ashley. We met. We studied. We dated. But it was a lot more than that. I joined Alpha Gamma Rho during fraternity rush week. Before you start thinking Animal House and all, AGR is also called Agro. We're the agricultural fraternity. Let's face it. I've always known I was going to be a rancher. I just didn't figure it would happen this soon. So, there's no pledge process. You join or you don't. I did. We're pretty active on campus, but our focus is on the agricultural and ranching business. The UW sports teams are The Cowboys. The brothers of Agro are the real thing.

Sigma Alpha is our sister sorority. These are girls who love the country and plan to stay there. Look at the promo pictures of all the sororities on campus. You have all these cute girls in short skirts or off-the-shoulder evening gowns, the Kappas, the Tri-Delts. Then you get to the Sigma Alpha girls all posing in their best blue jeans. Let me tell you, they do as much for blue jeans the way they pack them as any Tri-Delt ever did for a mini-skirt. I know the stereotype is loose sororities full of beautiful girls, but really—did you ever meet a college girl who wasn't beautiful? Sororities or not, just walking across campus while the weather is still warm will give a guy a boner.

By the time I got to college, I already knew the two women who could be the love of my life were equally unattainable. *Shit!* One was my first cousin and she'd lectured me soundly that I couldn't be pining for her this year when I got to college. Izzy had been fun, but Mary Beth was convinced that I needed to be looking for the woman who would share my home and ranch. I guess a guy will agree to anything when he's about to come in a beautiful, tight pussy under a moonlit sky. I agreed that when I met a girl this time, I wouldn't bring up Mary Beth right away. I'd focus more just on the relationship.

The other love of my life lived 100 years ago. How unattainable is that? There were days when I'd just go out riding through the high plains hoping I'd see a redtail hawk. But it seems they've gotten rarer as our little bit of wilderness becomes more urbanized. No matter how much I wished and prayed to be taken back to 1892, there was no answer.

Roped and Tied

I ADJUSTED TO campus life pretty quick-like. There were a lot of hands-on classes where we were working on the school ranch as a professor taught us about grading beef. I got a couple of used textbooks and I swear one had smudges of cow manure on the pages. I sure know it did after I was done with it. There was a class on accounting and finance that I really dug into. I'd been around the cows and horses my whole life, but I never got my hands on the ranch books until Dad and I had our little conversation.

While I was studying for my classes, I had the chance to do some independent research. All I knew about Joe Teini was that he showed up in a Corvette and stole my girlfriend when I was a junior in high school. There were times when I still had a pang of missing her if I let myself think about it. Things were working out well for her though. She graduated from high school without getting pregnant and was going to technical school this fall, but I didn't know what she was studying. That was pretty much the last I'd heard about Joe until Dad said he was offering to buy property in our valley.

Finding information about him was no real problem. He graduated from the same high school I did, but six years before. Mary Beth might remember him, but they only overlapped a year. According to all the things I read, he was dirt poor growing up in Laramie. His pa was a ranch-hand on one of the big spreads east of town and his ma took in sewing. School records were locked, of course, so I couldn't find out how he'd done. I looked through the yearbooks from the high school, though, and he looked like a nobody. There was never a picture of him with a girl. He wasn't listed as a member of any of the school clubs. And the day after graduation, he hopped a train out East. Nobody expected him to come back again.

Then three years ago, he shows up in a flashy car with a big bank account. Said he'd gone to stock brokers' school and had done well in the markets. First thing he did was buy the ranch where his dad worked and move into the big house. Alone. His parents still lived in the hired hands shack on the property and his dad now worked for him. It looked like Joe Teini had an axe to grind and was set on paying everyone back for what they'd done—or not done. Joe kept an office in Laramie and was brokering for some of the big-shots in town. Not bad for a 26-year-old former nobody. I was getting pretty suspicious.

Those suspicions turned to near panic when it was announced that our County Sheriff was in bad health and there would be an off-year election in November. Joe Teini announced his candidacy.

I looked at his picture in the newspaper with a new Stetson perched on his head and I swore I was looking at a younger version of Sheriff Cal Despain.

Of course, all that was taking place in my "spare time." My focus had to be on my studies and on training my horse. And on fraternity obligations. The first obligation was to show up at the Fall Cotillion sponsored by our sisters in Sigma Alpha. Sigma Alpha's big fall dance in early October was really just a mixer for the two organizations to get to know each other. But we were expected to dress our best and dance with a young lady. The dance was Western Formal. I had a pretty good suit with a Western cut jacket and boot-cut slacks, and of course I had my good boots. The young ladies all dressed in party clothes that would have been appropriate back in my other timeline in the 1890s.

There were some couples who were automatically paired up with each other, but in order to keep the event from being a typical high school dance where all the women lined up on one side of the floor and all the men on the other side waiting for someone to get so embarrassed they made a run for it, Sigma Alpha had a different method. The singles were lined up on opposite sides of the room promptly at 8:00. A hostess who already had a date then took the list of names and paired us up for the first dance. Us guys were looking over the line of eligible women and more than a few of us had already taken a sip from our hip flasks. By the way the girls were giggling, I guessed they might have been hitting it a little, too.

I hardly noticed my name had been called when I saw this absolutely beautiful blonde detach herself from the crowd and walk to the center waiting. One of the guys gave me a shove toward her. My head was doing all kinds of flip-flops and my stomach decided to get in on the act as well. The girl facing me brought up memories of hours spent on a sitting room sofa, carefully not touching, and not saying much as we got to know each other. This was the girl Kyle was falling in love with: Kat Tangeman.

"Kat?" I said as I approached her. She looked a bit shocked but then giggled.

"Well sometimes I'm a pussy and I do scratch, but I'm just a kitten if you make me purr."

"I'm sorry, Miss. I didn't get your name when they announced it and you look so much like a girl I knew a long time ago that I thought you'd just grown up and come here to UW and then I was so shocked when they called my name I didn't even realize I was supposed to come out and join you because you are without a doubt the most beautiful young woman at this dance and…"

"God! You do ramble! Are we going to dance?" she asked. Fortunately, they started with a nice medium-paced two-step and I was able to take the young woman in my arms and not make any more a fool of myself.

"Sorry. I really didn't get your name. I'm Cole Alexander Bell and I'm pleased to meet you Miss…"

"Miss Ashley Kay Brewer at your service, Cole Alexander Bell. Does your name mean you are related to the famous Alexander Graham Bell?"

"No, Miss Brewer. Alexander was my mother's maiden name. We Bells have been in Albany County for a long time. Where do you hail from?"

"Glenwood Springs, Colorado. And we Brewers have been around Garfield County for a *long* time." She laughed, making fun of me. I didn't mind. She was good company and beautiful and seemed to fit in my arms like she was made for it. I wracked my memory—or Kyle's—to see if Kat Tangeman was like this. Of course, he'd never held her in his arms quite like I was holding Ashley. Things moved at a different pace in respectable society back then and Kat was a school teacher. I supposed that meant she was about 19 or 20—the same as Ashley and me—but if I figured the times correctly, Kyle wasn't much more than 18 or 19. His timeline was moving at a different pace than mine.

"So, what does your family do out in Glenwood Springs that brings you to Laramie, Wyoming to study and become part of Future Ranch wives of America—I mean Sigma Alpha."

"Watch it there, buddy. My specialty is making bulls into steers." I laughed, a little nervously. My balls were tingling. "Seriously, we've been in the cattle business for years, but the past few years, we've been making more off of hay production than the cattle. My brother figures we could turn our remaining pastures into hay fields and not have either as much work or as much risk."

"So, he wants to turn the ranch into a farm."

"Right. That doesn't match my goals. I'm studying Agricultural Education, but I may double with Agricultural Business. You a rancher?"

"Indeed. My family controls about 6,000 acres west of here. Most of it is good grazing for cattle, especially in the high country. We run at least three cuttings of hay in the bottom land a year, though. If it doesn't snow too early, we'll often get a fourth cutting. As you know, it's a seasonal business. We run our own feedlot come winter and start shipping fat and healthy beef around mid-December."

"How about horses?"

"Well, it's not a business for us anymore. I hear in my great-grandma's day they were raising more horses than cattle, but there was a little break in the chain some years ago and when Dad started running the ranch, it was all cattle."

"Cole, I think I might like you. Now, keep in mind that's a big 'might.' You'll have to show me what kind of man you are before I make that definite."

"Well, Miss Ashley, I might just like you, too. Right now, I sure like dancing with you and talking to you."

And dance we did. I think we were the last ones on the dance floor when they called it quits at two o'clock in the morning. It had been a stimulating evening. We'd have a drink and catch our breath as we talked about everything from ranching to politics to economy to our love lives. Well, that last was a subject we tiptoed around a little bit. I did find out she was a year older than me and a sophomore. And when we danced those slow tunes, the cowboy was always at attention. Ashley never moved away from me though. The last dance was a slow one and Ashley pulled away from me just before we went into a clinch.

"Mr. Bell, before we go back to polishing your belt buckle, I need to know if there's a woman already in your life." I sighed. "Please, don't tell me..."

"Miss Brewer, we're going to get to know each other a lot better before we do more than polish the belt buckle and I'm looking forward to that. Let me say honestly that I'm single and free to make any commitments that I might wish. I will never lie to you about that, but I'm not ready to talk about everything that's happened in my life."

"Including your broken heart and the girl you're still pining for," she concluded for me. Well, that wasn't exactly it, but it was as good a place to start as any. She came into my arms and laid her head against my chest. I could feel her bosom pressed against me and the cowboy responded appropriately. He might have got in the way of the belt buckle a little.

"Ashley, would you consent to see me again? I'd like to take you out someplace where we can talk and get to know each other better. Maybe dinner on Friday night?"

"Cole, I'd like that very much. I've had a wonderful time this evening and yes, you are going to get kissed before you leave. But I'd like to take it slow from there if you don't mind. I hadn't really thought of taking up with a boy so soon after school started this year. I sorta had my heart broke last year, too."

"I think that's fair. No strings and no commitments, just a simple invite to dinner."

"Here's a simple yes," she said. She lifted her face to me and our lips made contact for the first time right in the middle of the dance floor. I'd never been that much into dancing, but I was beginning to think it could become a favorite pastime with a girl like Ashley. We kissed until that last number ended.

"Can I walk you home, Miss Brewer? Or drop you somewhere?"

"I live right here in the sorority house, Mr. Bell. I've had a wonderful evening, Cole. I know you came with a bunch of guys from AGR. Can you find your way back okay?"

"Thank you, Ashley. I look forward to Friday night."

"As do I," she said. Her smile and the sparkle of her eyes lit the room for me. Then she turned and went up the stairs. I watched her out of sight and then headed for the door my own self.

I HAD TO leave thirty bucks with Mom for the telephone bill because I spent all night Saturday night on the phone with Mary Beth. Honest to God, this was the first girl besides Mary Beth to really ring my chimes in this timeline. I loved dating Geneive. Who wouldn't love wild sex with a pretty girl like Geneive? She was so outrageous that it was hard not to fall for her. And Izzy had been the aggressor in our relationship, even to inviting Mary Beth to join. But Ashley made it hard to think of anything else. Mary Beth said she was happy and that I should see where it leads.

"Cole, will you want to… cool it with me so you can have a real relationship with Ashley?"

"Mary Beth! Please don't pull back from me. Before I have any kind of relationship with a woman, or if I should ever get married, it will be to a woman who understands I love you and will always have you in my life. We don't have to try to make things go three ways like we did with Izzy, but until you tell me to stop and go away, I will be with you, Mary Beth."

"Well, find out if she's the real deal before you go telling her all the details," Mary Beth said. "We'll deal with us after we figure out if you're a couple."

I DISCOVERED WE had the same economics class when Ashley walked in on Monday morning. She spotted me and sashayed over to where I was sitting.

"Is this seat taken, sir?" she asked. *Damn! I liked the way she filled out those jeans.* Levi Strauss could have made a fortune just by showing her in his pants. Or something like that. Not that he didn't make a fortune anyway. Hell, in 1891, Kyle had been wearing Levi's.

"Hey, Ashely. Please sit here. I realized when I got home that I didn't get your phone number or arranged when to pick you up on Friday. I was going to make a fool of myself and camp out on the sorority steps until I saw you." We laughed but didn't have time for any more chitchat because class was starting. I had to pay attention in this class. I understood accounting pretty well, but economics is more than just raising the price when demand is high.

"Government intervention in the marketplace. Good or bad?" Professor Saunders said. We're a pretty conservative lot at UW. You could hear groans in the classroom. "Let's take a look at the oil industry for this next example. Everybody loves to dig at the big oil monster. In 1985, oil hit sixty dollars a barrel. It was a thriving industry in the United States. Oil companies were hiring people left and right. There was huge pressure to deregulate the industry. Get government out of our business. But we hit a recession in the late 80s and by 1987, oil was going for ten dollars a barrel. Was that because there was no demand? Did people stop driving their cars and trucks? Did semis quit rolling down the Interstate?"

"Seems like people still needed gas," somebody down front said.

"Exactly. But the Arabs got together and established OPEC to regulate the price of oil they were selling. Prior to that time, the various Arab oil producers were competing with each other. OPEC changed the game. Now they competed as a group directly with American oil producers. They dropped the price to get more of the market. What happened in America?"

"Layoffs," Ashley said. "They couldn't afford the payroll, so the oil companies started laying people off. The economy just got worse."

"Bingo. Good old American competition, free economy, worked *against* our economic stability until the government stepped in and started placing tariffs on foreign oil. I'm not making a comment on whether that was good or bad. I just think it's interesting that the big oil companies were all of a sudden asking the government for subsidies and protections. Most of you are studying agricultural business. So, let's look at food. How much of the food you eat is imported from other countries?"

"Seems like all our vegetables in the winter come from Central America or Mexico," another student volunteered.

"Exactly. In fact, 35% of produce consumed in the United States is imported from foreign countries. But it gets worse. 70% of seafood is imported. That's a lot of sushi. Now, what happens if Mexico or Canada becomes the largest beef producer in the world and we start importing 70% of our beef from NAFTA countries. Even 35%?"

"We're screwed," the guy up front said. It wasn't eloquent, but the point was well taken. Most people were scribbling down notes, but not many were talking. I was thinking mostly.

"Right now, the National Cattlemen's Beef Association's number one concern is to stop government intrusion into the marketplace. But if Canadian beef imports rose from the current level of around three percent to as much as five percent, it would have an adverse effect on what you would get per pound of beef on the hoof. What would the NCBA's position be regarding government regulation then?"

"It would make sense that the NCBA would want the government to impose tariffs on imported beef to protect American beef producers," Ashley volunteered.

"Now what does that tell us about economic theory?" Saunders posed. There was quiet. He didn't volunteer an answer. I liked that about his classes. They really made you think.

"Are you saying a free marketplace only works in a closed system where the players are pretty much operating on an even footing? If someone from outside the system competes because they have lower production costs or government subsidies, then the entire marketplace is threatened," I said. It got a nod from the professor.

"That's economics," he said.

It got me thinking about what Joe Teini was doing. For some reason, he wanted to buy up land in Albany County. Dad and Uncle Angus weren't the only ones he'd made offers to. Now he was running for sheriff. If he was the other time traveler the old prospector had warned me about, as I'd begun to suspect, was his real goal simply to buy the county? It seemed like there was something else to it, but I couldn't make the connection. The prospector had said it was simple greed, but that just wasn't enough in my book. Now I was thinking about economics.

We MOVED INTO winter in earnest. Light snow started falling the first weekend in November.

I was making a trip out to the cemetery almost as often as I was having dates with Ashley. It was a short walk from my dormitory and just going to visit Caitlin's grave gave me a connection back to the people I knew in that other time. And while Ashley and I hadn't gone beyond some great making out, we were real close to calling each other boyfriend and girlfriend.

"Cole, are you going to be around Thanksgiving weekend? A couple of the girls and I were thinking about making a dinner at the house and I'd invite you if you want," Ashley said the Saturday before Thanksgiving.

"Ashley! It never crossed my mind that you wouldn't go home to be with your family for Thanksgiving."

"Glenwood Springs isn't that easy to commute to for a long weekend. I'll go home for Christmas."

"Well, why don't you join me and my family then? I know for a fact that Mom and Dad would love to meet you and I'd like you to meet my Aunt and Uncle and cousin, too. If you're uncomfortable about staying at the ranch for the weekend, I'll run you back to the house after dinner, but we've got plenty of room if you'd like to stay and I'd love to introduce you to my horses."

"You live that close that you'd run me back after dinner?"

"It's about thirty-five miles from campus out to our place. That's why I go home most weekends to work with my horses." The answer I got was a huge kiss. I guessed I was having company for Turkey Day dinner. I called Mary Beth the next morning.

The DAY CAME and when I pulled up in front of Sigma Alpha House on Thursday morning, Ashley came running out with a small suitcase in hand.

"I didn't know for sure if the invitation to stay for a day was still open, and then I thought that if we're going to work with horses I needed a change of clothes anyway, so I tossed some things in a bag, just in case, you know?" Ashley was looking at me with those big brown eyes that I loved. How could I resist. I pulled her in for a smooch.

"The invite is open for as long as you want to stay, sweetie. If you meet my family and get freaked out, I'll bring you right back. If you want to stay all weekend, I promise to be as much a gentleman as you want me to be." I grinned and she punched me in the arm. Under her heavy coat she was wearing a skirt and I glanced over at her legs. I took a deep breath. "Ashley, I also promise that if you want the whole story that I promised to tell you before we got serious, I'll tell you this weekend. I'm damned close to being serious right now and I need to tell you this stuff."

"Don't worry about it," she said. "What's past is past." I didn't respond. "Oh shit. It isn't past, is it? Maybe this isn't such a good idea."

"Ashley, please let me tell you about it before you decide that. I really want you to meet *all* my family first."

"Okay. You promised to be straight with me and the least I can do is listen to the story. Cole, please tell me my heart ain't gonna be broken."

"Ashley, honey, I will never intentionally do or say anything to hurt you. But if that interferes with my pledge to be honest with you, I have to choose honesty."

She leaned against me with both hands wrapped around my right arm the rest of the way home. I love the big bench seats in a pickup with a center seatbelt.

THANKSGIVING TURNED OUT to be fine. In fact, more than fine. I got dragged to the den with the men-folk where we chewed on cigars and watched the football games until the women yelled for us and the kids to come to the table. We professed our thanks for the hands that fed us and paused to consider the land, and then settled into a big yummy meal.

After dinner, the menfolk headed to the kitchen to do the clean-up. It's a family tradition. The women get the den, have sherry, and sometimes smoke. It's about the only time Mom allows smoking in the house. The men get the kitchen. We thanked God for the hands that prepared the food; they thanked God for the hands that cleaned it up.

When we were all finished, we went to the den to see what the score was. One glance around the room and I wondered *exactly* what the score was. Mom, Aunt Lily, Sally Ann, Brenda, and their kids on the floor. No Mary Beth and no Ashley.

"Um... Where's Mary Beth and Ashley?" I bravely asked.

"Hmm. Girl-talk, I think," Mom said. "Mary Beth said she wanted to tell Ashley all about you. They went to the barn to see your horses."

"Oh hell," I muttered.

"MB did say you should come out when you were done with the men's work," Aunt Lily said. "They're probably getting cold out there by now. They've been gone half an hour."

"Well, I'll just go tend to Bolt," I said. *Damn!*

It wasn't hard to find them. They were sitting on a bale of hay just outside of Bolt's stall talking intently. I involuntarily flinched when I thought about the fact Mary Beth and I had made love on that very spot on my graduation day. Well, it was a different bale of hay, but it was right there.

Ashley looked up at me with a curious expression on her face as I approached.

"Hey. What do you think of Bolt?" I asked, not asking anything I wanted to ask. *What the hell are you talking about?*

Before Ashley could speak, Mary Beth stood up and gave me a solid, for real kiss.

"I'll go in the house, hon. I'm cold and you and Ashley have a lot to talk about." She headed toward the barn door and I turned back toward Ashley. She had a little moisture in her eye, but I couldn't tell if it was just starting or just ending.

"Ashley..." She held up her hand and bit her lip. I braced myself for getting smacked.

"I knew," she said. "I knew it would be something like that. I had visions of it being your kid whose mother had deserted you, or a crippled sister you were committed to care for, or God! Just about anything. It wasn't what I expected, but I figured that it was going to involve some getting adjusted to."

"It's nothing either of us ever intended," I said. "But we're committed. We just can't be the couple that either of us would like to be. In fact, both of us want to have a happy normal life, but neither of us can imagine it without the other."

"Yeah. I understand that. Intellectually. Emotionally, I'm still a little adrift. But I ain't quitting. Not yet. Tell me, Cole, is there any chance that you could ever love me like you love her?"

"You mean the exact same way?" I already knew that I didn't love Mary Beth the same way I loved Laramie. That wasn't like I loved Caitlin and I'd hardly known the fiery redhead. "No." I said it with finality, but Ashley kept looking at me and waiting. "Ash, I've been in love a few times. Some that Mary Beth doesn't even know about. There isn't any two that have been the same."

"Yes, but..."

"No. Wait. There's more. I wouldn't *want* to love you like I love Mary Beth. I can tell I'm falling for you. I mean, really thinking you could be the woman I want to spend the rest of my life with. I know that sounds awful rushed. We've only known each other for a couple months. But there's something special about you. And..." I cut myself off. How could I tell her that my other self, Kyle, was falling in love with her other self, Kat? Kat probably wasn't even her other self, any more than Laramie was Mary Beth's other self. The fact that I had parallels going in a different time period only needed to confuse me, not everybody.

"There's more, isn't there, Cole? There's something hidden deep down inside that you haven't even told Mary Beth. I can see it in your eyes. I can see it when you go out and put flowers on Caitlin's grave."

"What? You... you know?"

"I wasn't spying on you, honest. I saw you go into the cemetery a week ago and thought I'd catch up and walk with you. I lost track of you, though, and when I finally saw you, it was in the really old section and you'd cleared the snow off her stone and left flowers. I was going to ask you why you were leaving flowers for someone who died 100 years ago but I never really had an opportunity. I decided I was really in the wrong place and I shouldn't invade your privacy."

I let it rest, hoping that we could move on to another topic—maybe back to Ashley and me.

"Oh my God!" she screamed and then clapped her hand over her mouth. "You aren't like one of those immortals like in that movie—what was it?—*Highlander,* who outlive their first love and go back to the grave hundreds of years later, are you? Please tell me that can't be so?" Christ! This was getting worse. I didn't make it better.

"She wasn't the first," I said softly then caught myself. "I'm not immortal. It's nothing at all like *Highlander*. Nobody is out looking for my head—at least that I know of. It's just… something different."

"Okay. That settles it then."

"I'm sorry."

"I won't push you about your mysterious relationship with a girl who died 100 years ago. It doesn't matter. What matters is that you have a very real relationship with your cousin right now. What matters is that you're asking me if I can put up with that and maybe even be a part of it. And what matters is that I've fallen in love with you. So, the answer is yes."

"Yes?"

"Yes, Cole. I'm freezing my ass off out here in the barn right now, so I'm not going to strip off my clothes and fuck you. But sometime this weekend, sweetheart. Sometime, we're going to find time to love each other. And I'm betting that Mary Beth is going to be right there with us."

Ashley crushed herself to me and kissed me with more passion than I could remember her showing since we started going out. It was breath-taking. We held hands as we went up to the house.

FRIDAY AFTER THANKSGIVING isn't that big a deal for us on the ranch. The idea of Black Friday means something different to us than it does to the retail industry. So, after I'd helped with the feeding and made sure the water tanks were open in the feedlot, Ashley joined me in the corral to work with Bolt. As soon as she came out, the big stud on the lunge line ignored me and stopped to look at her. Usually, I'd give him a tickle with the long whip to get him back on his pace, but this time I just broke down laughing.

"Some big stud you are," I laughed, gathering the lunge line in my hands as I walked toward the fence. "You see a pretty face and you forget all about what you were supposed to be doing."

"He's beautiful!" Ashley said. "I was watching for a few minutes before I came out to join you. I'm sorry I messed up his training."

"Oh, he knows what he's supposed to do and what he's doing. This big boy is smarter than I am."

"Hmm. I think I'll remind you of that sometime. When do you plan to ride him?"

"I could probably get on now. I put my weight on him sometimes. I work over and around him. But right now, I'm working on the gaits and cuts he'll need to work cattle. I don't really expect to sit in the saddle until early spring."

"Is it hard to know he's ready and not get in the saddle?" I looked at Ashley. There was a twinkle in her eye and a lift of her brow that let me know she was making references to more than one thing.

"Well, there's no question I'd like to get in the saddle if I truly knew he was ready. It's hard."

"Yeah. Poor horse is smart, but he can't actually come out and say, 'I'm ready.' Not like I can."

"Are you ready, Ash?"

"Scared, but ready."

I leaned over the fence and she caught my face in both hands so she could control how soft and gentle this kiss was. She let it gradually heat up and I was reaching through the fence to hold her waist when there was a blast of hot air on our faces and we turned to see Bolt snuffling at us. We laughed.

"Looks like this fella needs to finish his workout before he'll let me have mine," I said. "Watch him turn and cut." I led the stud back into the ring and damned if he didn't show off. Every little command I gave him to cut, turn, and jump, he went at with gusto. When we finished his workout in half an hour, we were both blowing steam as we puffed. Ashley applauded.

I led Bolt into the barn and Ashley joined me in his stall to brush him and cool him down. He just basked in our attention, eating a handful of oats that Ashley offered him. I didn't feed him much oats because it makes a horse hot. Still, in the winter he needed a few to supplement the hay. Ashley and I ducked out of the stall and she was immediately in my arms.

We kissed and for the first time, I let my hand drift down and grasp her butt cheek and pull her to me. She didn't resist and ground herself against me. Ashley is a nice height. She's a little shorter than Mary Beth, maybe 5'6" or 5'7", which to my 6'3" is still perfect. I just hugged her to me and tried desperately to figure out where to go that we'd be comfortable for our first time together. When we came up for air, Ashley turned away from me and pointed up the ladder to the hayloft. She started to climb and I gladly followed that shapely ass up the ladder. God, I love tight jeans! She sure seemed to know where she was headed.

When I finally pulled myself through the trap into the loft, I was greeted by two young women with an arm around each other, holding out a hand for me to join them. I couldn't believe what I was seeing. They weren't holding each other like lovers, but like friends who were about to share a meal. I guess I was the main course.

"Honey, Ashley invited me to be with you two. Is that okay?"

"Mary Beth, you know I always want you with me. Is it really okay with you, Ashley?"

"Cole, I've never done this before. I mean being with a guy who has another girlfriend. Together. Mary Beth and I talked, a lot, last night. And again this morning. Turns out, neither one of us is really into girls *that* much. But I don't mind company. Especially when I know we're both in love with the same man."

From that point on, there was more touching and kissing than there was talking. I was having a little trouble keeping my present-day mind separate from my 1890s memories. God, Ashley was so sweet and I knew exactly how hard Kyle was falling for Kat. And here I was with Mary Beth who was as close to a soul-mate as I was ever going to find in this life, but just like with Laramie, there was this huge gulf between us that we couldn't cross. Oh, we crossed it physically plenty, but we couldn't cross it socially. With Laramie, I couldn't just go and be with her, no matter how much I wanted to.

And that was something I needed to take care of, too. Someplace along the line I was going to have to tell both of them about my "other life." Even though my months spent in that other timeline translated to mere minutes or at most hours in my real life, I had months of memories. I was there. I'd made love to Laramie and to Caitlin. I killed a man. I'd hidden money that I came back to find this summer. It was all real and I needed to tell them.

But not right now.

Right now, I was busy learning about Ashley's beautiful body. She was a little shy about undressing, but I suppose we were all a little awkward.

Mary Beth was just going to lie back beside us and watch, but she took a hand and undressed to encourage Ashley.

"Kiss me, Cole. Please kiss me and show me that you mean it. I'm not asking for a lifetime commitment or a wedding ring. I'm just asking you to show me that you love me at least a little right now."

"Ka… Ashley, I don't say words like that lightly. You know I had two other girlfriends while I was in high school and I might have said 'love ya' to them, but no matter how intimate we got I never said, 'I love you' to anybody but Mary Beth because I knew it wasn't completely true. I might not be as *in* love with you as I will be, but there's no question in my mind that I *am* in love with you. I love you, Ash. I really think I love you."

I kissed her. I tried to tell her everything I had in my heart with that kiss. I tried to tell her that she'd be with me forever and that I'd always take care of her and love her and that we'd raise our kids on the ranch and everything would be fine. I tried to tell her all that with one kiss.

I don't know how successful I was, but we were lying together—the three of us—without a stitch of clothing among us. It was pretty chilly in the barn but Ashley and I weren't noticing it as the perspiration began to collect between our bodies and we kissed some more. I rolled us over so she was between Mary Beth and me. I knew Mary Beth would keep her backside warm while I continued to heat the front. That little extra contact, sandwiching Ashley between us, raised her temperature in more ways than one. We loved. We kissed. We were lost in our passion for each other and when I reached a hand over Ashley to caress Mary Beth, I found Ashley's hand already there. The three of us clasped our hands together as I entered Ashley for the first time.

If you've got any experience in such things, you will know there is nothing that compares to the feeling you get when a girl takes her shirt off in front of you for the first time. There is nothing you will remember more than the first time you kiss her naked skin. But the sensations are so intense, there is no way in hell you will be able to describe the first time your cock made its way into her pussy. It's the closest thing a man can get to complete sensory overload. My world reduced to a single point of contact. I felt every inch of me slide into her and felt her contracting around me as she came from the pressure I placed against her clit. And as her lips sought mine to muffle her cry, I came. The first time in this life I'd ever come in a woman unprotected.

I didn't care. This one was for keeps.

WITH THAT BEING the highlight of my freshman year, there isn't a whole lot more to say. I fell in love with Ashley, deeper every day. On our different spring breaks, Ashley and I went to Boulder and Mary Beth came to us in Laramie.

With the breathing room that an extra $400,000 gave Dad and Angus, they bought another two hundred yearling calves and we had the biggest herd ever to drive up to the high range as the snow started to melt. Ashley had her horse, a nice buckskin mare that looked good next to Bolt, shipped up from Colorado and I hired her to ride the range with me over the summer. Dad had a straight talk with me about keeping my mind on the job, but he was okay with it. He and Angus transferred the two ranches over to the new Alexander Bell Cattle Company as part of our giving them the gold and Mary Beth and I signing a note. All kinds of details had to be worked out, like ensuring Mom and Dad, as well as Angus and Lily, had a great retirement. We also had to be sure Mary Beth's sisters were cared for and got their fair share of the inheritance. The Bell property was close to three times the size of the Alexander property, but Dad had a lawyer work up a contract for deed for the two ranches. For all intents and purposes, Mary Beth and I became land-owners.

I wasn't even the boss up on the ridge. George did a great job of keeping the hands scheduled and things quiet while we rode. I took a tent that was a little larger than the tiny tents we usually slept in up on the range. I also got an air mattress that filled the bottom of the tent.

Ashley and I had ridden up to the high pastures already when Mary Beth got home from college. She graduated with honors. What a woman! Then she shocked both our families by calling them together and announcing her plan to ride up to the high pasture and join Ashley and me. She told them all they could call the place Sinners' Paradise for all she cared. She was going to spend at least one summer with the man she loved. And the woman who loved him.

Nobody blinked an eye. She saddled her roan gelding, threw her pack on the back and rode out. Was I ever surprised to see her! And delighted. Ashley didn't seem surprised at all as they stowed MB's gear in our tent. Mary Beth wasn't working the range for pay, so she just worked the same shift as we did and we rode and talked like forever. We made love in some combination pretty much every night we weren't in the saddle all summer long.

And eventually that summer, I told them about my "dreams."

I started, just telling tales, like I did when Mary Beth and I were up in the Big Horn. But the tales got more and more detailed and specific and then one day I took them over the ridge and showed them the old Douglas Fir. Both girls looked at me kind of funny and stepped away.

"It all really happened, didn't it, Cole?" Mary Beth asked.

"Caitlin," Ashley whispered.

I just stood there and nodded my head and busted out crying. It all really happened and I missed Laramie.

Before I could explain anything about how it happened, I saw a flicker of a shadow and that old hawk cried.

Traveling: Courting Kat

I'D JUST TURNED twenty in my real life. The Kyle I was thrown into had just turned nineteen. He was as serious and hard-working a man as I'd ever seen. He seemed to have outgrown his whoring and killing days. I'd learned on a visit some while ago not to distract him when I popped in. Not distracting him now was a good thing as he was helping lift a log into place, but his eyes involuntarily flicked up toward the hawk circling above. The log thudded into place about the same time I was tackled from behind by a five-and-a-half-foot tall Indian beauty.

"Kyle! You're back!" Laramie yelled. She hung on me and kissed me and I could see a couple other men look over with puzzled expressions.

"You men just get back to you work," Theresa Ranae snapped as she got down from the wagon that had just pulled up and lifted down my daughter. "You didn't see nothing."

I'd taken over Kyle's body before her lips hit mine and in that instant, I was a transformed man. I was at peace. I grabbed as many memories as I could from Kyle while I kissed my lover and discovered that Theresa had hired him to manage the building of their cabin on her new property. It wasn't that much, but it dwarfed what they'd lived in up over the ridge. Forty head of horses were running in a fenced pasture nearby.

"You did it!" I said proudly. "You got your land and you're building your home. Laramie, Theresa, I'm so proud of you both." I gave them another hug and picked up Kaylene. She was almost two years old and I'd missed her growing. I hugged and tickled the little girl until she giggled and hugged me back. "Where's our baby?" I asked Laramie. Her face fell.

"I'm so sorry, Kyle. I forgot you didn't know. There was a bad influenza went through town soon after you left last time. I got so sick I lost the baby. Oh, Kyle, our little baby is dead." I had a feeling Laramie had been holding in the tears the whole time until I got back. She couldn't hold them any longer and neither could I. I held her and wept for the innocent life I'd never met.

A mule trudged by hauling a good-sized log and I knew Kyle's responsibility was to build a house. I broke away from Laramie, helped smear the mud caulking, and joined the others in hoisting the lintel log over the doorway. We worked all afternoon as I managed to get caught up with Laramie between raising logs for the cabin. Soon—maybe tomorrow— we'd put up beams for the roof. Kyle had organized things well and had all the materials for the cabin prepared before the men started building. I knew these logs had come from the upper slopes, dragged down a trail to the building site on this promontory. Down below me, I could see the Little Laramie River and the rich bottom lands.

"How much did you get?"

"We managed to get over 3,000 acres purchased and 160 acres right here as a homestead. We have to build the cabin and occupy it for five years. We want the house over yonder where the barn will be, but that piece isn't on the homestead, so we have to build this temporary cabin."

"That's good. Even if you make nothing from the ranch, I can get you more money. You'll need some crops, though. It's too late to plant this season."

"We have a garden down near the river. The next thing the men have to do is dig a root cellar and then they'll start on the barn and corral."

"Sounds like you've got everything under control."

"Kyle does. He's really very good and kind."

When the day was done, the hired men headed back to Centennial where Laramie had put them up in a boarding house. They had moved out to Centennial when the building began so the men would only have a couple miles to ride to work. Otherwise they'd have been camped in tents on the homestead. Laramie had been busy as well. She and Theresa had left earlier, but Laramie rode her horse back out to the homestead late in the afternoon. The paint she loved so much, of course, had been sold before she and Theresa became 'Midwestern ladies'. Now she rode a roan mare that reminded me of Mary Beth's gelding. She'd changed clothes, too, and instead of the proper dress, she was now in buckskins.

"We will spend our first night in our new cabin," she announced, "and still be under the stars. Will you make me feel the things that I miss so much, Kyle? It is sometimes so hard to have you so near and it not be you."

"And you can tell. You certainly knew when I got here."

"I saw the hawk circling while we were still half a mile away. I drove the horses hard to reach you."

"Laramie, I love you. Even when I am not in Kyle I think of you every day and dream of you every night. I miss you." We settled onto our bedrolls and kissed. I loved the feeling I got when I slipped my hand under her buckskin shirt and let it find her tender breast. "You changed out of your dress."

"There are too many clothes and layers. Why do white women wear them with their husbands?"

I laughed. The question was a good one. I was certainly happier when there was just this one buckskin shirt to pass over her head and have her pressed naked against me.

We made love well into the night, stopping only long enough to eat the vittles she'd brought with her. We built a little campfire in the middle of the cabin and ate and talked.

"Some things have changed, Kyle," Laramie said as we held each other close. "You will want to go to the city Saturday night. Kyle always does."

"Well, he doesn't need to go whoring when I'm around."

"It is not that," Laramie said. "Kyle is courting a school teacher and he wants to build a cabin near ours so he can bring her out here to live and both of them work on my ranch."

"Kat Tangeman!" I said.

"Yes. There is considerable competition for her affection. We roomed next to each other at the boarding house in Laramie. She was so helpful and sympathetic when I was sick and lost the baby. She is a very proper lady, but also very passionate. She prefers Kyle because he is young, but a wealthy older man is also courting her. I think Kyle must act soon."

"You are all right with this? Knowing that it is really me going to court her?"

"You will know how to win her for Kyle, love. It will make him happy and you will be near when you arrive. He has been very good to mother and me and brought us more money when we needed it. He cannot show himself to be a wealthy man unless he leaves here and he will not leave. So, he works hard and has the men well-organized."

"I hate to go into town. I could get sent out by that sheriff."

"It is always a risk. Kyle has organized the men so they know exactly what to do and they are reliable as long as their wages are paid on Saturday."

I sighed. Everything she said made sense. It especially made sense now that I was with both Mary Beth and Ashley in my own time. The thought of courting Kat was not unpleasant. And Kyle had been good to Laramie. He deserved his corner of happiness.

We worked on the cabin for three more days and by the time work ended Saturday at noon, the roof was on and the men had put a door on hinges at the opening. Theresa planned to order glass windows for the two openings on the sides and another man was coming on Monday to close in the firebox and build a stone chimney. Laramie, Theresa, and Kaylene would have a snug home for the winter.

It was also well-known among the laborers and town folk that if anything untoward happened to the family, Kyle would mete out justice where it was due. Laramie was secure.

SATURDAY AFTERNOON, I joined four other riders on our way to Laramie City. I let Kyle take over.

"City" was a good word for Laramie. Since Statehood, the population had grown to nearly 7,000 people. It was still a rough place, but much more than a street of brothels and bars. The town was being cleaned up. Kyle went straight to a barber and got a hot bath and shave. His blond hair was pulled back in a tie behind his neck and fell to nearly his shoulder blades. He even washed his mouth before he headed toward the boarding house where Kat lived.

She met me at the door with a chaste kiss and led me to the sitting room. An old woman sat in a rocking chair next to the fireplace, even though in the July weather no fire was laid. We sat on a settee that was anything but comfortable, but was narrower than the big sofa on the other side of the room. The old woman would have to turn her head to look at us.

"I've missed you, Kyle. How were things at work on the ranch?" It was normal old married folk talk. I told her about the progress on the cabin and she told me about the new brick school and the number of teachers and children there will be, with a separate teacher for nearly every grade. "Let us take a walk, Kyle," she said at last.

I gladly offered my arm, thankful to be out from under the baleful gaze of the old lady. We walked up Second Street and down Main before she turned to me.

"Kyle, when will you take me to be your own? If you ask, I will say yes. I inquired and can teach in Centennial. They have only a dozen children and I will teach them whatever they need to know. But Kyle, my maidenhead is anxious to be gone. She would fly hither and be free. That blood that she leaves behind will be the only troth you need if you will leave your seed in exchange." Kyle was having a little trouble following that, but the fact that she wanted him to fuck her came through. He was baffled, though. He couldn't take her back to Centennial without a place for her, and in Laramie he'd moved into a single room over Mackenzie's Dry Goods. True, the stairs to his room were in the alley and they might be able to go there undetected, but he was self-conscious about bringing her to the lowly room.

"My room isn't very nice," he said, finally, "or I would take you there this instant." She took his arm and began to lead him to the alley where he lived. He was surprised that she knew the way.

"Any room with you in my arms will be a palace," she said as she hurried him along. Now that Kyle had agreed, she was wasting no time getting him there. When they arrived, Kyle stood in shock as he looked at the spotlessly clean room, fresh linens on the bed, and even a trimmed wick in his lamp. "Please do not be angry with me dearest. I went to Mrs. Mackenzie and convinced her that you'd hired me to clean your room while you were gone since I had no employment for the summer."

"Kat, I ain't a great catch. I don't know why you want me instead of that rich guy who's been a'courtin' you, but I promise on my knee that I will love and cherish you for the rest of my life. Will you bed with me and let me show you how much I love you?"

"Oh Kyle! That's the prettiest speech you ever made. I'm a little scared, so please go slow and tell me what I must do to show you how much I love you."

"I don't have a wedding band for you, but I will get one as soon as I can and we'll have the preacher announce our marriage. As my pledge to you, let me give you this." He pulled the watch the old prospector had given him and handed it to her. *Shit! I was supposed to find that. If he gave it away, how was I supposed to ever find it?* I jumped in. "My dearest, let this token be forever passed to our eldest child and his to show our unbroken line for all generations," I said. She looked at the watch and then fell into my arms to kiss me.

I stayed out of the rest of it for the most part. I slowed Kyle down a bit at one point, reminding him how it had been when he deflowered Laramie. Aside from that, he was a tender lover and I thought of Ashley as he and Kat became a real couple. He got no sleep that night and Kat slipped back into her boarding house, creeping up the stairs before dawn.

Kyle went back to his mattress and went to sleep instantly, but sprang awake when I nudged him as the church bells chimed on Sunday morning. He had promised to escort Kat to church and I wasn't going to let him miss his entire first day of wedded bliss. Even I had trouble staying awake through the two hours of praying and preaching. Kat nudged me and I tried to keep Kyle awake. With the two of us working on it, we somehow survived the morning. I suggested that we have dinner in the hotel dining room and Kat agreed. Just before we reached the fancy hotel in the middle of town, an urchin rushed up and blocked our progress.

"Kyle Wardlaw, Sheriff Cal said to tell you to get your ass into his office right now. He's been looking for you all morning." Then the kid was gone.

"Oh, Kyle. I know you do work for the Sheriff sometimes, just like you work for Miss Theresa and her daughter, but does it have to be on Sunday afternoon?" Kyle sighed.

"I have to go. Sheriff Despain is a tough man. I don't want him mad."

"You go ahead then, dear. I will be here waiting for you. Please come home soon and let us be off to our new home together."

"As soon as I can," he said. He kissed her. It was scandalous. They were in the middle of town with respectable people passing by and neither cared for anything but that kiss. "I love you, Kat Tangeman," he said.

"I love you, Kyle Wardlaw."

I headed for the Sheriff's office. I figured that I'd better sit back and ride and let Kyle manage this meeting. If Joe was riding in the Sheriff, I didn't want him to look me in the eyes and see me there. I didn't need to worry. Both Sheriff Despain and Joe Teini held Kyle in complete disdain. They thought of him as 'simple' and gave him no credit for craftiness. Despain laid the map we'd taken from the prospector on the table.

"Are you sure this was all the old man had on him?"

"Yessir," Kyle answered. "You told me what to look for and as soon as I found it, I took it and rode like hell to get out of those mountains."

"Then I must have sent you to get it."

"I beg your pardon, sir?"

"I said, I'm sending you to get it. Bring whatever is in this hiding place back here and get moving so you can get back before snow flies this time."

I groaned and so did Kyle. I didn't have to answer.

"But sir, do I have to go now. I'm about to get married next weekend."

"Ride hard and you can get married in three or four weeks."

WE RODE HARD. First to see Kat and explain that we had to get on the road right away if we were going to get back before snow fell in the mountains. It was the end of July, but we'd been known to have snow on that pass as early as September. Kat was sad, but I kissed her with meaning and then rode hard for Centennial. I reached Laramie's room and ran in without even knocking. She was rocking our little toddler in a chair and singing her some native song that I took to be a lullaby.

"Laramie!"

"Shh, Kyle. Kaylene just went to sleep." She laid the child on the bed and turned to me. "Oh dear, Kyle, what is it?" I explained that I was being sent west of the mountains and that I had to ride hard to get back before snow flies. "Oh no, Kyle. You just got here and I want more of your sweet loving."

"Oh, I do, too, sweetheart. I want to make another little baby in your womb and be with you to raise them on our ranch. But in order to do that, I need to get out of here and get back. I love you, Laramie. You are the light of my soul. I ache every day we are parted."

"Come back to me, Kyle. Just come back to me."

"You should know, Kyle proposed to Kat and we are to be married as soon as I return. She will teach at the new little school here."

"That is wonderful. We may have to explain to her... whatever we can explain. I don't know what it is, but I love you."

With a kiss that threatened to disturb our daughter on the bed, I took my leave and went to the stable to get my mule. I had supplies at the ready and I headed for the mountains.

THERE WASN'T MUCH for me to do. Kyle knew the way and I just sat back and contemplated what Joe Teini was up to, in this time and in ours. Here, he was accumulating wealth. In uptime, he was making a grab for power and land. I had to figure out how to stop him. I didn't think it was necessary for one man to try to own a county. What then? The whole state? The country? I supposed that with unlimited money you could about do anything you wanted. Unless somebody with more money stopped you.

It was nearly four weeks making the thousand miles from Laramie to Oregon where we'd picked up the map. Bolt might have made it faster, but a mule is smarter than a horse and when it's gone far enough for a day, it stops. We used the mule's good sense to break up the trip. And while Kyle controlled the journey, I sat back and studied our problem. It seemed that Cal Despain was more trouble than he was worth. It would be a whole lot easier on us if Joe Teini could no longer just drop into the past.

I won't say that I contemplated *killing* Despain. All I'd done was think about how we'd all be better off if he wasn't around.

It took most of another week to find the plot where the prospector had buried his stash. It wasn't that much. There was a chest, like the old man said. We already knew what was there, but I didn't understand Teini's haste in getting it right now. It was mostly filled with double-eagles and two hefty pouches of jewels. We didn't wait or look around for more. We split the loot between the mule's side bags and headed back east.

I was worried about making the Teton Pass before it was closed in. It was already the second week of September and there was definitely snow on the high peaks. Kyle turned south to head for the old Cherokee Trail that crossed Bridger Pass nearer to Laramie. Just before we turned north of Salt Lake City, I got the idea to take the train across the rest of the way. The Transcontinental ran from Salt Lake City right to Laramie. We booked passage and got our stock loaded. I decided to camp out in the stock car instead of taking a seat. If it was good enough for the horse and mule, it was good enough for me. Besides, I was transporting twenty thousand dollars in gold coins and a bunch of jewels. It seemed better to stick with it.

We weren't the only ones who traveled with their stock, and I was glad we were there. I was pretty sure any one of these hombres would slit my throat and steal my horse. It was only the fact that there was never just one other in the car and that I was always awake, even when Kyle slept, that kept us alive. If one of those strangers so much as stretched in the night, I woke Kyle up. I was finding that it was easier and easier for me to stretch my senses—what, my intuition?—when Kyle was asleep so I was aware of our surroundings without using his eyes or ears.

I'd always been limited by what his body could do. If Kyle's eyes weren't open, I couldn't see. If he was asleep, I could listen and smell things, but they were faint and I had to nudge him awake in order to do anything. On that train, I was beginning to expand my awareness. Maybe I couldn't exactly *see,* but I could sense more of what was around me—even where we were.

One thing had puzzled me. Despain/Teini didn't want us to bring the treasure back on our first trip out to get the map. Why did he decide to send us out now? I had to put myself in the shoes of the puppet master.

What could have happened in 1996 that drove Joe Teini to feel he needed Kyle to get the old man's treasure right away? I kept coming back to Schrödinger's Cat.

The famous theory was that if you placed a cat in a sealed box with a chemical drip that had a fifty percent chance of combining to create a toxic gas and a fifty percent chance of remaining benign, then as long as you kept the box sealed, the cat was both dead and alive. It was only when the box was opened that history branched and there was either a dead cat or a live cat.

What if Joe Teini had opened the box and found it empty?

I'd opened a box when I'd lifted the rock and brought ten gold bars down from the mountain. But I'd put those bars there myself. For whatever reason, Joe Teini chose to work through other people. I didn't think Cal Despain had actually ever been to see the treasures Kyle had piled up in the Medicine Bow. Teini had undoubtedly opened a box somewhere along the line in order to have the money he was already throwing around to buy the sheriff's office and the ranches he had. But he assumed the mother lode of treasure was what the old prospector had collected. There was a lot more treasure lost in the 1840-60 range than in the 1880-1900 range. So, if Joe had just memorized the map and gone to search for the treasure in uptime and it wasn't there, he had to assume someone already moved it. Best to send your own agent out to move the treasure, then.

Cal Despain was surprised to see me when I walked into his office the fifth of October. I looked into his eyes and could tell that Joe was not there, or he was hiding the way I was.

"What the hell are you doing here? Did you get it?" I nodded. "You took it to the cave?" I shook my head and hooked my thumb out toward my mule. "You brought it right here? You dumbass!"

"There's just one box. It's a good one, but didn't seem like I needed to make a trip out there for this."

Cal had me bring the mule around to his back door and the two of us hoisted the bags into the back office. We unloaded the coins and jewels and Cal looked like he'd never seen so much.

"Damn! This is good. Here, Kyle, have a handful. You earned 'em. Now go court your missus."

I realized at that moment that Despain was nearly as simple-minded as Kyle was. Apparently, there is a limit to the intelligence of the person who gets occupied by a time-traveler. But this could create problems. If this was the first time Cal had actually seen the big payoff instead of just the few coins that he usually received, he might get curious. This was going to be tricky.

Kyle headed straight to see Kat and I let him go, but in the morning, we were headed to Laramie. Unfortunately, I never got that chance.

How many times does a redtail hawk swoop right down in the middle of a city and scream?

Thar's Gold in Them Thar Hills

When I landed in my own body, I was cradled between two luscious breasts and hands were gently stroking my head. I thought for a minute I'd just jumped a little and Kyle was being cradled by Kat. Then I realized there were more hands than that. My eyes flickered open. The luscious breasts were Ashley's. Her hands were holding mine. Mary Beth was stroking wet streaks off my cheeks and whispering, "There, there. It's okay, honey. We're here for you."

"Did I… was I…?"

"You just cried yourself to sleep for a few minutes, baby," Ashley said. "It's okay. I… um… told Mary Beth about Caitlin. I mean her stone. I hope that's okay."

"Yeah." My eyes started leaking again. "I gotta find another one out there. My wife lost our second baby while I was gone. She's buried in the infant lot. There's no stone. I just need to go there."

"Your wife, Cole?" Both Ashley and Mary Beth hit it at the same time and I realized what I'd said.

"I guess we never got married. Never seemed to be time when I was there. Besides, my host is in love with someone else and it would be awkward for him to marry my love. God, it's so confusing sometimes."

"How many children do you have, Cole?"

"Just one I know of. I've got a funny feeling Kyle and Kat will be getting pregnant pretty soon, though. And who knows if anything caught with Laramie this time."

"This time?" Mary Beth asked.

"Damn. Didn't you hear the hawk?"

"Yeah. Funny thing. Screeched when you started crying and then circled around and came back a few minutes ago, just when you were waking up."

"I don't know why it is, but I figured out that it's Redtail's call that triggers me to switch places."

"You mean you were there? In the 1890s? While we were holding you?" I nodded. "How long?" Mary Beth asked.

"Two, almost three months."

"That's a lot of lovin'. One of those girls ought to be pregnant."

"That's the problem. I don't just spend my time with her—or them—when I'm there. This time I got sent on a trip to Oregon to recover a treasure. I dumped it in Laramie and Kyle was on his way to see Kat when I got called back."

"Kat. And I look like Kat, don't I? That's why you called me Kat the first time we met," Ashley said. I nodded. "Why do you suppose this happens?"

"Right. Why did you get sucked into all this?" Mary Beth added.

"Damned if I know. Don't seem like I'm a very likely guy to go out and fight Joe Teini."

"The Sheriff?"

"Yeah. He's one, too."

"Are there more?" Ashley asked.

"I met one other on my last trip. But his host died while we were there and I don't know his name in either time. He could be alive, or maybe he died when his host did. I just don't know. From what he said though, he wasn't actually from this time. I just don't know when."

"So, I believe Joe Teini is a scumbag, based on what Dad's been telling me," Mary Beth said. "But what's he up to? What's he trying to do?"

"I don't know," I admitted. "So far, all I can see is that he wants to buy all the land in Albany County and become God."

"That sucks. How are we going to stop him?" Ashley asked.

"We?"

"You've got Kyle, Laramie, and Kat in 1890 and Mary Beth and me now. The six of us ought to be able to come up with something."

I smiled up at Ashley and turned my head enough to nip at her tit through her shirt. She and Mary Beth both started giggling.

"I think what 'we' are going to do right now involves at least two of us getting naked," Mary Beth laughed. She reached to unsnap Ashley's shirt.

"I think we should all three get naked," I laughed, popping the snaps on Mary Beth's front.

"Oh, I was thinking just Ashley and me," Mary Beth said with her eyebrows raised. "Are you sure you're up to it?" Ashley's hand was in my crotch and I was definitely up. Mary Beth leaned across me and took Ashley's face in her hands. "I know I said I prefer boys to girls, but Ash, I do love you." The two girls kissed over the top of me and my cowboy went wild with anticipation.

I HELD MY two naked lovers against my body. Mary Beth's pussy was still pulsing around my cock and I was leaking the last drops of my second load. Ashley was holding my balls and had played with both of us all through our loving. The girls didn't go down on each other, but they were active partners in turning me on and turning each other on. I turned my head and Ashley met my lips. Mary Beth snuggled her head against my chest and squeezed her pussy muscles on my cock as Ashley and I kissed.

We could just walk away from it all. We could sell the ranches to Joe, send our parents on an around the world cruise, and buy ourselves a big spread up in Montana—just with what I knew we were lying on under the roots of that big tree. Why should we fight a battle over land? If I cared to open Schrödinger's box, I knew where there was a bunch more treasure, assuming nothing untoward happened in the 1890s. I'd come up here with the intent of opening one of those boxes today. We needed to make sure the ranches were safe for the winter, and that meant more money.

Ashley's kiss became more intense. I heard a slurp and looked down to see Mary Beth nursing on Ashley's nearest tit. There's just something about a girl who's wearing nothing but her neckerchief. Somehow, we'd never taken that red bandana off. The sun was low, even on this western side of the ridge. We had the early shift on the herd in the morning. I guessed I'd dig for buried treasure later.

Later didn't come that week. I left Schrödinger's box unopened.

WE WERE CLOSE to the end of the month. Grass was getting scarce and the nights were cold. Some of us had to get back to school. We were planning to drive the cattle down to the lower pasture and start separating them out for early feedlot after the weekend but Friday, I got a radio message from home.

"Cole, your dad's been in an accident," George said when he caught up with me riding herd. "You need to get back down. Go out to the trailhead. Your mom is sending Jack up with the 4x4."

"Let me grab Ash and MB," I said. "I'm on my way."

I rode uphill toward where my girls were and explained what was going on. I needed to get down to the house.

"I'm a hired hand," Ashley said. "I can't just take off and go with you. We'll be down on Tuesday or Wednesday and I'll see you then. I love you, Cole. I'm praying for your father while I'm riding herd." God, I love that woman!

"Hon, I better stay here with Ashley," Mary Beth said. "I trust the guys, but it's just safer all around if there's two of us girls up here. And it's only a couple days. Go take care of your Mom and Dad and tell them I love them and we're all praying for Uncle Earl and Aunt Sarah. I love you, Cole."

"I love you, Mary Beth," I said as I nudged Bolt over next to her roan and kissed her. I moved up next to Ashley and she practically threw herself out of her saddle reaching to kiss me. I looked at the two girls, turned my horse and headed for the trailhead.

THINGS WERE BAD. Dad was in intensive care and was still listed in critical condition. His truck had gone off the road coming back from the co-op meeting late Thursday night. The ranchers had started complaining that winter food was going up in price and they were going to have to sell off their cattle before they could be fattened up. This was already driving the price of beef down. We were all expecting to get $2.00-2.25 a pound live weight, but the market price at the moment was down to $1.85. This was going to cause a massive sell-off before winter.

One of our neighbors north of Centennial had been traveling the Snowy Range Road a mile behind Dad when a dark car blew by him at close to a hundred miles an hour. It went so fast that our neighbor couldn't even identify what kind of car it was other than small and fast. Its lights were off. Just at Porter Lake, he came upon Dad's truck crashed through the guard rail. So far, we were all wondering if it was an accident or if he'd been run off the road deliberately. The Sheriff's office just said they were investigating. I knew how hard they'd be looking into it if Joe Teini was behind this.

I joined Mom at the hospital in Laramie and just held her in my arms as we waited for news about Dad. We were allowed to go into ICU for just ten minutes at a time, once an hour. There was no change in Dad. He had tubes in his nose and mouth, tubes in his arms, and monitors connected to his chest. There was no change between our visits.

I finally got to talk to a doctor about dinner time.

"There's really no change," the doctor said. "We got him in about eleven last night and have done everything we can to patch him up, but he's not showing signs of waking up yet. His head was pretty banged up and he broke several ribs when he went into the steering column. His left leg was snapped in three places from the impact with the guard rail. If he doesn't show signs of regaining consciousness by morning, I'm going to have to say he's entered a coma. Usually, I'd call that now, but there's no difference in how we treat him. He's staying in ICU and I'm not upgrading his condition. He's critical because we're actually supporting his life. Without that, he'd die. I'm sorry to put it so bluntly, but that's the fact."

"Thanks, Doctor," I said, not knowing what I was thanking him for. There wasn't anything in what he said to be thankful for. Except Dad was alive. I prayed hard that it was a good sign.

I STEPPED INTO managing the ranch in Dad's absence the next morning. I was twenty and technically, Alexander Bell Cattle Company already owned the combined spread on a contract even though they were still managed separately by Dad and Angus. The important thing was to make sure we were ready to receive close to two thousand head of cattle when they came down from the high range. Between that and supporting

Mom, I had my hands full. Uncle Angus and Aunt Lily took turns going up to the hospital to sit with Mom. I was a little surprised when he turned to me and told me that he and Dad had already signed papers handing the management of the combined ranches over to the Alexander Bell Cattle Company in anticipation of us coming down on Monday and that I should assume management of his part of the herd and not bother separating them out. Like the other ranchers, he figured we were going to take a big loss this year with the shortage of winter feed.

This was also part of ranching economics. It's expensive to feed cattle over the winter in the best of times. When you bring them in from the range you can have strong healthy cows but they don't have the quality fat marbling for Prime Grade beef. You have to fatten them up. From what I was seeing, we weren't going to last longer than a month before we had to start selling cattle off to Midwestern feedlots. That meant shipping and lower wholesale prices. We might be lucky to get $1.25 a pound on the hoof net. Everyone in Albany County seemed to be in the same fix. Even Sheriff Teini had spoken up at the meeting about not having feed, though no one felt sorry for him.

I went back to the hospital every day and every day the news was the same. No change. Dad was existing there because they had him plugged in. They'd moved him into a private room where he could still be monitored, but because he was stable they no longer had him in ICU. Stable as a vegetable. I never let Mom see me weak, but I went home at night and cried. On Monday morning, I got the radio message that the herd was moving. George estimated it would be Wednesday midday before they arrived. I told him to bring them all in together. We weren't cutting our cows from the Alexander's. We'd just funnel half into their feedlot and half into ours. It wasn't unexpected after Angus and Earl had ordered the fences removed from between our property early last spring.

What started worrying me, on top of having no feed for the cattle and Dad being a vegetable, was that school was supposed to start the following Monday. On Wednesday morning about the time I could see the herd clearly from the back steps, I called the admissions office at UW. I explained the situation and said I would not be able to enroll this fall. They made the appropriate sounds of sympathy and told me not to worry. I had protected admission and could take up to a year leave before coming back. I optimistically told them I hoped to be back for the winter term, but the truth was I knew better. Even if Dad started to recover, I was a twenty-year-old manager of a producing cattle ranch. If I got more schooling, it was going to be night school. I kind of regretted that, but I loved the ranch and I loved what I was doing. I'd make it work and hope Ashley would stick with me.

WEDNESDAY AFTERNOON, I was mounted when the herd started into the lower pastures. I rode with the hands and barely had a chance to get a quick kiss from Mary Beth and Ashley. I did switch to Bolt, though, and he performed like the stud he is. Uncle Angus and his lead hand, Bill, had joined Jack and me most of the morning, making sure there was water in all the tanks and that our hay was ready to move when needed. We'd only managed three cuttings that summer, but the lower pasture was still green and lush. Our thousand heifers and calves that hadn't gone to the upper range could graze for at least two weeks on what was growing.

Usually Mom and Lily handled food for the crew when the cattle came in, but knowing the condition we were in with Dad in the hospital, a team of neighbor ladies showed up with chili, cornbread, and beer for all of us at about six. By eight, we were sweaty and dirty and hungry. Many of the neighbor men showed up as well. Mary Beth and Ashley were on best behavior because even though our hired hands and family knew how we lived on the range, none of the neighbors did.

I was surprised when three of the neighbor men cornered me with a beer.

"Cole, what are you going to do about selling off?" Obert Calhoun asked. He owned a spread east of us and was maybe fifteen or twenty years older than Dad. He grazed all summer in his own pastures and bought only the hay that was necessary to get them to market. He usually got a good price for his grass-fed beef.

"Little early for me to make that my decision, Obert. I've still got hopes that Dad will be here telling me what to do."

"Don't take this wrong, son. We all want your father back here and healthy. I'm proud to call him a friend for more than thirty years. But we also all know he's been grooming you to take over. He even credited you with saving the farm last winter, though none of us know how you did that. Even if it was just giving him hope, it was the right thing to do."

"Thanks, Obert. Give me a week to get my head around what I'm going to do here. I've already told UW I would be taking a year off to manage the ranch while Dad recovers. I know as well as you guys that it will take him a long time to get back to normal."

"Well, I'm glad you've got a head on your shoulders. If I had to depend on my son, I'd already be bankrupt. What are the chances I could mate him up with that filly cousin of yours? At least then I'd know there was one brain in the family."

"Well, who Mary Beth mates with is her business, but if you ask her about it like that, you should probably have a doctor present. One you trust because you're likely to be in the bed next to Dad's." The guys all laughed and I breathed deeply so I didn't give away any real feelings I have for my cousin. The laughter relieved a little of the tension and we just sat around jawing about some of the daily news.

When we'd all eaten our fill, the neighbors had left, and the guys had gone to get hot showers, the three of us went into the house. It was strange having the house to ourselves. Mom was staying in Laramie as long as Dad was in the hospital and I would go in early in the morning. It was way too late tonight. We enjoyed our showers and there wasn't a drop of hot water left by the time we were through. I loved washing Ashley's hair. Mary Beth got her hair washed by my girlfriend and we turned around and worked it the other way. Ashley got conditioner while I got shampooed. Then MB and I got conditioner at the hands of Ashley.

Sure, we played around a bit, but we saved most of that for bed. When I was about 15, I made a suggestive comment to one of the older guys in town, saying we missed something with not having horses and buggies when we were dating anymore. Not that I'd know. I said, "The horse knows the way..." and left it hang. The geezer—not any older than Dad—said, "Speaking as a man who's been married fifteen years, I'd rather have 256 horses under the hood and a soft bed waiting at home."

Well, my bed wasn't standard since I'd reached my full height two years ago. Mom and Dad consented to get me a king size bed, so there was plenty of room now for me to crawl in the middle and hold each of my girls close beside me. I was planning to welcome them both home with some good loving, but they were so tired and so relaxed after their showers that they fell asleep on my shoulders before I could get something started.

I went to the hospital in the morning and stood beside my Dad as he passed away.

I KNOW MY dad wasn't perfect. But let me tell you about my dad. His mother died before he could recognize who she was. He was taken by the neighbors and raised as one of their own while they managed both ranches and kept things solvent for twenty years. He married the girl he grew up with and her brother was like his brother. He served in the Army and survived Viet Nam. He did his duty for his country and came back with an honorable discharge from a grateful service. And then he got this ranch re-established as one of the leading cattle producers in the county and worked with his neighbor brother-in-law to rise above the tides of fortune.

Sometimes I regret giving him all that money, because I took away the opportunity for him to solve the problem himself like I know he could have. I opened Schrödinger's box and that set the reality.

I've figured out that I can't do anything in the past that changes anything that happened up to the present. All I can do is make the choices that affect what comes hereafter. Being in the past is just like being in the present that way. I couldn't save the old prospector's life. Nothing in known history changed. His body was found next to that of his faithful mule. There was nothing of value on his person or on his mule. I didn't change anything. Joe Teini opened the box and discovered the prospector's treasure wasn't there. He acted to make sure the reason it wasn't there was because he'd recovered it. Still no change in the outcome.

My dad made a difference. He created who I am. He changed the course of the future.

Why am I so upset, other than that my dad is dead?

Because right now, I'm trying to decide who else has to die.

7
To Be or Not To Be

OF COURSE, I read Shakespeare in Senior English Lit in high school. Who didn't? I just suddenly found myself identifying with the melancholy prince. A father killed. A usurper on the throne. What's a prince to do?

I was convinced my dad had been murdered and I was ready to lay it at the feet of Joe Teini. The bastard actually came to the funeral on Labor Day and when he went through the receiving line he offered my mom two million in cash for the ranch. At the fucking goddamned funeral! The bastard.

"Mom doesn't actually own the ranch now," I said, stepping between them. I kept my attention on Mom and avoided looking him in the eye. There was a chance he could recognize a time traveler just by looking him in the eye. "I'll be sure to let you know if the owners ever want to sell."

"Just thought I could make things better," Joe sneered. "I wouldn't want anyone else to end up like your dad."

The son of a bitch! He was as much as threatening my family. This was going to stop. I was going to cut off his source of funds or his balls or both.

I wasn't sure yet, but I had a feeling that it was going to happen soon. Things in the western part of the county were looking bleak for everybody and I figured I needed to get my act together pretty soon or everything was going to hell.

Just let me bury my dad first. Okay?

Family Bible

WE USED THE backhoe to scrape out Dad's grave up on the promontory with the other Bell family members. When I helped lower the casket in the hole, I wondered about all the other ancestors who were buried there and how long the ranch had been in our hands. I was pretty sure Laramie's ranch had not been far from here, but the landscape had changed enough that I couldn't identify things. I'd only found the site of the hut because of the thermal spring. I'd kept hoping that I'd discover that we had another neighbor who was maybe a descendent of our child, Kaylene. But whatever happened, I didn't find anything.

That just wasn't what I was focusing on. I had people who were depending on me in two timelines. I needed to figure out how best to protect both of them and it was all coming down to getting rid of Joe Teini.

Folks finally left after the carry-in dinner and after our refrigerator was filled with food we only needed to warm up for the next few days. Mom looked up when she saw that Mary Beth and Ashley were both still there.

"Oh. I suppose you're waiting for Cole to take you home," Mom said.

"Mom," I said as gently as I could. "Ashley and Mary Beth are staying here tonight. With me."

"Oh. Well the guest room…"

"Mom. With me. Ashley is my girlfriend and if she will consent to be my wife I will marry her before Christmas." Ashley rushed to me and kissed me deeply, right in front of my mom. I wasn't embarrassed by it at all. I held out my hand and Mary Beth took it. "Mary Beth is my cousin and I love her with all my heart. She will live with me and with Ashley for as long as she wishes and holds us in her heart like she does now. Mom, we're going to be one family and while we don't want to advertise things to all the neighbors, we're not hiding it from our families."

"Oh. I suppose I knew all that. Your father did. Both your fathers. I just thought that when you got serious about a girl she would be the only one. I can see, though that you are all three in love. I don't understand these things, but I'll just go to bed now." Mom hugged each of the three of us and it really did feel like she loved and accepted us. "Cole, will you write it in the Bible? I got it down yesterday, but I just couldn't open it."

"What Bible, Mom?" Well sure I had a Bible. We all had Bibles even if we didn't go to church much. But I wasn't sure what she wanted written in what Bible.

"The Bell Family Bible," Mom answered. "I got it down last night and put it on the desk, but I couldn't write your father's death in it. It's really your responsibility as head of the household now." I didn't even know we had a family Bible. It was common enough for each family to have a record of their family in a Bible. I'd looked at enough of them at the Family History Library. Apparently, the last event that had been written in ours was my birth. I kissed Ashley and Mary Beth goodnight and told them I'd be up in a bit. Then I headed toward the office and my dad's desk. I suppose it was going to be my desk from now on.

I MUST HAVE seen the big book sometime in the past, probably when I was a little kid, because it looked sort of familiar. There was a marker in the middle of it and it opened to the page where my Dad's information had been recorded. It was pretty complete information. It started with his full name and birth date. Below that were his date of graduation from Laramie High School. Then his dates of service in the United States Army, 1973-1975. Next came his marriage to Mom and her birth information and parents. A number of lines below that had the caption children, but only my name appeared. I was surprised to see a line above mine marked with the simple words, "Infant girl. Stillborn. March 10, 1974." I never knew I had a big sister. It made me remember my own baby who was buried somewhere in the infant field at Greenhill. At the bottom of the page was space where the single initial "d." indicated where I was to place his death information. The next page started with my name at the top and my birth date. I wrote the date and place of Dad's death, but it seemed that there was a lot of space left and I wondered what I was supposed to write there.

I turned back a page to see if my Grandmother's entry was there. It was. Mildred Arlene Bell, b. 5/10/1925. At the bottom of the page were the words, "d. 12/5/1955 She loved a soldier who was taken to war and did not return. When she had delivered their infant son and she knew he was safe, she hurried to join her love." The only child was Earl Thomas Bell, my dad, born August 7, 1955.

I turned back to Dad's page and thought about what I should write. My handwriting was certainly nothing like the flowing script on the previous page and I wondered who had written that. I thought and then wrote. "Earl Thomas Bell, faithful husband, respected father, cherished friend. All those who knew him miss him." I got it now. That's why the stones in our family plot were blank. Our stories were in this book. I wondered how my story would be filled out.

I turned back a page to Mildred's information and read it through completely before looking at the previous entry. The writing was more difficult to read, but I stared at it long after I'd read it.

"Kaylene Redtail Bell, born March 10, 1889. Lived with Robert Hood, 1925 by consent. Died October 5, 1945. No church heard their vows, but they loved each other and brought a beautiful daughter into the world."

It couldn't be. It had to all be coincidence. Still I knew what I'd find when I turned the page. I had opened Schrödinger's box.

"Laramie Wyoming Bell, born summer of 1873. Beloved of Kyle Redtail, 1889. Mother of Kaylene Redtail Bell. Died December 24, 1929. To the very end she listened for the cry of the redtail hawk."

Oh God! I was hyperventilating. Laramie Wyoming Bell was my great-great grandmother. I was my own great-great grandfather. I stumbled out of the study and ran out the back door of the house with the Bible clutched against my chest. Before I reached the family plot I heard it slam again and a flashlight flicked across me as I ran to my father's grave. I didn't understand when we laid him to rest what the meaning of the short rows were. Here were the generations of my family. My father and baby sister. My grandmother Mildred and her soldier lover. My great-grandmother—my daughter—and her common law husband. And three stones together. Laramie Wyoming Bell, the child we lost... and me. Above us, a single stone. Theresa Ranae Bell who ran off to marry a Cheyenne brave named White Horse.

I lay down on that stone that I was sure was my Laramie and screamed into the night. Hands were on my shoulders and I looked up into the eyes of my lovers—into other eyes a hundred years ago—and cried.

My cry was answered by the call of Redtail.

Traveling: Passing

THE LIPS I was kissing were sweet. The release of my balls made me cry out in a mix of joy and agony—a little death in which I was joined by my beloved... Kat Tangeman.

I wanted to jerk Kyle away and rush him to Laramie's bed, but I couldn't do that. It wasn't Kyle's fault that he fell in love with Kat while I loved Laramie. The truth was, I loved Kat, too. I'd given up trying to figure out how I could love so many women so completely. When I looked into Kat's eyes, I saw Ashley and there was no question I was in love with that girl. I was anxious to get to Laramie, but now that I was here and was suddenly sure I'd be with Laramie until we died, I didn't mind relaxing in the back of Kyle's mind while he made love to Kat.

I looked through his memories to find that it was only a day after I'd been sucked out of Kyle's body the last time. I wondered what it meant that the time was so close. My whole experience had been over just three years in 1889-1892, but in my own timeline, over four years had passed. I was happy that I would continue my own story so soon after I had left. While Kyle feasted on Kat's fat, round nipples and rose to excitement again inside her, I let the exquisite feelings flow over me as I thought out how to manage the two relationships in downtime. Somehow, Kat would need to be let in on the fact that he/I was also involved with Laramie. I think she suspected it already, though I'd been discreet. If Kyle and Kat lived in the foreman's house on our ranch, then his body would be convenient for me to visit Laramie and live with her. We could work that out as we progressed.

What was more important was that Sheriff Cal Despain had to disappear. I'd looked him up in the City history and there was precious little about him. He was an almost non-entity sheriff in Laramie for ten years. At the end of his tenure, he rode out of town and was never heard of again. If that were the case, it was a safe bet that Joe Teini had moved the treasures from his cave and then found a way to dispose of Despain. I'd been to the cave three times and there was more treasure there than I could let Joe Teini have in the twentieth century. He had the resources to ruin and buy out every man woman and child in Albany County, include the 30,000 plus citizens of Laramie, Wyoming.

Having given Cal a rich treasure without the controlling influence of Joe, I may have inadvertently opened a crisis situation. And if I was arriving back in Kyle more quickly, Joe could be arriving back in Cal more frequently as well. I had to make sure that Joe didn't find what he wanted when he opened the box.

"Kyle, are you listening to me?" Kyle was still dreamily reliving his last orgasm deep in the pussy of his beloved. I'd been drifting. I jerked Kyle around to make him pay attention.

"Kat, love, I was so overwhelmed that time that it took me a minute to come back to you. You do things to me I've never experienced before."

"Don't you lie to me, Kyle Wardlaw. I know very well that you have done more things than most men dream of. I know where you lived for the past nineteen years, and I don't hold it against you."

"My love, it ain't the physical things you do to me that I'm talking about. You do something inside me that I can't even say." Kyle was emotional and I was glad. He'd turned out to be a good, if slightly slow, man.

"Well, here's something else that I'm going to do to you. Kyle I'm going to have your baby. You were gone for two months and I haven't bled in all that time. I'm sure I'm pregnant."

"And it's mine?" Kyle asked. I mentally slapped him upside the head.

"What do you think, Kyle Wardlaw? Do you think I'm a whore who doesn't know the father of her baby?"

"No! No, Kat, you took me so much by surprise," I said, taking over. "That's wonderful news. We need to get married. Right away. We'll ask the preacher to say the vows Sunday after church. Kat, you make me so happy. I love you and I want to take you to Centennial and have a whole bunch of children with you. Please say you'll marry me, Kat."

The answer I got was a tongue almost all the way down my throat. When either of us could speak again, Kat said, "Oh yes, Kyle. You know I'll marry you. Sunday is good. I'll see the preacher and make arrangements. I love you, Kyle. I'll always love you!"

"I'll always love you, Kat Tangeman."

ON MONDAY MORNING Kyle and I rode hell-bent for leather back to Centennial and out to Laramie's cabin. She knew as soon as she saw us on the trail to her that I was back. She came running out in her buckskins and threw herself into my arms as I dismounted.

"Kyle, you're back!" she said. In answer, I buried my face in her hair and kissed my way up her neck and to her lips. The other workers were already at work on the barn and scarcely glanced toward us. I held her close to me and looked at all the progress that had been made. Laramie showed me the root cellar and pointed to the new barbed wire fencing.

"It hasn't been finished yet," she said. "I hired a crew to set posts and stretch the wire around the 160-acre homestead. They have about four hundred yards yet to stretch and we can turn the horses loose in here. They'll have the barn to winter in and look at that windmill! A dowser came out and found the perfect spot for our well."

"You have been busy the last two months."

"I wanted you to be proud, Kyle," she said. "Even if you came back as Kyle Wardlaw instead of Kyle Redtail, I wanted you to be proud."

"It wouldn't be a hardship for you to live with him, would it, Laramie?"

"I'd always be waiting for you to return. But he's a good man, Kyle. He's been a hard worker and I'm fond of him even when you aren't here."

"Well, we've got a bit of a problem," I said. "Kyle just asked Kat Tangeman to marry him next Sunday."

"I like Kat. I told you that. It isn't uncommon among my father's people for a man to have two wives. Men die in battle and in the hunt. Women have adjusted to the need to share a man."

"Well, I don't know if Kat will be as willing as you, but it is something we need to deal with. There is something else even more important that we need to talk about, though."

"Can we do it on the sleeping furs? My beloved, I have missed you."

I saw nothing wrong with having our discussion on the sleeping furs when Theresa took Kaylene out to ride the new fence. I looked at my little girl and giggled. "Hello great-grandma," I whispered.

The cute little girl giggled and said, "Papa." I was stunned and when I set her down, she ran off to ride with her grandma. Laramie and I settled down in the cabin and it was only a few minutes before we were skin-to-skin in a lovers' embrace. I pushed the thought of the cold stone on the promontory out of my mind before tears could flow. I was here and Laramie was here. Here we would stay. Seeing that stone had given me new confidence. If I left, I would be back. We would grow old together and die together. Our stones were together on the hill.

I kissed my way down her dark skin paying special attention to the soft roundness of her belly. She was still lean, but two pregnancies had stretched her middle. Her tits, dry from the milk she no longer fed Kaylene, had softened as well. They would never be the firm round globes of a sixteen-year-old again, but they were attached to the woman I loved—the woman of my dreams—and so were perfect. When I reached the junction of her thighs she sighed and let her legs part for me. There was no taste I craved more than the fluids of her pussy. I didn't think cunnilingus was all that common in the 1890s, but we both sure enjoyed it. She cried out softly, muffling her voice with her shirt held closely to her mouth. She pulled at me when I would have gone on again and begged me to enter her and give her another child. I was all too willing to do so.

My cowboy was up for the occasion and penetration was easy. Loving was even better. I could feel Kyle in the back of my mind, curious as to how he could feel so much for two such different women and wondering how he could manage to satisfy both of them. At least for the time being he didn't need to worry about that.

I LAY THERE, stroking Laramie's soft skin, and letting her presence overwhelm my senses. I inhaled deeply of the scent of her body and hair. Hygiene was different when you lived in the wilderness. Not bad, but less stringent than in uptime. Laramie's scent was earthier. Natural. Arousing.

"Love, we have to run an errand. I'm going to tell you things that will help you on the ranch now, but you have to be very careful of them. You have to never let anyone know you are a rich woman."

"People already think mother is rich because of all we have bought."

"There was a reason for the kind of wealth you have shown. You were simply turning a farm in Iowa into a ranch in Wyoming. But this is more money than anyone living can imagine."

"Why do we need this wealth, Kyle? Is our home not enough?"

"It is. But this wealth must be guarded so that no one can use it to harm others. It is a sacred trust to our family."

"Then we will bury it and leave it."

"Yes. But first we must move it to a place that only we know about."

"Where is this wealth?"

"Not more than a day's ride from here. There is a place on our ridge where we can hide it and forget about it."

"We will leave in the morning, my love."

"Late tonight. I do not want the workers or the people of Centennial to know we have gone."

After dinner, we told Theresa that we were riding out and would be gone three days. I just hoped that I got to the stash before Sheriff Despain, or more especially Joe Teini got there.

I hitched the six draft horses to the Conestoga and tied the two mules behind. Laramie and I sat on the big seat and she leaned against me as we drove off into the night. These wagons were made to haul two tons of household gear—furniture, clothing, plows, tools, stoves. Everything went into the wagon when people moved west. Running empty the Morgans scarcely noticed the weight.

"Is there so much?" Laramie asked. I just nodded.

WE TRAVELED OVERLAND. Most of the range was still open and there were wagon tracks that we could follow north toward Medicine Bow and then east along the ridge. No one would ever know that just a few hundred yards from this track lay a fortune that would make Midas jealous.

When we pulled the wagons into a copse of trees, there was no sign that anything had been disturbed. It took me a minute to get my bearings, but Kyle nudged me over to the right spot. I detected that he'd decided that this wealth should not belong to Sheriff Despain either and was happy that I was hiding it and not planning to use it. He was fine with getting enough money to live on and not disturbing anything else. He was a good man.

It took all day to load the Conestoga with the chests of gold and jewels and whatever else was there. There was no telling what was in some of the suitcases and trunks that had been stowed. Mostly they were lighter weight and probably contained some poor traveler's clothing. But we moved everything. It looked like we were carting a wagon of household goods like any other settler. Even with the big Conestoga, we couldn't clear the cave completely. We left suitcases and lighter items in the cave, assuming they would have less value. We couldn't pull out in the dark, so we made camp to spend the night. I was wrapped in the arms of my lover and soul mate again.

"Well looky what we got here," I heard behind me as I was tying the mules to the back of the wagon in the morning. We'd used them to help move things from the cave to the wagon and their packs were full. I turned to see Cal Despain holding a rifle. "Why is it that the cave is almost empty and you got a full wagon?"

I wasn't too surprised to see the Sheriff, though I had hoped to be clean away from here before I had to deal with him. The fact that he was holding the rifle at an unwavering point to my chest, though, was unnerving. Laramie was unarmed and behind the Conestoga. Maybe she hadn't been seen yet. My Winchester was under the seat.

"Sheriff, two riders were scouting this area last time I was out here. You told me to move things over below Rawlins about five miles where there's a cave nobody knows about. You even gave me a map."

"You are full of more shit than a prize bull, boy. You know the order was bring it here and don't come back. Looks like you decided you needed a wedding present. Or are you fooling around with that squaw you work for. She's a little red, but I bet she's got a prime cunt."

I was getting pretty pissed and Kyle was ahead of me. Without realizing it, I'd loosened the safety strap on my right gun where Despain couldn't see my hand.

"Stand straight and turn toward me, boy!" the Sheriff snapped. I did as ordered. I wanted to be in this position anyway. I now had my hand and my gun where I needed them. "Drop them gun belts!" I wore a gun on each hip, but each had its own belt. As a result, I could loosen my left gun and still have the right ready to draw. I kept watch on Despain as I felt the buckle loosen. I saw his eyes flick to the side as I tossed the belt to my left. My right flashed to my side and I fired before my mind had caught up with the action. I felt the sting in my gut. The Sheriff was falling backward, a hole in his chest as I was falling forward with my guts spilling out.

"I'm sorry, Kyle," I whispered. "It wasn't supposed to be like this."

Laramie ran from her cover with my Winchester and put another round in the Sheriff's head before she knelt beside me. I was fading fast.

"Kyle. Kyle, don't die. I need you, Kyle," she cried as she held me.

"Honey, listen. I ain't got much time. I love you. I love you, but you gotta drag that son-of-a-bitch back into the farthest corner of the cave. His saddle, too. Set his horse free on the back range. I showed you where all this treasure has to go. You gotta take it there and never let anybody know about it. Do that for me Laramie honey. Our children and grand-children depend on it. I love you."

"Don't go Kyle. I love you. I love you."

I didn't know what happened if you were time-traveling and your host died. The old prospector hadn't known either. It looked like I was about to find out. I found myself pulling away from Kyle's body and heard his voice one more time.

"Please. Tell Kat I love her." Then Kyle was gone.

THERE WAS NO hawk's cry heralding my departure from Kyle's body. The pain in my gut ceased and the last thing I felt was Laramie's hot tears falling on my face.

But I was still there.

I was present, but I didn't have any way to really be there. I no longer had Kyle's eyes to see with nor Kyle's ears to hear with. My senses were cut off, but I could still *sense* what was going on. I knew Laramie held Kyle for a long time and then managed to hoist him up into the wagon and cover him. She was a big strong girl, but I'd just given her a task that was near impossible. Still, she managed to drag the body of Cal Despain back into the cave where the treasures had been hidden. It was a deep cave and she shoved the body into a crevice head first. She found his horse on the other side of the cave and stripped the saddle, blanket, and bridle from it and dumped it all in the back of the cave with the Sheriff. His saddle bags she hoisted into the wagon with my body. It took her a few hours. I could feel her sense of satisfaction, though, when she'd smoothed out the ground around the cave and erased all signs of our camp and the track to the cave. She led the Sheriff's horse and tied him by a lead rope with the mules and climbed aboard the Conestoga. She whipped the horses to life. When she reached the point where she could join an established, if ill-used, trail, she backtracked and erased the signs of the heavy wagon coming down from the ridge. It felt like it was late at night by the time she was satisfied. But she didn't let up. Under the heavy load, the horses moved slowly, but they kept the pace until dawn. She was near the Divide when she pulled away from the road, erased her tracks, and watered the stock.

Then Laramie wept.

Her pain was a palpable thorn in the side I no longer had. I was drawn to her. I loved her and I reached out my mind to comfort her. I just said over and over, "I'm here. I love you." I don't know that I had any effect, but eventually her sobs quieted and she slept soundly.

WHEN YOU ARE traveling with a heavily loaded wagon, seven horses, and two mules, it takes a while to get camped and to break camp. All the animals have to be cared for before you get food. It takes a good hour when you are alone to get them all hitched and ready to pull. And neither horses nor mules are particularly fond of traveling through the mountains at night. Laramie knew the way, and gathered all the reins in her small hands and got them moving. I think she knew the mountains better than either Kyle or me. Well, she'd lived and hunted on Centennial Ridge for years. She knew a different trail, down on the west side of the ridge and then back up toward the peak. The horses plodded slowly through the night, stopping only for water that Laramie carried to them. I imagined in my mind what it must look like for six black horses pulling a Conestoga with a dirty and blackened canvas through the night on the ridge, followed by two mules and a riderless horse. I would guess ghost stories would flourish.

She pushed on at daybreak and two hours later came to the site where years ago I'd found her hut. What Laramie had to do next took days. If I'd been there in body to help her we could have finished in maybe two days, but it took Laramie a week. She unhitched the wagon and hobbled the horses. Cal's horse she led down the western slopes until he was in a wooded area and set him free. It was pretty unlikely he'd ever get back toward Laramie. There were closer barns on the west slope in Carbon County and horses are prone to find the easy way to food. She dressed the mules in their side packs and then emptied one box at a time into the packs to take down the trail to Kyle's hiding place. There, she stacked the boxes and reloaded them before returning up the hill to get the next load.

When she'd finished her task and cleared the area of any further evidence of a path, she re-hitched all the teams and headed back down to the small town of Centennial. Her wagon creaked through town in the middle of the night, returning home the same way we had left.

She headed the mules toward the barn.

When Laramie pulled the wagon up to the cabin, her mother and daughter came out to greet her. So did Kat Tangeman. After Laramie had hugged our daughter, she looked at Kat and opened her arms. There must have been words that passed between them, but the communication was between their hearts. Together, the three women and child drove the wagon up to the promontory I now knew as the family plot. They took turns digging in the hard ground but eventually had a hole suitable for a grave. They lowered Kyle's body into the ground without removing the canvas he was wrapped in.

I wondered what was going to happen to me now. Everywhere I'd been since the shooting was in the company of Kyle's body. Now that he was in the ground, would I be stuck here, haunting this plot forever? Would I have to wait until the soulless body of Cole Alexander Bell was laid to rest before my spirit would find peace?

I followed Kat, Theresa, Laramie, and Kaylene back to the cabin that Kyle had built for them. I understood what they talked about, even though I could hear no words. I knew Kat was distraught. She was carrying my child. I reached out to her with my mind and, as I had done with Laramie, kept repeating, "I'm here. I love you." Kat calmed. Perhaps I had some effect after all.

Laramie was not only a strong woman, she was a smart woman. What she couldn't figure out, her mother could. They were a formidable pair. I understood their plan. Laramie simply told Kat that Kyle had been working for land and that the 1500 acres next to the Bell ranch would be placed in Kat's name. With that, she was to go see her other suitor and ask him to marry her. It was a bold move, but both Laramie and Theresa were confident that Arthur would overlook the short term of Kat's baby in exchange for the lush ranch she had just inherited. I wondered who the man was and reached back into Kyle's memories that I still carried. Arthur. Kat's other suitor was Arthur Alexander. They would live on the ranch next to the Bell ranch. He would treat Kat's son as his own, even naming him after himself. In a sudden insight, I realized that I had once again become my own great-great-grandfather.

Mary Beth would get a kick out of the fact that I was her great-great-grandfather. Of course, I was dead, so that might put a damper on her sense of humor.

It was close to a week later that Laramie, Kat, and Theresa moved a flat slab of limestone over Kyle's grave. Next to it, they placed a smaller marker and I knew it was to be a memorial to the baby Laramie had lost, though there was no body. The three women and my little daughter, my unborn son in Kat's womb, stood at the grave and Theresa wrote the words in the Bell Family Bible beneath Laramie's name. "Beloved of Kyle Redtail."

They stood in silence as a shadow flicked across the grave and Redtail called my name.

Natural Resources

I AWOKE WITH a cold compress on my forehead, feeling as though my fever was breaking.

"Cole! You're awake. Oh, darling, I was so worried," Ashley said. "Mary Beth!" I heard footsteps in the hall and both Mary Beth and my mother charged into the room. "He's awake."

"Honey, you had us all so worried. How are you feeling?" Mary Beth asked as she snuggled next to me. I was in my own bed with the two women I love most in this life at my side. My mother sat at the foot and placed a hand on my leg.

"It's a fool thing to do going out in the middle of the night and catching your death," Mom said.

"I'm sorry I worried you all," I managed to croak. Mary Beth held a glass of water to my lips and I drank greedily. "How long have I been sick?"

"All night after the funeral, all day today. It's after three now," Mary Beth said.

"Wow. I'm hungry. Can I eat?"

"Sure. Are you strong enough to stand or should we bring you something in bed," Mom asked. I shook my head and tested my limbs.

"I feel fine. Just hungry. I'll come down."

I *was* just fine. I ate and went out to check on the stock. I was really going to have to do something about that soon. We were in the same situation as the rest of the ranchers. No winter feed and over three thousand head, including steers, heifers, and calves, in our pasture. I knew what I was going to have to do. I just wasn't sure I was up to it. I knew for sure, though, that I'd cut off Joe Teini's unending treasure and his access to going back in time. I was sure he hadn't been in Cal Despain when I killed him. Oh, there was still some treasure left in that cave, but it wasn't the billions he thought he'd have.

That night, I cuddled with my cousin and my fiancée in my big bed. There was slow gentle loving aplenty. I held them both and assured them that I was all right. They'd heard the screech of the hawk in the night when I collapsed on Laramie's tomb and knew I'd been taken back in time. They had made themselves my keeper and kept Mom from calling in a doctor. They made up all kinds of stories about how this flu bug was knocking people out in town and I must have picked it up visiting the hospital and it would be best to stay away from there so the illness didn't get worse. They admitted that if I hadn't been awake by the next morning, they'd have had no choice but to call the doctor.

"So, what happened while you were away? You were gone a long time. Is it always going to be like that?" Ashley asked.

"I don't think I'm going back," I said softly. My eyes filled with tears for the loss of my sweet Laramie and my loving Kat. I choked them back.

"Cole, what is it, honey?" Mary Beth asked.

"I'm dead."

I told them about what had happened and about the shoot-out with Cal Despain. I even explained why Despain had to die and the role Joe Teini had in everything. The only thing I didn't tell them was that I'd moved a treasure onto our property and that Laramie had hidden it.

"Wait. Ashley, get the Bible," Mary Beth said. I watched my lover's bare ass as she popped out of bed and ran to my dresser to get the big family Bible. When she returned and I saw her pretty tits and waiting pussy, my cowboy sprang back to life. It hadn't been that long since he'd been buried between those thighs, but I was ready again. Mary Beth felt the movement under the sheets and wrapped her hand around my cock.

"You are way too sexy, girlfriend," Mary Beth said to Ashley. "You've got him all riled again."

"Well here, then," Ashley said. "You hold the Bible and I'll hold the cowboy." Ashley crawled over the top of me and settled down onto my cock. "Now what's in the Bible that you wanted to see? Are you going to marry us here on the spot?" I jerked inside Ashley. "Cole likes that idea. And so do I. Do we have to wait till December to get married, Cole?"

"Sweetheart, I'll marry you right now in this very bed. Mary Beth, tell us the vows."

"I think all I have to do is write it here under your name, cousin. But this is what I wanted to read. 'Laramie Wyoming Bell, born summer of 1873. Beloved of Kyle Redtail, 1889. Mother of Kaylene Redtail Bell. Died December 24, 1929. To the very end she listened for the cry of the redtail hawk.' Cole, are you Kyle Redtail?"

I nodded my head. Ashley sat back on my cock and drove it as deeply into her as she could. She held still.

"Does that mean you are your own great grandfather?" she asked.

"Great-great-grandfather," I said.

"And Laramie... Oh god, Cole. What year did Kyle die?"

"October 1892."

"Poor Laramie. She listened for the call of the redtail hawk for... for thirty-seven years!" There were tears in both Mary Beth's and Ashley's eyes. I'd have wilted if it weren't for the constant pulsing around my cock.

"That's not all," I said. Might as well get this in the open as well. "I'm your great-great-grandfather, too, Mary Beth."

"What? Great-great... Arthur Alexander the first?" Mary Beth knew her family tree a lot better than I knew mine. Of course, there had been three Arthur Alexanders.

"Not exactly. Arthur's wife, Kat Tangeman, was already pregnant with Kyle Wardlaw's baby when she married Arthur."

"You were Kyle Wardlaw, too?"

"Kyle Wardlaw was the body I kept being sent to. When I was there, Laramie called him Kyle Redtail. But when I wasn't there, Kyle Wardlaw fell in love with Kat Tangeman. Unfortunately, I got us killed before they could get married. Arthur agreed to marry her and raise her son as if he was his own in exchange for a strip of 1,500 acres next to Laramie's homestead."

"The Alexander Ranch. It was part of your family's home all along. We are going to put it back together, Cole. This is going to become one ranch again," Mary Beth declared.

"This is so exciting," Ashley squealed. We weren't sure if she was talking about my revelation or the fact that she was now pounding down on my cock. Mary Beth leaned over and caught one of Ashley's nipples in her teeth and Ashley flooded me with her juices as she belted out her orgasm. My juices just pushed more of hers out and down my balls.

"Mmm. I'm going to have another of those before this night is over," Mary Beth said dreamily as she hugged Ashley and me together. We lay in a heap panting together. It was an odd time, but I just thought of something.

"Mary Beth, do you or your dad own an antique gold pocket watch?"

I WASN'T READY to open the box that Laramie had hidden, but there was adequate to save our herds in the stash under the Douglas. The next day we took two ATVs and a picnic lunch and headed up to the high range. I managed to navigate us all the way to the tree without a mishap.

"Laramie/Kyle," Ashley said as she touched the initials carved in the tree. "Why was the brand changed?"

"I don't know," I said as I began to dig under the root. "The Bar-B has been our brand forever, it seems. Hmm. At least for cattle. Laramie started out raising horses. Maybe they changed it when they started on cattle."

"What are we digging for?" Mary Beth asked.

"Buried treasure," I said. "We have a couple ranches to save."

It took about twenty minutes to uncover the box. The tree roots had grown around it. I knew I was damaging the root to get to the box, but it couldn't be helped. And the truth was, there wasn't much of a box there. Pretty stupid burying a wooden box under a tree. Once I hit something solid, I started clearing the dirt off with my hands. Then I started handing the bars of gold to Ashley.

"Is this gold?" Mary Beth asked as Ashley handed them to her one at a time.

"Genuine." I worked at dislodging the bars and handing them out of the hole.

"How many are there?" Ashley asked.

"Count 'em." I said as I came out of the hole with what I thought was the last one. "If there aren't a hundred, I need to keep digging." There were 100 two-pound bricks of gold.

"Cole, how much is this worth?" Mary Beth asked.

"Last I looked it should be around five million."

"Dollars?" Ashley exclaimed.

"I could probably get a figure in Euros if you want."

"She-it!"

"But how do we get rid of it or explain it?" Mary Beth asked again.

"We don't have to. It's gold. Dad got a dealer account set up last year when we sold ten bars."

"So that's how we all managed to pay down the debt and get the extra steers. And now it looks like those extras we bought are going to cost us a fortune if we have to put them down."

"Wait. I get it," Ashley said. I grinned at her and we all sat around the tree to eat our lunch before heading back down the ridge.

"Well, go on," I said. "We took the same class."

"Okay. So, if there was a foreign influence on the open market that suddenly drives the prices down to where all the ranchers are going broke, there'd be an outcry for government subsidy or tariffs on the imported beef. But the Beef Sellers don't want the government to interfere in the open marketplace if it isn't a foreign intervention. They figure the market will support what they want to sell without regulation. But they never anticipate that some circumstance would arise domestically that would deflate prices and threaten the livelihood of all the ranchers in the area."

"That's just what's happened here," Mary Beth said. "There's no winter feed so all the ranchers are going to have to sell off their stock at a loss. We're likely to have a panic and everyone will lose their ranches unless they've got a big enough bankroll to take the loss. And nobody does."

"Nobody but Joe Teini," I said. "Who has been offering to buy up every ranch in the county? The only ranch that's outside his scope is the Boswell Ranch and that's only because it's on the National Register of Historic Places. Eventually he can probably get hold of it, too."

"But all the acreage in the county—that would cost millions."

"Then we need billions to fight it. But our first step is to start subsidizing the local ranchers. We send to Omaha and Chicago for feed. Even

Spokane. Buy up everything we can and have it shipped in. Some of the guys are already paying a premium to get feed from Carbon County and Laramie County, but it's getting short there, too. We pay for the shipping and sell to the ranchers at normal market prices if they'll give us a guaranteed option on their cattle at two dollars a pound live weight in January. If the market goes up, then we've got all the beef in the county for a profit."

"And if the market goes down?" Ashley said. "If Joe Teini can keep the deflated prices going through the winter season? Then we lose everything. It would cost over $30 million to buy all the beef in the county and we've already spent most of our four million on winter feed. Cole, how much more of this do we—I mean do you have?"

"You had it right the first time, sweetheart. It's *we*. The three of us. As to how much, I don't rightly know. I haven't opened the box."

We headed down into the valley and made it back to the ranch just about dark. I got Dad's army footlocker out of the attic and we loaded the gold and took it up to my room. Mom was on the phone when we came downstairs.

"YES, ANGUS. THEY just came in. God knows where they've been all day. It's a good thing we have George. The ranch would fall apart. As it is, I don't know how we'll make it through the winter.— Yes, Mary Beth is here, too.— Sure. Mary Beth, honey, your daddy wants to talk to you." Mom handed the phone off to Mary Beth. We used the radios when we were on the ridge in the summer, but never thought to turn them on for our little afternoon adventure.

"Hi, Daddy.— Really?— Sure. We were going to grab a bite, but…— Okay. Ashley hasn't had Mom's meatloaf yet. We'll be right over."

"You're invited, too, Aunt Sarah. Mom's waiting dinner for us."

We piled all four of us in the front of my truck and drove the half mile to Mary Beth's home. Lily did, indeed, have a delicious meatloaf ready with mashed potatoes, green beans, and thick milky gravy. After dinner, Angus called the three of us into his office while Mom and Lily chatted in the kitchen.

"First of all, Cole, you know how I feel about your dad. I lost my brother when you lost your dad. I get choked up every time I think about it. I also know you got the money for us to pay off our debt last winter, and although it looks bleak again this year, I thank you for it. You need to know I'm going to retire now. I'm ten years older than your dad was and I want to take time with my wife before it's too late."

"Uncle Angus, you're still a young man. What happened to Dad was a freak accident."

"You and I both know that was no accident. I'm scared, Cole. Joe Teini offered to take all our cattle at $1.50 a pound. It wouldn't begin to pay the debt, but the Wyoming Homestead Act would at least save the house and ten acres around it for Mary Beth. You should take his offer, Cole."

"Dad," Mary Beth began. She glanced at me and I nodded to her. However much she wanted to tell her dad was okay with me. He was family. "We're not going to lose the ranch. Cole and I created the partnership and Ashley is joining it. We have both properties on contract for deed from you and Uncle Earl. If you want to call the contract, we'll meet the offer price Joe Teini has made. You and Mom and Aunt Sarah are all taken care of and can live here as long as you want. I plan to live and die on this property or Cole's and you might as well know that I'll be sharing that life with Cole and Ashley."

"Baby girl, Earl and I have known for a long time that you and Cole had something special and we figured you'd find a way to work it out. Ashley, everything I've heard about you tells me you'll be a wonderful daughter-in-law or however you kids want us to refer to you. Earl and I already sold you the ranches on contract. We'd signed an agreement giving over management to Alexander Bell Cattle Company as a surprise for when you came down from the upper range. I don't know where you'll get the money for this, Cole, but your daddy said he knew you had more," Angus said as he leaned back in his chair and bit a plug off his cigar. He chawed a little and then got right back to us.

"I'm worried about that Joe Teini. You kids are going to be targeted by him and he plays rough. Don't tell me your daddy wasn't killed by that Sheriff. He's got bad blood. How does a boy who was raised without a cent to his name go to a big-name Ivy League school out East and come back so rich he can buy anybody out he wants? You kids gotta be careful."

"We'll be careful, Uncle Angus. But pretty soon it's Joe Teini who's going to realize he's the target. I'm not going to let anyone run the ranchers out of Albany County," I said. Angus nodded his head.

"Just be careful. Now, Missy, you asked me this morning about a watch. I reckon this is what you were looking for." He reached in his desk and pulled out a cigar box and opened it. Inside was a simple gold watch with a leather fob. "As far as I'm concerned, it goes with the ranch. Always has. I reckon it's yours now." He handed the watch to Mary Beth. It was plain and didn't look like much. Mary Beth looked at me and I nodded. I was sure that was the watch. The old prospector had shown it to me and Kyle had given it to Kat Tangeman. She reached for the cigar box and put it back in the protective handkerchief it had been wrapped in.

"Thank you, Daddy. I don't know why, but it's important. We'll figure it out."

8
Hunting Treasure

JUST BECAUSE I live out west doesn't mean everything is cowboys and Indians. I was a pretty normal kid, even if I did have more access to horses and had an hour of chores before school each morning. You get a lot of opportunity to play pretend things when you live miles away from everything else. I pretended pirates, explorers, and army, just like most kids.

I guess "pirates" was my favorite. And of course, where there are pirates, there's buried treasure.

I remember the day I dug a hole in the paddock, looking for buried treasure. Dad explained—with his belt—how dangerous it was to dig holes just anyplace I felt like. To make sure I'd learned my lesson, after I filled in the hole and tamped it down so the ground was solid, Dad made me go into the barn and apologize to each horse for creating a danger to them. Lastly, Dad brought me to a stall with a new horse in it. Once I'd apologized to the horse, who stood looking me in the eye the entire time, he made me promise to care for her and keep her safe.

That was my introduction to Buttercup.

It was also my ticket to greater freedom. I couldn't lift a saddle high enough to saddle her by myself, though she'd take the bit from me with no trouble. Then Dad introduced me to the joys of the bareback pad. An inch-thick cloth pad with a cinch. I could toss it onto Buttercup if I was standing on a stool and it didn't have to be cinched as tight as a saddle. I had freedom of the ranch.

Buttercup was about the same age as me and much better trained. I made the mistake one day while riding in the paddock of turning her tightly around at the fence and giving her a nudge with my heels. She took off like a bat outa hell—or a cutting horse after a calf—and left me sitting on my ass on the ground by the fence. It took her about three steps to realize she no longer had a rider and slide to a stiff-legged halt. Then she looked back at me as if she was trying to figure out where the calf was I'd roped and hog-tied.

Well, I learned and Buttercup taught me. She added a new dimension to my treasure hunts. We explored all over the mountain, looking for caves where Spaniards had hidden their gold. Never mind that Spaniards never got to Wyoming.

I've often wondered what would have happened if I'd stumbled on Kyle's treasure cave when I was eight or nine years old. What would I have found? I reckon this would have been a different story.

Gold Watch

WE ALL GOT home from the Alexander's and Mom went on to bed. The three of us went to the office and Mary Beth placed the cigar box on the desk.

"Now, tell us what is so important about this watch," she demanded.

"Before I say anything else, I've been puzzled about something. School started at UW yesterday. I'm on leave for a year. Ashley, when do you have to be back?"

"I'm going to be forward, Cole. I understand waiting till Christmas to marry so our families can all be together if you insist. But I'd rather do it now. In lieu of that, I want to live with you and Mary Beth. I don't think I could bear to be apart from you two anymore. I arranged my classes so they are all on Tuesday, Wednesday, and Thursday. You know I'm a year ahead of you and it wasn't difficult to get the classes I wanted last spring. I guess I was planning ahead. I've missed a couple days of classes, but I can make it up. Can I live with you, baby? Will you two take me to bed with you every night and love me like we've been loving all summer?" My grin liked to bust my face. I couldn't get to her before Mary Beth had her wrapped in a hug. When she got free a little, I kissed her right to the tip of her toes. "I guess that means yes?" she asked.

"It sure does, Ash. I'm worried about you commuting every day, though. Even if it is just three days a week."

"If I need to, I can stay in the sorority house those two nights a week and only commute in on Tuesday and home on Thursday."

"That might be good. I just don't want any more accidents and what we're about to do is going to make somebody really mad."

"Oh my God!" Mary Beth said. I looked at her. "I didn't even ask you if I could move in with you. Ashley, you are so cool. I just assumed that I was by-God going to live here and only thought about how to tell our parents. I never thought to ask you two if it was okay."

"Do you remember the size of my bed, hon?" I asked. "I think Ash and I would get lonely with just the two of us. What do you think, Ashley? Is she in?"

"Damn straight she is." We hugged again and all sat back down on the leather sofa in Dad's—my—our—office.

"Here's the story. I'm not the only one who has been time traveling." I went on to tell how I'd first discovered that someone was traveling back and taking over Cal Despain. He was sending Kyle out to get the treasures and hide them where he could get at them. Then I told about my encounter with the old prospector and that he was a time traveler and warned me about Joe. "I never did figure out who the prospector was, but just before he died he gave me—or Kyle—this watch. When Kat and Kyle first got together he gave her the watch as his pledge because he didn't have a ring. She promised it would be passed down from generation to generation."

"So just before you became my great-great-granddaddy, you gave my great-great-granny this watch. But what are you supposed to do with it now that you found it?" Mary Beth asked.

"I don't know. Joe Teini was after the prospector's treasure. Joe told Kyle to only bring the map the first time we went out. I think that sometime in the past year or so Joe went to get the old man's hoard of treasure and found nothing there. It's the old Schrödinger's Cat thing. Once he opened the box, the cat was either dead or alive. In this instance, it was dead. The treasure he expected was gone. So, the next time he came back, he sent Kyle out to get it and store it with the others. He didn't expect Kyle to walk in and toss a sack of gold and jewels on Cal's desk when Joe wasn't in control. I don't think Cal was ever supposed to know the extent of the treasure Kyle was stacking up for Joe."

"So, without Joe there to control him, Cal went to see the treasure and found Kyle stealing it?" Ashley asked.

"Pretty much."

"So, where did all the treasure go?"

"Laramie followed Kyle's instructions on where and how to hide it. She probably took some to survive the depression in '96 and the range wars. I'm guessing the rest is still there waiting for us, but until we open the box we won't know for sure if the cat is dead or alive."

"And back to the watch." Mary Beth prompted.

"I think in some way or another it is the map to the old prospector's real treasure. He wanted me to have everything I needed to fight Joe Teini. Let's take a look." I unwrapped the watch. It was more than 100 years old, I knew. I didn't know how long the old man had had it before he gave it to me. It was a plain gold watch on a leather fob. I suppose that even if someone had seen it on the prospector's body they would have simply pocketed it and still said "Nothing of value." I opened it. It wasn't running, but it was clean. There was engraving on the inside of the case.

"I need a magnifying glass and better light to see this," I said. I turned on the desk lamp and grabbed Dad's magnifying glass. "Phile. Morgan, Esq. Salem, Oregon." I looked some more. "I don't see anything else."

"What about taking off the back. They do that to clean them and replace the crystal," Ashley said.

"The case is solid. I don't see how to open it and get at the works. Maybe we'll have to take it to a jeweler."

"There should be a ring that twists inside the frame that will release the crystal. Try turning the crystal." I did and a ring popped out. So did the crystal, which I barely caught. When I turned over the watch, the face and works fell into my hand. We all looked at the inside, but there were no further messages.

"I guess that's it. Now we have a pocket watch in pieces."

"My hands are smaller. Let me try to put it back together again." Ashley took the pieces from me and deftly replaced them. "All better." The watch was actually running.

"But we still don't have a clue," Mary Beth said. We all sat there and finally wrapped the watch up and decided to go to bed. I looked at the stack of mail on the desk that I hadn't dealt with yet. One piece caught my eye. A statement from American Gold and Silver Exchange regarding the account Dad opened last year. I smiled. The address was in Salem, Oregon.

ASHLEY AND MARY BETH were lying naked on my bed when I walked into the room. They were holding each other, not particularly sexily but like two best friends who just loved to be in contact. They looked askance at me, still fully dressed.

"It seems I'm overdressed for this party," I said.

"Why aren't you in bed?"

"I called directory assistance on a whim," I said. "Morgan, Morgan, and Morgan is the oldest law firm in the city. Founded in 1872 by Philemon Morgan, Esq."

"Philemon Morgan?" Mary Beth said.

"The apparent original owner of your watch. I'm going to go to Salem Monday. I think you should come with me, Mary Beth. It is your watch, after all. I'm sorry, Ashley. I know you have to be in school on Tuesday."

"No. You're right. But with both of you gone, that's going to leave a hole in ranch management. I will come back here each night next week. We'd better let George and Harold know what's going on so they know they can come to me and keep me informed."

"I love you," I said. I stripped off my clothes and crawled over Ashley to lie between her and Mary Beth where they made room for me. My lovers came to me and our lips came together. I think a kiss is the most sensual thing in the universe. I've kissed a few women. Certainly, Laramie learned kissing quickly and loved it. Kat was an enthusiastic kisser. Geneive and Izzy were frantic and insatiable kissers—all tongue and open mouths. But encountering the combined lips of Ashley and Mary Beth—all of us touching and freezing, not knowing what to do, but unwilling to let the electric tingle through our senses dissipate—was the most sensual encounter I'd ever experienced. We were truly one being and when a tongue tentatively passed across my lips, I was lost in wonderment. We joined in the kiss together, unwilling to move any other part of our bodies, lest the magic of that first touch be lost. We each explored the other two—touching, tasting, receiving. And as we breathed the same air, there was moisture on each of our cheeks. The love we three had together was greater than that of any two of us. I was flooded and overflowing with affection.

I WAS TWENTY years old, a college drop-out, co-owner and manager of over six thousand acres. I had a fiancée, a cousin girlfriend, a widowed mom, and panicked Uncle. Out there someplace there was a greedy bastard who was trying to drive all the ranchers in the county into bankruptcy. And more and more, people were looking to me to save them.

We always used to say you tell a pioneer by the arrows in his back. Yeah, I know that's racist and I only bring it up because you can tell a savior by the nails in his hands. I wasn't looking forward to the kind of pressure that was building.

Joe Teini had the advantage. He had a four-year head-start on owning the county—and my former girlfriend. He had public office and had shut down the investigation into my Dad's death before he was dead. He'd already acquired a huge spread in the north county and was running thousands of cattle. For all he spoke up at the co-op meeting complaining about feed supplies, the rumors said the shortage was because he'd bought everything that came into the county. All ranchers had was the hay they raised on their own lands.

Every Friday we saw a drop in the price of beef on the hoof as a thousand to five thousand head were put on the market for a nickel less than the previous price. You might think a nickel isn't much, but every time a thousand head went on the market, it represented a loss of another $50,000. I had no proof, but it seemed that if no other rancher stepped up to sell undervalued beef, Joe Teini did.

People were another problem. I had good loyal ranch hands, my cousin-lover, and my fiancée. Joe had the entire Albany County Sheriff's Department, at least fifty ranch hands and an office full of bean-counters and lawyers. I couldn't see how we could match that and just hoped the old prospector, or whoever it was that time traveled back to him, had a plan and that I'd find out in Salem. We were going to need a lot more than the gold in that trunk to fight what was happening.

MONDAY MORNING, I secured the trunk of gold in the back of Dad's Explorer and Mary Beth and I headed for Oregon. I remember clearly taking this trip in 1891 with a mule and a horse, crossing through mountains that were already filling with snow. This time we hit I-80 west to I-84 and northwest to I-5 then south to Salem. It was eleven hundred miles at seventy to eighty miles an hour. We made the trip in two days and booked into a hotel in Salem so we'd be ready for tomorrow. I decided I really wanted to get rid of the gold as quickly as possible, so we set up an appointment at the Exchange at nine in the morning.

Dad set up the original account with me as a joint owner with right of survivorship, so all I had to do was show my I.D. and Dad's death certificate and the account was mine. There was about $25,000 dollars left in it from the bail-out last winter. Mr. Jenkins, the broker, looked at the gold bars and was very pleased.

"Are these from the same manufacture as the last batch your father brought in?" he asked.

"The same period of time, but there may be differences in the composition. I assume you will do an assay?" I asked.

"Yes, of course, but based on what we have here, I'm sure we can transfer at least 50% of the estimated value into your account immediately. It will take several days to assay all one hundred bars. We will mark the price as of right now." He turned to his computer. "The price at this mark is $1,770.40 per troy ounce. There are 14.5833 troy ounces per pound and the scale shows a generous 2925 troy ounces. A little more than 200 pounds. That is $5,178,420. Less our commission of 15%, your projected net is $4,401,657.00. It is likely that like the previous batch your father brought us, this will not assay at 99.999 fine. Nonetheless, why don't we advance $1.5 million into your account for immediate use and the balance after the assay is completed?"

"That will be fine, Mr. Jenkins. Do I need to transfer funds to my local bank in order to use the money or can I make purchases directly from my American Exchange account?" I asked.

"We are not a bank, per se, so you cannot write checks on this account. However, if you are making a purchase of more than $250,000, we can make a wire transfer directly to the party."

"That's good to know. There is one other question. How much gold can you handle?"

"My God! You have more?"

"It seems my great-great-grandfather was a bit of a miser." I thought Mary Beth would choke.

"We have a market capitalization of $8.4 billion. There is always a market for gold. Transportation of significant quantities is always of concern. I would suggest you hire an armored truck for the purpose rather than carrying more in your suitcase."

"Thank you, Mr. Jenkins." I took the receipt that he filled out along with the account balances. I added Mary Beth as a signer on the account. Joint tenants with right of survivorship just as Dad had originally set up the account with me. I didn't want the account going through probate or to be held in limbo if anything should happen to one of us. We would get Ashley's signature added to the account on the next trip through.

WE LEFT THE building and turned up the street. I'd made an appointment to see the youngest of the partners at Morgan, Morgan, and Morgan. I'd said merely that I wanted to discuss a matter regarding a historic watch engraved with Philemon Morgan's name. I had thought about making all kinds of excuses to see someone at the law firm, but it seemed best to come right to the point.

When I announced my presence to the receptionist, I expected to be kept waiting an hour or two. I was surprised when she picked up her phone, said, "Mr. Morgan your eleven o'clock is here," and then stood to escort us directly to a large office where a man about twice my age by my guess hurried around his desk to greet me.

"Welcome, Mr. Bell, Ms. Alexander. I'm Phil Morgan. No, we ran out of numbers at 'the third' and my name is Phillip, not Philemon." He was a pleasant man with a balding head but not too wrinkled. Instead of sitting behind his desk, he led us to a conference table where a soft cloth and a jeweler's loupe were laid out. "I understand you have a watch that may have historical value," he said. "May I see it?" He wasn't big on small talk. That's okay. I wasn't either. Mary Beth handed over the cigar box. He opened it and unwrapped the watch, fastening the loupe in his eye and examining the case. He opened the cover and read the inscription. We just waited. When it looked like he'd examined as much as we had, he looked up at us. "How did you come to have this watch Miss Alexander?"

"It has been passed down through my family from my great-great-grandfather. Several things have happened lately that made my father decide to pass it on to me now rather than will it to me when he dies." Nicely put. I was getting the feeling, though that Mr. Morgan really didn't know all that much about it.

"And you, Mr. Bell? What is your interest in this bit of history?"

"That's rather complicated, Mr. Morgan. Perhaps we should go now, unless there is actually someone here who knows about this watch." Phil Morgan stood up and for a moment I thought we were being dismissed. He went to a side door in his office and opened it.

"Grandpa? I think this is what you wanted to see. It's real." An old man, using a cane but walking erect and proud entered the room. He dismissed his grandson who left through the same door.

"Well, you've finally made it. I've been waiting a long time for this," the old man said. "Miss Alexander? May I ask you precisely who gave this watch to your family as a family inheritance?" He apparently had been listening in on our conversation. Mary Beth glanced at me and I nodded. I'd already recognized the old man.

"My great-great-grandmother, Kat Tangeman, gave it to her son, Arthur Alexander Junior. Kat received it from Arthur Junior's real father, her lover Kyle Wardlaw."

"It's nice to see you again, Kyle," he said turning to me.

"In this life, it's Cole, sir. It's nice to see you, too."

"Phile," he answered. "The third. And how did you happen to find Miss Alexander?"

"We're first cousins and next-door neighbors. It turns out that Kyle is both of our great-great-grandfathers, in two lines."

"You were busy back then, weren't you?" We all laughed.

"Kyle was kind of a randy kid, especially when I wasn't around."

"And how goes the challenge of this guy Joe? Are you in the fight now? I never learned his last name and I withheld mine just like I did with you. It was a real shock to die, though, and then come back to life sitting in my office."

"How long ago was that, if I may ask?"

"Sure. It's been close to twenty years now."

"Hmm. For me it was just last summer. I've figured out who Joe is.

He seems to have unlimited wealth and is trying to buy out or drive out all the ranchers in our county."

"Why would he do that?"

"I don't think he's figured out who I am yet specifically, but in general he knows Kyle cheated him."

"Certainly not that sack of gold I sent him after!"

"No sir. I decided that Joe Teini shouldn't really have all the wealth he'd amassed out in his secret cave. So, I went and stole it and hid it where I could find it in this life on my property."

"You did that? And is it there?"

"I haven't opened that box yet, sir. But I'm pretty sure Joe thinks the treasure is somewhere in western Albany County. He's just trying to acquire all the land so no one can claim he took something of theirs."

"He was always looking for treasure. He thought getting it was the point. When I realized what he was doing, I came back here to Salem as Bill Campbell and set things up with the man who would become my grandfather, Philemon Morgan. You see the big problem has never been accumulating wealth. There was so much gold and jewels being mislaid in the 1800s that it would have made the entire country wealthy. And yes, I acquired far more than that bag of double-eagles I left for him. The problem has always been how to transfer the wealth from one time period to another. Have you done any of that?"

"I've moved some gold bullion into cash using the company that is here in town. Oh. And I'd guess that Joe never got the bag of coins and jewels you left for him. Kyle dumped it on Cal's desk when Joe wasn't in control. Cal had it in his saddlebags when he came out to see the rest of the treasure and killed Kyle. And got killed. Laramie tossed his saddlebags into the wagon with the rest of the treasure."

"Very good. It is much harder to move coins. Oh, it's easy if you just have a few. But if you have a thousand or ten thousand or a hundred thousand, it is almost impossible to do. So, as I was saying, as Bill Campbell, an old prospector, I went to my grandfather, Philemon Morgan, Esquire. I presented a memorial watch to my grandfather inscribed with his name. This one." Phile pulled a gold watch from his pocket that looked exactly like the one on the table. He opened it and laid them side by side. They were identical. "I told him that I'd made one myself and I wanted him to keep my wealth and pass it on to my heir who would walk in the door with the match to this watch. My grandfather thought the request was a little foolhardy but he was an honest man. When I told him that if the money and gold and jewels I left with him had not been claimed by the time of his grandson's death, then it was to be converted to a philanthropic foundation. There was already a good example of that with Carnegie building libraries. I knew already that I would own the watch and that we would be managing a great deal of money. I simply didn't know where it came from."

"So why didn't you just use the money yourself? You didn't need to fix it so that I could come for it," I said.

"Oh, we've certainly used some of the money for philanthropy, but after meeting Joe, my objective was always to save the bulk for the battle to come. Besides which, I already knew that in this life I was as well-off and as happy as a man had any right to be. And I could set up the foundation the way I wanted to before I died. But when I met Joe and saw what kind of man he was, I determined that the wealth I had gained would be used to stop him. Is that what you intend to do, Cole?"

"Yessir, it is."

"Then we have the resources to help you."

The old man went to a safe in the wall behind his desk. He opened it and extracted a large envelope. He emptied the contents on the table. It was mostly pages of account numbers in the name of Gold Watch Corporation. This corporation had vast holdings. I recognized accounts at the same gold exchange where I had mine, but also bank accounts in the U.S. and around the world. There were keys and deeds to a dozen properties from Washington to Florida.

"Gold Watch Corporation is managed by a blind trust on behalf of its anonymous owner. The reality is that the owner can be named the trustee. Not only that; the actual resources of the trust are not public knowledge. Therefore, as soon as I file the papers naming you as the trustee, you will have all these resources at your fingertips. You will need to be cautious as to how you handle it, but you should have enough to save every ranch in your county and make sure it is safe for the future. You can transfer your own wealth, even your ranch into the trust and not be exposed for the fortune you have."

"I don't know what to say. I'm overwhelmed. What about taxes?"

"The corporation pays capital gains taxes on investments in the United States. Since the corporation owns it all and you are merely the trustee, you have only the direct income that you wish to draw for your personal expenses. I think that, like me, you are not the kind of man that will need millions for your personal benefit. You will direct the Corporation in its good works."

"I still don't understand why you didn't just do this all yourself?" I asked. "With the extra time you've had building this fortune, you could have put a stop to it all before Joe Teini got a handle on it."

"It's the limits of time travel," Mr. Morgan said. "I had a first name, but when Bill died and I stopped traveling, I didn't even know *when* this Joe lived. You might not believe this, but that was nearly twenty years ago. You were just a toddler and this Joe Teini had never been heard of. By interacting with the two of you, I was getting a glimpse of the future, but it was incomplete. I couldn't directly manipulate it. I really didn't know who or where or when it was. It was a gamble on my part to assume you'd get here before I died, but I thought you were probably a contemporary of mine. I had no idea I was dealing with the future. But you want to do good with this money. I could see that when I looked into your eyes back in 1891."

"Yessir, that I will. I'm starting by ordering winter feed for 100,000 head of cattle and supporting the price of beef on the hoof through the winter. In the spring, we'll see if Joe Teini can still make a grab for the Albany County land."

"Just be careful, Cole. Have Phil make the arrangements through the trust. No one will know you are behind it. Phil is a good attorney and I've taught him as well as I can to be trustful for this event. This Joe Teini has already shown himself to be ruthless. Don't let him catch you unawares."

THE PAPERWORK TOOK most of the afternoon. Phile called Phil back in and gave him instructions on what was to be done then wished us luck and left.

"I'm eighty-nine years old," Phile said. "I think it's time I retired."

Phil proved easy to work with. Mary Beth and I spent the entire afternoon with him explaining what we wanted to do. We set up the new board of directors and officers of the corporation as Mary Beth, Ashley, and me.

I had to call Ashley to get her Social Security number, but it didn't require a signature. Phil would continue to act as administrator, administering the funds according to our directions. I had the impression that Phile III had been training Phil for this job from the time he was born. He knew the purpose of the trust and the corporation and he intended to administer it according to the way his grandfather wanted. We sent orders to Omaha, Chicago and Spokane for winter feed and hay to be delivered at a critical time. Even Billings had hay we could ship in. Phil would send in a team to negotiate with the ranchers quietly. There would be no trainload of feed dumping at the co-op nor a caravan of trucks carting hay. It would come in a little at a time from different directions. I would be kept out of all the transactions and it would look like I was taking deals the same as any other rancher in the county. I liked doing business this way.

On Thursday, Mary Beth and I headed back toward Wyoming. We got an early start, but even switching off drivers every couple of hours, six hundred miles a day is a lot of ground to cover. We were southeast of Boise, figuring we could make Twin Falls before we had to pull over for the night. It had been a beautiful late-fall day and we rolled down the windows to let the air flow in and keep us alert. That creates a hell of a wind at eighty miles an hour, but we were happy about the prospects. We'd been talking all day about what else we could do with the money we had access to after the current crisis was resolved.

Over the whistling air currents, with my hands still on the wheel, I heard Redtail's call.

Traveling: The Bridge

I KNEW WHAT was happening, but it was an odd feeling. Always before when I'd made this transfer, it was into the living body of Kyle Wardlaw. This time there were no eyes, no ears, and no cock plunging into my lover. I kind of missed that. Instead, I was in a disembodied state in which I could feel what was happening around me, but I couldn't actually hear or see anything. I'd learned something the last time I was here when Kyle died, though. I could use my meditative state to visualize what was going on around me. If I relaxed myself enough, it all became a real world and I could see in my mind's eye exactly what was going on.

Hearing was different. It was like listening to that little voice in your head. If you are asking yourself, 'what little voice?' that's it. I've never known anyone who didn't talk to himself in his head. Listening to what was going on around me was like that.

"Kyle?" Laramie's head came up and she looked around the room. Her heart was beating faster. She'd heard the hawk and knew… just *knew* that I was there. I didn't know how to communicate with her, so I just kept thinking in my mind over and over, "I'm here. I love you." Laramie relaxed and I could feel her smile. I extended my awareness and found my daughter, Kaylene. My God! She was fourteen years old and what a beauty! I just wrapped my love around her and repeated again, "I'm here. I love you."

"Papa?" How could she know? She was three years old when I was killed. The last time she'd seen me alive was the first time she ran to me and said "Papa." My last memory was of her standing over my grave crying. All I could think was, "I'm here. I love you." Kaylene beamed her joy and I stretched myself to feel what had called me to them at this time.

"Redtail? Is that you?" Theresa's ragged voice spoke. I found her and settled my love around her. "Have you come to show me the way?"

"I'm here, great-great-great grandmother. I'm here and I love you."

"So that's where you came from. Show me, grandson. Show me what it will be like in that long time."

I thought about everything I could. My life, our ranch, my beautiful cousin who looks so much like Laramie. My fiancée who looks like the neighbor, Kat Tangeman Alexander. I didn't hold back and told her of the death of my Dad and all the problems we were having. And then I told her how we were fixing them. We rode in cars and even on an airplane, but I showed her how I still loved to be on a horse. When I'd shown her everything I could, I whispered, "I love you, grandma. I'm here and I love you."

When I finished, she sighed. "It will be all right," she whispered. "The story, grandson, is all in the Bible. Finish the story so we all rest in peace."

"Mama?" Laramie said. She moved to Theresa's bedside.

"It will all be just fine," Theresa said. "You are doing good, Laramie. Kaylene, you're doing good. It will all be fine. I've seen it, and I'm happy." She sighed again and her soul slipped from her body. For an instant, I was standing in front of my mother-in-law/great-great-great-grandmother. She was young and beautiful like an eighteen-year-old princess. A hand reached out and White Horse guided her on. Then she was gone. In my mind, there was a whisper. "Marry her, grandson. Marry the girl soon."

I was a little surprised that the hawk didn't call me back that moment. Laramie and Kaylene bent over Theresa's body, both of them shedding a few tears, though they'd known for some time that this illness would take her from them. I thought of myself wrapping my arms around them and just telling them again, "I'm here. I love you."

"Thank you, Kyle. Tell mama we love her," Laramie whispered.

"I love you, Papa. I love you, Grandma," Kaylene said. They set to work preparing Theresa's body for the burial they would have tomorrow. Kaylene left the room to tell the hands that Theresa had passed and to send word to the neighbors.

The house was quiet. House. I realized this wasn't the cabin Kyle built a dozen years ago. This was a frame farmhouse. I was pleased. Laramie and Theresa had done well and after the five years on their homestead had expired, they had a house built down nearer the lush pastures and bottomland. It was the same house I'd grown up in though it had only one floor.

I hovered near my wife and daughter the rest of the evening. They ate a quiet meal. Occasionally they would look at each other and smile. They'd had an exhausting couple of days, though and soon Kaylene said she was ready for bed.

"Good night, daughter," Laramie said as Kaylene headed to bed.

"Good night, Mama," she said then whispered, "Good night, Papa."

"Good night little love," I whispered in my head. "Sweet dreams."

Laramie sat at the table for a while longer, just letting me hold her in my mind. She was sleeping peacefully in my arms in my mind. Was this all just imagination, run away with me? Would I awaken the next time in a hospital where they put people who spoke gibberish? I didn't care. I was back with my love. She might be my great-great-grandmother, but she was still my love. I nudged her and suggested she go to bed. She nodded sleepily and went toward the back of the house to her own bedroom.

Once finished in the bathroom—she still marveled at her indoor plumbing—she stood for a moment at the foot of her bed. It was not large—certainly not by my standards. Slowly, my wife deliberately undressed. She wore the conventional clothes of a ranch woman instead of the buckskins she'd grown up in. She'd complained once about all the underwear women had to wear. But she removed each article of clothing and folded it carefully before laying it aside. All the time she kept looking at the bed. When she was fully naked she faced the bed and just stood there.

"Do you still love me, husband?" she whispered. "Do you still like my naked body? Would you still touch my skin and my secret places? Would you kiss my lips?" She approached the bed. She was beautiful. Still a woman of only thirty years, she was kept thin by the work she did. No other babies had suckled her breast nor stretched her womb. No other hands had touched her body. I met her before she reached the bed and caressed her lips with my own. I remembered so well the taste of those lips. She held me in her arms and we fell to the bed, holding, kissing her naked body.

I held the picture of her in my mind as I caressed her beautiful breasts and sucked my lips against her nipples. I thought of her earthy rich scent when we made love in the wilderness, or in the roofless cabin with the stars above. The sound of her breathing as her arousal sped it up and the thud of her heartbeat against my cheek. Her body so hard from life in the wilderness, but her skin so soft beneath my fingers. And then as I reached her center, the gasp of pleasure as I touched her sex. I listened to her as she rose to her peak and shrieked her climax to the sky.

And then there were tears as she continued to shudder through after-shocks and I held her in my arms and thought how much I love this amazing woman.

"I try, Kyle. I try so hard to do the right things. But with you gone and with Mama gone, how will I survive? Kaylene still needs me. But, my love, not a day goes by that I don't want to crawl into the dirt beside you. Help me, Kyle. Help me be the mother I should be, like my mother was. Help me be strong and run the ranch the way we wanted to together. I love you. Every night I lie awake and call your name. Do you hear me, Kyle? Do you ever hear me calling?"

"Laramie," I thought to that voice in my mind. "My love for all times, I think about you every day. I come to the place where you will lie beside me and I still weep. You are strong, my love and I will always hear you when you call. Even when I cannot answer, know that I am near you and I will help you."

It was the best I could do. She slept, her skin still tingling from the sensations of my touch.

THE FIRST TO arrive to help in the morning was Kat Alexander. She still looked so much like Ashley that it threw me, though since I only had the feel of her and not an actual visual, I could have been superimposing Ashley on her. She just looked a little older and more mature. She'd had a daughter with Arthur who was just three years old and hanging onto her mother's skirt. Her son, eleven-year-old Arthur junior had driven the wagon and was outside "with the hands."

I wanted to go to her and hold her, but I hadn't been Kyle Redtail when I was with her. I'd been Kyle Wardlaw. I wasn't sure if it would be the same, though I could feel the warmth of Kyle's memories mixed with my own and with my feelings for Ashley. I brushed her cheek and she looked around, lifting her hand to her face curiously. More women arrived and set about the task of preparing a large meal. Theresa had become a fixture of the rural community and was well-known in the town of Centennial. The preacher arrived just before noon and the rest of the men-folk followed soon thereafter. The hands had constructed a simple casket and Theresa's body had been moved into the sitting room where the service was held and the men carried the casket up the hill to the open grave. It was at my head, just where I knew it was when I buried Dad.

The graveside service was blessedly brief after the sermon the reverend preached in the sitting room. The men were hungry and anxious to get back to work. The women would sit with the family for a while after dinner. Laramie and Kaylene were escorted back to the house after she whispered, "I'll be back." Kat held her son by the hand, preventing him from joining the others.

"Mother…"

"In a minute, Artie." When the others were out of range, Kat continued. "You see these two stones? That one on the left is just a marker for the baby that Aunt Laramie lost when we were living in the same boarding house. This other one, though… There's a man buried there.

He was a good man who loved with his whole heart. And he died long before his time. If things had been different, Artie, he would have been your daddy and he would have been so proud of what a fine young man you are. And I believe he's happy that Art Senior is your father. But there's something that he would have wanted you to have and I'm going to give it to you. This isn't to carry around with you or to show to your friends. You take this and keep it for your son or daughter that takes over the ranch from you like you will from your father." She pulled the gold watch out of her handkerchief. "I wanted to give this to you here, but I'll keep it safe for you so you can go join the menfolk for dinner. When you think of this watch, Artie, think of the man that lies beneath this stone."

"What was his name, Mama?"

"That don't really make a difference now, does it? He'll know if you think of him."

I wrapped myself around the two of them in my mind. I had no idea if this would work, but Artie was as much my son as Kaylene was my daughter. I just stretched my mind around the two of them and thought, "I'm here and I love you. And I'm very proud of you." I repeated myself until I was exhausted, though it seemed to only take a moment.

"What was that, Mama?" Artie asked. Kat had tears streaming down her cheeks.

"That was a wonderful message, Artie. Hold it in your heart for as long as you live. I will."

I knew it was coming. I wanted so much to spend just one more night with Laramie in my arms. *Oh, please don't call me now!* That hawk screeched and all I could do was whisper again, "I love you."

Proposal

I SNAPPED INTO myself with the Explorer idling beside the highway. Mary Beth was sprawled half over me with her hands on the steering wheel and her foot on the brake. She had her hand between her legs and it took me a minute to realize she was shifting into Park. I shook my head a little to clear the call of the hawk out of my ears.

"Mary Beth. Darling, I'm here."

"Oh God! Cole, you scared me. One minute we were talking and the next you just weren't there. I thought you weren't going back there anymore." Mary Beth started crying and beating on my chest with one hand while she hugged me with the other. I patted her back to comfort her, but there was no time to explain. Flashing lights were pulling in behind me. Mary Beth pulled herself into her own seat, and I got my license and registration out. The windows were open, so the officer came to the passenger side. It was dusk and he shone a flashlight quickly through the window as he approached. As soon as he reached the window, I held out my license and registration with my other hand on the steering wheel.

"Thank you. Are you folks okay? I saw you swerve to the shoulder and stop. Ma'am, are you in danger?" He hadn't taken my license and I realized he had one hand on his gun.

"I'm fine officer. We just had a scare. Did you see that deer?"

"Deer, ma'am? No. I reckon I was too far back to see that. Is that why you jerked to the side?"

"Yes, officer," I said. "It came out of nowhere and I thought we were going to hit it. We just missed."

"Well, you are lucky. You have insurance?"

"Yessir. May I reach to the glovebox?" He agreed and kept the flashlight trained on my hand as I opened the glovebox and pulled out the insurance card. Dad was always meticulous about keeping every vehicle updated and the cards where they belonged. I should have pulled that out when I got the registration, but I'd forgotten. He looked at the registration, insurance card, and my license.

"This vehicle is registered to Earl Bell. Your license says Cole Bell."

"Yessir. It's my dad's car. He passed away this week and I haven't had time to re-register it."

"Would you step out of the car, son? Come to the back so I can talk to you."

I got out of the car and walked around the back with my hands held out at my side. I didn't want him to have any chance to think I was armed. When we met, he shone the light directly into my eyes. I flinched a little, but I knew he was looking for signs of drugs.

"There wasn't any deer back there, was there, son?"

"No sir," I said meekly. "I fell asleep at the wheel. We've been driving all day to get back home."

"Well you aren't going farther tonight. Your girlfriend drive?"

"Yessir."

"Put her behind the wheel. There's a cheap motel at the next exit. Get off the freeway and go to sleep. I know what kind of stress a death in the family puts on people. Don't make it two. Do you understand me?"

"Yessir." He handed me back my license and papers and motioned me to the passenger side. I opened the door and Mary Beth went around to drive while the officer watched the exchange.

I breathed deeply and leaned back in the seat as Mary Beth signaled and we got back underway. We took the next exit and found the cheap motel. At least it was a national brand and had clean towels. If we'd made it into Twin Falls, I might have sprung for a place that was a little nicer. Mary Beth and I fell into each other's arms and flopped on the bed.

"Don't scare me like that again," Mary Beth said after she'd kissed me soundly. "Now get Ashley on the phone and tell us what happened this time."

I called Ashley, but it took a while before we got around to my trip back in time.

"Someone has been following me," she said as soon as I had her on the line. "Cole, I'm scared.

"Where are you now?" I asked. I was ready to get back in the car and get to her yet tonight.

"I'm home. Uh… your place. Our place. There was this creepy guy on campus that seemed to be near me a dozen times today. I reported him to campus security because he didn't look like he was a student. Apparently, half a dozen other girls have noticed him, too. Campus has all kinds of security alerts out and the frat guys are escorting any woman who is out after dark. I had an escort from your AGR take me to my car after class this afternoon. But I noticed a car following me as I pulled out onto 130. I thought I'd seen it behind me a few times but he followed me right through Centennial and out toward the ranch. When I turned into the drive he cut a donut in the middle of the road and sped back toward town."

"Did you get a license number or description of the car?"

"It was a dark sedan. I couldn't see the make or license. Should I call the sheriff?"

"Don't bother," I said. "We know what he'd say. Probably something like you shouldn't dress so provocatively."

"I'm wearing jeans and a work shirt!"

"'See, that's what I mean,' says Sheriff Teini," I said. That got us to loosen up a little. "Sugar, how soon can you get your parents to Laramie so we can get married?" I asked. "Or do you want me and Mary Beth to fly to Glenwood Springs so you can have a bigger wedding?"

"Married! When are we getting married?" she squeaked. Mary Beth was looking at me with her eyes wide open.

"As soon as you say yes and set a date. I'm free starting tomorrow night when I get home."

"Then I'm buying a wedding dress and calling Mom. We'll have the ceremony right here at the house where I plan to live with my husband and my... wife. And Mary Beth, you better fuck him good tonight because tomorrow night I'm going to wear him down to a stub!"

That lightened all our moods a little and Mary Beth told Ashley about my episode on the highway and why we were in a no-tell motel in Mountain Home.

"So, what was the trip?" Ashley asked.

I told them about the whole experience and being able to be there like it was all in my mind but I wasn't really seeing or hearing anything. I didn't go into detail about making love to Laramie, but I figured that wasn't as important to them as my seeing Kat give the watch to her son.

"The strange thing is that just as Theresa was leaving her body, I saw White Horse taking her hand to lead her away. That was so peaceful and comforting. But I heard this voice as clear as it could be saying, 'Marry her, grandson. Marry the girl soon.' There's only one girl that could apply to."

"So, you want to marry me just because your grandma said to?" Ashley asked. I could hear the pout over the phone.

"No, sweetheart. I want to marry you because I love you. I want to marry you *soon* because grandma said to. At least sooner than what we kind of planned."

"You know you haven't really even asked me."

"And I'm not going to over the phone. You set the date and get your parents here. I'll take care of the rest when I see you." We had a fair amount of kissy noises and I love yous before we finally said goodbye. By then, Mary Beth and I were naked and I was betting Ashley was, too. When we finally disconnected, MB did her best to make sure there was nothing but a stub left when we got home to Ashley.

I HADN'T EXPECTED to ever go back again, but now that I had, I was pissed. It had been almost twelve years on their timeline, even though for me it was only a week. I felt so crappy Laramie had been waiting for me all that time and I'd just shown up in time for her mother to die. And Kaylene was fourteen! I hadn't been there for any of it. My son, Artie, had just turned eleven. I'd gone from visiting every few months to years between visits and that just plain depressed me.

I guess that's about when I started dreaming again like I had a couple summers ago. First, let me tell you that I know the difference between what I'd experienced and a dream. Dreams are a little bizarre. You skip from one thing to another and sometimes repeat them. Sometimes you can identify bits or pieces as triggered by specific memories. And people get transposed in dreams. I could be dreaming about Laramie one second and she'd turn into Mary Beth the next second. Dreams are like that. They don't have a continuous storyline or timeline. At least mine don't. This was like what they call *lucid* dreaming. Every detail was crystal clear and I remembered it all, even when it was disjointed.

There were moments when I actually felt like I was in Laramie's arms and I could feel her breath on my cheek. Sometimes I'd wake up and still feel the warmth of that breath and realize that it was Mary Beth or Ashley snuggled up to me. And once or twice when I woke up, I was sure I heard her whisper, "Kyle," as she lay asleep on my shoulder. The result was that even though I was feeling rested when I got up in the morning, I was spending more time with Laramie, Kaylene, and even Kat in my sleep than ever before.

Do you call that wish-fulfillment? Was I just assuaging my guilt for not being there by pretending that I was?

Damn! It drives me crazy.

9
Engaging the Enemy

SOMETIMES I think I'd give anything for a normal life. You know. One where I grew up, married my high school sweetheart, lived on the ranch inherited from my father, and raised half a dozen kids who gave me grandkids before I was too old to recognize them. At the same time, I would never trade my life with Laramie, the love I experienced with Kat, my cousin's passion and commitment, or the unbelievable young woman who consented to be my bride.

You know, when I got home I found out more about her stalker on campus. That sweet woman had taken a flower to Caitlin's grave for me. She'd done that because she knew how much it meant to me to remember that sixteen-year-old whore who died in 1890. It might have been my baby she was aborting. Well, Kyle's. We were given to understand that she was already pregnant the first time I rode along. But she was a sweet girl who genuinely cared for Kyle, and I believe he had deep feelings for her. To think that Ashley had put herself in danger to make my remembrance to Caitlin for me! How can you ever love someone enough when she shows that kind of compassion?

I can honestly say I gave my heart to Ashley. And I'm glad we got married when we did.

Wedded

EVERYTHING HAPPENED THE last weekend of September. Saturday after we got home from Salem, I took Ashley into town and we chose a simple wedding set. As soon as the clerk handed me the box, I got down on my knee.

"Ashley Kay Brewer, I love you. You are the woman I want to spend my life with. Will you marry me?"

"Cole!" She grinned and cried at the same time. "Yes. Oh God, yes!" I slipped the engagement ring on her finger. There was a bit of applause from the jewelers. When we left the store, Ashley led me down the street to another store. She pointed out another simple wedding set and I bought that one, too. The jeweler could clearly see the ring on Ashley's hand, so he was a little confused but he didn't refuse the sale. We rushed home to show Mary Beth.

"It's so pretty!" Mary Beth said hugging Ashley. I wrapped my arms around them and Ashley told her how I'd got down on my knee in the store to propose. Mary Beth was happy for us, but there was a sparkle of tears in her eyes. She and I *couldn't* marry. She loved Ashley and wanted us to be happy. But there was still just a little sadness around the edges.

When we got ready for bed that night, Ashley took care to undress Mary Beth herself. The girls were always loving with each other, though both were clear that they preferred what was between my legs to what was between either of theirs. So, I think Mary Beth was a bit surprised at how lovingly Ashley removed her boots, her shirt, her bra, her jeans, and her panties. Mary Beth kept glancing at me, but I sat back in the side chair as I slowly undressed and watched my two princesses.

When Mary Beth and Ashley were both undressed, Ashley sat Mary Beth on the edge of the bed and knelt in front of her. Mary Beth looked a little worried as Ashley had never made a move that was so suggestive. But it wasn't what Mary Beth might have thought.

"Mary Beth, we live in Wyoming. I came here from Colorado and I'm proud to call this my home now. I have met and loved not just one, but two wonderful people. But Wyoming law says you can't marry your first cousin. And even though it was the first place in the country to give women the right to vote, it won't let them marry each other. But Cole and I both love you. I know that we each love each other differently, but it's love just the same. You all taught me that. Mary Beth, even though neither of us can marry you, will you stay with us forever and love us till death do us part?" With that, Ashley slipped the second engagement ring off her finger and placed it on Mary Beth's. I joined Ashley on my knees in front of Mary Beth, took the hand from Ashley and kissed each finger. I turned it over and kissed her palm. Mary Beth was crying and nodding her head and sniffling. When Ashley moved up to the bed to hold her and kiss her, MB's legs sort of parted in front of me and being who I am, I sort of worked my way up there until I found that honeyed slit where my tongue had something to do.

ASHLEY'S PARENTS SHOWED up on Wednesday before the wedding. I'd met them before, both at Christmas last year and again when they came out with Ashley's horse last spring. The first thing her dad did was call the two of us aside.

"Now we've been expecting the two of you to get married ever since we came out here last spring, but what's the hurry? Ashley, are you pregnant?" We laughed then got serious again.

"No Daddy, I'm not pregnant, but I will be as soon as I get out of school and convince this guy to do the job. There's a lot happening out here and we are in the middle of it. We need each other and we need to be together for this."

"I'm sorry about your dad, Cole. I thought he was a fine man. That's not what's driving you to this, is it?"

"No sir. I admit that Dad's passing has made me aware of exactly how vulnerable we all are and how fragile life is. And I don't want to waste a minute of it. But I want Ashley here by my side as my partner in running this ranch. I promise I'll support her in school and we'll both finish, though we might not be able to do it as quickly as we'd have liked. This is a critical time and an important decision for us."

"Support her? I know you must have inherited the ranch, but are you able to make that commitment?"

"Yes. I think you'll find I have adequate resources to do whatever is necessary, including pay for the rest of her education, if you'd like."

"That's not necessary and I wouldn't ask it of you. I'm a father. I just want what's best for my daughter."

"Mr. Brewer, on that account, your goals and my goals are in perfect sync!"

"It's Chet, Cole. You're going to be a fine son-in-law. Welcome to the family."

THAT WASN'T THE end of it, of course. Mary Beth and Ashley had all three moms tied up with wedding plans and multiple trips into town for last minute needs. I needed to make sure Chet Brewer knew exactly what was happening and I needed Angus with me.

"Dad and I used to come out here occasionally to have a cigar," I said as I led Chet and Angus to the ruined stone chimney that I recognized now as the remains of the log cabin Kyle built for Laramie. "Care to join me?" I asked offering them one of Dad's best. They accepted and we took a few minutes to cut them and light up. Well, Angus bit his off like Dad had. They'd both agreed they needed to stop smoking when Dad was told his lungs couldn't take it anymore.

"It's nice to get out here away from all those women for a while," Chet laughed. Angus nodded and I grunted.

"You okay, Cole?" Angus asked.

"I'm nervous as a bronc rider," I said.

"Oh, she's not gonna be that hard on you," Chet laughed. "And if she is, I don't want to know about it."

"It's uh… It's not that, Chet. It's you all I'm nervous about."

"I thought we covered that."

"There's a few pieces you don't know about yet and to be fair, you need to know this." I told him what was happening in the county with the prices of beef and the condition of the local ranchers.

"How are you going to survive that?" he asked.

"First, we're going to buy all the hay you can ship up here," I laughed. "I have the resources to outlast the downturn. But we're going to be targeted by the bad guys and I don't want Ashley in a position where she isn't protected. We suspect that Dad's accident wasn't just an accident."

"Maybe I should take her back to Colorado with me. Are you putting my daughter in danger?"

"We're all in danger, Chet," Angus broke in. "I agree with Cole that this is one of the best ways to keep her out of danger. We've got a good-sized clan here."

"Actually, that's something else I need to tell you, sir." I don't know why I got all formal with him again, but his threat to take Ashley back to Colorado really got to me. "Ashley is already one-third owner of the Alexander Bell Cattle Company. That partnership, which includes Mary

Beth and me, owns both the Alexander ranch and the Bell ranch, and all the nearly 4,000 head of cattle here."

"Whoa! Angus? You don't own your ranch?"

"I sold to Mary Beth and Cole last winter when they bailed us out. He's telling you the truth, Chet. He has the resources to last and we'll all be here to help."

"Let's see. You and Mary Beth formed a partnership and bought the ranch. Then you made Ashley a one-third owner in it as well?" Chet asked. "How does Mary Beth feel about giving up a third of her family homestead to my daughter?"

"That's another bit of what I need to tell you, Chet." I took a deep breath. "Mary Beth lives with Ashley and me. We have a three-way partnership that is more than just a business relationship. I hope you'll be able to accept Mary Beth along with me, just as Angus accepted both Ashley and me."

Chet stood up. He turned toward me and started to speak but turned toward Angus and started again. Then he walked away. He didn't go far—just to the other side of the stone chimney. Then he turned back and flopped himself down on his log seat. He let out a big sigh.

"Celia already knows about this, doesn't she?" he said, referring to his wife.

"I was forbidden to discuss it with you before Ashley had talked to her."

"Yeah. I figured it was just wedding stuff or money that she was talking about when she made me promise not to get mad when I talked to you today. I never imagined this." We sat there in silence a few minutes, puffing on our cigars. Angus pulled out a hip flask and handed it to Chet who took a pull and handed it on absently to me. I took a little slug of Wyoming Whiskey and handed it back to Angus. "You remember when I said that if she was that hard on you I didn't want to know about it?" he asked me. I nodded. "Well this is something else I don't want to know any more about. You'll all three be welcome in our home and we will never say a thing about it, but I really don't want to know any more. Okay?" I nodded again. Angus handed him the flask again and we passed the rest of the hour discussing our strategies for surviving the cattle depression.

AND THEN IT was Saturday and I stood with Uncle Angus beside me in the living room and watched Mary Beth come in from the dining room and take her place as maid of honor. The family was all standing because we didn't try to put chairs in any order, but when Ashley came through those doors there wasn't a dry eye in the house. Her dress was knee-length linen with a single row of buttons on the left that went from her collar to her tiny waist along a center placket with ruffled edges. It was topped by a western yoke. The skirt was full and, with the number of petticoats she had under it, it looked like she was ready to go dancing. Especially when my eyes got down to those high-heeled boots.

But I could only spare a moment to look at her pretty legs. Her face was glowing. Her blonde hair hung in ringlets beneath the brim of her white Stetson. Those sparkling eyes, just took my breath away. I hardly noticed her father walking with her until he placed her hand in mine.

"Take good care of her, son," he said. "You're not the only one who loves her."

I looked into those beautiful eyes for the whole ten minutes it took the preacher to bless our rings and have us repeat our vows. When he said I could kiss the bride, I sure did, right there in front of God and everybody. I sure wished Dad was there to be with us. And I thought, why not? *I bet the whole family is here. See what I got, Dad? Theresa, I did it. I married her. Laramie, doesn't she remind you of Kat?* They were all there and they were all happy.

Early Sunday morning, Ashley's brother took us to the airport. He had to catch a flight home so we were on the first leg from Laramie to Denver together. It was going to take almost as long to get from Laramie to Salem by flying as it did driving. But Ashley and I were on our honeymoon, so we booked a couple nights in a fancy hotel in Portland and then Phil had a car pick us up for our business meetings in Salem. We went back to Portland the next day and enjoyed three more nights of loving before we faced the flights home. It was sweet.

MEANTIME, MARY BETH got to experience firsthand what all the ranchers in the county did that Sunday afternoon. A man knocked on her door after they got home from church and Sunday dinner that Mary Beth took her parents, my mom, and the Brewers to. It was timing on her part to be sure we'd made it to Portland. Angus answered the door.

"Mr. Alexander, I represent a company interested in purchasing your cattle at premium prices. May I speak with you?"

"Never hurts to listen," he said, letting the man into the living room. "Mary Beth, you need to come listen to this."

"Actually, Mr. Alexander, in order to proceed with our discussion, I must speak to you under a signed confidentiality agreement. You should really not have family members present."

"Well, in that case, I'll be leaving."

"Wait, sir."

"No, you don't understand. I consigned all my cattle and ownership of the ranch to my daughter's new partnership, Alexander Bell Cattle Company. She owns this ranch and the Bell ranch next door. Technically, she is the person you need to have sign your paper and I'll leave unless she wants me to stick around."

"Oh. Ms. Alexander? I'm Howard Case. You have partners in this business venture?"

"Yes, but they are on their honeymoon. If you have a proposition to make, I'm the one you need to talk to. I'll ask my father to also sign your confidentiality agreement if he will stay here."

"And are you authorized to make agreements on the part of the partnership?"

"I am, Mr. Case. Let us take a look at this agreement." Angus sat with his daughter and looked over the confidentiality agreement.

"This provides some pretty stiff penalties for breaking this agreement," he said.

"That is why we are trying to keep the number of people exposed to this conversation to a minimum. This is a very sensitive matter." Angus and Mary Beth signed the agreement, MB on behalf of the partnership so she could discuss it with her partners.

"Very well," said Mr. Case. "I represent Gold Watch Cattle Company. We are a new company that was created by a prestigious think tank in

Chicago. You might recognize this name. Our investors include some of the wealthiest men in America. Our focus has been on international trade and the effect of one country dumping products on the international market in an effort to destroy the other's economy—essentially, economic warfare. You can imagine that this could be pretty serious."

"And that led you to create a Cattle Company?" Mary Beth asked.

"In a way. We've often seen the cycle as it plays out, but studying and observing are only beneficial if they lead to action. In this instance, we have decided to take action."

"Against what?"

"We believe a foreign influence is flooding the Albany County market with cheap beef. This seems to be a contained effort and is unlikely to affect the commodities market in general, but could have devastating effects on the economy of this county. You may have noticed both a drop in beef prices and a scarcity of winter food."

"Who hasn't noticed that? We'll probably cut our losses and sell out if the price doesn't pick up by mid-October." Angus flinched. This was news to him, but he knew that Cole had the resources to start over if necessary.

"We don't want you to do that. How many head are we talking about?"

"We have 2,537 tagged for market plus our heifers and calves for next year."

"We would like to place a guaranteed option on your marketable beef of $2.00 per pound on the hoof. One-third payable in January, one-third in February, and one-third in March. By March, your young stock should be ready for summer pastures and you'll be able to buy more stock for the next season."

"We were getting $2.05 in August."

"Yes, but the market price in this county is now $1.80 and falling. We believe $2.00 is a fair offer."

"But if the market picks up in January, then we'd be out our profit." Mary Beth was making Case work for his sale. She tried to keep her smirk hidden.

"You will notice this clause," he said. "The guaranteed option is at $2.00 per pound or market price, whichever is higher. You have no downside."

"This sounds too good to be true. Do you work for Joe Teini."

"Ma'am, we believe Joe Teini is being used as the funnel for cheap beef in this county. He has offered 5,000 head a week at a nickel below market since the end of August. And he still seems to have the same 50,000 head on his ranch. He is the enemy. That is why it is so critical that this offer and these terms do not get out. Our intent is to cripple this foreign influencer on the open market so that they cannot sustain their losses and withdraw."

"Well, there's just one little problem. Your offer is for live cows and all ours will be dead by first snowfall. We can't get feed or hay."

"Since we would effectively own all your cattle, we wouldn't want that to happen. We will ship in feed monthly to supply your needs."

"This is expensive. There's no local feed and it costs a dime a pound more to ship from Omaha. Why are you guys doing this?"

"Ms. Alexander, there are some men who have grown very wealthy in this world through other people's labor. Their wealth is legitimate, but it is really more than they and their heirs combined could ever spend. So, they give to research, health, science, and any other way they can find to better humanity through their good fortune. The think tank has identified this as a way to support an economy in a new and untried way. Let me assure you that we will also have inspectors visit with every delivery of feed to ensure that you are complying with the terms of the agreement and that our cattle are healthy and accounted for."

"Sounds like you have everything thought of. Would you excuse me while I phone my partners? They should have arrived at their hotel by now and I might catch them before they are indisposed."

Of course, Ashley and I were waiting for her call. Mary Beth told us all about the presentation and that any rancher in the county would be a fool to pass it up. I agreed. I was looking forward to seeing the numbers on Wednesday when we got to Phil's office. We kept Mary Beth on the phone and Mr. Case stewing for half an hour. Most of that time, Ashley and I spent teasing MB about what we were doing to each other and would do to her when we got home. Mary Beth was flushed when she returned to Mr. Case.

"My partners have authorized me to sign the agreement," Mary Beth said. "You understand that this covers all the cattle from both the former

Alexander Ranch and the former Bell Ranch next door, correct?" He nodded. "Then it looks like we need to get some papers signed and the inventory done."

I wasn't sure exactly how he'd done it, but Phil had placed 183 agents in Albany County at once. They came from different directions in different makes and models of cars, none of which were linked to the company. They made simultaneous presentations to all the ranchers in the county but two. One was Joe Teini and one was in the hospital. Two ranchers were getting ready to cut their losses and retire by selling their ranches to Joe. They accepted a cash offer of exactly twice what Joe had made and on Monday the deeds were transferred at the County Recorder's office. One stubborn old guy said he'd never taken charity from anyone and he was determined to fight this on his own and Joe Teini and Gold Watch Cattle Company could both be damned. He agreed, however, that he would keep the terms of the confidentiality agreement.

By eight o'clock Sunday evening, the only agents left in the county were the two closing on property the next day. Gold Watch Cattle Company effectively owned over 120,000 head of cattle. Now if we could just keep it quiet until Joe Teini gave up.

That wasn't to be. Suddenly no one would talk to Joe about buying out their ranches and no one was putting cattle on the market except Joe. By November, the price of beef in Albany County was down to just over $1.50 a pound and our observers noticed that Joe's herd was finally beginning to dwindle. Joe didn't like that.

On November fifth, Harmon Hayes' house and barn were burned and seven hundred head of cattle were killed. Harmon and his wife died in the fire.

It was the beginning of the second Wyoming Range War.

GOLD WATCH CATTLE Company hired armed guards for every ranch in the County, including ours. Since we had two homesteads, we had double the guards. What nobody knew was that we also had a small army camped in the foothills. The next attack, though, wasn't on a ranch. Thanksgiving weekend, three hay trucks were firebombed as they crossed the county line in three separate locations. As it happened, a deputy's car was approaching each of the locations at the same time and flagged all the drivers over and got them out of their trucks before the tanks exploded. There was no doubt in our minds that Joe was using the Sheriff's office as enforcers. They ticketed the drivers for unlicensed transport of flammable goods.

We responded by putting a tail on every County Mounty. Two deputies resigned and left the county. The county prosecutor opened an investigation into the increased number of 'accidents' that were occurring and complaints about the Sheriff's Office responsiveness. It looked like a stand-off because neither side could openly declare itself. I was going through money—or Gold Watch Trust was—at the alarming rate of close to a million dollars a week. Phil assured me that we could afford it and Phile talked to me to tell me that's what he collected the money to do. We just tried to keep a low profile while we kept ranchers from going belly-up.

CHRISTMAS EVE. SILENT night, holy night. I'd just come in from the barn handing out bonuses and wishing all the hands a Merry Christmas before they took off for the day. I was changing clothes for dinner when a rifle bullet tore through my bedroom window. It looked like Joe had figured out that I was the enemy and was firing a warning shot.

I stared out the broken bedroom window—daring the son of a bitch to shoot again. Instead, a shadow flicked across the opening and I heard the call I always waited for but never expected.

Traveling: Spirits of the Land

I WAS DISORIENTED, not finding myself with Laramie. The room seemed to be empty. I stretched my senses and realized I was in what would eventually become my office. There was the stone fireplace, though the absence of a fire let me know it was summer. Laramie's bed was still in the room, but there was a desk there, too. I sensed the presence of something pulling at me—something that was always a part of Kyle. On a hat tree in the corner hung my guns. They called to me as much as if they were a part of my soul.

I was happy to be near them and to find they had been kept clean and ready in my leathers. I could feel the fresh ammunition in them, though something told me they hadn't been fired recently. I hadn't even known that Laramie kept the guns. I assumed they'd been buried with Kyle's body. There was something soothing about having them here where they could protect her.

Protection. That was why I was here. I had to protect my family. But I had no body. What good would my guns do me?

I heard gunfire at a distance. Doors were slamming and there were footsteps in the house. People were shouting, inside and out. The door to Laramie's room flew open, but it wasn't Laramie who entered. It was an old man, breathing so hard that I thought he'd collapse on the spot. He looked wildly around the room until his eyes lit on my Smith & Wessons.

"I know you're still here, Kyle," he said as he approached the hat-tree. "I know you watch over them—us—all. I'm not as much a man as you were, but I love Kat. And I'll die to save her and Artie and Bonnie. And Laramie and Kaylene, too. We're all family and I'll fight for them now." My awareness put it together. This was Arthur Alexander, the man who gave his name to my maternal line and to Mary Beth. He had to be near seventy. He broke down wheezing and coughing as he reached for my gun belts. "You got to help me, Kyle," he continued. "I don't know how to do this. Help me save them." As soon as he touched my guns I flowed up into him and wrapped myself around his old body.

This was different than any time I'd been back. I couldn't read his thoughts because I wasn't inside his mind. I wasn't dreaming him because I could feel every aching pain in his old body. What I understood was that our wives and children were in danger and Arthur Alexander was asking for my help to save them. That was a call stronger than that of Redtail. I just took control. I could hear him sigh as I moved his hands and fastened the buckles. I cracked his old arthritic knuckles ignoring his winces of pain. I released the safety straps, straightened the old man's back and walked out of the room.

"Artie!" I commanded as I walked to the front of the house. "Take the women to the back room and stay low. Put out the lights. Here." I handed him the shotgun that hung above the mantle. "Anything comes through that door, kill it."

"Arthur?" Kat said as Artie responded to my command and began hustling the women to the back of the house.

"Kat, never forget I love you and our children. Never forget." I wasn't sure if that was me or Arthur speaking. I gave her a quick kiss and a gentle shove toward the back of the house. Kat's daughter Bonnie and my Kaylene followed. Laramie paused and looked me in the eye.

"Be careful, Kyle," she whispered. "We all love you." She always knew. I nodded and opened the front door.

Six riders were circling their horses and parading around in front of the house firing guns into the air. It took a minute before they realized I was standing on the porch.

"Look heah!" one shouted. "Arthur's come out to give us numbers. Who gets first choice, Arthur? I already decided I'm gonna fuck the Indian girl. She owns this spread and I figure that'll make it mine."

"Grant," Arthur's voice croaked. I took over.

"Grant Slocum! You get you and your boys off my property and stay away from my women."

"Don't you talk big now, Arthur? You don't understand the way things are. You're an old man. Hell, I tell you what. When you die, I'll take your little wife along with the others. And I figure now you're likely to die tonight."

"I've warned you, Grant. Go now or die." There must have been something about the way I was talking or the way I stood that let the horseman know I was serious. He hesitated a minute then holstered his gun and turned his horse so his gun hand faced me.

"I give you a fair chance. You coulda died an ol' man, Arthur," he said. "Well, hell, I guess you are an old man so dying won't be that tough."

His hand went for his gun. His shot rang out an echo of my own and his bullet raised dust in the ground at his horse's feet as his chest blossomed in blood. He fell back from his saddle. I saw other guns turning to bear and my left hand took two as the right dropped two more. In a heartbeat, five riders fell from their saddles and one stood stock still with his hands raised in the air.

"Don't shoot me, Arthur. I didn't want to come. You know how Grant threatens people. Don't kill me in cold blood, Arthur. I'll go and never come back."

"Bill Towson," Arthur said softly.

"Bill!" I hollered. "You ride hell-bent for leather back where you came from. This ground is forever protected. Even if I am dead and buried, I will be here to protect my women and my land. Ride out of here. Warn everyone you see. The spirits of this land do not rest. And we are deadly when we hunt."

Bill turned his horse and spurred him to a gallop away from the house leaving the carnage behind him. I heard the door bang open as Kat's voice screamed, "Arthur." There was nothing I could do to keep the old man from collapsing on the porch in her arms. I supported him as well as I could and spoke to him alone.

"You are a brave man, grandfather."

"You know as well as I that my blood does not run in your veins," he said to me. I knew his lips were moving, but I thought no one else could hear.

"The spirit that runs in our descendants is stronger than the blood. I am proud to call you my ancestor and my friend."

"Show me the way, Kyle." I saw his spirit pulling away from his body. "Goodbye, Kat. I have always loved you and our children. Raise them well." Then he was standing before me as a young man. A young woman came to meet him—his first wife, I understood.

"You did well, Arthur. Don't worry, we'll meet them again." She held out her hand to him.

"Rose. You still remember me."

"How could I ever forget?"

They turned and walked away, but I heard him clearly as he said, "We'll be waiting when you come."

"Art? Art! He's gone," Kat wailed.

"Pa?" Artie wasn't looking at his dead father. His eyes were searching around him. I reached out with my mind and hugged him.

"I'm here. I love you," I said. In a moment, I had all my family in the arms of my mind as they knelt over Arthur Alexander's body. To each I whispered, "I'm here. I love you."

Laramie lifted her head. "I love you, Kyle. I dream of you every night. I knew you would be here in our time of need."

"I love you, Papa," Kaylene whispered. "Thank you."

"You helped a brave man, Kyle," Kat whispered. "I never stopped loving you. Thank you."

Bonnie looked uncertain, but I just hugged her and Artie as well and said, "Always remember what a brave man your father was."

Then I heard Redtail.

War

ASHLEY RACED INTO the room to find me standing in front of the window just seconds after the shot. She dove at me and took me to the floor with her, but no more shots were fired. I could hear Mary Beth shouting into her phone as she talked to the 911 operator. "Shot through the bedroom window. Cole! How bad, Ashley? Send an ambulance." I raised a hand and waved.

"No ambulance. He missed. Nobody's needed," I said. Mary Beth sobbed into the phone and relayed the message. She was assured that help was on the way and to stay away from the windows. We crawled out of the room, though I doubted there would be any more shots. I hadn't been visible when the first one was fired. It wasn't aimed at me, but rather at my bed.

It was odd that Sheriff Teini was in Centennial on patrol when I called in the report. He showed up at the house fifteen minutes later.

"Sheriff," I said as I let him in. "Didn't expect the boss to show up. Usually there are just deputies around."

"Christmas Eve. At least one deputy gets the night off to be with his family."

"How kind of you."

I showed him the broken window. He made a production of tracing the trajectory, finding the tear in the foot of the mattress, and pointing up toward the ridge.

"High caliber from a long way away. Could have done a lot of damage to a person in the room." He pulled out a knife and cut into my mattress to pull out the slug. "Well, no harm done. It looks like someone was just trying to send you a message." He stuck the slug in his shirt pocket while I watched.

"So, what do you plan to do, Sheriff?" I asked.

"Well, there's not much we can do tonight. Tomorrow in daylight we might be able to send a team up there to look for tracks. No way we could get up there to hunt a man at night, though. He'll be long gone, of course. Be a shame to spoil people's Christmas with a fruitless manhunt."

"It's a hard place to be in winter," I said. "We'll probably find his bones when we drive cattle up to the range this spring. Wild animals can get really hungry in the winter."

"You still figure you'll be in the cattle business? Seems like a dangerous profession." I itched to have my guns in my hands.

"How about you, Joe? How long can you last? January? February? You're eating up what you have."

"Why don't you ever look me in the eye, Cole? Afraid I'll recognize you?" I looked him square in the eye and we held it. He found what he was expecting. I found someone scared. "It was a dirty trick of you to steal my treasure."

"I died too young to do much of anything. You sure it wasn't Cal Despain when you weren't there? He never struck me as too trustworthy."

"I found his saddle and his boots with a skeleton and the remnants of a treasure that should have made me a king. I want the rest of it now, Kyle Wardlaw. I won't rest until I have it." I shook my head. If he'd never been back, I wasn't revealing that I'd continued to travel.

"I didn't live all Kyle's life, Joe. I was only there for a few fun bits. Just like you. It was fun while it lasted but it's over. I once saw two men shoot it out with each other until they each killed the other with their last bullet. Is that what you want, Joe? We're running out of ammunition. Bag it. There's no more treasure to be found. You can't hold out long enough to make me sell, or any of the others either. You're just wasting what you've got."

"I can't quit. It's my life." He turned to go but hesitated. "You be careful out there, Cole. You wouldn't want that pretty young bride of yours to be a pretty young widow."

I grabbed Joe's arm and spun him around to face me. The words echoed in my mind like generations of Bells and Alexanders using my voice.

"This ground is forever protected. Even if I am dead and buried, I will be here to protect my women and my land. Ride out of here. Warn everyone you see. The spirits of this land do not rest. And we are deadly when we hunt."

Joe's head popped up to look at me in horror as he backed out the door and left the house, taking the bullet from our torn mattress with him. There was never an official report filed.

I looked out the window when I saw two flashes of light up higher on the ridge. There was darkness for a minute and then the two flashes again. I went down to my office in time to meet my security chief coming in from the back.

"The threat's been eliminated, Mr. Bell." I nodded and he left.

No, the shooter had been eliminated. Not the threat.

Joe Teini had to die.

I WONDERED WHERE Kyle's guns were now. I'm not really a violent man but if I had been Kyle, Joe Teini wouldn't have walked out of my bedroom alive. Hell, the times I had control of Kyle's gun hand weren't legendary. We'd finally ended up dead. But I'd killed seven men, including just taking control of Arthur Alexander's body and shooting down five who threatened our families. I couldn't tell one of my 'soldiers' to go off Joe Teini. If I did that, I'd be the same as him. But he'd threatened my family and I was by-god going to protect them. My hand reflexively clenched as though I had the Smith & Wessons at my side.

MOM MOVED IN with Angus and Lily, back to the same room she'd had when she grew up next to Dad. By New Year's I had reinforced the master bedroom wall with a double coat of fiberglass and ¾" plywood paneling. It wouldn't stop a high-powered bullet, but it would slow it down. For the time-being I bolted a sheet of ¼" steel over the window. No one could see whether a light had come on in the room. I'd make it pretty when this war was over. We moved my king-size bed with a new mattress into the master bedroom. Mary Beth moved the rest of her things in with Ashley and me. It was funny. It was her room at the Alexander's that Mom moved back to. Mary Beth hadn't slept in it in months. There was little I could do if someone was coming after me from inside the house. That's what a shotgun was for and I had one in about every room. We all knew how to use them.

"You said he was scared," Ashley said as we were painting our new bedroom.

"Definitely. But scared like a cornered dog. Dangerous scared."

"It doesn't make sense. We've never threatened him—only responded. What's he scared of?" Ashley persisted.

"And why the hell does he keep upping the ante instead of retreating?" Mary Beth joined in. "Maybe there *is* a foreign influence that's pressuring him. I thought we made that all up for Gold Watch."

"Let's look at what we know," I said, tossing my brush in a pail of water. "Poor broke Joe left school the day after graduation. Nobody hears from him for six years. Then he comes back to town in a sports car with a bundle of money and steals my girlfriend. For which, by the way, I am eternally grateful because that made it possible for me to have the two most fabulous women in Wyoming to share my bed and my life." I got kissed from both sides. "He sets up a brokerage office, saying he went to brokers' school and did well in the market. He attracts a dozen or two of the richest men in the county to let him handle their accounts. Two years later, he has a strong enough base of support to run for Sheriff and win. In the meantime, he buys three ranches or more, including that huge spread up north."

"Where did all the money come from?" Ashley asked. "Even if he was successful in the market, you have to start with something and according to your version of the story, he didn't have two nickels to rub together when he left."

"We could rub *our* nipples together if you want," Mary Beth teased. "I mean in the shower. Now. To get clean." We laughed, but kept talking, even when we were rubbing various body parts together in the shower.

"County plat map," I said when we were drying off.

"Huh?"

"There's a county plat map in the office. It shows who owns all the ranches and farms. We used it to identify who should be contacted with the bailout. I want to see exactly where Joe's land up north is." We went to the office and unrolled the huge county map. It wasn't hard to see where our ranch was. There was open range managed by the BLM between our southern border and the Bosworth Ranch in the southeast. It extended west across the ridge and bordered about a mile of our land on the west. I was interested in the north county where Joe's ranch was.

"Look, this isn't where Joe lived when he was in school. That's the ranch he bought over here on the east side of town when he came back. I think it's still where he and Geneive live. The north property is all pasture. There's close to twelve sections of it." I traced the outline with a yellow marker. This Medicine Bow area includes a radical land change along a cliff that creates the northern border of his property. Along in there someplace is where Kyle kept stashing the treasures until the night we loaded them all in the Conestoga and moved them to our property. At least I hope it's on our property."

"We already figured that Joe went to the stash after Cal Despain died and found the cupboard bare," Mary Beth suggested. "That's probably why he's targeted our ranch. He must know this is where Kyle was building Laramie's cabin and he's trying to get his treasure back."

"Which begs the point of where the money came from to get him started. How much did he have access to before Kyle emptied the cave?" Ashley asked. I thought about it for a minute trying to access as much of Kyle's memory as I could.

"As far as I can recollect, Kyle only took two batches of money directly to Cal Despain. One was the gold and jewels the prospector left for him. I think Laramie took it when I killed Cal. So, it wasn't in the cave either. Then there was the suitcase full of currency that we sent by train and that Kyle carried to Despain."

"How much?"

"Probably a hundred thousand. A lot of money in 1891. But Phile Morgan said he met Joe on previous trips. He could have been getting cash from any number of sources before he recruited Kyle to do the legwork so Despain could be sheriff."

"That brings us back to step one," Mary Beth said.

"Not necessarily. Hiding gold is one thing, but hiding currency is something else," Ashley said. "A hundred grand in 1891 is a lot of money. In 1996, not as much. How much do we know Joe has spent?"

I looked up the property values we'd compiled so we knew what each ranch was worth in the county. Those that had sold had sale prices listed.

"The Medicine Bow acreage went for $3.5 million. The first ranch east of Laramie was $1 million. And the little property between the two went for $750,000. That's $5.5 million."

"Plus, what it's costing him to maintain his operation and dump cattle on the market," Mary Beth added.

"And Kyle can only account for $100,000 in currency that was deposited in a bank so somehow he could get access to it in this century. Whatever he got before he started using Kyle has to be considered, but he might have hidden that in the same cave as the stuff Kyle stole," Ashley said. "Joe might be leveraged out as far as he can get. He might be broke."

"And if he took out loans based on finding his lost treasure, he could be desperate. Shit!" Mary Beth said.

"I think we have to assume that when the January purchases are made, Joe might be bankrupt. If he has an 'investor' who has backed his venture, things could heat up even more," I said. "We've got to be careful."

THANKS TO THE Gold Watch security force, the other ranchers were feeling safe and still refused to buckle under pressure as the January sales got under way. Instead, Joe focused all his efforts on me now that he knew for sure I was the enemy. We were followed whenever we left the ranch. It was possible he had people in the hills above our place. I certainly did. I had my cars all scanned each morning to make sure there were no explosive devices that had been hidden in the night. Phil sent me three professional drivers and no one left either ranch unless they were driven. That included our parents, Mary Beth, and Ashley.

When Joe put up 5,000 head at $1.49 a pound, Gold Watch put up 5,000 at $1.45. Joe suddenly found out what it was like to be undersold. The other ranchers in the county watched the results as they counted the $2.00 a pound they'd been paid. We lost three-and-a-half a million on the sale of 40,000 head, but no one else lost a penny. Except Joe Teini. This time it was him that had to drop to a lower market price. It was going to be an interesting co-op meeting at the end of the month.

"COLE, I THOUGHT you ought to know there was a gun battle on your upper range last night," Phil said when he called. In general, I had no contact with the mercenaries Phil had placed on our upper range. It was our most vulnerable side and he'd decided to station ten men up there to protect our western frontier. I only dealt with the security staff we had near the house and the drivers. "The force repelled six marksmen headed toward the trail down. They were professionals and have disappeared. You need to stay alert."

I kept wondering over the next week what it meant. "Repelled six marksmen." "Gun battle." "Disappeared." I didn't even know how I'd tell the good guys from the bad guys. But it was obvious that we were targets and should take precautions. Of course, I figured I was immune. What is it about guys that make us think nothing can touch us? I'd already died once. I should have known.

I ARGUED ABOUT it, but was overruled. When I went to the co-op meeting on the last Monday of the month, a professional drove my truck. He stayed in it and I came out of the meeting with even more questions on my mind. Most of the ranchers were in a good mood, which was a mystery to the Co-op manager. The news he had certainly wasn't that good. Cattle had sold each week this month at a record low, but no one seemed to be concerned. Well, why would they be? Gold Watch Cattle Company had bought their January share at two dollars a pound and sold it at a dollar forty.

Joe didn't show up for the meeting. He sent his wife, Geneive Murrieta Teini. She looked great. She'd always looked great. She merely nodded her consent when others talked about holding out, even though everyone figured Joe was behind the price drop. The truth was Joe had been undersold and took a bigger hit than anticipated in getting rid of his cattle. They were already on the block and sold when he realized the going price wasn't the one he set. The ranchers were all so paranoid about the terms of their confidentiality agreements, though, that they wouldn't even talk about why they were holding out with each other. Still, they were a united front.

The meeting ended with a weather forecast for the coming month, planting tips for spring, and what we should be ordering now so we were ready. It was stuff most of the guys already knew and the meeting broke up so folks could get into small groups with a cup of coffee and whisper.

"Long time, Cole," Geneive said as I filled my cup.

"'Tis," I said. "Looks like life's been treating you well."

"You mean Joe. Yeah. He gives me anything I want. Except the one thing neither of you would give me." She reached across me, poured a cup of coffee, and stirred creamer and sugar into it. In the process, her shirt gapped open and I stared down on those little tits I used to love to suck. Somehow, knowing that Joe's lips got all over them now turned my stomach.

"What's that?" I said as she straightened up. What was it she said? Neither of us would give her something?

"A baby. The damned fool got himself snipped before we were even married." She made a face as she drank the coffee. She'd never liked coffee.

"I'm sorry to hear that, Geneive, but frankly I don't like the idea of little Joes running around."

"What about me, Cole? Don't you know that's the only thing I ever wanted? I'd give you little Coles running around."

"Geneive! Didn't you hear I'm married? I'm not going to be your sperm donor."

"Yeah, I heard. Congratulations." She sighed. "I didn't figure you'd buy that. But we had some good times, didn't we?"

"Oh yeah." Geneive looked sad. She started to say something and then changed her mind.

"Geneive…"

"Goodbye, Cole," she cut me off. "We'll always have Bertha's."

"Goodbye, Geneive."

Now what the hell was that about? I was wracking my mind to remember any Bertha's we'd ever been to. I didn't know of one even now, unless maybe she used to call my old truck Bertha. I couldn't remember, but we did have some good times in that truck. I smiled and headed for the truck, nodding to a couple of the other ranchers as I left. The nice thing about having the Gold Watch confidentiality agreement in place was that nobody's attention but Joe's was particularly on me anymore.

I was still thinking of Geneive when my driver swerved to the left and touched the guard-rail. He turned sharp to the right and I heard the metal crunch as I felt the impact. The truck spun one-eighty and I felt the contact with another vehicle again. We slid backward off the edge of the bridge and jammed against the abutment.

What the hell? This was the same place Dad had his accident.

"We better see if he's still alive," my driver said.

"Who?"

"The guy in the black 'Vette and no lights that just tried to run us off the road." Shit! I hadn't even seen the other car. There was only one black Corvette I knew of. Joe Teini was trying to take me out the same way he took my father. I got out and walked around the back of the truck while my driver radioed base to call 911. The sports car was pinned sideways between the truck and the bridge. The driver's airbag was already deflating and I could see Joe Teini struggling to breathe.

I motioned my driver to pull the truck forward as I leaned into Joe's shattered window.

"We'll get you out of there, Joe. We've called for help. An ambulance is on the way."

"Don't trust 911," he wheezed. "That's how you get me."

"There are still some services that come no matter who you are."

"It's a good thing. No one would come for me. Not even my wife. It's over, Cole. You win." He tried to laugh and coughed up blood. There was no way I could get him out of the car. His side was completely crushed in and his legs were pinned under the dash. I kept working at the door anyway, trying to get it open.

"Take care of Geneive, Cole. She still loves you, you know."

"Why the hell did you ever want her in the first place?" I asked. "You didn't even know I was involved back then."

"You'll have to ask her, Kyle Wardlaw. You'll have to ask her." He was quiet and I managed to free the door of its latch but could only open it a few inches.

"When did you first know I was Kyle?" I asked as I worked. I was just talking to keep him alert. He was silent. I reached over to check his pulse and his head lolled to the side, his eyes open and unblinking. "Joe?" There was no answer. "Rest in peace," I said as I reached over and closed his eyes. I could see flashing lights coming down the road, but on this stretch you could see a couple of miles. I leaned back against the car.

The war was over.

10
Another Generation

I ALWAYS FIGURED one day I'd grow up and have a family. You know. A boy to carry on the family name and a girl for me to dote on and spoil like a papa ought to spoil his daughter. Well, I got the daughter in another time and she turned out to be my great-grandmother. How fucked up is that?

You see, I met Laramie Wyoming Bell as a young man meeting a beautiful young woman, falling in love, and letting nature take its course. Kyle could have left Laramie and been happy with Kat if it hadn't been for me interfering and getting him killed. I felt damned bad about that. I ruined that kid's life. But I didn't know Laramie was my great-great-grandmother. It didn't feel like incest or anything. I just loved that woman. But I could never have felt that way about Kaylene. Hell, she was my daughter. Yes, I know she was my great-grandmother, but she was still my little girl. I loved her like a daughter. I just wished I'd been there to see her grow up. The feelings I had for her weren't the same as the feelings I had for a great-grandmother. I got so confused.

In my dreams, I still made love to Laramie. For that matter, I made love to Kat, too. After Arthur died, she was alone with two kids and they were often with the Bells. I felt Kat and Laramie held each other together and they were both happy for my visits.

So how does that work? They were both my great-great-grandmothers. Was my mind just whipping me around to justify stuff that never happened? Do our dreams let us be with people we loved a hundred years ago, or are they just random firings of our synapses that give us a measure of wish-fulfillment? I didn't get snatched out of my skin, but I continued to dream.

I got the shock of my life when Ashley and I had just managed to give Mary Beth an orgasm that was probably heard at her parents' house half a mile away. I was still pulsing in her vagina and could hardly breathe.

"She was here!" Mary Beth gasped out. "She was here with me!"

"What are you talking about?" Ashley asked. "Who was here?"

"Laramie Wyoming Bell," Mary Beth panted. "I swear she came as hard as I did. I felt her. It was like she was inside me, just repeating over and over, 'I'm here. I love you.' Cole, she was giving us her blessing. I felt it. I know she was here."

That shocked the hell out of all three of us and we were crying and confused and trying to figure out what it meant. Laramie visited Mary Beth? And not me?

Revelation

I GUESS NOTHING is ever over. I was sitting in the office going over the books for the ranch. Our buyout of stock in March had been two cents above the guaranteed option. Beef prices were strong and Joe's cattle were auctioned off with his estate. Turns out he'd borrowed against the assets of his brokerage clients and they were pissed. Geneive did her best to delay things, but there was too much pressure to settle. The land went cheaper than it deserved because of the quick sale demanded by the bank. I didn't bid. I didn't want any of the property he'd grabbed. We had enough back in our little homestead.

The extra guards were dismissed the middle of April, though two of my new ranch hands had extra responsibilities the others didn't know about. One would be responsible for security for our herd when we drove them to the upper range in May. The other would be permanently on staff at the ranch, responsible for security at both homesteads. I wasn't cutting our parents loose to be on their own. I owed too much to Angus, Lily, and Mom. Our drivers were the last to go when it was deemed that we were safe. That was after Phil's investigator decided Joe had acted on his own to hire thugs and wasn't into any major crime syndicate. We breathed a sigh of relief over that.

The inquest ruled Joe's death an accident, even though it was obvious he didn't have his headlights on. I guess it was an accident that *he* died instead of me. There wouldn't have been any benefit to having him declared a murderer or attempted murderer. Dead is dead. I don't hold with trying to punish a man's memory. It wasn't Geneive's fault and she'd be the only one to suffer. He was stupid to use his very recognizable sports car to try to run me off the road. The F350 dually weighed more than twice the Corvette.

"COLE, WE'D LIKE you to run for sheriff in the special election," Obert said. There was a delegation of ranchers from our side of the county standing on my front porch. "We know that whatever it was that happened this winter, you were at the heart of it. Not that any of us would say anything about it, but we just know. You could win this election hands-down."

Shit. That would be just what I need. An interim sheriff had been appointed by the governor and a new sheriff would be chosen in a special off-year election in November. Like Joe had been. I really didn't want anything to do with it.

"Obert, Jack, Josh, thank you all for expressing your faith in me. But guys, put on your Stetsons. Which one of you would give up your ranching to be a sheriff?" They all shook their heads. "This land, them steers, that's what I love. I'm only twenty years old and I don't want to hold the keys to a jail. I want to ride the range and love my wife. I'd like to finish college and that's already been delayed at least a year. I appreciate what you're saying about me, but I'd be a lousy sheriff."

Ultimately, they agreed and wished me well. They all said if I changed my mind they'd support me, but they understood and said my dad would be proud of me.

The contest was heated with both sides pledging to clean house. I forget who won. It doesn't matter.

The Gold Watch Cattle Company had taken a pretty severe loss on feed, subsidies, and hired security, but it wasn't as bad as it could have been if prices hadn't sprung back. That was another thing I really didn't care about. It was only a few million. When things settled down, we'd look for another way to use the billion dollars we had in reserve. I put the Gold Watch Trust report in the safe.

ASHLEY AND MARY Beth came into the office, dressed in parkas and boots.

"Come on, Cole. You promised. It's the first of May. The slopes on this side are clear. We've got the ATVs sitting by the back door all packed. Come on," Ashley nagged, pushing at my arm playfully. I laughed.

"Are you sure you want to do this? When Joe went to his secret stash the cupboard was bare. Hell, for all I know, Kaylene used it all in the Great Depression. We don't even have partial records."

"But we'll see where," Mary Beth said. "We've been waiting all winter."

"And you're sure you want to stay out there tonight?" I asked. "You know it still gets close to freezing that high up at night."

"We've got our love to keep us warm!" Ashley sang. Well, there was a reason that Ashley only mouthed the words to hymns in church. She sang that one line in at least three different keys. I kissed her rather than risk another bar.

"Okay. I'm trustin' you two. I haven't looked at any of the supplies you packed. If I freeze my fingers, I'm going to put them someplace warm."

"Here. Wear your gloves."

"Nobody loves me and my hands are cold," I whined.

"God loves you and you can sit on your hands," Ashley shot the standard response back at me. We went out the back and I took the ATV with the supply wagon while Ashley and Mary Beth took the two-seater. In a matter of minutes, we were running up the cattle trail, ostensibly to check the conditions of the upper range. I don't think there was a ranch hand who didn't know what was really going to happen when the three of us camped for the night.

What they didn't know was that we were going treasure hunting. And it was going to be a challenge. The last time I was here, I was dead. I know we'd approached the narrow track below the ridge from the direction of Laramie's old hut. That was where we planned to spend the night. We could make the distance on the ATVs that we couldn't on horses. It was still slow going.

When we got to the old hut site on the west side, it was still pretty snowy but there was water in the thermal spring and we could have taken a bath if we were crazy. We could set up camp in the open on snow, go back over the ridge to our usual summer site, or head into the shelter of the woods. We opted for the woods and then cleared a pit for a small fire. It was hard to get stones dug out to line it, but with the help of the ATV, I hauled a dozen from the east side of the ridge. Our camp was beneath the old Mountain Douglas that had Laramie's and Kyle's initials carved in it. In a way, that made it feel like home. Once we had warmth and food, we crawled into the tent and piled on top of each other on the air mattress and our sleeping bags. The little tent was surprisingly warm the way we heated it.

"We both want you tonight out here in the wilderness, husband," Ashley said. "I want to feel you moving inside me and filling me while our lovely Mary Beth holds us tightly. Then I want to hold you both as you light up our tent with your love."

"What got you so poetic, tonight, lover?" I asked. "First you were singing—no, you don't have to do it again—and now you're talking like a romance novel. What classes are you taking this spring?"

"Cattle breeding. Just lie back and I'll tell you all about it," she said. Both her hands were on my chest, just like mine were on hers, so it must have been Mary Beth that was stroking my cowboy up to his full potential. I let go of Ash's left tit to reach out and pull Mary Beth closer to us. She kissed me, then raised up and kissed Ashley.

"You ready for this big boy, sweetie?" she whispered.

"Honey, I'm so ready for it I'm leaking. Put it in me, MB." Mary Beth stroked my cockhead through Ashley's wet slit then held it steady for her to sink down on it. I noticed, she didn't pull her hand away, but kept it between us and stroked my cock when Ashley rose and her clit on the down stroke. "Oh, I like this so much, loves. I am ready to burst."

"Let the dam break, wife. I'm here to catch your flood and to flood you in return," I said. I wasn't so awful bad at romantic talk. I guess it was enough, anyway because Ashley started moaning and squealing and the way she clamped down on me had me spurting on the next stroke.

"I feel it!" Mary Beth said. "I feel it going into you, honey. You're both so wet." I think Mary Beth had a little come, too. Her other hand was down between her legs.

We just lay there and kissed and hugged while Ash and I caught our breath. It got a little chilly and we pulled the blankets over us. I held both girls as close as I could and counted my blessings.

"Cole, it's nice to cuddle up to you in spoons, but my front-side is cold. Isn't there a way you can warm up my front?" Mary Beth complained. By this time, she could already feel that my cowboy was reviving and was poking her in that very warm backside.

"Sure, honey. You want to roll over on top of me?"

"No. Then my back would get cold. I want to use you as a blanket." Ashley was giggling against my back and pushing at me to help out "poor Mary Beth." Mary Beth rolled toward me and I settled down on her, supporting most of my weight on my arms. It's hard to get purchase on an air mattress, but I was working on it. Ashley was doing her best to help, having reached between us to grasp the cowboy and get him in position.

"I love you, Mary Beth. I would never let you get cold if I could help it."

"Just start moving so you heat up the rest of the tent," Ashley giggled.

"Is this what you want, honey?" I asked as I pressed forward.

Every time. Every time I press my hardness into the soft core of Mary Beth's body, it's like the first time. She consumes me, bit by bit, until I'm buried in her and all my senses focus on that pinpoint at the center of our being that holds us together. She was right in sync with me.

"Do you remember our first time, honey?" she asked. "I love all the ways we make love and all the combinations of the three of us. Don't forget I love you, Ashley. I'm just so absorbed in our man right now. I like everything we do, but when you are on top of me like this and so deep in my puss, it's always like the first time and I'm so happy." We were building up. Mary Beth was panting as I plunged in and out of her with Ashley's hand gently caressing my balls. "This is our first time, honey."

"Is it, Mary Beth? Is it our first time?"

"Yes, Cole, my love. It's the first time I ever made love to you knowing I was pregnant with our child."

And then that damned hawk screamed.

Traveling: Grandma

"BABY?" I SCREAMED. I love coming back in time to my family, but damn it! This wasn't the most opportune time. Mary Beth just told me she was having our baby. *Holy shit!* I was going to be a daddy in uptime. For real, with me there to love and protect her and see her grow up to be a fine young woman. Don't ask me how I knew my firstborn would be a girl. I just knew!

"Papa?"

"Kyle! You're here." The first voice was my little girl, my Kaylene who was struggling in bed. She cried out again. The second voice was Laramie, my beloved, hovering near Kaylene to help her through.

Through what? *Please, don't tell me you brought me back here for another death. Not my baby!* I wrapped my spirit around the two women and was immersed in Kaylene's pains. Not dying. Giving birth. I whispered to them, "I'm here. I love you." For having no physical senses, the agony that burst through my awareness as Kaylene pushed her daughter through the narrow channel almost sent me back to my own time without the damned hawk.

"That's it, baby," Laramie soothed her daughter. "The head is out. Just push one more time and I'll have my grandchild in my hands." That push came. It was less agonizing than the last and I just kept soothing and comforting my daughter as if I was really there. I wanted to be holding her hand and wrapping her in my love, so that's what I did.

"Papa's here, baby. Papa's here and I love you. You're going to give us a beautiful granddaughter."

"Papa," Kaylene whispered. "My baby girl?"

"She's here," Laramie said proudly and laid the baby on Kaylene's tummy.

"Oh, she's perfect, Mama. I have a perfect little girl."

"I heard you, Kyle," Laramie said. "You knew it was a girl. I'm so glad you're here to be with us. I dream of you every night and I listen for you every day, Kyle. Every day."

I could feel a noisy car approaching the house. Car? What year was this? If this is my Grandma Mildred being born… God! I've been gone seventeen years.

"Oh Laramie, darling. I didn't know it had been so long. I love you and I miss you and I didn't know it had been so long. I love you like the day we met." A door slammed and two men came through the house and opened the bedroom door.

"Kaylene, I got the doctor," said the first. "Look at there! We've got a baby."

"Robert, meet your daughter," Kaylene said.

"Well, it looks like I wasn't all that needed," the other man said. "Ranch wives always seem to get things done on their own. Let's just take a look."

"Uhn!" Kaylene groaned.

"That's just the placenta giving way and coming out, girl. You've seen enough cows give birth to know what's happening."

"Do I have to lick it and chew through the cord, Doc?"

"Well now you have to talk to your Mama about that. I don't know how you Indians do it. I usually just tie a knot in the cord and cut it off."

"That will do, Doctor," Laramie said stiffly. "My mother and my husband were white as you are."

"Now don't get huffed, Miss Laramie. You know I was just kidding. Don't matter to me what color a man is, just how well he lives. I'm sorry I never knew your husband."

I wrapped my spirit around Laramie to soothe her and wondered how much racist crap she had to put up with in 1925. It pissed me off, but I kept that to myself as the doctor continued to clean things up and check the baby's health. Robert kissed his wife and left to take the doctor back to town. I was impressed that Centennial even had a doctor, but I sensed that he was old and not really practicing much medicine anymore.

"Look at my baby, Mama. Isn't she beautiful?"

"Well, she will be after we clean her up a little," Laramie laughed.

"I never thought I'd have a baby, Mama. I'm thirty-five years old. And then Robert came along."

"He means well," Laramie said. I wasn't sure she was that pleased about her son-in-law. "He just isn't that dependable. The doctor would have been here in plenty of time if he hadn't insisted on finishing the chores first. You know you'll have to raise this little girl mostly yourself, baby."

"Just like you raised me, Mama. I knew what I was getting into."

"And what is the name of this little treasure? She's trying to get her lips around your fat teat. Help her a little."

"Ow! Oh, she's gonna be a handful. I'll name her Mildred after Robert's mother. Write it in the Bible, Mama."

"I'm ready to take a little walk right now, baby. We'll clean the two of you up after you've rested and she's had her fill. You have a glass of water here. You need anything else?"

"No Mama. You take Papa for a walk. I love you, Papa. Thank you for being here."

Laramie left the room and I paused to hug my daughter and her daughter in my mind. "I love you, too, Grandma," I said. Kaylene giggled a little. "I love you, little girl," I repeated to Kaylene. She sighed.

I caught up with Laramie outside. She was walking toward the promontory where the graves were. I was thankful to see none had been added. She spread her skirts and sat next to my stone.

"The ranch has grown," I whispered as I wrapped her in my arms.

"New barn. Second floor on the house so Kaylene could raise her family. Close to a thousand head on their way to the upper range for the summer. I come out here and talk to you all the time. I know you're not there, but I keep hoping you'll come back and talk to me again. Hold me in your arms. You wouldn't want to kiss these old lady lips or suckle my saggy breasts anymore. I'm getting old."

"Love, I still see you as young and beautiful as the day we first made love. Every day I long to kiss your lips and suckle your breast. Every day I miss you and would be here with you."

She relaxed in my embrace, dreaming of when we were young. I gave her a feather caress across her lips and down her body as I passed her breasts and her stomach and ruffled the hairs around her cunt. She sighed.

"Are things all right here on the ranch?"

"Oh yes. We have a good life for two women and a scatter-brained man. And now a baby. Kaylene wanted this so badly. He sleeps in the house most nights, but runs home to his Mama on the weekend. I don't think Mildred even knows she has a new granddaughter. I should go to town and tell her myself. She doesn't approve of our Indian blood."

"Is there a lot of that thinking?"

"They still pay good money for our cattle."

"Do you have plenty of money?"

"Not as much as we once had, but we have the ranch and the house now. Even a truck that Robert drives around as if he owns it. I went to the new college and learned about investing. I'm buying some stocks as we can."

"Laramie, next year, start taking all your money out of the bank, sell the stocks, and keep the money in a safe place. Don't do it all at once and leave a little there so you look poorer. If you need more money, go up to the cave and take what you need. Don't let any of the hands go with you or see where you go. Hard times are coming."

"I'll do what you say, Kyle, but I don't know why. Tell me, in your place, are you happy? Do you have a wife and children waiting for the call of Redtail? What do they say about me? Do they know?"

"I have two wives, much as we would have been together with Kat if… if things had been different. One is pregnant with our first child and she swears you were with her when we were making love. We are happy and they both know about you and wish they could be here to love you, too."

"Mary Beth," Laramie whispered. "I heard you call her Mary Beth in my dream. I told her I loved her. You brought a good love to me, Kyle Redtail. Hold me and love me like you did before. I'm old now, but I still remember."

I held Laramie in my mind and silently loved her. Loved her until she was at peace and knew she was loved.

I felt his presence before the call came. I had long enough to tell her again, "I'm here. I love you, Laramie."

Opening the Box

"Laramie," I called, just as I erupted in Mary Beth. Her climax was so close that she couldn't stop it, even though I'd just called out the name of another woman. Ashley just rolled back in shock.

"You were there! I knew you were there. I could feel the tenderness and love. Oh, Cole, do you love me that much, too?" Mary Beth cried. "Do you love me so tenderly that I want to cry and curl up in your protective arms and never let go?"

"I do, Mary Beth. I love you that much and more. It was just like that first time we made love and that hawk came by. Mary Beth, everything I said and everything I felt goes for you and our unborn daughter and for you Ashley. I love all three of you from the bottom of my heart. Every night I fall asleep thinking I can't love you any more than I do, and in the morning, I prove myself wrong. Now tell me about our baby, Mary Beth. I thought you were on the pill."

"I told you years ago those things weren't 100% effective. Even if they are 99.9% effective, we banged a thousand times without protection since Ashley joined us. I think it was the night Laramie came and blessed us. I'm sure she gave us this child. I wouldn't be surprised if Ashley's got a bun in the oven before the summer's through."

"And you knew about this, too, didn't you?" I said turning to Ashley. "Are you okay with it, sugar?"

"Of course I'm okay. It's why we wanted you up here on the mountain before she told you. I'm only disappointed that it wasn't my pill that didn't work. But I'm off them now. You get your seeds ready for planting."

"You want a baby that much?"

"Oh, Cole, yes, I do.

"I love you two so much I'm gonna bust!"

"Cole, you said 'our daughter' a minute ago. Did you see something? Are we going to have a little girl?" Mary Beth asked. I had to stop and think about it. Yes, I'd said that. I wondered why.

"I don't remember seeing anything about our baby," I said carefully, "but it probably had to do with what I saw while I was gone."

"What did you see?"

"I saw the birth of my granddaughter. That's Kaylene's little girl. Um… that's my grandmother."

"Only you, Cole. Only you could have your granddaughter be your grandmother."

"Well, you know genetically I'm not her ancestor. Kyle Redtail Wardlaw was. But it still felt like I was her grandfather. Kaylene giggled when I called the baby 'grandma.'"

We talked long into the night, huddled together with all our blankets on top of us but not a stitch of clothing between us. In the morning, we laid a new fire and made coffee and a range breakfast of sausage, beans, and eggs. We almost didn't come out of the tent because we had to dress first, but once we were out, we got moving pretty quickly to stay warm.

"ANY IDEAS WHERE we start?" Ashley asked. "You've been here before."

"Well, I think it's over that way. But the last time I was here, I was dead and didn't have physical senses. I was getting feelings. And it was more than a hundred years ago. Kyle started putting stuff here before that, but nothing actually looks like Kyle's memories."

We wandered in the general direction that I thought the cave was. It was rocky going. The drop into the next gully was sheer. We went down into it and then back up to the ridge. We weren't getting anyplace.

"I've got an idea," Ashley said as we got back to camp to eat some lunch.

"Shoot," Mary Beth said.

"Blindfold him," Ashley responded.

"For my execution? I'd rather not walk off the edge of that ravine. I know you'll be a rich widow, but we ought to find the rest first."

"I don't intend to be any kind of a widow," Ashley snapped. "You are going to keep fucking me until there's a baby in my tum."

"Do I have to stop then?" I mourned. She threw herself at me and I caught her up and held her in my arms.

"I love you, Cole. There's been too much death and dying in your history. Let's don't be talking about that anymore. Mary Beth and I will guard you to keep you from falling, but you got to just think about what the path felt like when Laramie walked it that last time. Think about that and walk and we'll get in your way if you are about to trip or fall. Do you trust us to do that, Cole?" Ashley was dead serious and even had moisture on her cheeks when I kissed them.

"I trust both of you, not only with my life, but with the lives of our children," I said.

We finished up our lunch and they tied a blindfold around my head. They did a good job of it. I couldn't see anything. They stood a couple feet away from me and I just stood there. I'd learned a lot of meditation techniques when I started traveling and discovered I could be awake for months at a time. The problem with most meditation is that the intent is to free the mind from the body. After Kyle's death, when I traveled my mind was always completely free of my body. So I relied on memory. I'd been conscious after Kyle died. I just didn't have any physical sensations. I let go of my body and just let my mind wander into the past where my memories of Laramie leading the mules away from the Douglas took me. I'm not sure when I started moving. Twice Mary Beth or Ashley touched me to keep me from running into a branch or a tree. That jerked me back for a second, but then I recaptured where I was and continued. The going was slow.

"Cole, stop!" Mary Beth's voice cut into my awareness. I froze. She and Ashley were next to me in a second and they removed the blindfold. I was standing on a narrow ledge. A misstep would have taken me down fifty feet or more. "There's no sense using the blindfold here," she said. "There's only one way to go."

I agreed and we started along the ledge. It sloped downward slightly. I suppose a sure-footed mule could navigate this path, but there better be a wide spot to get him turned around. He couldn't go backward all the way we came down. A well-trained mule can turn around in less than half the length of his body but this track didn't allow that much. I was still in a bit of a daze, hanging on to the remnants of my memories. I even risked closing my eyes once or twice to feel around me.

We'd gone a slow and torturous quarter of a mile when I froze. This was it. If there was still any treasure left, this would be where it was found.

"Here," I said. "It's here in the cliff someplace." We started parting the shrub and vine covering on the canyon wall, thrusting a long stick into the wall until the stick kept going. I almost lost my balance and fell forward. "We're here."

We looked for a way through the thicket without damaging anything, but eventually, I had to cut a narrow passage. The good part was at least this wouldn't be the den of any kind of large animal. When we had a narrow space to get through, I poked a flashlight through and looked around. The little cave was dry and protected and there was no sign of animals larger than a fox. It seemed to have been deserted even by those. The flashlight didn't penetrate far into the hole, so I pushed through and finally got a better look around. This was the cave. In the back around a bend were stacked wooden crates. It was amazing. I had no idea what was in most of the crates, having never stopped to look when Kyle was collecting them.

Ashley and Mary Beth came through the opening behind me and their flashlights joined mine in scanning the contents.

"This is what Joe Teini was looking for," I said. "He was willing to buy every ranch in the county to find this."

"If those chests all contain gold, it would have been a good purchase."

"Well, let's see." I went to the first crate and lifted it to the floor. It was heavy I wondered if it had gold in it. I used the hammer and prybar we brought with us to loosen the top. We looked inside.

"Pots and pans?"

"Iron skillets and Dutch ovens," I said. "Kyle never stopped to look at what was in most of the boxes he collected. He just went out and found the treasure that Cal sent him after. I suppose pots and pans had to be shipped out west and got lost, too." In fact, the next six boxes we opened had cookware in them. The seventh box was light and we discovered clothing. I shuffled the first row of boxes aside, anxious to see what else was there, but not willing to go through a lot of domestic goods to get to the next row. These boxes and crates had been carefully organized. Far more carefully than Kyle would have done. Laramie must have sorted and arranged what was in here.

The first box of the second row I opened held rifles. There was a good market for antique weaponry. This, at least, I knew we could sell. There were other boxes of firearms and ammunition. I reached over and pulled a box from the third row deep in the hoard. It was slightly smaller than the front trunks but weighed more than even the boxes of pots and pans or guns. I got it to the floor of the cave and pried the lid open. Mary Beth and Ashley shone their lights in the box.

"Cole? Is that… gold?"

"Looks to be, darlin'. By the count, ten bars across by ten bars deep. One hundred bars at two pounds apiece is two hundred pounds of gold."

"I just know you've got it all worked out already. What's it worth, Cole?" Ashley asked.

"Depends on how pure it is. Looks like about five million in a box."

"How many boxes like that one are back there?" I looked. They were stacked six high and five across.

"Looks like about thirty boxes like this, but there's more behind it."

"More? That's like $150 million!"

"Might be more than that. The bottom crates are bigger. They might have larger bricks in them or more of them. And there are more behind. I guess we found what we were looking for. Now what?" I asked.

"I think we should take a couple bars with us to send to our friends in Salem and have them assayed. Then we should talk to Phil about bringing a secure crew here to remove everything and take it someplace where we can inventory everything and get appraisals where we need them. This is like uncovering Fort Knox," Mary Beth said.

"Um… could we keep one? I mean in the house?" Ashley asked. I looked at her. We had at least three thousand gold bricks. If she wanted one to wear around her neck, I'd give it to her. "I mean, just so we can have one to see what a real gold brick looks like?" she finished.

"Darlin', if you want, we'll take the legs off the bed and stack them up just to hold the bed up," I laughed. I got punched from both sides. I looked over the boxes and crates as much as possible. Laramie had unpacked them all and carted the contents and the boxes down here with two mules, then repacked everything when she got here. She'd organized it all. It surprised me there was no paper money in the cave as far as I could tell. I bet she took the notes home and gave them to Kaylene to get through the depression with. Then I got to thinking. There could be all kinds of things still in the house. I had to get my dates straight, but Mildred was born in '25 and Dad was born in '55. The Great Depression hit in 1929 and its effects lasted well into World War II. Kaylene might have done anything with the warning I gave Laramie. They'd come through, but Mildred, my grandmother/ granddaughter had died soon after Dad was born and the house had been locked up for twenty years with just the annual cleaning before he got out of the service and married Mom. The house itself could hold many secrets.

"How far are we from camp?" I asked. I'd been blindfolded and had no idea how long we'd walked.

"About a mile, I'd guess," Mary Beth said. "It was a lot deeper into the woods before you turned back into this canyon."

"Are we still on our property?"

"Yes. I've got the GSA topo map. We're clearly on the property, just not where we could ever graze cattle."

"Okay. I should be able to carry ten of these in the backpack out of here. Let's put everything else back in some semblance of order and head back to camp," I said. As I started to shift things back in place I saw an old pair of saddlebags. "Wait. I think I know what those are," I said. I had to climb halfway over the crates to reach them and pulling them up was a strain. The bags were old, but in good condition. I was going to feel like a pack mule hauling them out of the cave. I didn't bother to open them. Mary Beth and Ashley put five gold bars each in their day packs. I was afraid my lightweight pack wouldn't take the weight of the bags, so I slung them over my shoulder. We headed back to camp after we restored the foliage around the entrance to the cave the best we could. I kept having to shift the bags from shoulder to shoulder and was the last one up the trail.

An extra ten pounds in your pack when you are hiking up a narrow ledge is more than it sounds like. Mary Beth and Ashley were puffing pretty good when we got back. *I* was about done in. I figured those saddlebags must weigh close to a hundred pounds. I dropped them in our tent and stood straight for a minute before I started a fire and Mary Beth and Ashley put together our dinner. The steaks that left the house frozen yesterday were just thawed enough that they seared nicely on the outside while leaving the inside warm and red. We were past the equinox, but it still got dark early and we headed bed before the fire's embers had completely died.

"So, what was so important about those saddlebags?" Ashley asked as she pulled my shirt off. "Oh my god! You are raw and bruised back here."

"Oh, poor baby," Mary Beth said as she kissed my shoulders. I winced a little. "How much do those weigh?"

"About a hundred pounds, I reckon," I said.

"What's in them?" Ashley said.

"A thousand gold coins. And if I'm right, a bag or two of jewels."

"The last of Phile's treasure?" Mary Beth said.

"Yep." I opened one of the bags and pulled out a handful of Double Eagles. "I don't know the value of each one, but $20 gold coins from the late 1800s sell for anything from $2,000 to $150,000 each."

"So, at a minimum you just carted a million dollars up here, up to maybe fifty million. Right?"

"Just a guess. We won't know until we have every date checked and find out what condition they are in." I poured the coins back into the saddlebag and kissed my ladies.

It didn't take long for the three of us to get naked—it's the way we slept most nights. I gave Ashley a long luxurious kiss that left us both panting. I whispered in her ear and we both rolled over Mary Beth.

"What are you two doing?" she asked.

"We're on a baby-hunt," I said kissing her. "Nope. Sweet but no baby there." Ashley was loving both Mary Beth's breasts, kissing and sucking on them, one after the other.

"Hmm. No baby here," Ashley said. I nuzzled right into MB's left armpit and Ashley dove into the right as Mary Beth squirmed.

"No baby here," I announced.

We progressed to her hands, one of us on each side, each sucking in her fingers and kissing her palms. We looked up at each other and grinned.

"No baby here," we both repeated. Mary Beth was giggling as we reversed ourselves and attacked her feet.

"Ticklish!" she gasped. "Oh please. Help." We didn't actually try to tickle her feet, but we did make sure every toe had been kissed and her feet had been loved right up to her ankles.

"I didn't find a baby. Did you find a baby?" Ashley asked.

"Nope. No baby here." Then things got interesting. I didn't know how Ashley would respond to this, but she followed along as we kissed our way of Mary Beth's legs, making sure we'd kissed or massaged the whole way up. There was another ticklish spot just behind MB's knees and she nearly threw us off of her when she jumped. I moved up, spreading her left leg to the side and licked her slit from her rosebud to her clit. Damn but I loved to lick her. I started to say something, but Ashley pried Mary Beth's right leg to the side and dove right into the junction.

"Oh, oh, oh!" Mary Beth moaned.

"Oh God, Mary Beth. You taste better than I do. I mean, not that I go around tasting myself all the time, but sometimes there's some left on Cole when we kiss, you know. I mean, I've never really done that before but…" Ashley paused as she swooped down between Mary Beth's legs and took another long slow lick, flicking my cousin's clit. Mary Beth went wild and when Ashley emerged, I caught her face between my hands and kissed her before licking her lips thoroughly.

"But did you find a baby?" I asked.

"No. Where could that baby be?" she panted. We leaned down and started kissing Mary Beth all over her tummy. At two months, there was no bump there yet, but I was pretty sure we covered the area well enough to have kissed over that little girl at least a couple of times.

"Oh, there's the baby," I said, continuing to kiss. "I love you little baby. I can't wait to hold you in my arms and tell you all about the amazing love between your mommy and me."

"And I love you, sweetheart," Ashley continued. "I'm going to be your other mommy and I'll love you as much as if you came out of my own tummy. And I'll love your mommy and daddy forever." We moved back up to toward Mary Beth's head, stopping to kiss her nipples on the way to join all three of us in a kiss. There were tears on Mary Beth's cheeks.

"You two are so wonderful. I love you both so much," she sobbed. "Will you really love me and love my baby like you said?"

"Now and forever, Mary Beth. I'll love you always and I'll always love our children."

"Sweetheart, I never imagined I could feel for a girl what I feel for you. I still won't say I don't prefer Cole's big old cowboy, but I find something when I'm holding you and when we're all making love that I never could imagine before. I will always love you and your children will be my children if you'll let me."

"Oh. What are we going to do?" Mary Beth asked in a panic. She sat up straight. "We kept all this quiet for so long. Now everybody will know. Will we go to jail for incest, Cole? Oh, God!"

"Easy, girl. We're okay. I looked it up. Yes, Wyoming State Law forbids marriage between first cousins, but its incest laws don't offer any penalty for first cousins who commit a sexual intrusion. I plan to be on this child's birth certificate as the father and if you will consent, she'll bear my last name," I said.

"Cole, I love you!"

11
Aftershocks

I UNDERSTAND WHAT aftershocks are now. You know when there's an earthquake and then later you get knocked on your butt because the earth hasn't really stopped shaking. I kept waiting for it. I kept expecting some Federal prosecutor to issue a warrant for my arrest for manipulating the market, or for murdering Joe Teini.

Phil sent us a security team and we led them to Kyle's treasure cache. Either Mary Beth or Ashley or I and sometimes all three were at the cave inventorying exactly what was taken out. They moved it to a secure storage facility in Salem and I followed behind the two armored trucks, put a padlock on the door and sealed it. We made three trips to Salem over the summer to sort out what was in the storage unit. We transferred half a billion dollars' worth of gold bullion to our account at American Gold and Silver Exchange. There was over fifty million in gold coins that we decided to keep on deposit there, too, but we'd sell them just a few at a time as we found coin investors. I wasn't interested in depressing the numismatic market by dumping a bunch of rare coins.

The rest of the stuff was interesting from a historical perspective and some of it was valuable, but it wasn't like it was another fortune. I puzzled over that. Kyle had just picked up whatever was at the site he'd been sent to without checking to see what was there, but he'd mostly been sent after gold or currency. Apparently, in the days when Joe was doing his own treasure-hunting, he'd been less discriminate about what kind of treasure he went after. Any abandoned wagon or cabin was game for him. I wondered how long he'd been at it before he started using Kyle. Still, for all the effort there wasn't nearly as much there as the old prospector's treasure and I had to wonder about it. Phile was still hanging around and getting a kick out of what we found, so I asked him point-blank how he got so much more treasure than Cal and Kyle did.

"Oh, I didn't," he said. "There's much more here than I ever saw. There's a Bible-story about it. The master of the house called together his three servants and distributed his wealth among them according to their ability to manage it. He gave the first five talents, the second three talents, and the third one talent. Then he went away and told them he'd be back. The first invested the five talents and when the master returned he had five more talents. The master made him the manager of his whole estate. The second traded with his three talents and when the master returned he had three more talents. The master made him the manager of his business. The third buried his talent and when the master returned he gave him back the same talent the master had given him. The master fired that servant and gave the one talent to the servant who had ten. That's what happened here. Joe buried his treasure and when Kyle took it, he didn't last long enough to do anything with it. So, it stayed buried. There's been appreciation in the value of gold, but that's all he got. I put my fortune in the hands of my grandfather to manage and invest and my family has been doing it for a hundred years. It more than doubled. In fact, it's probably doubled ten times."

"I guess I'm the worthless servant," I said. What a disappointment. I just hadn't been smart enough for this game.

"No. You just didn't have time to manage the fortune. If you'd been there, I'm sure you'd have done as well as I did. Remember, I didn't last there, either. I just gave it to someone I already knew could manage it. And you have time to do the same. Somehow, with a fortune this size, I can't help but think you'll need it in the future."

I guess that satisfied me. It wasn't like I needed anything more. We were already giving away money as fast as we could. Still, every time I went to Salem or even rode up on the range, I was looking over my shoulder.

We kept waiting for the other shoe to drop. But it wouldn't be a shock if it came when you expected it. Time went by and I thought we were all clear. That's when you get the shock.

Birth of a Baby

I WENT BACK to school part time in the fall like I said I would. I was a year behind and likely to get further behind at the rate I could attend classes and still manage the ranch, but I didn't care about that. Ashley would graduate this spring, assuming her either with a baby in her belly or on her tit. I think I nailed her Labor Day weekend.

Fortunately, Angus was willing to help out as we got our feet on the ground at the ranch. It wasn't too difficult to get back into the swing of things at school. It's different when you are applying the lessons immediately in the real world. I was also able to contribute a bit when it came to the economics of the open market for ranchers and farmers. What we experienced in the cattle business last year was just as applicable to sheep, pigs, and even cash crops. I was careful not to divulge any information covered by the confidentiality agreement. The time period on that agreement was five years. We didn't want a bunch of people talking about the think tank that saved Albany County.

I attended classes Monday and Thursday. It wasn't quite as convenient a schedule as Ashley had worked out last fall, but at least on Thursday we could commute back and forth together. When I came to school as a freshman, I figured I would live on campus so I'd get an experience of living away from home. Now I lived in my own home and I had a wife, a cousin-wife, and two babies on the way. I wasn't staying away from home any more than I had to.

It was Saturday before Thanksgiving and Ashley had a sorority function to review the new pledges. Even though she wasn't on campus, she was still a senior member of the sorority and participated in its activities. We'd gone to the fall cotillion in October, just like the first year I was in school. The difference was I took her home and made love afterward.

I figured I'd study in the library until she was done with her meeting and then we'd go home. It turned out to be a bright sunny day—a rarity for November—and I found a study carousel on the third floor near a window. I guess that was a mistake because I couldn't keep from looking out across the parking lot to the vast snow-covered park. It slowly seeped into my mind that I was looking at the cemetery and I got to thinking about Caitlin again. After Ashley had been stalked in the cemetery, she hadn't gone back to place flowers like I used to, and since I got back to school, I confess I hadn't thought about it either. But sitting there in the library on a beautiful day, I was moved to go find a flower and take it to her. I found one at the Wyoming Union and headed across the parking lot to the cemetery. At the main entrance, I walked down the Avenue of Flags about a hundred yards and turned left to get to the Old Potters Field. I suppose I could have just wandered across the cemetery and around the stones at that end, but for some reason I always stay to the paths. Eventually, that brought me to the field from the east.

I was surprised to see another figure standing near Caitlin's stone. As I moved forward, I was even more surprised to find it was Geneive. I cleared my throat as I approached and spoke her name. She turned abruptly, almost like she was afraid to be found there. Well, there had been stalkers last year.

"Cole! What are you doing here?" She looked at the flower in my hand and started crying. I had no idea what was going on, but as I approached she wrapped her arms around me and buried her head against my chest and wept. She was directly in front of Caitlin's grave. "You remember her," she sobbed. "You remember."

"I… Geneive… how do you…?" I wasn't really sure what I wanted to ask. I glanced up in the sky to see if there was a hawk flying out there someplace but nothing appeared.

She pulled away from me and said, "I'm sorry."

"Nothing to be sorry about, Geneive. I just come out here when I can and give a flower to this poor girl who had it hard back when Wyoming was just becoming a state."

"But you remember her. You remembered her and found her. You wouldn't believe how long it took me to find her."

"How do you know about Caitlin, Geneive?"

"I… She was… I'm like you and Joe, Cole. Or I was. I was till she died."

"My God! I didn't know."

"You never recognized me. I knew. Caitlin was already head-over-heels in love with Kyle. I knew as soon as you taught Kyle that trick about where to kiss me and then to go down on me. I was so scared that when I got back, I broke up with you."

"Right after Christmas."

"Then I wanted to get back together with you. I wanted you to know that it was me. We were sharing something so special being together in two different times."

I laid the flower on Caitlin's grave and took Geneive by the hand. "I always say thank you to Caitlin and tell her that I miss her," I said. We paused a minute and I led her back toward campus. "Let's get something hot to drink and talk a bit."

She followed docilely as though she had lost her will. We went back to the Union and I ordered her a hot chocolate the way she used to drink it back in high school, with marshmallows floating on top. We sat and she stared at her drink.

"You remember everything, don't you?" she said. "I haven't had one of these in three years. It wasn't sophisticated enough for Joe." I snorted.

"For a kid who grew up in a hired hand's house he didn't know that much about sophistication."

"I know he was ruthless, Cole, but he was good to me. He made me a better woman."

"You were always a good woman, Geneive. Why did you leave me?"

She sipped at her cocoa and a tear dripped into it. I reached out and wiped the tears from her cheek with my thumb. She flinched with the contact, but relaxed into my hand. She sighed.

"Because you never recognized me, even after... even after I died."

"I'm sorry, Geneive. I don't know what to say."

"When I was fourteen, Billy Sanders convinced me to let him put his hand in my panties. He was sixteen and knew stuff. He said he'd teach me. His finger in my pussy was just the start and while he pushed his cock into my virgin pussy, I heard a bell ringing far away and all of a sudden, a dirty old cowboy in a whorehouse was ripping his way through my maidenhead. I was flat on my back on a smelly bed crying while he pumped into my dry pussy and left me three pennies for a tip. Caitlin was thirteen." I looked at her in horror. I knew Caitlin had been a whore for longer than the little time I knew her, but I didn't know the extent of her abuse. Thirteen! *Shit!* "I don't know why I was sent into her. Maybe it was punishment for my sins. I visited her at least twice a year. The first time was just long enough to feel the pain and horror. The whorehouses that you went to—don't tell me it wasn't you, but Kyle; you were there—they were never houses of pleasure. They were always houses of pain. I don't blame you. When you showed up in Kyle, I thought that was why I was there. I was there for you and you would rescue me."

"Um… thanks, or I'm sorry, I guess."

"When you came back and cried for her—for me—I just wanted to find you and love you the way I knew it could be. And then in the morning, you left. You went to find that Indian girl. I knew then that I'd lost you. Except that Kyle came back and made a stone for me. It was the first time I knew how much he cared. Not you. Kyle. The first time I'd been able to leave the room, and I did it with him. It gave me hope. When Kyle stopped coming to the whorehouse, I was lost. It seemed like I could only leave with him. But he went out west to help the Indian girl and I didn't see him again."

"Shit, Geneive. How long were you out?"

"There, months and months, trapped in that whorehouse bedroom. I lost track of time. Here? A few weeks. You remember. You tried to call me but my mom broke us up."

"I thought you'd used her to break up with me. Then when school started, you were mad at me, but we got back together again. For a while."

"It was weird. It was when the first bell rang in school that day and I saw you in the hall. It was always a bell that rang when I shifted. I'd been released from that hell, but you still didn't recognize me. I thought if I did some of the things we'd done together back then, you'd see it was me, but all the things we did were things you'd already done to me. I couldn't understand how you couldn't recognize me."

"And then Joe. He recognized you?"

"Right away. The first time he looked at me at the restaurant, I knew he was a time traveler. And he knew I'd been there. He had Cal's memories of fucking Caitlin. I had Caitlin's. They weren't all that pleasant for me, but they were this special secret only we could share."

"Do you still go back?"

"Go back? Cole, is Kyle still alive? Can you still go back?" There was a trace of excitement in her voice for the first time. "Can you take me? Cole that's all I wanted from Joe. I thought he could maybe somehow take me with him when his coyote howled. I want to go back to before Caitlin got pregnant and stop the little bitch from aborting. Can you do that, Cole? Can you take me?"

"Oh God, Geneive. If I could do things like that, I'd go back and stop Kyle from getting killed. I'd stop Caitlin myself. I'd probably kill

Cal Despain right away. We can't change the things that happened. Even when we're back there the past is the past."

"You got everything, Cole. You got a wife and child back then and you've got a wife and your cousin is pregnant. I know she's the one I always shared you with. I found out a long time ago. You still go back, don't you? The only thing I ever wanted—the little baby to hold in my arms—she threw away and I can't have. I hate you!" Tears were streaming down Geneive's cheeks. I had to do something.

"Come home with us tonight, Geneive. Let us be with you and talk about things. You don't have to suffer out here alone," I said.

"Oh Cole. You're great really. But you've got a wife and... and another wife. Neither one of them would be that happy about having your ex-girl-friend who happens to be the widow of your worst enemy show up. I've got money. Joe bankrupted himself fighting you, but I managed to hide enough that I'm not penniless. I'll go somewhere. There's no reason to stay here and no reason to live in the past. Either past."

Geneive got up from the table and walked away. I didn't know what to do. I just let her go.

WHEN ASHLEY AND I got home about an hour later, Mary Beth was not at the door to greet us as she usually was.

"Mary Beth? Are you here, love?" I called. In answer, I heard a scream from the bedroom. Ashley and I ran.

Mary Beth was stretched out on the bed clutching a pillow to her. Her knees were in the air and spread, but she still had her pants on. We rushed to her.

"Coming. She's coming," she gasped.

"Hell. Not with your pants on, darling," I said. I unfastened the pants and pulled them off with her panties.

"Oh! That feels better. I forgot. I'm thirsty. I haven't been able to get up for half an hour." I ran to get water and towels while Ashley got MB out of her Shirt and bra. I started hot water running in the bathtub then tempered it to medium warm. As soon as the tub was full enough, I went back to get Mary Beth. As soon as the war was over last winter, we had the master bathroom remodeled and put in a tub we could all three get into. Ashley and I supported Mary Beth and got her into the tub. "So much better. So much better."

"Did you call Ava Dickinson?" I asked. She was the local midwife and had talked to us a few times about the coming birth. The tub was her idea.

"No. It came so hard and all at once that I laid down without ever thinking of the phone."

"I'll take care of it." Ashley was already stripped and in the tub with Mary Beth, supporting her as she leaned back. If it weren't for what was happening, I'd have just stayed there to watch them. They were so perfect together. I went out of the room and called the midwife. Ava said she'd be there in half an hour and to just stay calm and help Mary Beth relax.

Relaxing wasn't in the cards. This baby wasn't waiting for any midwife. Mary Beth had thrown herself back against Ashley and was gripping both her hands tightly. I looked down in the tub and could see the top of the baby's head. I stripped off my shirt and scrubbed my hands nearly to my shoulders in hot water and germicidal soap. When I was clean, I reached down between Mary Beth's legs and touched my daughter for the first time.

"She's almost here, honey. I'm touching her head. You take a deep breath when you're ready and give us one more good push. We're about to have a baby Mary Beth." Ashley was whispering in Mary Beth's ear and helping her with her breathing as they clutched their hands together. Being between Mary Beth's legs and touching the head of my own child beat the hell out of delivering calves. Mary Beth took a deep breath and started to push. "Keep coming. Keep coming," I said. I had her head in my hands and the rest of the little girl was making her way out of my precious cousin's opening. "One more push!" and then our baby was floating in the water.

I pulled her up and placed her on Mary Beth's tummy, letting the cord float in the water. Ava made us get a kit prepared for this and I finally had a chance to open it. I looked for what I wanted and found that little bulb squeegee that sucks mucus up. In the barn, we just use a big old turkey baster. I quickly sucked any gunk that was in her nose out and rubbed her back with Mary Beth and Ashley until we were sure she was breathing okay.

I keep saying she. I'd decided long ago I was having a daughter and they say the father decides. I don't know what we'd have done if she'd come out with a cock and balls. But she didn't. She was perfect. We bathed her in the water that was warm enough to be like mama's womb.

"Her eyes are open!" Mary Beth said. Ashley looked over her shoulder and I leaned over. Open and hazel with gold flecks like her mother's. I checked and the cord had stopped pulsing, so I took out the clamps from our kit and cut it.

"Time for that last big push, darling," I said. "We get the nasties out and then we can get you and our baby into the big bed and warm."

"Oh, Cole. Thank you for giving me the most beautiful present in the world! Thank you!" She gave another big push and I scooped the placenta out in a kitchen strainer. As long as Mary Beth and Ashley and the baby were comfortable, I didn't want to disturb them, so I ran to the kitchen and put the kettle on for tea. While I was still there, Ava knocked on the door.

"Well, let's get this show on the road," she said as she walked in.

"To late, Ava," I laughed. "Curtain already went up. Mom and baby are still in the tub. Go on up. I'm making tea."

"Already? That must have been one of the shortest labors on record. Don't go thinking every one is going to be like that." Ava was off and up the stairs to the master bath while I finished making tea for everyone. I chuckled to myself over Ava's comment. Every one? I wondered just how many there were going to be. I supposed I should call the parents, but once I got Ava out of the way, I wanted a little time with my family before everyone else got there. I took the tea up to the bedroom and Mary Beth and Ashley were already cuddled in the bed. Ava was standing right beside them and did the health assessment on the baby while they dried and got into bed. She wrote the baby's length and weight on a form with a five-point checklist of vitals and then she tucked the baby right under the covers with Mary Beth and told her to start sucking. I guess she knew what that meant because Mary Beth's nipple went into that baby's mouth like into a vacuum.

"Well, you all done good," Ava said. "You've got a healthy baby girl, a healthy mama, and you, mister," she said turning to me, "have three naked ladies in your bed. I'll leave and you can get in there, too." With that, she gulped down one of the cups of tea and said, "I don't think Joyce Kenworth's delivery is going to be that easy, so I'm headed over there. Give me a call if anything changes or if you have any questions. I know your mamas will be here soon." She put her cup on the tray and was gone.

I already had my shirt off, so I stripped off my boots and pants and crawled in next to my wives and my daughter. She'd sucked her fill and was lazily toying with the nipple, her eyes mostly closed. I know I talk like all this took five minutes, but I suppose it was a good three hours since Ashley and I got home. It's just that things went so fast it was hard to keep track of the time.

"I think your little girl is ready to meet her daddy," Mary Beth whispered. "You hold her while I rest a while, Cole. Tell her how much you love her. I'm going to lean on Ashley and just rest a while." I took the baby and she tucked her little legs up like she was a frog and went to sleep on my chest. Mary Beth drifted off and I just marveled at the life in my arms.

And wouldn't you know, Redtail called.

Traveling: Blessing

I KNEW I was on my way to see Laramie and I held the feeling of my baby in my arms as I quickly looked to see where my love was. I was lying in the bed right beside her.

"Kyle?"

"Look, Laramie. Isn't she beautiful? She's the next in our line, my love, and she was just born."

"Oh Kyle. So beautiful."

"I'm here, Laramie. I love you." I swear both the baby and Laramie sighed contentedly.

"Are you here to show me the way, Kyle? Will you take me home now?" she said.

What? What was going on? I stretched my senses. I was in the same room as I'd been in the present, but Laramie stretched out still beside me. Kaylene was nearby and little Mildred, my granddaughter/grandmother was holding her grandma's hand.

"Papa?" Kaylene said. "I knew you'd come. Mama, he's here. You can feel him, can't you, Mama."

"He's here with me, Kaylene. Kyle has come to take me home, haven't you, love?"

"I'll be here with you, Laramie. I'm always here with you. I love you. I love you. I love you." Laramie's breath stuttered and she was floating with me, young and beautiful and full of life like the first time I saw her when we were making love. With us, too, were Theresa and White Horse, Kyle and Kat. They were all waiting for Laramie with their hands outstretched. I didn't know Kat had passed away, but I was thankful for a chance to see her again. They all came to bless my little baby before they turned to go.

"I'll be waiting here for you and all our family," Laramie said. "And I will always be with you." I felt the wash of a love so warm and joyful that I cried out, "Laramie!" and felt her presence withdraw. I wept. I held my little daughter in my arms and wept for the loss of her ancestor who died seventy years ago.

My daughter. How had I brought her with me? She was in my arms as surely as if I was holding her. I couldn't just let go of her. I had to protect her and care for her. I had to hold her till Redtail called me back again. I was scared, but I was doing my best to be strong and calm for my baby. She didn't seem to have any problems with it at all and was still cooking on my chest where I'd held her.

"Thank you, Papa," Kaylene said softly as she pulled the sheet up over her mother. "Goodbye, Mama. I know you are at peace now." Kaylene paused as if expecting something to happen. "I know you are still here, Papa. I know the place. I'll show you now."

I followed Kaylene down to the den with the original stone fireplace in it. Only it looked different than it had when I'd seen it before. Maybe I was thinking differently since I really had no sense of sight. It was just the feeling was different. Then I realized that the fireplace was more like the one we currently had.

"Mildred, go get ready for bed now. It's going to be a long day tomorrow."

"Where's grandma, Mama?"

"Grandma's gone to be with Grandpa, baby. Tomorrow we'll take her out to lay her beside him."

"Oh. She's not alone then. Okay." The little five-year-old girl ran out to put her pajamas on.

"Mama hid our cash from the bank here, Papa. She said we'd need it to pay people and keep the ranch going while times are bad. But she said to put her box of papers here, too. She said you'd know what to do with them. So here they are." Kaylene took a locked metal box from the desk and placed the key on top of it. She moved a stone near the back of the fireplace and pushed the box behind it. I stretched my senses and felt my Smith & Wessons still hanging from the hat tree. Kaylene seemed to feel it. "I don't know what she put in the box for you, Papa, but she said you'd know what to do. I'll put these in there, too. It's a different world now and we won't need them again." She put my leathers and the guns behind the stone and pushed it back into place. "Don't worry about us now. We've got money and good hired hands. Mildred is a good girl and Robert is still here most of the time, unless he runs off after another new invention that will make all our lives easier. Would you believe we've got a washing machine? Don't be hard on him, Papa. He's a good man, but I'll never marry him and let him have the ranch. It will all go to Mildred."

"What goes to Mildred?" my granddaughter asked coming back into the room with her footie pajamas on.

"Everything goes to Mildred, baby. All my love. All Grandma's love. And all Grandpa's love. Everything goes to Mildred."

"Who you talking to?"

"I just like to talk to Grandpa, sometimes when I know he's near. I think Grandpa needs to know we love him and we love the little baby in his arms. Now that they aren't here with us anymore, you have to say goodnight in your heart and mean it, baby."

"I love you, Mama. Goodnight Grandma. Goodnight Grandpa. Love you!"

Kaylene took her daughter out of the room and I heard Redtail call me again.

Naming

"OF COURSE, COLE. It's perfect." Mary Beth said softly. I filtered through my memories of the past few minutes as a tear rolled down my cheek. I'd been gone. I saw Laramie die and I knew where the papers were that she wanted me to find. I'd continued to hold my daughter in my arms as I'd gone back and shown her to her ancestors. And I'd called out Laramie's name.

That was it.

"Wait, Mary Beth," Ashley said. "He's been gone. Didn't you hear the hawk?"

"I thought I was dreaming it," Mary Beth yawned.

"You took the baby with you, didn't you, Cole?"

I nodded. I told them about seeing Laramie greeted by Kyle, Kat, Theresa, and White Horse and her promise to meet me and all our family when it was our time.

"That makes it an even better choice," Mary Beth said. "She's been blessed by both our grandmothers. Ashley, do you object?"

"What? That you're not going to name her after me? Don't be silly. I even know what I want my son to be named."

"And when is that going to be?" I asked.

"In about six months," Ashley said. "Laramie needs her brother to grow up with her."

"Laramie?" I said.

"When I asked you what we should name her, you practically shouted out 'Laramie!' I think it's perfectly beautiful."

"Laramie Wyoming Bell," I whispered. "My daughter."

"And when her little brother comes along," Ashley said, "we already know his name will be Kyle Redtail Bell."

12
A Letter from the Past

THANK YOU. I guess I'm normal now, but it helped to have someone to tell the story to. I haven't been back since the birth of my daughter. I don't reckon I ever will go back again. I don't have an anchor anymore. That's why Geneive and Joe and even Phile never went back after their hosts died, I think. They didn't have an anchor in that life like I did. Once Kyle found Kat, he stopped going to Bertha's. Geneive just didn't have anyone to go back to. I had Laramie.

They'll all be waiting for me when I die. I've got a little girl and a little boy just six months younger. They are the most fun I've ever had. Ashley says they're too young to have horses already, but I figure the horse ought to know his rider from the beginning. It's like the two black geldings already know them.

I managed to open the stone in the fireplace. A few years ago, Dad had it tuck pointed so the mortar would all look nice. I had to chip away the new mortar in order to release the stone. Inside there was a box with several hundred dollars in it. Not a big find, but a few of the bills are collectors' items. The rest we'll just put in the bank eventually. I pulled my guns out and they felt smooth and natural in my hands. I got them cleaned up and now they hang on the hat tree that's still in the corner of the office. The locked metal box, though, was different. The first thing in it was a letter from Laramie.

My darling Kyle Redtail.

You never told me what the name of my great-great-grandson would be, so I call you by the only name I know. I'm sure you will find this letter and the other things I have left for you. I left everything in the cave except the currency. There was such a lot of it, though. I know Kaylene has enough to get through the hard times and Mildred will have

*the ranch and plenty to work with. But that left quite a lot
of cash and coinage.*

*I went to the new College in Laramie before Mildred was
born and they taught me about finance and economics. Armed
with the knowledge I acquired there and your warning of what
was to come, I began traveling and making purchases. No one
asked where I got the money so I guess that will be your problem
to deal with. Herein are my purchases.*

*Kyle, I love you with all my heart. I listen each day for the
call of the redtail hawk and dream of you each night. We may
not see each other again in this world, but I will wait for you in
the next. And bring your wives and family. I will love them all.*

*As I write this tonight, I think of the first time we met when
you taught me the pleasures of love. I will smile throughout the
night as I relive that moment.*
With all my love,
Laramie Wyoming Bell

The contents of the box were negotiable securities. There were shares
of companies that were still new in the 1920s like Ford Motor Company
and the Minnesota Mining and Manufacturing Company. There were
bearer bonds, treasury notes, and other items. Some proved to be worthless, like the five thousand shares of Studebaker Corporation. But by and
large, she'd made good decisions and more than half of her purchases
were worth a great deal. Close to a billion dollars, in fact. She was a good
and faithful steward, in Phile's words. I gave everything to Gold Watch
Trust to maintain and liquidate if necessary. We all went to Phile's funeral
last year. He was ninety-four and lived to see the good works that his
time-traveling had enabled.

Mary Beth, Ashley, and I draw a healthy salary as the board of directors and we are putting the money to use wherever we can to help people.

And we work the ranch.

Neither of them will be going up on the ridge this year. They are both
pregnant and that is something no mere ranch hand should have to deal
with. Ashley is still a bit miffed that Mary Beth's first labor took less than
three hours and hers took closer to twenty. Ava warned us. But Kyle is a
healthy boy and follows his sister Laramie everywhere.

I still believe this ground is sacred and forever protected. Even if I am dead and buried, I will be here to protect my women, my children, and my land. The spirits in this land do not rest. And we are deadly when we hunt.

No. I'm okay with not going back in time anymore. Who would I see? I know how the story ends. I just couldn't get that across to Geneive, though God knows I tried. She set out for California to live the good life, but she never made it. I cried when I heard the news and I went to Caitlin's grave with two flowers instead of one. What more could I do. Not everyone's story ends happily.

So, I don't think I need to come back again, at least any time soon. I've got a lot of work to do on the ranch and two pregnant wives at home.

Did you know that pregnancy makes some girls horny?

 **The End**